*My Chocola*

Christopher Hope was born in Johannesburg and grew up in Pretoria. He was educated at the Universities of Witwatersrand and Natal. His first book of poems was *Cape Drives* (1974), which received the Cholmondeley Award, and his first novel, *A Separate Development* (1980), won the David Higham Prize for Fiction in 1981. A collection of stories, *Private Parts & Other Tales*, was given the International P.E.N. Silver Pen Award in 1982, and published in a revised paperback edition entitled *Learning to Fly* in 1990. His long poem *Englishmen* was dramatised by the BBC in 1986. His next novel, *Kruger's Alp*, won the Whitbread Prize for Fiction in 1985, and the *Hottentot Room* was published the following year. *Black Swan*, a novella, followed in 1987, and in 1988 he published his first work of non-fiction, *White Boy Running*, which won the CNA Award in 1989. Christopher Hope has lived in London since 1975.

CHRISTOPHER HOPE

# My Chocolate Redeemer

Minerva

**A Minerva Paperback**

MY CHOCOLATE REDEEMER

First published in Great Britain 1989
by William Heinemann Ltd
This Minerva edition published 1990
by Mandarin Paperbacks
Michelin House, 81 Fulham Road, London SW3 6RB

Minerva is an imprint of the Octopus Publishing Group

The epigraphs come from the following sources:
The *Autobiography of Kwane Nkrumah* (Panaf Books, 1957);
*Selected Poems of e. e. cummings 1923–1958* (Penguin, 1967);
'The Song of Lawino' in *Modern African Poetry* (Penguin, 1984).

A CIP catalogue record for this book
is available from the British Library
ISBN 0 7493 9058 1

Printed in Great Britain
by Cox and Wyman Ltd, Reading, Berks.

For Balthus

*Seek ye first the political kingdom . . .*

Kwame Nkrumah
(known as 'The Redeemer')


*– listen: there's a hell of a good*
*universe next door; let's go*

e.e. cummings

*Waq*

Atkins International Airport, outside the city of Waq, in the country of Zanj, is something of a surprise. The traveller who steps down onto the tarmac after bouncing over hot air currents for hours in a racketing, shivering turboprop has been buffeted into grimfaced acceptance and deafened. This happens to those who have tried putting their hands over their ears during the flight, only to find that this sets up a vibration running from the elbows through the wrist bones to the finger tips, as if the nerves have turned to ants which march along the neural pathways into the brain via the ears. Waq is a 'request' stop where the pilot's door, which sags on its hinges and flaps during flight, gapes shamelessly as the plane taxis to a halt to show you the Jordanian pilot leaning back from his controls, yawning and scratching his grizzled grey hair while the Taiwanese stewardess says, 'Hurry up, darling,' as she swings open the hatch. The passengers rouse themselves from their torpor and stare at the back of the departing passenger and one of them says quite distinctly, 'Well, I hope she's got her head screwed on.' The air of Africa enters the plane, hot and dry, smelling memorably of dust and salt. A paper cup, still with a few drops of orange juice adhering to its sides, falls down the steps behind you and you wonder whether it has been thrown out deliberately.

And then you're on the ground and the spongy humidity wraps around you as you walk to the terminal building, passing a collection of planes parked on the tarmac with weird designs on their tails and names like Ba-rozwiland Air and Monomatapa Freight Services. Biggest of all is a jumbo jet of Zanj Air in the national colours of black and pink, a livery unexpectedly elegant in the bright winter sunshine, though as you get closer you see that the cockpit windscreen is broken and the plane is mounted on concrete blocks on one of which is written in white paint the words: *Crew Training Module*. You know that this plane is not a hive of activity – even before you arrive on the other side and see that it's propped up with poles of the sort used to stop walls from falling down.

Why am I telling you this? You know it all, you'll have been here before, you who direct and control my movements, you've thought this through. But you see those of us who have to visit out-of-the-way places for reasons of love or duty, or upon your iron whim, are not always prepared for the trials ahead. I take it that you're watching over me. At least I hope and pray so.

I dressed carefully before leaving Rome on my flight to Kinshasa, with a connection for Zanj. Whatever the occasion was to be, black seemed a suitable colour for funeral or feast. I chose to seem undecided, a straight black cotton skirt and turtle-neck top, a jaunty swing-coat in dogtooth check, a black straw picture hat and white gloves. That way, if I stood up as tall as possible I was a woman of the world, and if I crouched a bit I was just a little girl dressing up in Mummy's clothes, and if I tottered on my small heels and threw out my feet when I walked then I was just a crazy kid lost in the world and far from home. You looked at me and you took your pick. I was determined to be pliable.

I did not stay for the funerals – my grandmother's was to be used as a recruiting drive for the Party. André's cremation was to be presided over by Father Duval, naturally – with a squawk and a flap of his wings as the coffin entered the flames. My Uncle Claude, in his capacity as Mayor, demanded immediate disposal, as a health precaution. Twice-incinerated André, hoping no doubt for a third purging down below, entered his reward. Ambition for unhappiness is far stronger than longings for bliss. My uncle confiscated my silver chocolate trunk and had it dusted for fingerprints.

Please don't be surprised.

A man who kidnapped a crippled doll would stop at nothing.

Three months ago work began on the conversion of the Priory Hotel in La Frisette. It disappeared into a steel cage, a larger version of the kind they use for massive fractures of the skull. The old wooden beach by the lakeside burns

4

ash-white in the autumn sun – empty forever of its load of oiled, expensive human flesh laid out for the inspecting hawks floating high above the headland of the little bay. The interior of the Priory has been ripped out and is being made ready for the new technology, which is the boast of the Party – only the façade remains. Our newspaper *Les Temps* celebrated the event: A MIRACLE AT THE PRIORY! By now they'll know where I've gone. They will whistle to discover I've left my music. They will find my silver trunk beneath my bed, still smelling of chocolate, stripped of its dollars – I guess Granny Gramus meeting Old Laveur at the bakery will say, 'Madame Dresseur's granddaughter has fled to Africa!' and Old Laveur will say, 'It serves her right!'

# La Frisette

# 1

I take my ease upon our private beach. 'Relax Bella,' I tell
myself, 'you're among friends.' That's not quite true – but
then if you can't tell yourself stories, who is there to talk
to? You should know!

Although it's called, rather grandly, a *plage privée* it's really
a semi-circular wooden platform, or jetty, by the lakeside,
specially reserved for guests of the Priory Hotel. A notice
warns trespassers to keep away. The wooden slats are grey
with age, warm and deeply grooved, and through them I can
see the baize-green water, striped with dusty silver where the
sun falling between the slats strikes the surface. In the shade
the green blackens and thickens but in the shallows where the
sunshine pierces to the sandy floor, the water is brilliantly clear.
Over to my right is a mountain covered with trees and scrub
through which the grey rock shows. Rearing several hundred
metres above the lake, it is part of the chain of mountains
curving behind the hotel and the village of La Frisette. Jutting
out into the water, this natural headland forms a small bay
where the weekend yachts ride at anchor, stripped of their
sails, each wagging a naked mast like a warning finger. To
my left the lake opens up, stretching to the further shore
and the distant mountains with which this vast reservoir is
ringed, and behind those mountains are greater mountains
still. Alps. In the distance power-boats rip the lake to tatters
with skiers criss-crossing the foaming wakes. Closer to shore
the windsurfers lean back pulling on the wishbone spar of the
bellying sail, keeping their difficult balance; backwards and
forwards they ride, displaying the remoteness of ploughmen.
Nearest of all float the severed heads of the swimmers. With
the hazy glitter of mid-morning the further shoreline vanishes
and the mountains beyond are a smudged outline. This great
stretch of water is a thoroughfare where all traffic rides,

including the big ferries connecting the little towns around the lake.

Our corner of the lake is a backstreet, a parking lot, quiet and secluded. These qualities undoubtedly led the monks to found their monastery in the village of La Frisette. From its high point, the Church of the Immaculate Conception, the village curves delicately down the mountainside to the water's edge where the Priory stands looking out across the lake. All roads lead to the lake dipping between crumbling walls held together by climbing roses. Once it would have been difficult to reach this spot, except by water, in the days before the little road ran the length of the lakeside as it does now. Mountains behind, water before, a fine defensive position. The little road divides the hotel behind me from the wooden *plage privée*, continuing around in a curve which ends abruptly when it comes up against the rocky lower slopes of the headland. The little lakeside road gives access to the big houses carved into the mountainside, neighbours of the Old Priory, which was so fabulously wealthy before the Revolution that it took the wrecking parties, chosen from amongst the peasantry, three days and nights to burn its manuscripts, brocades, miniatures, its silver candlesticks and golden chalices. They spared the Priory, though, and allowed an empty house swept clean of monks and vanities to fall into gentle ruin. It must have made the rich really sad when the Priory closed down. All their pretty things were burnt. They had invested so much in the monks' house. It was like money in the bank, only it was better than money in the bank because it stored up treasures in heaven. The rich are still here, in their triple-storeyed summer houses set well back from the little shore road, with wonderful views across the lake. But the monks are long gone.

The Priory's the grandest hotel hereabouts. There has been a church on the spot since the ninth century when an unhappy queen, deserted by her husband, settled here and devoted herself to good works. At least that's the contention of André, its owner, who loves it like a mistress. Perhaps, considering its origins, it would be better to say he loves it like a wife. Or a sister. Or a madonna. For the Priory is after all holy ground and retains something of its odour of sanctity, thanks to André who has spent years preserving and refurbishing it. He wants

10

to retain its monastic qualities, eased, but not overwhelmed, by certain comforts. Clearly this is an impossible task since there are demands made by guests who come to a luxury hotel groggy with dreams from the glossy magazines – which centrally heat the minds of the rich – stoking up expectations which the fabric of a sixteenth-century Carthusian Priory cannot provide. And it costs him too much.

André has fought off several attempts by Monsieur Cherubini to buy the Priory as a home for his political party, the *Parti National Populaire*. André's answer has been one stiff finger, an astonishingly violent gesture in a gentleman. Monsieur Cherubini's paper, *La Liberté*, has run hostile stories headlined: WHAT ALIENS BLOOM IN THE GARDEN OF THE CARTHUSIANS? This despite the fact that the Priory has no gardens unless you count the inner courtyard with its old well and statue of a mother and child. But *La Liberté* has never let facts spoil a good story and, between you and me, it's an attitude I rather like.

André has the cheeks of a shelled boiled egg, full fleshed, tightly gleaming. His eyelashes are long and lovely. Although he modernises the interior little by little, he insists on preserving the spirit of the place. This is contradictory, as I'm sure he realises, yet he persists, giving that soft apologetic smile to all objections. André's need to avoid giving pain is so deep and genuine it actually encourages the feelings it is supposed to prevent: it makes you feel bad when you realise how hard he's trying to spare your feelings, and how many feelings there are to spare. For example, the old cloisters are glassed-in against the wind and dust so that the guests look out on the wild green courtyard in the centre of the building as if peering into a glasshouse. Here the priors of the monastery were buried though their graves have vanished. An old well, overgrown with climbing roses, stands in the corner. In the Priory's heyday it was the vegetable gardener's privilege to grow the roses. On a low wall, the life-size stone madonna presides with the sacred child. The baby redeemer plays with her rosary and she looks down at his foot which she holds in her hand – it's a fond yet professional glance. She might be examining it for injury or deformation – in fact the foot is very beautiful – or she might be a saleslady assessing his shoe-size. It would have been more sensible to cover the open courtyard,

*11*

to put a roof on it, but that, says André, would have been to damage the architectural unity of the Priory. And this he will not have, he declares in the same quiet, sorrowful tones in which he told me he was once a Parisian stockbroker.

'I was a monster of the Bourse.' And if that was not enough to shock a girl, he added, 'With offices in Lyons.'

There was no mistaking the wistful note of regret, of shyness, of shame, with which this very ordinary statement of fact was offered. Please note: he said 'offices'. At first I thought he must mean branches, and said so. But he was gently adamant.

'With *offices* in Lyons,' he repeated.

These dread offices lay heavily on his mind. Did he mean perhaps that the geographical location of the offices reflected badly on the status of a Parisian stockbroker? Or was it because, though claiming Parisian attachments, in fact he had been based at Lyons and was forced to commute? That seemed unlikely. After thinking about it for some time it appeared more probable that André had, in his Parisian days as a monster of the Bourse, possessed offices in both Paris and Lyons and for some inexplicable reason the second set of offices caused him agony and humiliation. For the life of me I cannot think why this should be so. Does it mean that although he had turned away shuddering from his old life in Paris, he was always haunted by the knowledge that it had not been enough for him to yell, grab, stuff his pockets on the Market, that so great had been his greed and ambition that he had flung his net over half of France? Perhaps it is memories like these that make him confess: 'I was a terror, once.' And then with a quiver of downcast lashes which give his face that eggy, Humpty Dumpty about-to-fall look, he adds, 'Of course, you're too young to understand. I don't mean you're at all immature, quite the contrary. You're a young woman now, Bella — '

In my experience a middle-aged man who couples confessions of his former terrorism with compliments on my maturity is usually being dead bloody boring and is at the mercy of his erectile tissue. But there is nothing of this in André's pale blue eyes. He smooths his hand across the few crispy grey hairs remaining on his shell of a head and looks at me as if I were the Virgin descending. Ferocity seems very unlikely in

12

one such as André in his pink shirt and midnight-blue pants, his espadrilles and his gentle, apologetic smile. Indeed, he is so self-effacing and shy that he is frequently taken to be a member of the staff by guests visiting the Priory for the first time and is to be seen cheerfully carrying suitcases up the great stone staircase, passing the weeping wooden Nereids who guard the front door, with eyes averted. I shall also say it's probably unavoidable since the young cretins he employs as bellhops, baggage carriers and waiters have only the wispiest idea of their responsibilities and no great desire to sweat for their wages. The big, heavy suitcases having been unpacked from the boot of the Mercedes or the BMW in the dusty parking lot behind the hotel, the astonished guest will find the bellhop apparently inviting him to divide the load between them – always of course offering the guest first choice.

'Will Monsieur take this case, and I the other? Or does he prefer the other?'

These boys, Armand, Tertius and Hyppolyte, are hired (need I reveal it?) in Lyons in the summer months when the hotel is full and the permanent staff cannot manage without extra help. They're not bad, if somewhat loutish and far too young to be really interesting. But what can André do? Though I know it embarrasses him horribly to see his guests treated in this cavalier fashion, he has no option but to run along behind the perspiring arrival, snatch the heavy case from him and glower at the young idiot so lacking in grace and consideration.

And yet he considers himself guilty of monstrous crimes. He seeks forgiveness for wolfish deeds. He shudders to think of himself in the days when he was a beast on the Paris Bourse, with offices in Lyons. He must have ravaged his private clients, or his clerks, or the buyers from the big institutions, or terrorised his staff in the office in Lyons and done something so horrible that it caused him burning shame. But what these crimes were, what blood was spilt, what scalps taken, what hideous dreams disturbed his sleep, no one can tell. He seeks salvation, he goes about in pink and blue, all gentleness and humility. He wishes to repent; the deeply appealing and sympathetic thing about André is his need to make an act of public contrition. Naturally this is virtually impossible in our age. What is one supposed to do if one wishes to proclaim one's penitence? Go on a pilgrimage, or fight in the crusades, or endow a monastery?

Well, not quite. But in taking over the old priory and converting it into a hotel, André has done the next best thing. And by being always so humble and self-effacing, talking as little as possible, eating sparingly, tolerating the whims and excesses of his guests and dealing with such exemplary kindness with his novice baggage boys, he does his best to reflect, in a modest way, the lifestyles of the former inhabitants of this old grey-stoned Carthusian retreat under its roof of pale red tiles. The milky flagstones of the cloisters are worn smooth by generations of patrolling monks.

'I was a terror once.'

How those words of André's haunt me! What does he mean, *terror*? And where is it now? When you stop being its possessor or its victim what happens to this terror? Does it die? Or go into hiding? I know about terror in books. The Terror of Robespierre and Marat. Blood and more blood. I remember the leg of Princess Lamballe, after her body was ripped to pieces, stuffed in a cannon, her head on a pole, and her heart roasted and eaten. That was the official Terror – written up – from the books we knew it, always from the books. You visit it like a public monument. You walk around it. When you're tired you go home. Only when I begin to think, when I feel for the people pulled from their houses and accused by the Committee of Public Safety, when I hear their cries and screams as they were dragged to the guillotine, then I begin to be frightened. That was the Reign of Terror. How strange that there should be a reign during a revolution which killed a king! It's as if other people's terror is not open to us. We all need our own.

But first we must hear the call, and wake, alone, to face our fear. Through the wooden slats I can see shoals of tiny fish darting past. These little silver fish teem in the lake and are a local delicacy, fruit of the lake, fried and eaten sprinkled with lemon juice and black pepper. The shoal flicks this way and that, nervous, forever vigilant. No doubt they are programmed for this anxious slipperiness. At every moment extinction threatens. A state of useful terror developed by nature preserves the group. Quite right too. For at this moment they are being watched by one who would kill them and eat them. Cheerfully.

On this warm, wooden, private island human sun-lovers have no such fears. These naked, oily, delectable morsels of flesh fry gently. They know nothing will fall on them and tear their livers. No plague or brimstone will strike. No eagles will drop from the sky. The modern human animal is blithely self-confident. I must say too that the guests of the Priory this summer are more than usually fearless. They are healthy, they are enjoying themselves, they are on holiday and of course they're rich. They could not afford the Priory otherwise. Two elderly French lizards sit in deckchairs, facing one another, their heads thrown back, eyes closed. They are both excessively burnt and I suspect they have come on here from Sardinia or Monte Carlo. They know the tricks. They apply oil liberally to each other every hour or so. He even rubs some on his bald spot. Clever touch that. Their bodies are almost blue-black and deeply wrinkled after many summers spent tanning their hides. They must be in their late sixties, possibly in their seventies, though it's hard to tell for they have good crops of blue-white hair. Well versed in this pursuit they constantly move their chairs to catch the full force of the sun, then settle back again and close their eyes. They're awaiting the call, but it's only the call to lunch, a buffet in the garden beneath the chestnut trees, pink tablecloths and bottles of chilled rosé . . .

I heard the call, just as St Augustine of Hippo in the fourth century heard a voice saying to him: *Tolle lege*, 'Take up and read!' Well, maybe it didn't say *exactly* that to me because I mean – who uses Latin any more? Except possibly that mega-super group Giuseppe and the Lambs who were so big a few years ago with their reworking of Virgil, a great mix of *a capella* and skate-punk and wah-wah guitars – 'Electronic Bucolics' – in the original Latin, of course. They followed it up with a real winger. *You* remember. Of course you do!

Anyway, so I heard this voice and it said something like, 'OK, what's the story, baby?' though not in so many words, and even if sixteen hundred years have passed since the *Tolle* business back in Hippo, the upshot's the same when you hear something like that – when the call is for more than lunch.

It is on this authority that I name the people around me. For instance I name these elderly lizards Alphonse and Edith. Do you approve? It really doesn't matter. I have named them and the names will stick, not for ever, but for as long as is necessary to make the world make sense, the little world of the private beach. *Make* is the operative word here. You know that, you who have made us in your image and likeness, you will not mind if I take a leaf from your book. Thus I baptise them Alphonse and Edith in the name of the author of us all, we who populate this little wooden world by the lake for a few weeks each summer.

Naked we came into the world, naked we go out. Once that was a threat, now we're just talking suntans. All, that is, except for he who arrived weeks ago and has still to be seen to be believed, but is said to be black! Black as a coal-hatch, according to Father Duval, black as night says my Grand-mère, black as the dark matter which is said to hold together the universe, according to my Uncle Claude, black as the words on the page, say I. Seeing is believing said doubting Thomas, or words to that effect. But between seeing and believing comes saying. You see, I say, *they* believe. So I say that the elderly lizards turning their leathery skins to the sun are called Alphonse and Edith. Who do you say that they are?

And I am Bella. Who do you say that I am? In the absence of an answer, I will just have to continue to say I am little Bella, always big for her age, fifteen last September and when I look into the water I see her looking at me: there is a shine to her face that reminds me of cheap plastic: she has reddish hair (not really visible in the water), eyes like hot slate, a whitish grey (also not well reproduced in her watery reflection), good legs, ugly knees, racking period pains and a heavy menstrual gush in one so young (really, it's a virtual geyser once a month). The hair around my ankles rather worries me. For some reason it grows rather heavily on the lower parts of my legs. I'm scared to shave it in case it encourages growth. From the onset of puberty I have been – well – rather *tufty*. I always shave before wearing a bikini – even then it's awkward. I am

*16*

wearing a pair of headphones which gives her (the Bella I see) a slightly scientific look she certainly doesn't deserve or want. And she is listening to – but you guessed it! – Giuseppe and the Lambs in their chartbuster from a few years back called – see, you *do* remember! – simply 'Blood!'

In six chairs against a low wall that divides our wooden beach from the lakeside road running behind us, sit the family of Germans. The father is very tall with a substantial belly which he wears proudly. His name is Wolf. He is reading *Charlemagne*; yesterday it was *Frederick the Great*. His wife is half his age and looks Scandinavian. She wears her dark hair in a plait and has a square handsome face. I've decided her name is Gudrun. Their three daughters sit beside her, surprisingly pale, thin and nervous little girls to come from this confident, wide-hipped young woman and the big man. These little girls, as yet unnamed, do not leap and shout like the other children who come down to the platform and swim and dive. They sit quietly, often wearing blouses or even jerseys over their swimming costumes despite the heat, and they gaze anxiously across the lake. There's a little boy, as well. He can't be more than two, very beautiful with thick golden curls, who sometimes sits on the sixth chair and sometimes on his mother's lap. When she wishes to swim she passes the boy to one of the little girls and he sits on her lap. Then the mother in a solid and stately fashion descends the iron steps into the water and pushes out gracefully. The girls watch their mother unhappily. The father turns the pages of his book and ignores them all.

Over to the right the Dutch people have their little colony. Father, called Willem but known to his friends as Wim, never swims. He sits in his chair smoking his pipe and reading his paper. His wife, Magda, and daughters, Beatrice and Ria, have beautiful breasts which they display proudly. Watching the girls is a young man with dark greasy hair and an old-fashioned bottle-brush moustache. He has big muscles in his forearms and rather short, thin legs; at least this is so below the knees although they widen beefily and, I must say, rather unpleasantly, around his thighs. The pair of grey trunks he wears are clearly army issue. I have decided that he has escaped from the Foreign Legion. His name is almost certainly Raoul. His

17

eyes are hungry and seldom leave the breasts of the Dutch girls. He pretends to be watching the water-skiers ploughing their watery furrows but I can see through that. Of course he's wasting his time. Those breasts are not available. They are not for handling, or motherhood or even for show. They are exposed in the interests of uniformity; in order that the upper half of the body may be evenly browned. The young man is barking up the wrong tree, as my poor father once told me. The fashion for going bare-breasted in Europe is cosmetic. It is not derived from any wish to be free.

'Do you see women removing their brassieres in libraries? Of course not! Bear my advice in mind, Bella. If ever you have breasts do not expose them in the presence of the printed word.'

It set me thinking. Papa was right. You did not see bare breasts in libraries. What could be more provocative than unclothed flesh among books? Words and flesh do not mix. However, in Africa, my father said, many women still uncover their breasts quite naturally. But then, he added, 'However, though their breasts are free, everything else is in chains.'

Papa knew about these things. Not even Grand-mère quarrelled with his knowledge of Africa. Papa died in Africa three years ago. He'd always wanted to end his life in Africa. So that was lucky, but then I suppose he was a fortunate man. People do not choose where they are born. That's common enough. What is perhaps not realised is that they seldom choose where they die. I was put in mind of this when we were summoned, Mother and I, to the Foreign Ministry in Paris to be told of Papa's accident.

'Who are you and what is your function?'

That was the question I threw at the horrid official who saw us, a sleek robot with a face that showed about as much animation as a shoehorn, with the same smooth sheen. I should add that I wore that day a little black dress and long black lycra gloves, an ensemble suited to the occasion, I thought, enlivened by a choker of amethysts and emeralds (a present from Papa), and that my appearance threw the downstairs flunkies, who took us perhaps for a visiting starlet and her chaperone, into considerable confusion. People do tend to stare at me. A lot. I think it's the way I walk. The civil servant ignored my challenge and concentrated his attention on my mother.

'I am afraid, Madame, that I must confirm the death of Monsieur Dresseur. He died somewhere in Central Africa. There've been political disturbances. Details are sketchy.'

'Philippe?' My mother shook her head as if she hadn't heard. 'Gone?'

The shoehorn nodded and the light skidded off his cheap plastic forehead.

Then, still insisting she hadn't heard: 'Completely?' She opened and closed her hands as if to grab hold of something. Then again: 'Utterly?' as if the nothing my father had suddenly become was unthinkable. 'There were absences. He travelled. But we met later, always. Isn't that so, Bella? We have our own professions, you see.' She displayed her cameras hopelessly. 'My subjects are often old; they fade like fruit left too long in a dish.' A look of panic-stricken cunning appeared in her eyes. 'There will be a funeral — soon?'

But he was too smart for this. 'Utterly,' he repeated.

'Bella don't cry,' my mother said. 'There must be *something* still.'

'You will be informed if anything comes to light,' said the plastic man. 'He was attacked, we understand, somewhere in the bush. There were dissidents in the area. Soldiers. The new regime had severed relations with France. Communication is difficult. We will know more in a week or so. Perhaps.'

'I might be in Chicago,' said my mother vaguely, 'or L.A.'

That was when I put my question again. 'Are you a wave or a particle?' It derived, as I'm sure you know, from quantum theory and the study of the atom. I had stolen it from Uncle Claude who used to pursue me with the question when he still thought there was a chance of my salvation for science. The particles that make up the atom may be thought of as two things at once, points or waves. An atom is composed of a nucleus orbited by electrons. When studied at rest an electron, say, can be thought of as a round little globe, like a ball-bearing or a billiard ball. But when it's moving we must think of it as a wave, as a little packet of energy, as a field of force smeared around the nucleus. Now that was the purloined thought behind the question I put to the shoehorn. Was he a wave or a point?

'I am a spokesman for the Department of Foreign Affairs, Mademoiselle,' was his wet and boring answer.

It didn't much matter. I had already marked him down for a particle. He could only be considered a wave if you thought of him as part of the onrushing momentum carrying Mama and I towards our destiny.

'Then speak to us,' I demanded.

But the interview was over, though I noticed that he looked at my amethyst and emerald choker with little piggy eyes.

My mother took the news with terrible composure. She was, at the time, about to fly out on a new project in which she would be photographing film stars for an American magazine and her schedule was hectic. Nonetheless she found time to wind up my father's estate, sell off our apartment in Paris, remove me from the local school and take me with her to England where I was enrolled in the North London Academy for Girls to the great pain and chagrin of my dear Grand-mère, who regarded the removal of a twelve-year-old 'daughter of France' to England to be nothing short of kidnapping. She referred thereafter to my mother as the 'child stealer'. No doubt, she said, this was how Joan of Arc had been stolen by the Goddams. The Goddams was her way of referring to the English.

'There are mothers walking across Europe who have seen their children stolen by their Algerian husbands. They walk to draw attention to the theft. I will join them to protest at the taking of Bella to England.'

'But Maman,' Claude protested, 'your arthritis!'

'Very well, I shall go by wheelchair, and you may push me. No, on second thoughts, you are too busy. You are Mayor now – and mayors cannot go walking whenever they please.'

I remember asking Mama if there was to be a funeral and she explained that without a body this was not possible. However, she promised me that on her return from New York she would arrange a memorial service for friends and family. Sadly, she was delayed in the States where her project, brilliantly transformed into a photographic essay on the oldest female film stars in America, 'The Eye of Aquinas', was a great success and when she returned to London some months later she confessed that she had forgotten all about the memorial service.

'Your Papa would have understood, my little Bella.'

We took a flat on the northern heights of London overlooking a square. It went by the name of Pond Square though it was neither watery nor square but was in fact an ovoid of solid earth covered with tarmac and surrounded by elderly plane trees. Boys played football against the wall of the public convenience which stood rather proudly at one corner having about it the air of an old auberge, rather comfortable and welcoming, or perhaps the sort of modest bar you'd find in some small, out-of-the-way French village.

Appearances deceive. That is their function, particularly in England. I have gathered together a number of useful proverbs which attest to this truth during the course of my English classes at the Academy where I have made reasonable progress over the past three years since we moved to London. I know for instance that beauty is only skin deep, that it is in the eye of the beholder; that handsome is as handsome does. I make my annual visit to my grandmother in the thin house at the top of the village of La Frisette, every July. 'French leave' Mama calls it. Like many English expressions it disturbs my grandmother. And when I translate these for her she treats them with disbelief and loathing. Her lips tighten and compress into a hard, thin line, a crack so narrow it would not admit even a coin, and when she sniffs, short and hard, her nostrils pinch together. Her skin is very fine and she looks like a delicate creature flinching when she does that. Anemones, or butterflies' wings, are not more delicate than the little indentations of distaste registered on my grandmother's nostrils when I come out with such expressions.

Now I'm back in La Frisette for the duration. Ever since Mama disappeared into America. I suppose she must have found herself – and lost me. She communicates regularly; I get dollar bills, sometimes pretty large denominations, from Tampa and Dallas. She used to scrawl a few lines across the notes: *'Beauty is always so appropriate – but so fast. Must rush!'* Or: *'We will have the funeral, one day. Promise.'* But soon the messages stopped and just the bills arrived. I keep the money in the silver trunk under my bed, with my chocolate supplies. I'm saving up, for something.

# 2

Each glittering summer in the house high above the lake, between the church and the Bellevue Hotel, overlooking the village square; ever since I was a tiny girl I have come to the house in July, on my own, and been welcomed by my French family of Grand-mère and Uncle Claude.

When I was little Grand-mère carried up the stairs every night a cup of hot chocolate with which I was soothed before going to sleep. She cupped it in her palms and this made the steam seem to rise from her hands. Long before she entered my bedroom, long before I even heard her feet on the stairs, the milky fragrance reached me, the warm sweet genie left the mug and communicated with me. On the cup, which was white with a thick lip and a generous ear, there appeared the picture of a man in a top hat leading a bear on a chain. The bear was muzzled, and padded behind the plump gentleman in his frock coat who put his feet down with complete confidence. When I saw the picture I always felt sad for the bear, but then I would drink my hot chocolate and drowsiness soaked up sorrow like blotting paper. All that was human was to be found in the downcast face of that plodding bear; everything that was most beastly in the fat proud man, beginning with the hard shine on his top hat and going right down to the hatefully confident angle of his little feet. I believe that had it not been for the chocolate I would have tossed and turned and dreamed of the bear. But however much that picture moved me, the chocolate took away my worries and I never dreamed of the bear.

I dream now. Sometimes I think that if only we could return to those times, those evenings, my grandmother and I, then the dreams would stop. I eat large amounts of chocolate but this does not have a soothing effect, in fact, quite the opposite, for the taste of the chocolate, sweet or bitter, reminds me that the cup, the man and the bear are forever out of my reach.

23

When my father died and it was announced that my mother was selling the apartment in Paris and moving to England, my Uncle Claude broke the cup.

He dropped it on the stone floor of the dining room, a complex pattern of octagonal black-and-white tiles that reminded me, when I was younger, of the eye of a fly I saw hugely magnified in the photographic exhibition held to celebrate the opening of the old Mairie, restored by Monsieur Cherubini in the days when he still spent his money on restoring old monuments and did not give it all to that disgusting party of which he is the principal benefactor and guardian angel.

The *Parti National Populaire* is, against all expectation, increasingly successful and claims it will win seats in the National Assembly at the next election. It has already found favour in our village. Party backing ensured that my Uncle Claude received the nomination for mayor. It was in fact on the day that he was installed in office and took up his sash in the newly renovated *mairie* that he dropped my bear cup on the kitchen floor, where it did not so much smash but exploded with a dull crump. That day also happened to be my tenth birthday. It was the only time that Uncle Claude actually marked my birthday. In a few weeks' time I will turn sixteen and I can tell you I won't be surprised if Uncle Claude celebrates by burning my clothes or hiding my tapes. He insists that I attend the big rally to be held in the village square by Monsieur Cherubini on Saturday. Monsieur Cherubini, says my uncle, is the true guardian angel of the Party and a model for any young person.

'A paragon of strength, purposeful and honest, a vital force,' remarked Uncle Claude. 'A simple, passionate follower of science and truth.'

Men are the fools boys grow into. It's not enough that Uncle Claude should have spent his life shut away, contemplating the mysterious origins of the universe and then one day think he is fitted for the job of mayor. But he is also determined to woo converts. From his bedroom in my grandmother's house, where he still lives, he has been catapulted into the brutally refurbished *mairie*, an elegant house built before the Revolution into which the Guardian Angel has introduced his ideas of preservation. A steel brace supports the roof, great glass panels prevent access to the central courtyard though they allow a glimpse of the gleaming interior, polished like a tooth; the façade is stripped to what he insists is its original severe purity. It looks like the face of an ancient actress caught in the cold light of dawn before she could apply her makeup. It's cruel, what they've done to the old house, even picking out its birth date, 1673, in gold paint on its scrubbed face. My Uncle Claude goes to that place every morning and pretends to be busy. There really is nothing to do. He places the cards showing the temperatures of the day in their wooden slot; he squares off the maps of the lake and the mountains; the time-table for the ferries that cruise between the villages around the lake is moved a little to the left or the right; the prices of the tennis courts and the times of the church services are similarly adjusted and then he sits in his new office for a few hours signing papers. At twelve o'clock he goes to his room and his real work.

Uncle Claude is an atheist and a cosmologist. The order is important because the first depends for proof on the second. He studies the latest developments in the search for the origins of the universe with great excitement. His talk is all of the Higgs Transition. He is determined to prove that belief in God is so much 'intellectual excrement'. This is Uncle Claude's mission in life.

'I have now advanced to the point where it seems to be clear, and will seem to everyone else undeniable, that God has been beaten back to the very rim of time and is clinging there by his fingernails. A terminal figment. It cannot be much longer before he is released from his misery and drops unlamented into the abyss. And the further the faster!'

I do not like this view of things. Taking a different tack, I hear noises, I hear his scream. It changes pitch as he falls. This is called the Doppler effect. A similar observation, applied to the movement of galaxies by the astronomer Hubble, showed the famous red shifts. The red shift told Hubble the galaxies were rushing apart at many thousands of kilometres a second. The most distant galaxies were travelling at the greatest velocities – or, in Uncle Claude's words: 'The further, the faster!' Another is: 'The earlier, the smaller!' This refers to the fact that as we trace the inflation of the early universe back through the first few minutes, it becomes smaller and smaller until it gets to a point so tiny it may not exist at all.

What concerns cosmologists is what they call the first four minutes of creation, beginning at zero time, or T equals nought, when the very young universe begins to expand furiously, fifteen to twenty billion years ago. During this very early, fabulous period of expansion there was created all the matter in the universe which became in time the great swirling clouds of gas and dust from which evolved all the galaxies, all the stars, suns, comets, asteroids, planets, all the solar systems, all the heavenly bodies (if we can still use this phrase without embarrassment), all the worlds that are or ever will be. Zero time marks the point when there occurred the unimaginably violent primary explosion known with rather affecting understatement as the 'Big Bang'. This is the chosen field of Uncle Claude's enquiry. But in a sense, the bulk of these four minutes is not very interesting to him, for while the most extraordinary things happened in that time the actual business of creation was already under way, the show was running, the clock had started and most of the really important developments took place in a period of time so brief it is quite impossible to imagine. Uncle Claude will say that it was about a millionth of the time it takes light to cross a photon, or the first billion trillionth of a second after Big Bang. But then that's Uncle Claude's opinion and of no use to anyone. At any rate the really important thing, it seems, is to get back to the moment when it all begins, to push back through the four minutes to that fragment of time, that alpha point at which absolutely nothing very suddenly became something. It is essential to press back towards this point in order to deal with religious fanatics who claim that no matter how big the bang, someone had to set it off. Who demand to know why there should be anything at all and not just nothing.

'Childish, metaphysical ignorance! We will answer them once and for all when we can push back to the earliest moments. We can get back now to the fragment of time when the universe was about a millionth of a second old. But that's very late in the day, Bella. By then, the universe is already about the size of our solar system. The time of the quarks. But we must get back further, to the very first beginnings of the flash. Then we will find answers to what we already know to be the case. The unity of all the forces.'

Uncle Claude believes that in the beginning there was GUT, and in GUT there were contained the four Universal Forces: the 'weak' and 'strong' nuclear forces, the electromagnetic and gravitational which, in the old times, were one. GUT is also called Grand Unification Theory. Before the creation of the universe and before the beginning of time unity existed in the divine speck of nothing, or next to nothing. And only then. When the speck exploded, GUT went with it, the four forces of the apocalypse broke up and galloped all over the universe. Ever since then people like my Uncle Claude have been trying to put the forces together again.

'When we do that, we'll have TOE! The Theory Of Everything! What do you think of that, Bella?'

I think I'd like to smack his face.

Uncle Claude only asks questions to which he knows there are answers. The answers send him crunching towards the 'shivering figment' clinging to the precipice of time by his fingernails. The tread of Uncle Claude's boots echoed through my dreams. In my dreams I saw them cruelly studded, nearing the edge of the cliff where the fingers clutched, the blood blushing beneath the divine nails. I heard the cry as the poor figment plunged into the abyss and I woke sweating and crying and Grand-mère would bustle up the stairs in her pink flannel gown and sit by my side smoothing my hair until I had calmed down. To add further to my fear Uncle Claude made sure that I knew from a very early stage that the universe was not infinite, nor was it eternal. Our sun would one day run out of nuclear fuel, grow into a huge red giant and incinerate all life; eventually it would shrink and grow cool and dark and dead. So would we. Then also there was no point in snatching at some dream of the universe as expanding forever, infinite in size, unending in its glory. The universe had an edge. Astronomers were reaching out further and further with the electronic cameras and would soon be bumping up against the very limit of the universe, millions of light years away.

But what is this edge? Is it what a fly must feel when it is trapped in a bottle and bumps against the sides?

'Bella, stop being foolish. With you everything is birds or flowers or bees! There is no bottle. There is no fly.'

'Then what is there?'

'There is nothing. The universe simply runs out.'

This is it then. At the beginning, according to Uncle Claude, there had been nothing and then the next minute there was something. There was a speck of matter, which exploded, then there was a lump of matter about the size of a grapefruit which kept on inflating and suddenly everything came into being. At the end of space time, says Uncle Claude, where there was something, there will suddenly be nothing.

'That's it. There we are. Or rather, there you are.'

He gives an impish smile when he says this, as if his pronouncements contain a delicious irony, but one which can be savoured only by atheist uncles.

'You ask stupid questions, Bella,' says Uncle Claude. 'It's as well you have your looks, my girl. Because you're going to need them. There is nothing beyond the edge. Nothing!'

It was in this mood of spiteful glee that Uncle Claude abused me when I was small. Not physically but arithmetically, not with his fingers but with figures. He would watch me slyly, sneaking up on me when I was playing with my doll, Gloria, and he knew I was utterly absorbed. Gloria was a plump, porcelain creature with silly red hair, much darker than mine, and grass-green eyes, perfectly lashed. She was also far older than me and some accident had robbed her of three fingers on her right hand. I played hospital with her, being both the doctor who gravely shook his head and called for bandages at the sight of Gloria's poor hand, and the nurse who put her to bed and bound the injury. I would feel Uncle Claude's presence before I saw him because his shadow fell on me as I played in a corner of the garden beneath the great chestnut tree. I wore white often in those days – it made me feel medicinal and Grand-mère would tie my blue sash around my waist in a plump bow, with a matching ribbon in my hair.

My darling Gloria! She lost her fingers in not one but in a series of tragic accidents. Once she had been sailing on a lagoon in Tahiti, leaning back on the purple cushions of a barge and trailing her hand in the water when a shark had taken the fingers. Then she had been waylaid in a dark wood on the way home after selling her grandmother's last pig at the market, a silver coin clutched in her hand. She ran home to the hovel where her poor, ailing grandmother lay in bed calling weakly for the soup that would save her life when suddenly a cutpurse, reeking of woodsmoke and onions, stepped from the shadows and seized the coin. Gloria bravely resisted and the thief sliced off her fingers with a razor. Finally, she had also been a violin prodigy until a mysterious wasting illness infected her hand and the doctors were forced to amputate – oh! how dreadful! Whenever she heard the Beethoven Violin Concerto her fingers miraculously bled. I began unrolling my precious strip of bandage, rather grubby I fear, and retaining only the merest hint of its old antiseptic aroma. The doctor (whom I became) gave instructions to the nurse (whom I would become) and Gloria's green eyes shone with love and gratitude.

'Would you like some of these?' Uncle Claude's familiar words when he proposed an assault. And what were 'these'? These were always the same: golden coins stamped with the head of Napoleon and the frieze of the Arc de Triomphe all silvered with sugar button eyes, or bicycles with spokes so fine you felt they had been spun by spiders – but always *chocolate*: white, brown, dark, sweet or bitter. He chose his moment. He knew my weakness. How could it be otherwise? Each summer I sailed through the blazing months like some tiny craft on an ocean huge and empty, glittering like a mirror in which I saw few faces but my own. Papa was in Africa, Mama was photographing America and Gloria was ill with a damaged hand. Of course he knew his moment.

And so I went with him to his room. Den might have been a better word. Or lair. There among his books and journals on stars and quasars and mu-mesons, he prodded me with his figures.

'If nine men with ten wheelbarrows excavate an area of eleven cubic metres in twelve days, how long does it take three men to excavate the same area?'

The warm sweet taste of the chocolate was still on my tongue, guiltily cloying, as I forced my mind to go down this path. I got no further than the first two figures. Never.

After that my understanding darkened, sweat broke out on my upper lip. I was lost.

At about this time I began growing my nails. Grand-mère objected: 'At your young age, you cannot do that. What do you want with long nails?'

'I'm frightened by some men.'

'Which men?'

'Claudistes.'

My uncle gave me that grim and yet strangely happy, tight smile. 'Come Bella, let me hear you. At least let me *feel* your thinking.'

I grew to resist this assault. To fight back tooth and nail. I learnt, bit by bit, how to reprove his heated probing and teasing. I *thought*, yes – I thought of the nine men. Were they fat or thin? Short or tall? I saw their hands calloused from the heavy barrows, their boots thick with the dust of the soil they excavated. Were they married? And did their wives love them? Did they not object to being sent to work by Uncle Claude? Set in motion to satisfy a mathematical whim?

'What are they called?'

'That's besides the point.'

'What's their nationality? Are they Turks?'

'There are no men, Bella. They have no names. They are just words I used to explain the problem to you.'

'Then shall we say they're Turks? Or Arabs?'

There it was. They were created by him just to illustrate the workings of numbers. These men could expect no help from Uncle Claude. Just as the poor figment clinging by his nails to the precipice could expect no mercy as the stubborn boots crunched closer and closer, and I awoke crying in the dead of night.

There was also the damn grapefruit. The conceptions of the universe, as I remember them from my earliest years, changed, according to Uncle Claude's teaching, in the light of new discoveries. When I was very young I remember his saying to me that the universe probably began in its very earliest stages as a lump of matter about the size of a grapefruit, fourteen or fifteen billion years ago. Everything that now is was compressed into this ball. Of course even then, and I couldn't have been more than five or six, I learnt not to ask what size the grapefruit was, and whether it was the small African variety or the fat pink fleshy fruit from Florida. For I knew the answer to that – 'Bella, there *is* no grapefruit!'

Then there was the problem of how life came to be. We came, Uncle Claude taught, out of the primeval soup which existed on the cooling planet aeons ago. In this soup were, among other things, proteins and nucleic acids. Necessity and chance mated in the watery Eden and life grew out of this chemical brew, evolved into microbes and gave rise to us. We are the result of collaborations of the first primitive cell creatures. We are their cathedrals. Cells are machines for translating messages. Molecules associate and life emerges. And what is the meaning of the message contained in the elementary proteins from which we are formed? Why – *we* are the meaning of the message.

Can you truly say that you're surprised that I talk, and sometimes walk, in my sleep! 'Amino acids!' I cry, to the alarm of my grandmother who speaks no English but rises hurriedly from her bed seizing her black walking-stick with its silver duck's head handle, knocking over the photograph of Marshal Pétain, and calling on my Uncle Claude to save me from the 'ameenos!' whom she believes are in the pay of the hated English. Chains of DNA, pulsing like jellyfish, swim through my dreams!

There you have Uncle Claude's two lessons. In the beginning, the universe grew from a grapefruit; and man is descended from soup. There is the difference between us. Uncle Claude believes in equations, I believe in God. My problem, too, is that it is a lot easier to believe in God than it is to believe in Uncle Claude. And a lot more interesting. I fought back. I read his books. Reading is revenge! I found out about something called the Planck Wall. It seemed you could go back only so far into the very first moments of the Big Bang; at $10^{-43}$ seconds after ignition you hit the wall. Everything broke down. Nothing could get past the wall. Next time he picked on me I said:

'So what about the Planck Wall?'

He got really shirty then. 'Who told you about that?'

'Nothing can get past the Planck Wall. We'll never know what's on the other side.'

'You're too young to talk about such things!'

One day Gloria disappeared. I think I know what happened. Just as Uncle Claude had smashed my favourite cup, he had kidnapped Gloria, stolen into my room one night while she slept beside me and carried her away. I was so convinced of it I expected a ransom note:

*'Stop lying about the world. Do your sums or Gloria gets it!'*

I searched Uncle Claude's observatory at the top of the house where he scans the heavens for comets – he is determined to have a comet named after him – and where he does his experiments into the origins of life on earth, a smelly mixture of chemicals in a glass tank he calls 'the soup of life'.

In my dreams Gloria appeared to me in grainy videos, looking thin and pale, with a sign around her neck: PRISONER OF THE CLAUDISTES. I'm sure he tried to get her to learn the names of all the sub-atomic particles, to confess that soon all the world would recognise the historical necessity of the rule of quantum-mechanics.

But I knew my Gloria. She was brave. She had her nursing experience to fall back on. And if she had kept her fiddle she would cheer herself by playing defiant snatches of the Beethoven Violin Concerto.

Still, I knew she was gone. And I could not even send her notes, or money, the way Mama did. One day she would turn up in a shoe box, or a drawer, or at the back of a cupboard, or in a car boot . . . with her neck broken, or a bullet in the back of her head.

It's mid-morning and the sun is blazing in a perfect sky. Over the rocky mountain that forms the curving right arm of the little bay, the hawks are hunting. At first they are so high above the mountain that they appear like specks, floating scraps of blackened paper after a fire. It's only when they swoop lazily lower that you realise that these are serious killers. They spread their wings and glide lower still, like planes waiting to land. I know they will hunt all day, rising and falling on the thermal air currents, suddenly plunging for the kill. An unobservant creature might imagine them to be wind-blown specks, distant, unimportant and harmless. Such creatures, no doubt, make perfect prey.

Beneath the slats of the wooden jetty the lake water curls and slides like dark green silk. In the sunlight it has a thick folded quality, while in the shadowy corners it ripples like black cream. Ria and Beatrice, the young blonde daughters of the Dutch couple, have removed their tops and are taking it in turns to oil each other's breasts. The mother, Magda, is tall and auburn-haired with a fussy, aggressive manner; she bullies her blonde daughters on whose perfect faces there appear no traces of emotion. They are as smooth as soap. Magda resents their shining perfection; she sends them back to the hotel time and again for her wrap, her book, for drinks, for more suntan cream. She is one of those curiously shaped women with very long legs, though the upper half of her body is packed into a black swimsuit and has a dense, oblong look. Her bottom is spreading and there are wrinkles around her neck. She wears white mules with thick heels which emphasise the distance between her shaggy footwear, which gives her the look of standing somewhat bizarrely up to her ankles in snow, and the tops of her thighs where rolls of brown and rather leathery flesh mar the line of what are otherwise very good legs. Her husband, Wim, reclines beside her in his deckchair; he wears short white socks and sandals and he studies *De Telegraaf* through large, gold-rimmed glasses. A handsome man who seems younger than his wife, he is clearly the source from which the daughters derive their blonde good looks. Doubtless this is a constant source of frustration to the mother who gazes down the long length of her legs to where her daughters sit on their towels rubbing oil into their breasts. They have the most perfect breasts. Beatrice must be about seventeen and her breasts have the dense, chubby compactness of peachflesh. Ria would be about twenty or so and is very fully developed. Her breasts have a lovely lolling quality to them, firm yet elastic with delightful natural bounce. Now that they are oiled and gleaming they lie back and close their eyes and offer their breasts to the sun. The mother was beautiful once and that is surely the real source of her dissatisfaction. That is why she bridles at the unruffled surface her daughters present. That is why she harries them for drinks, books, attention. The daughters speak seldom and seem joined in some secret which faintly amuses them. When she can't stand it any more, the mother pulls the costume to her waist and her pendulous dugs tumble alarmingly into view.

Raoul, the escapee from the Foreign Legion, is watching the girls. He cannot keep his eyes off their breasts. He pretends to be watching the water-skiers, the windsurfers, the hawks overhead, but I can see what he is really watching and what he is thinking. He wears a pair of rather wide, full, very old-fashioned swimming trunks. The impact of those breasts on Raoul's imagination is being registered in the centre of the swimming trunks which appear to be made from some material resembling old and grubby parachute silk. There I see the pointer or indicator or dial of Raoul's emotions rising noticeably, deep within his deeply unfashionable swimming trunks. In this manner I imagine Red Indians once raised their tepees. Poor Raoul! Does he not understand that those breasts are not the objects of desire he imagines? They are exposed solely and simply for browning beneath the solar grill. Their aim is not to seduce, they rebuff glances as they would a caress. They are not here for that. His swelling prologue lacks a theme. Uncle Claude would explain what is happening in basic, biological terms. He would recognise that erectile tissues are responding to the stimulus inspired by well-oiled mammary glands. What could be more natural or inevitable? The boy's organ is responding to signals, a nervous reaction takes place, his penis rises. Simple, natural – and what is natural gives Uncle Claude fierce joy. Doubtless, he would say, the boy's brain tells him that he likes the look of the Dutch girls, or that their breasts are beautiful, but these are pretty strategems by which we humans trick out brute reality. The girls are just bait, flowers for the bee.

Uncle Claude worships the understanding. He believes it is omnipotent, he believes his own eyes, though of course he is willing to change his mind in the light of the evidence. Evidence means a lot to Uncle Claude, the facts of the case. There were, for instance, the facts of the case of the postboy Clovis and me in the bar of the Priory Hotel a few nights ago. The bar was rather cold and so we were sitting close together in the corner booth with its pink plush benches and marble tables. The ceiling is low and groined, short squat pillars support the roof. Were it not for the bar in the corner you might think you were in a crypt. You'd not be very far wrong because the bar of the Priory was in fact the infirmary of the old monastery where the sick and dying lay under the eye of the infirmarian, according to the very strict rules of the order. For everything in the house of the Carthusians was ordered, written down. Indeed, a visit to the infirmary was likely to be the only time the monk ever left his cell, except for his visits to the chapel for lauds, matins and vespers. For the rest they were always alone in their hairshirts and their silence. Dying, however, was a communal affair, particularly if illness attended one's departure. Dying was a time of bells. If one was very weak, a time of soup and perhaps a little fish, even a taste of meat, forbidden on all other occasions. When a brother lay dying he entered what they called 'the agony'; the monks came to pray by him and the Paschal candle smoked in the corner. Now it was Clovis and I who sat in the old infirmary and Clovis had something almost like the agony on him. But there was no priest, no candle, and only Emile the barman fiddling with his drinks up at the other end. As Clovis leaned his head on my shoulder, I held his hand. It wasn't much but I felt for Clovis and that's not surprising. The idiot had this enormous black boot he was forced to wear because of the polio he had contracted when a child. His right leg was not more than a stick of bone and he dragged it behind him with a great heavy hoof attached to it which made him walk as if he were continually beginning to climb a flight of stairs and missing his step. The bar was cold, clammy, damp and dull – but we drank beakers of Emile's *coupe maison* as if we hadn't noticed. Clovis had dyed his hair bright green and wore it in a stiff wedge, like an axe-head of grass.

'The Party is anticipating a wonderful rally in the Square,' Clovis told me excitedly. 'The biggest ever. Speakers will come from many large cities. Lyons, of course, and even Paris. You and your family have honoured places on the platform. I am to act as an aide as well as to help direct the cars to their places. The chief of police is designating the entire village a parking area. I am to have a new uniform' – he pressed his mouth to my ear - 'even a new boot! Of crystal!'

'People park everywhere as it is.'

'Yes, but this time no one will be permitted to complain.'

'The Angel has arranged this?'

'Naturally, together with the Mayor.'

'The Angel is a shit.'

'Bella, I implore you – speak softly.'

Clovis buried his head in my shoulder as if this would hide him from anyone listening.

Note the ostrich logic. The silly fool was at the mercy of the world and as if having to drag around that great black weight at the end of his withered leg were not enough, long suffering had made him simple and his wish to be loved had placed him in irons.

Uncle Claude entered at that moment and believed the evidence of his eyes. He brushed past Emile the barman, who endeavoured to cheer him up or slow him down, or perhaps (am I unworthy in my suspicions?) to ingratiate himself by offering him a 'cup of the house' which was, I should say, a subtle blend of lime and kiwi fruit on a base of sparkling wine spiked with vodka and garnished with a sprig of peppermint, an apéritif of his own devising offered with a full heart to guests of the Priory. He needn't have bothered. Uncle Claude brushed him aside with an expression of exasperation and disgust, as one might reject the salaams of some beggar or street drunk. Just as well none of the guests in the hotel was present in the bar to witness this display of rudeness – not, I fear, that my uncle would have cared a straw if there had been – but I felt for myself, my family and the unfortunate Clovis on whom my uncle bore down with a look of puffy self-importance that made me want to shriek.

He planted himself in front of our table. 'I'm despatched by your grandmother with instructions to escort you home.'

Clovis lifted his head from my neck at the sound of my uncle's voice and blinked with the sweet bovine glassiness of a cow lifting her head from the manger. Poor dear fellow! It is true that he pressed close to me. It's true that he was stroking my arm, but in the way that a child will do, in order to give comfort to himself not to stimulate me.

'Good evening, Monsieur le Maire.'

My uncle ignored this salute and as he did my look of extreme displeasure mingled, I hope, with contempt. I went with him not out of any sense of obedience, but because I knew he was capable of causing a scene and Clovis did not deserve that. But I ignored the arm Uncle offered me and side by frosty side we passed out into the night. Emile the barman caught my wink and lifted a glass of the 'cup of the house' in ironic salutation. Clovis stared after us with bloodshot eyes.

What Uncle Claude hates about Clovis is his limp. His boot. That's strange, given that my uncle laughs at the foundation of the world and stamps on the fingernails of the divine figment until blood spurts all over his shoes, and shrugs about the heat death of the universe as he blows on his coffee. The sun may expand into a red giant and cook us all, or the universe may reach the outer limits of its expansion, may go into reverse and deflate like a child's balloon popped at a party, running backwards into a point of singular nothingness – it can do all this and Uncle Claude will look on with a grin and a wink. But show him a boy bitten by a bug in his babyhood and my uncle throws his hands to his eyes and runs away like a medieval peasant faced by a leper. It makes him feel ill, unclean.

'Nothing distinguishes us from the more primitive life forms – except perhaps the number of accidents in the replication of the genetic material over a very brief period – cosmically speaking.'

You heard him say that? You're my witness, aren't you? And I tell you, it stinks. Because it sounds like science and all it is is a complaint about behaviour.

'Uncle Claude, does a virus have a conscience? Can it sin?'

'Don't be silly.'

Do you understand the nature of the lie being told? Every blink of his eyes is a lie.

What drives scientists is the same thing which drove priests long ago. Power. Knowing secrets.

'Clovis is my friend. That's all.'

'The lad's no good for you. A fugitive from reality. So much space in his attic you could fly owls up there.'

'The Angel thinks he could be useful.'

'Monsieur Cherubini, if you please. The *patron* takes a wide view. Political considerations, Bella, make for unexpected associations.'

'Strange bedfellows.'

He shivers. 'I beg your pardon?'

'It's an English expression.'

'Of course. Someone said that wisdom begins with the rejection of English ideas. The point is that you're here now with us, in France. Your family. What do you think I feel if I have to go out at night and find you drinking with the postboy in the Priory, which is full of strange types. Some of the worst among the management. Closely followed by some of the guests. If you won't consider my feelings, think of your grandmama. She feels the responsibility since your mother left.'

We were walking slowly up the hill to our house at the top of the village. The air felt warm and fat and carried the smell of jasmine. In the moonlight the lake kept its large eye on us.

'I wish you wouldn't always personalise issues, Bella. For you everything must be individualised. That's bad because it prevents clear thought. Remember that evolution only takes account of transmissable mutations, exterior forces acting by chance, over time, on strains within the population. Single deformations don't count. Freaks are a sideshow. Bad science.'

I reach up and touch his neck suddenly in the moonlight and he flinches.

'You jumped! You're frightened of freaks, you think you'll catch something! Shame on you!'

'Don't do that, Bella!'

'I'm your prisoner, aren't I? Like Gloria.'

'Gloria?'

'You know who I mean. I know you stole and hid her. Well I'm not staying for long, I promise you. I'm just waiting.'

'And for what might you be waiting?'

'For Mama to come back.'

'I don't think she will, you know. She's left for good.'

'Then I'll wait for Papa. When he calls.'

'From Africa? What makes you think so?'

'I don't think so, I know so.'

I knew nothing of the sort but I said it all the same and I made it sound as if I meant it. I think I did mean it.

'Now, Bella, don't cry,' says Uncle Claude. 'I know it's hard to be young. I was young too.'

*

Another lie. My uncle purports to be my father's younger brother. By five years! What a bloody joke that is. When Uncle Claude was a boy he must have looked exactly as he does now, stooped, lined, his little sharp beetle face pecking at the world. He'd be much shorter then, that's all, a middle-aged dwarf, who went about terrifying his friends as soon as he could talk. Telling them that there was no bright heaven presided over by a loving father; instead the universe was a dead loss. It wasn't even particularly majestic, or infinite or filled with zillions of worlds. It was dark, cold, empty and probably stone dead. I saw big-little Claude jumping out of the bushes with questions about whether the universe was open or closed. When he was a young-old man they thought it was closed. Now that he's an old-old man, they say it's probably open. Big deal!

Much more important seems to me his complete misreading of Clovis. The boy is too wild, too weak-willed, to be trained for the sort of thing Uncle Claude and the Angel have in mind. His problem isn't love, it's drugs. Wherever he gets them, whatever they are, he takes them all the time and jumps on his yellow post-office autocycle and tears up and down the streets of the village like a madman, his face ice-white, the wretched little two-stroke machine bucking and coughing like the sad mechanical incompetent it is, not the modern invention the post office passes it off as. Mind you, to Clovis in his bombed-out, smashed state of euphoria, I suppose it's a celestial steed, a Pegasus, and he is Hermes, messenger of the gods. His long green hair scything the air has the sheen you see when the wind presses and polishes a patch of grass. He moves too slowly to be much of a danger, except perhaps to the hard of hearing, and the very old, as he putters through the hidden lanes, covered in clematis and ivy, climbing roses and bougainvillaea, which run between and behind the lakeside hotels, and connect the few steep roads plunging to the waterside, riding with remarkable composure, but absolutely gassed to the eyeballs. Owl-eyed, rigid with dignity, out and about on his business as if commanded by some heavenly general. There's a big number 4 on the front mudguard of his bike. This does not mean that there are three other postboys, no – there is only Clovis, rushing at heaven knows what speeds down what his stoked-up head tells him are the boulevards of his dreams. And likely to write himself off, sooner rather than later. Now the Angel has told him he is also an integral part of their new political movement and that at the very next rally he'll be in charge of the motorised communication division. What worries me is that Clovis just doesn't sniff and smoke his drugs, he injects them as well, and he has no money for fresh needles. If hepatitis doesn't get him, something worse will. Uncle Claude thinks that I make love to Clovis. This shows pretty clearly how very little he really knows about the world. Who makes love nowadays? What I give Clovis is cash intended for clean needles, because I worry about him. But he spends it on more pills and powders. It's not myself I press on Clovis, it's my money. The Angel and Uncle Claude and their Party wish to employ Clovis when they have made their revolution. He tells me that he will be dressed in 'light' colours when they have, as they say, 'chastened the channels of communication' of which the postal services, being the most democratic and closest to the people, deserve the fiercest attention. 'Pornography clogs the mails just as foreigners bloat the slums' — that's the cry of the Party. Clovis and the police chief Pesché, for their own reasons, are recruits to the Party.

My father detested and scorned these dreams. If he could see how the Party has grown in strength, the rallies, the looked-for seats in the Assembly, he would turn in his grave, that's if he has a grave in which to turn. It's odd that someone should disappear so completely. His grave is unknown, his memorial service forgotten. Our apartment in the sixteenth arrondissement sold and the officials in Papa's government department shrugging their shoulders and looking blank whenever we ask them for news of what was happening to him, or where he lay buried, for Papa's disappearance from the face of the earth and from the memory of the government he served is total. He is as if he never was. 'Lost in Africa', the shoehorn official told us after we sold the apartment and he added, as if this would encourage spiritual acceptance, 'and Africa is a big place'.

It was with Papa's death that I discovered we had been rich. I learnt this when we suddenly became poor. The second-floor apartment in the rue Vandal with its rare collections of antelope masks from the Ivory Coast, masks with weary, hooded eyes carved of black wood; soap-stone sculptures of old men taking their ease on small chairs; Bundu masks from Sierra Leone with their funny squashed faces and helmets like knights; grave-faced Basuku masks, dreamily sedate faces with wooden birds perched on their heads and great straw beards – all sold from under our feet and the proceeds seized 'pending investigation'. What investigation? And my mother, beside herself with worry (who could blame her?), stole away to England – as if she recognised her status had been diminished.

I was just twelve and at twelve one doesn't have many alternatives. One puzzles, wonders, weeps and perhaps learns the sounds of idiomatic English at the North London Academy for Girls even if the food was so bad that my appetite began to fail. One reads and talks to oneself, and grows up fast.

It was at about this time that I began to depend more and more on chocolates. My tastes are pretty catholic: *Praline, After Eights* and *Rolos*, as well as *Lindt Excellence, Côte d'Or 'Extra Dry'* and *Cadbury's Bourneville Dark*. I'm not a chocolate snob, I'm a chocolate catholic. It began as a comfort but it became my salvation. Faced by the barbaric custom of feeding children at school which the English adopt, faced by little cow-pats of grey meat between buns; or the minced remainders of yesterday's lunch floating in a greasy soup covered in an elderly thatch of potato and called a 'pie', I turned to the corner shop and there among the racks of chocolate found how to save myself.

My mother took the diminution in status quite well. She would work at becoming an independent, fully rounded human being. Once, many years before, she had been a beauty queen, she told me. This came as a surprise because she is now a short, rather squat woman with a small nose, a large mouth and no shape worth mentioning. There were one or two false starts on her way back to self-sufficiency. She laid aside her camera and became for a while a follower of the Bhagwan, dressed in purple, and came home at odd hours smelling of herbs. But that passed, I'm pleased to say, when she picked up the camera again. She did this while showing me pictures of herself in her days as a beauty. In the late sixties she had been Miss Torquay and even as late as 1969 she'd been crowned Queen of the Coast by the Mayor of Bournemouth. The photograph showed her wearing high heels, the sash of office and her crown tiered like a wedding cake. In the photograph of her enthronement as Queen of the Southern Region she is being kissed on the cheek by a man who presents his bottom to the camera while he pecks her cheek. She grins at the viewer with a frighteningly rigid smile. The man who is kissing her was apparently a well-known television personality. For what he was well known she could not remember. Even though I find a man's bottom is possibly his most revealing feature, in this case it gave nothing away.

'That was a competition organised by the Railway Service of the Southern Region, Bella. In Britain the provinces are called regions, as you will discover.'

For a while, after leaving the Bhagwan, Mama was a feminist and when I was twelve she decided we should both attend body awareness classes. These took place in a private room in a local gymnasium. About twelve women met there and took off their clothes and examined themselves minutely in front of large mirrors while in the background Vivaldi played on tape. I found it rather dull. I saw in the mirror what I saw every morning in the mirror at home: a somewhat thin, leggy girl with nice but small breasts, boy's hips, rather flat ugly knees, body hair beginning to sprout, even then I had this early shading of hair just above the ankles, like the top half of a pair of socks! A square open face in which the eyes were possibly the best features, large and grey with lashes I'm really quite pleased with, a recurrent patch of acne around the right-hand corner of my mouth which is reflected more faintly in about the same place on the left. I have noticed that spots on one side of the face frequently have their doubles on the other side, only slightly less severe and about five millimetres or so higher. Pretty boring really. I looked at myself in the mirror but there was so little to see. The other women were older and perhaps read more into themselves. To see them stroking and cooing to their calves and elbows, and doing what were called 'touch and appreciation sessions' was really quite eerie. There followed something called 'naming of parts'. We were invited to give new, loving, non-abusive names to our most-loved and secret parts. The women came up with names like Daisy and Mick and Honeypot. We could write songs or poems about them. One woman composed a hymn to her breasts which she sang to us. Several of the group wept and felt deeply religious and no one was surprised when the lady told us she had once been a nun. The next phase was to be the use of the speculum to examine ourselves internally.

I was relieved when Mama decided we had seen enough. We left these astronomers of their inner selves, searching their secret places. I was pleased when we came away. Frankly I had had more fun when I was seven and the grocer's son Henri bribed me with toffee and nougat to take my clothes off in the old stables of the Priory Hotel, which are now the garages above which the staff live in cramped rooms. The offer was irresistible and the look on Henri's face as I slid the cotton drawers over my hips was more fun than anything I saw before, or since. The minutes in front of the mirror with the sisters of Narcissus at their internal inspections did not appeal to me. Besides, I thought the speculum would do me damage. I could hardly tell the other women that I was a virgin. I knew just by looking at them how embarrassed they would be. I'm sure they would have blamed my mother.

I want to say, and I know that this is going to sound terrible, really *terrible,* but I haven't done it, not can't, but haven't, yet, don't rule it out but won't, not for a while. It came as a terrible shock to Mama to find out.

'What? Not even once? But darling!'

'It's OK. Really. I mean there are people around who – haven't.'

'But darling – oh you poor thing!'

My mother had been liberated, you see. Well, of course you see. She took the pill early and got a lot of experience. It kept her busy and feeling good. And at the time she was beautiful. This was before she woke up one morning and found herself little, dark and plump and her beauty vanished like a dream. And it was that sort of time, the sixties and seventies, whenever that was, anyway centuries ago when time blurred and everyone did it in the road, if you believe the lyrics. So I didn't expect her to understand and I couldn't bear her sympathy.

'Actually, I intend staying this way until I find a man I love and then I plan to give myself to him.'

My mother clutched her heart, shocked speechless.

It was shortly after this that she set off on her quest to discover the meaning of beauty and went to the States and I never saw her again. I used to enjoy the first handwritten pages from distant hotels as Mama rode her lens deep into the heart of America. Then the letters stopped and the money began. A little to begin with but then the flow of banknotes increased enormously, envelopes full of dollar bills with '*Love Mama*' scrawled beneath the portrait of George Washington and, occasionally, a line like '*I hope you got my note?*', a kind of long-distance joke, I suppose, to indicate that things were going well, or maybe just because she was in a hurry. With Mama wit and haste were always difficult to tell apart.

Maybe beauty is a memory of the way we were? We see something that reminds us of how we were when we were holy and we say: 'How beautiful!'

Maybe that's why there are no ugly saints.

In terms of particle physics, according to the gospel of Claude, my mother can be compared with the neutral pion, neutral and invisible, born from the decay of a negative kaon.

Mama rediscovered the camera and set off in search of beauty, and I was saved. She was determined to discover the source of her missing looks, her departed glamour, and no Livingstone in search of the Nile was ever more fiercely determined. She had time for nothing else. Her shiny camera case packed with expensive machines, her nervous cigarette smoking, my short, dark Mama became the investigator, the very private eye whose mission in life was to track down that elusive genius that she had once possessed, which we called 'loveliness'. Where did it go, Mama's beauty? And where is the terror André once was when he kept an office in Lyons?

# 3

About twelve, when the hawks float above us like spots before the eyes, so close to the sun do they fly, Monsieur Brown descends and joins us on the private beach. He has been with us now for three weeks and always appears in a white towelling robe, fluffy and soft, with a great gold B emblazoned on the breast pocket. The gown is tied with a scarlet cord. He wears most elegant dark glasses, a smoked windscreen for the eyes. The jetty moves beneath him when he arrives and he sinks into a deckchair without removing his gown or glasses. The jetty moves under every new arrival, I know, but somehow it moves more graciously beneath the carefully dignified tread of Monsieur Brown. He gets his name from the B on his pocket, from his colour and from the wide variety he offered me on our first meeting. André refers to him only as 'my guest', with a peculiar little grimace when he says it, as if he had just swallowed some unpleasant medicine. He has taken over the entire upper floor of the hotel, that is to say some twenty rooms are now at his disposal, rooms once the cells of the monks who lived on either side of the long oak gallery. For one man to take over half an hotel struck me as needlessly expensive but one would not have expected André to complain. Surely it's money for jam? The position of the other guests is more complicated. I can see they're pleased to have among them a man who can afford half an hotel, but rather uneasy about such alarming profligacy. You can see it in the way they look at Monsieur Brown – 'Who is this guy?', they ask themselves, 'that he should be spending money like there is no tomorrow?' Some say he's an eccentric millionaire, others whisper that he is an African potentate who chooses to live in seclusion. I say nothing, I am not even a guest here, I merely visit the Priory to sunbathe on the private beach by kind permission of the owner who is very fond of my grandmother.

He sits for a few minutes while the sweat gathers in his eyebrows and the little white hairs which salt his dark curls, stand out crisply. Then he rises and slowly removes his robe. He is so black that his skin has purple shadows in places. True, he is a little wrinkled around the neck and near the armpits, his body sags here and there and his waist is several rolls of flesh too wide, but then he must be in his late sixties at least, and all things considered he's in pretty good shape. He wears a pair of white trunks which set off the smooth, dark, satiny texture of his skin. He lies back in the sun. Is this wise, I ask myself? Every cook knows that chocolate should never be exposed to a naked flame. Even if you're using nothing more than cooking chocolate – *Nestlé's Chocolat Noir*, or *Baker's German Sweet* – it is still a shadow of the sacred substance, gift of the feathered snake god, Quetzalcoatl, royal beverage *xocoatl* the Aztecs drank in the courts of Montezuma in a highly spiced bitter froth of holiness.

And there he sits as if he is on a throne, or something. You can tell that the others do not like it. Not one little bit. It is a plump, solid way he has of sitting, as if he expects crowds to roll up and begin bowing and scraping, it is there in the cock of his chin, in the blind way he squints out across the lake. He hasn't come to sunbathe, to laze away a few hours, he has come to be adored! He looks strange, haughty and lost all at once. His manner makes the regulars on the wooden beach nervous. The Dutch father lifts his paper to his eyes and squints. The little German girls cluster around their mother and stare at the black man. I go on reading, we all go on reading, or pretending to, even Wolf, the German, turns the pages of *Hannibal; A Life* with an especially solid regular flapping rhythm which tells me that like everyone else he is watching the man. I am reading an article in a fashion magazine which guarantees to tell me what type of guy I attract: the high-flier, the whizzkid or the wimp. I tick my responses with eyebrow pencil and find when it comes to checking my score that I can't read the results because my eyes are full of tears.

It comes on me, this crying sickness, at odd times and it has been like this ever since Papa died or, at least, went away forever. Why it should have started again some weeks ago when I looked up and saw an elderly sunbather, plum purple and glistening, sitting on our private beach, I do not know. Maybe he reminds me of Africa, maybe Africa reminds me of Papa. As I cry, pushing my head into my arms and letting the tears drop through the wooden slats to mix with the water and be swallowed by the little silver fish, I also feel something else: I feel hungry. In all the questions in the quiz that promise to tell me what kind of man I attract, not one asks what sort of man makes me feel hungry. Perhaps we all need to eat someone, from time to time . . .

Papa usually came home at Christmas – or was it that his visits just made it seem like Christmas? He breezed into the apartment as if he had never been away. I would get home from school to find him walking about the place with his hands behind his back, humming under his breath and touching new things my mother had brought home, articles of photographic equipment, expensive lenses in gleaming black leather pouches, an assortment of the latest light meters which she would leave scattered about, a cluster of tripods, or he might be parading around the room beneath one of those white umbrellas photographers use to reflect light. He had a playful nature. Or he'd be standing beside the new compact-disc player, one of the discs in his hand, seeing if he could make the multicoloured surface reflect light on the ceiling. He'd be wearing a big blue coat and a red scarf and his face was always so incredibly brown for the middle of winter. When I first caught sight of him I thought he must be ill. He looked so odd, suddenly reappearing in European winter clothes, looking like a cross between a time traveller, a detective and an intruder. When Mama installed the new video phone I found him gazing into the blank screen as if it were a mirror, or a holy picture.

'When your Uncle Claude and I were children they showed picture phones like this in the American comics we bought. They were so small they strapped to the wrist. I remember Claude got very excited. "That's what we'll all have one day, just you wait!" It sounded like a threat.' He kissed me. 'Will they reduce this phone machine in size, Bella? So we can wear them on our wrists?'

'We will probably all be ordered to wear them. Won't Uncle Claude be pleased? Welcome home, Papa!'

He wrapped me in his warm arms. 'Dear girl, you're well? Has anyone told you that you have the teeth of a contented cannibal?'

I must have been about nine or ten at the time. I cannot believe that he has been gone so long – already. Is it four years, or five? I don't care to remember. I do not wish to count.

He would have brought a suitcase full of African gifts: masks, wood carvings, pelts, musical instruments, and would unpack happily in his bedroom which was a kind of museum of his travels. He would stay with us over the holiday and my mother would accept him as a rather interesting foreign relative, consult his tastes in food and wine very anxiously, as if he were quite unused to our ways. She would see to his material comforts and then retreat into her darkroom for longer and longer periods, and Papa and I were left alone.

At Christmas there were presents and walks about the city. Mama always received jewels to add to her beautiful collection. For reasons we do not understand, today these are all under government lock and key. No explanation has been given. With father's death we experienced a kind of big bang. Before it there was nothing very exceptional, but after it there was chaos. When I turned nine he gave me a diamond pendant. A big perfect blue diamond cut in the shape of a heart which I wear on a silver chain around my neck. The government snoopers never saw my pendant and I certainly don't intend to tell them a single word about it. Not bloody likely. They took all the rest, though.

I guess Papa must have reported to his superiors in the government department during these brief visits home, but he never mentioned it to us. Never said he was going to the office, or spoke about what he'd been doing in Africa. Soon after New Year he vanished, from one day to the next. We took this to be quite normal. Some people went to the office, Papa went to Africa. From the walls of our flat his latest trophies looked down on us: a royal chair from Cameroun carved as a seated man, his legs spread wide, his arms resting on the heads of two female attendants, the seat supported by elaborately carved wings of trolls, tigers, and slaves – a handsome seat for a chief; there was a hollow wooden figure from the Fang tribe,

48

a curious mannikin which mixed the foetal look of a tiny baby with a curious suggestion of age, a repository probably made to hold the bones of the dead; and an ivory bracelet of snakes and toads from the Congo. These new trophies were signs that my father had been and gone. During these brief reappearances he would not visit my grandmother with whom the break was complete when he married my mother, 'the English woman'. This was a fairly polite way of referring to Mama.

I always missed Papa when he disappeared though there was a curious kind of relief in knowing that however odd it all seemed, these visits were regular and could be counted upon. There seemed no reason why the arrangement should not continue indefinitely. Papa might have been absent for much of the year but he left behind so much to remind us of him. When I was very small the Bapuna mask which hung upon my bedroom wall frightened me. Particularly in the dark when its white face gleamed. It had a chalky complexion with curious slit eyes which gave it a faintly oriental appearance, and two parallel eyebrows above each eye, and a strange set of bumps on the forehead. The face was round and flat like a shallow soup dish, with jug-handle ears. Sightless, sleepy, slit-eyed, bumpy, the Bapuna mask on my bedroom wall haunted me. But it was, after all, Papa's gift, so I could hardly throw it away and after a while, very gradually, I became less frightened of it and eventually I grew fond of it. Over the years it hung on my wall I began to see that the nose was long and sensitive, that the lips were full and generous and that the mask had an expression of dreamy tension that was very appealing. I began to feel sorry for the poor pale creature. I took to calling him Rolo and even tucked him beside me in bed until Mama found us together one night and I woke to the sound of her screams. 'Bella! How can you put that horrible thing in your bed? Who knows where it's been!'

I remember that at the time my mother was working on her project called 'Collectors' Wives' in which she was investigating whether rich old men who collected objects of great beauty collected women in the same way. I remember her temper during that period was not good.

I was far too young, and in any event it was far too difficult for me to try to explain my change in feeling towards

49

the Bapuna mask and, in fact, this surging sympathy I felt for its blind, pale dignity was more difficult to deal with than the horror I had once felt for it. But there it was. For as long as I can remember I've had the feeling of being what Mama calls 'otherwise'. I would have much preferred not to have been this way. I remember Mama had told me once of a friend who had, she said, 'resigned' from the Foreign Ministry; 'he put in his letter and, Bella, that was that'. It seemed a very good idea to me and I, too, wrote a letter: *'I, Bella, resign from being otherwise.'* I carried it around with me for months but I never found anyone I could post it to, and I knew then that I was going to have trouble with these feelings.

Among the first of the picture books I'd been given as a baby was the story of Jack and the Beanstalk, and my sympathies were all with the Giant. Ugly, pop-eyed and oafish, he sprawled across his table, knocking over his soup which spattered his green doublet as he made a despairing grab at Jack who sped nimbly away clutching the Giant's speaking harp. The Ogre's thick red hair was all in a tangle, his eyes were moist and his face dark with rage and pain. Jack was fresh-faced and beaming. He had already stolen the bag of gold, he was proud of his speed and his spoils. Now he had the speaking harp, and he would be back, I knew, for the goose that laid the golden eggs. And when that happened, with the lumbering, snivelling Giant in hot pursuit, he would lure him to the tip of the swaying, miles-high beanstalk and then, quite deliberately, murder him. Jack was the sort of boy who ought to be locked up.

'What you love becomes beautiful,' Papa told me. This used to infuriate Mama who would reply with a saying of her own: 'Charity begins at home.' Papa would fall silent, and a few days later he would disappear back into Africa.

Since my Papa no longer spoke to his family I became the go-between. Each summer I went to stay by the lake with my French family. My Uncle Claude would come to Paris to fetch me and before we left to drive back to my grandmother's house he would look gloomily around our apartment at the new display of my father's trophies, the exotic accumulation of another year in Africa. And he would shake his head and click his tongue disapprovingly as if he were a teacher who had discovered one of his dimmer pupils has been writing on the walls.

In my father's bedroom, which was a kind of African shrine, there were photographs of men just like him who had spent their lives in Africa. These pictures were taken in the last century and showed traders and their houses. Some of them lived on houseboats moored on brown, broad rivers, clearly settled there for good because the boats had been roofed over and become permanent trading posts. There were pictures of the surprisingly comfortable and immensely cluttered interiors. The fashion was for many rugs and coloured glass in the windows, tables with twirly legs, a variety of lamps hanging from the ceiling, vases galore, leopard skins on the floor. Everyone in these pictures wore hats, it didn't matter whether you were a master or a servant, the head went covered if it was to be decent: hats of straw, hats with ruffles, cockades, plumes, bowlers, toppers, hats made of hair, or rope, or rags. But hats. Every head was roofed. Without doubt the head was then regarded as the seat of wisdom and if you went out with it not properly protected and respected, who knew what might fall on it.

These pictures offended Uncle Claude particularly. He would pause in front of one of them and demand loudly, 'But what is the use of it all? We went to these places and interfered. We stirred up the mud and now the mud is coming home to stick. The fair body of France is obliged to suffer the rubbish slung by those who delight in her humiliation. This is what radical politics have reduced us to. France beyond the seas is diminished, France at home is humiliated. Is this what we want, Bella?'

Being perhaps seven or eight at the time, I had no answers to these bitter questions. My mother was always careful to be out when my uncle came to collect me for my summer holiday. She was at that time photographing the female models of famous painters, in their old age. Could anything of their original beauty be found beneath the accumulated grime and varnish of the years?

When my father died somewhere in Africa, and nobody knew anything, we lost our apartment in the rue Vandal, our clothes, our car, our jewels. I continued these summers beside the lake in my grandmother's house, although my role changed and I was no longer the go-between and became instead, in the houses of both Mama and Grand-mère, a hostage. I was never sure until the last moment whether each would release me at the end of my time. My mother hinted darkly at some terrible war-time secret which was the real cause of the rift between Papa and his family, while Grand-mère declared furiously that when my father had died, Mama had stolen away with me to England.

'Would you run away with a child to Devil's Island, or some grim police state?'

'But Grand-mère,' I protested, 'England is not either of those things. Why don't you come and see for yourself? We would love to have you visit us.'

'Too much coal,' she sniffed. Her beautiful nostrils flexed.

'She gives the same reason as I believe Renoir's mother used,' my Uncle Claude explained.

I enjoyed being in both places. I liked being with my mother, except during her feminist phase. I enjoyed the freedom of having the little flat in England all to myself, while she was away on her shooting assignments. I studied the life in the little square beneath my window. Besides the boys who played football against the toilet wall, I took particular interest in a man who came most days and sat on a bench drinking from a bottle wrapped in brown paper which he kept in his pocket. His hair was thick and grey and his shoulders under the dark blue donkey jacket were broad. I think he saw himself as king of this little island. And you can't be king unless you advertise. He liked particularly to abuse the passers-by, waving his fists and shrieking incoherently at the mystified pedestrians who blushed and hurried away when his ranting began. He stood swaying on the kerb of the square which I realised presented for him some kind of outer boundary of his territory, bellowing thick, incomprehensible oaths at the reddening necks of retreating locals – who preferred to pretend he did not exist. The boys playing football on the square he demonstratively ignored, perhaps feeling that they were on the island first and therefore native to it. It was those others across the street, the outsiders, the foreigners, invaders whom he wished to repel by his aboriginal war dance. To make his point even clearer still he brought along with him one day an old and rather tattered Union Jack which he flew from the roof of the public lavatory, tying it to a pipe which is there to carry away noxious gases. Each morning he came back to the square, somewhat the worse for wear as his drinking grew heavier and after a while he no longer bothered to hide the paper-wrapped bottle in his pocket but took to swinging it by his side like a club, his thumb rammed down its throat. He put on weight steadily, his face turned mauve and when the boiling hatred inside him bubbled out, he yelled huge oaths. Always a shuffling, lumbering figure, his movements became slower and more painful. One morning he turned up with a walking-frame but still he managed somehow to patrol the perimeters of his island with achingly slow persistence. Quick to spot threats of invasion by housewives out with their shopping, or men walking their dogs, he would manoeuvre the triangular legs of his aluminium walking-frame to the very edge of the kerb, lean on it like a priest in a pulpit, rather in the way that Father Duval does in his pulpit in our village by the lakeside, and trumpet defiance.

One day things were different. A group of youths suddenly turned and faced him across the road. A stone arced through the air and landed beside him. The next hit him in the face. Even from my window I could see the blood. By the time I got downstairs he was bleeding freely from the gash in his face but he still waved his bottle and shrieked at his tormentors. When the boys saw me they ran away. The man smelt of wine and terrifically old cheese. All the time I wiped away the blood from his face he kept up his tirade and took no notice of me. What he shouted was quite incomprehensible, even close up. They were not words, they were bellows of a beast in agony.

I got the worst of the blood off his face and then still muttering, he limped away. He never came back to the square. Maybe he died of his injuries, or the drink. His flag hung there for months, getting drabber and limper until one day the lavatory attendant tore it down and used it to polish the copper pipes which came up beautifully, in a pinky-orange glow.

One saw so much through the window of my flat on the square during our time in north London that I didn't really think of myself as lonely, even though Mama was away so often. Sometimes it seemed that, rather than my staying with her, she was the occasional visitor who popped in from time to time and stayed with me. In this she began to resemble my father and I suppose in a way I was used to it. Mama was always slightly guilty about her absences and tried to make up for it by organising small soirées to which she invited friends whom she imagined might keep me company when she was off somewhere else. We went and had our hair done by *Catherine the Great of Finchley: Premier Hair Care!* She did wonders for my slightly greasy hair with dried Moroccan mud. Best damn hairdresser in the world. Not Russian at all, actually. Cypriot!

I knew Mama meant well when she gave these little parties, but then she had such high standards that whenever I caught the eye of one of the guests she would immediately warn me off: 'Yes, darling, he's friendly enough. But I'm afraid he's one of those bitter, sex-starved English atheists who unaccountably turns to poetry and writes verses about cricket and dog-shit . . .'

I suppose the truth was that we missed Papa horribly. Sometimes I caught her eye while we were washing up after one of these parties and we fell into each other's arms and howled like wolves.


The weeks go by in a daze of sunshine at my grandmother's little house at the top of the village, with its fine view of the square and the Church of the Immaculate Conception where that fat despot, Father Duval, presides. How I detest him, puffed up on his perch like a vulture above a burning ghat. Since my mother disappeared Grand-mère looks on my perhaps permanent return to her as a sacred gift: she is to reclaim me for France. There are times when I think she considers my father's death as part of the price he paid for deserting his family and compromising his country by marrying my mother.

'Poor Philippe. Your papa was such a dreamer. French women were not good enough for him, he had to choose an English girl. France herself was too small for him. He had to lose himself in Africa. Our village was too suffocating, he must have Paris.'

My grandmother lay in bed surrounded by the holy trinity; she smoothed her silky white hair and spoke to me of my uncle

with tears of pride in her pale blue eyes. At first I thought this
was because he had stayed at home and obeyed her. But even
when he got involved with the Angel, she doted upon him. She
believed that Monsieur Cherubini felt for him the 'strong love
of father for son'. Her mind moved to and fro in time like a
butterfly, touching on this and that. Never staying long. War
memories. The bombing of the French fleet at Meriel–Kabir by
the treacherous English. The nobility of Marshal Pétain, that
'man of iron'.

'He said to us: "I make you the gift of my person." Some
of us felt it an honour to return the gift – in the service of
the Marshal, at the service of France.'

Increasingly Monsieur Cherubini, successful, fanatical, sensible – with his nougat and his Turks and his big plans – takes
over her mind.

'Work, family, motherland! That's the way, Bella!'

'Who says so, Grandmama – Monsieur Cherubini?'

She thinks for a moment. 'No, the Marshal. But he is
a wonderfully public-spirited man, that Cherubini. Rich, of
course, but delicate. Claude responds to his quiet gravity.
Although it is true that just like his poor brother, Philippe, my
Claude has his head in the clouds and longs to discover worlds
as different from ours as Jesus Christ is from Buddha, yet, I am
proud to say, he has a sense of duty. A man of iron. He serves
his country. He has heard the call of Monsieur Cherubini and
he comes!'

Well, that's a matter of opinion. I mean anybody can hear
a call, there's nothing so wonderful about that. But what of
the nature of the calling? There's the rub! At a whistle from
Monsieur Cherubini my uncle leaves his study of the universe,
of everything that exists, of the immense void in which swirling
clouds of stardust, ghosts of long-dead suns, materialise into
new suns and solar systems, flare into life, shine a few billion
years, swell, glare and explode, consuming moons and melting
planets, and then die to icy black cinders; or, over periods so
long the teeth ache to think of them, in regions so far away
the ears ring with their remoteness, inflate to red giants, or
collapse into tiny bodies so heavy that a teaspoonful would
weigh more than the earth, white dwarves, or neutron stars,
or simply disappear altogether into black holes. All this my

uncle puts down the way a kid puts down a book, or a dog drops a ball – and runs away to play with the Angel, games of running and jumping and fists called 'Protecting France for Future Generations!'

I believe we exist in order that the universe should have someone to register it. The universe exists in order that we should have somewhere to project our fantasies. 'Nothing but physics and necessity!' says Uncle Claude when asked about the nature of the cosmos. He might as well reply, 'Baseball bats and knuckle-dusters!' Or is it that the universe exists in order that Uncle Claude can make people do as they are told? Five billion years since the birth of the sun and all that time spent preparing for Uncle Claude to bully the rest of us. It seems such a waste really.

'Bella,' says Grand-mère, 'why are you crying again?'

'I'm sorry, I can't help it.'

'But you must help it! Imagine what would have happened if Joan of Arc reacted as you do when she stood before Orleans? Or Pétain at Verdun? Or your dear brave grandfather when he faced the firing squad?' And she waves a hand at the holy trinity on her bedside table.

My grandmother's holy trinity comprises a lovely small statue of Sèvres porcelain in which blessed Joan of Arc sits astride a white horse and lifts her sword to the skies, the divine maid about to charge into battle and rout the accursed English. There is also a large photograph of a man wearing lots of medals, whom Grand-mère touches with a finger, a slim white finger like a wafer of ice, in a kind of tender salute and who she says is Marshal Pétain; and there is a young man in sepia who looks somewhat blurrily out into the world, as if the photographer took him by surprise just as he was on his way elsewhere. Because he wears a uniform and cap it is not possible to see much of him anyway, except that he is dark with a fine curved nose and bold eyebrows, in his early twenties. Grand-mère was deeply in love with him, she tells me, and in deference to her feelings I have never pressed her as to why he died in this savage fashion. But I did once ask her if she had been desolated by his death and she said: 'Absolutely. I loved him more than the world. But, alas, he loved honour and his country more.'

I was less sparing in the case of Uncle Claude. He is the sort of person who needs hard questions asked of him, so one day I said: 'Does anyone know why Grandpapa was executed by firing squad?' To this my uncle gave a surprising answer. 'For reasons of loyalty.' He added: 'His molecules are now dispersed in new patterns, that is all.'

What can anyone do with a man like that? What I want to know is: where are the new blasphemers, those who spit on the certainties of science? I mean, it's common enough, even boringly familiar, to encounter entire phalanxes of people who take for granted the non-existence of God. So tell me, where are the *new* atheists? Where are the black masses performed by naked research assistants upon the tomb of Einstein? Who practises self-abuse in a particle accelerator? Who has been known to mock the muon, the gluon or the quark? Why does no one deny the existence of Rutherford?

Well, then, is it any wonder that I go around most of the day with a pair of earphones playing pretty loud sounds of one or the other heavy mob, like In Extremis, who are simply great! Do you hear that . . . *great*! I don't care what the papers say about their being into sadomasochism, and I don't believe all that rubbish about that dead girl fan being found in the toilet or wherever it was with whip weals, or chain marks, as the papers say. In Extremis are heart's core stuff, the heaviest metal in the universe!

My grandmother lies back on her pillows and closes her eyes, but her mouth is open wide. 'For heaven's sake, consult Father Duval, child, he will help you to stop this incessant precipitation which waters no flowers and grows no leeks. And listen how you make me raise my voice!'

It is only when I take off my earphones that I realise she is raising her voice.

'When was Grandpapa killed, Grandmama?'

'At that most predictable of times, at dawn. Just as it is done in books. Believe me there is no way crueller of killing people than as it is done in books. He was taken into a square in a village not far from here, in the closing days of the war, and tied to a stake. We were all there, the families of the men to be executed. We crammed the viewing area which was roped off. It was like a farm show! The poor victims were led out like

57

cattle and tied to their stakes. Everyone was there, the De La Salle sisters, old Brest, dead these twenty years now, father of the present young Brest, the butcher, and of course the entire family Gramus who in those days were still the undertakers for folks in these parts. They were at ease with death, collectors of it, and this was a variety they had not seen before. Death by firing squad. I knew then what the friends of the condemned felt during the Revolution when they watched the business of the guillotine. Young Old Laveur was with me that dawn. He nearly married me once, you know, and he was so gallant. He said: 'If I could take the place of Victor, I would do so, Justine, my dear.' It was raining that morning. Hard. Even the shots sounded wet.'

'Now you are crying, Grandmama.'

'But my tears cannot be treated. Promise me you will see our good Father Duval. Tell him what is in your heart.'

'I'll go and make us some chocolate. And then you must sleep. We have Monsieur Cherubini tomorrow night.'

'And the great party rally on Saturday morning. What a time that will be! Monsieur Cherubini is a giant among pygmies.' My grandmother lay back and her tears began to subside. She looked younger, even the mention of Cherubini's name had this effect on her. When I returned with the chocolate, we sat sipping it in silence. She cupped her hands around the mug and looked into the sweet, steaming depths of her chocolate and she smiled sadly.

'On the morning I lost him, in the rain, I saw on the wall above our heads a great advertisement painted, for chocolate. *Cémoi*, I recall, in letters big as giants. It would have been the last thing he set eyes on.'

This was the first time she had told me about my grandfather's death and I was utterly astonished. I knew that the Maquis had been active in the mountains round La Frisette and the little villages by the lake and I imagined my poor grandfather's horrible, heroic death. I could see she was sleepy, so I'm sorry to say I took advantage of her.

'Who killed him, Grandmama? The Germans?'

'Germans!' Her eyes widened. 'Certainly not! He was killed by the French!'

# 4

So I go to consult Father Duval. The crying sickness has made me desperate. After all, that's what he's there for – to counsel troubled souls. 'Your priest is here to help, forgive, save,' says Grand-mère. Which is fine if you merely listen to those words, but if you write them in your mind and look at them as you would words on a blackboard – 'Help, forgive, save' – and try and make them apply to Father Duval, then it's very hard not to giggle. You're *supposed* to believe what the words are supposed to mean. But you're inclined to say, 'Sod this! I'd rather be watching telly,' as the English sometimes put it. To use certain special words some people ought to have to apply for a damn licence! But having been allowed his badge without a test, Father Duval became responsible for counselling the fearful: and I am one of those. Thus – I fear, and he counsels. Both of us conform to our definitions. Definitions are stormtroopers of science: they used once to work for theology, when she was queen, but they switched sides after the coup. They arrive unexpectedly and presume obedience; they hint at consequences, if we do not do what they tell us. It's odd, considering the damage science has done to the old faithful, to realise that scientists are among the hottest of the new believers. Look at Uncle Claude. He'll believe almost anything – until he's proved wrong. And then he'll believe something else. A search for certainty passed off as the spirit of fearless enquiry. It's bloody pathetic. Certainties have, of course, nothing whatever to do with Father Duval and me. But sometimes all we have left is to pretend that they do.

And, oh, what a wanker! – as we liked to say at the North London Academy for Girls. He would have made a good manager in a medium-sized cement factory; he could have run his own florist shop; I dare say he would have made a fine local councillor. He might, in other circumstances, in more extreme societies, have been one of those deputed to dispose of the victims of some death-dealing regime. Just to look at him gives me the confidence to say that the methods he would employ would be scientific, modern and, wherever possible, humane. No doubt he would have disapproved of wanton cruelty and brutality. Such excesses would have seemed old-fashioned and therefore inefficient. Whatever he touches becomes a manageable, small-scale, smiling world. The thing Father Duval likes to do is 'to spread a little cheer'. He would have felt the same whether he'd run a bar, or a mortuary. Make the best of things and get on with it! he preaches from the pulpit and you feel – yes – he'd do just that – whether dressing a corpse or pouring a drink. He implies, though he never says as much, that this is the real meaning of the Gospel and it's surely just a matter of time before his congregation, his flock in the Church of the Immaculate Conception, grasp this truth. In the meantime all he can do is to root out superstitious phobias to which the mentally delinquent are prone: hopes of love, dreams of death and eternal punishment; medieval legalisms about the profit and loss of grace – in short all the bad old psychological terrors of the past two millennia. And he does his work of destruction, not of course with any unpleasantness, but like a bank manager cordially turning down sadly unrealistic would-be borrowers. With a shake of the head and a firm smile he shows them the door. How many frail and pitiable human phantoms, what dreads and nauseas are disposed of by his cheerful modesty? What a deathdealer!

The Church of the Immaculate Conception is built of grey stone beneath a red tiled roof and dominates the village, which falls away below it in twisting streets crowded with a bewilderingly rich assortment of houses, hotels, parks and gardens down to the broad lake shore. La Frisette lies like a delicate tendril of vine fallen at the feet of the mountains.

The church was used as a munitions dump during the Revolution and had been shut throughout most of the war after the German invaders arrested the parish priest for hiding gypsies in the crypt (gypsies were detested almost as much as priests in the village of La Frisette and most villagers approved of the arrests). After that, through the fifties and sixties, the church had been allowed to slip gradually into decay until, that

60

is, the appointment of Father Duval in the seventies and his ambitious programme for modernisation. The broken stained-glass windows were replaced with clear glass, the Stations of the Cross on which doves had roosted were plucked from the walls and replaced with photographs of famine victims from distant parts. The organ has gone and in its place is a small music area for guitars, synthesizer, and gamelan; and South American sambas and Eskimo dances replace the more conventional musical element of the mass. What hasn't changed is the vast churchyard, a great, stony, yellow, bald patch of ground which surrounds the church on four sides rather like an area of quarantine. And I think the sewage drains are perhaps in need of repair because the smell is strong enough to carry into the church, when the wind is in the north. The altar, of course, has been turned in order to allow the priest to face the congregation and the expression on Father Duval's face when he does so is almost worth attending mass to see. There passes across it a mixture of fear, uncertainty, regret and defiant pride that I have not seen since I watched on television a trio of generals, the ruling junta of some South American dictatorship, obliged to take their place in the centre of an arena crowded with thousands of their countrymen, since the local team had just pulled off a sensational victory over a foreign rival and the generals were required to show their approval in person. They left the tank-ringed safety of their presidential palace and ventured into the lions' den of the popular football arena and their looks of tremulous, white-lipped bravado were precisely a triple version of the smirk which is to be seen on the pink, square face of Father Duval each Sunday morning as he stands in the pulpit, dressed in the only other parish asset, a set of new vestments designed for him by a famous Paris fashion house, a gift from Monsieur Cherubini. And here, with his mixture of bravado and good sense, with his pleasant, pragmatic, no-nonsense manner, he attempts to coax and jolly and bully his congregation out of their hide-bound superstitious ways.

There is a madonna in our church who survived the Revolution but not the deconstructive powers of Father Duval who moved her to the back of the church where she lives in gloom. She is plump and her square, honest face wears a perturbed, almost frightened, look as if she has just seen

*61*

a ghost. One of her hands is broken and the missing hand adds to her air of trepidation. She gives the impression that if another ounce of suffering is added to the load she bears she will burst into tears. She looks like a mother should, careworn, anxious. Her nose is very beautiful, full and flared. I pray before her sometimes. And she is in every way so much more friendly than the little statue with which Father Duval has replaced her on the altar steps, a Hollywood madonna, a child starlet, a flawless complexion, jet-black hair and a rosary over her arm, a pretty little chit of a girl utterly unlike the ample matron with her broad body, big hips and missing hand. Whether by accident or design, the dethronement of the madonna and her banishment to the shadows has had one advantage because she stands now directly beneath a stained-glass window depicting the Assumption of Mary. God the Father in a beard, a handsome son with the look of someone who would have found his niche somewhere between the stockbroking profession and veterinary science, together with the Holy Ghost, a shapely white dove, await her. Soon they will be assuming her body and soul into paradise, queen of heaven returned to the Redeemer.

I find the Pol Pot of the pulpit in shirtsleeves and shorts, polishing the tomb of some grand lady who lies buried in the smiling, sleepy loveliness of her marble effigy as Father Duval's yellow duster passes briskly over her lips. How little the feet of noble ladies must have been, if we can believe the tombs! The Church of the Immaculate Conception, despite Father Duval's modernisation, is slowly falling apart, and placed prominently in the aisle, where visitors run straight into it, is a notice saying: *Our Church is beautiful, but beauty will not preserve her. Give generously and may God bless you!*

'Such a frown on a young face! And one so pretty! Please, no frowns! You illuminate, if I may say so, the darkest corner of this medieval house of bad dreams. This stone barn where we humans in our foolishness huddle for warmth and comfort. From the time of Peking Man, *Pithecanthropus*, half a million years ago, with his extraordinarily narrow forehead and his appetite for raw brains, man has built fires in his caves, although for warmth, or worship, we do not know. So, too, some hundreds of thousands of years later did Neanderthal

62

Man, though his fires were for food as well as warmth and he drew pictures on the walls of his cave-church. And here we are today. It's somehow a poignant, pathetic continuity. What are we to do about it? This lady who lies here – do you know who she is?'

I say I do not.

'Nor do I! Nor does anyone. Some worthy, the wife perhaps of some obscure noble. She was once thought by the devout of these parts to be none other than St Frances of Rome. Such is the shield of ignorance, pilgrims came to kiss her hand. They believed it would cure dropsy, palsy and all manner of illnesses. How much infection would have been spread by this practice! Look – look down there!'

The flagstones are hollowed and polished, a shallow furrow stretched back some ten metres; this was where a shuffling line of human hope and misery had moved closer to the sleeping saint. It is possible to feel their reverence. The lady is both serene and confident with her hands joined on her breast, her grave smile and her tiny feet. The kisses of the faithful have worn away the back of her left hand, lips have rubbed away the marble.

'Doubtless there were those in authority who knew, even admitted, that this lady was not the saint in question. For St Frances of Rome is buried in the Church of Santa Maria Nuova! Now called, I believe, Santa Francesca Romana. Apparently she saw her guardian angel perched on her shoulder. Fictions devoutly held are proof against truth. Yes. I'm afraid you'll find out as you grow older. Now what can I do for you? Have you come to tell me about the rally? Monsieur Cherubini's in full cry. He promises us something we'll never forget! In the matter of angels, something of a medieval debate has taken hold of the press. That tool of the reactionary left, that gutter news-sheet, *Les Temps*, is at it again. Do you know what the idiots write, Bella? It's called blasphemy. Do people realise, *Les Temps* demands, that the angel is sitting on the *left* shoulder of La Frisette? They refer to Monsieur Cherubini not as a guardian angel, who, of course, sits on the right shoulder, but as the devil who sits on the other! Impudence! But our people on *La Liberté* fired back. Oh yes! We asked if people had noticed how frightened the socialists were. They see ghosts in corners. 'Some see devils everywhere . . .' said *La Liberté*. I thought that was good. Damned good!' And he slaps the shoulder of the stone lady in his enthusiasm.

'Father Duval – I have these feelings.'

He begins polishing even harder, the yellow duster covers the sleeping face of the stone lady.

'You have – what, exactly?'

'Urges.'

'How old are you now, Bella?'

'Fifteen.'

'I would have thought you were older.' He does not say why.

'Just fifteen. And I keep crying.'

'We have, as I say, these emotions, which we cannot control when we are at sensitive stages in our lives. It's not uncommon.' He looks relieved.

'But it's like an illness with me. I do it in private and in public and it's so embarrassing. Suddenly, for no reason, I simply howl!'

'Nonsense! A few girlish tears. A kind heart, perhaps, a certain emotional excess. Well, why not? If you wish, cry often and loudly. As I'm sure you know, there are more difficult urges, as you call them, than this.'

'Such as?'

But he doesn't answer.

'And then there are the prayers. I feel the need to pray. In the street. Everywhere. To get down on my knees and talk to God. He haunts me! The worst is when I am praying and crying all at once.'

He stops polishing. 'Now that's rather more serious. I do not like the sound of that. I must think about that.'

He is pocketing the yellow duster now and banging his hands together, and I see motes and flecks of dust smoking in the shafts of light that pierce the stained-glass windows and splash Father Duval's white shirt red and green. Suddenly there is a great deal of shouting in the porch and a bunch of little kids, dark-haired and dark-eyed, come streaming into the church. Father Duval's feathery laugh flutters among the roof beams.

'Kemal! It is not permitted to ride on the altar rail!' He gives me a smile. His smile conveys how life presses in on

64

him, he who is in the main a free and willing spirit, who would really get on and do things if only spiritual duties did not so weigh and drag. 'My catechism class from the nougat factory. These children were delivered into my keeping – with the demand that I instruct them in the Catholic faith. Monsieur Cherubini immediately warned me of a trap. This was possibly a scheme to establish a bridgehead. He has the eye of an eagle, that man! Duval, he says, the workers in Turkey will hear of the conversion of their brethren in La Frisette and will follow in their footsteps. So what happens? You get Catholic children in Muslim communities? This makes the deportation of illegal immigrants more difficult, repatriation less likely. Clever! Monsieur Cherubini acted. He bought the nougat factory. He plans to restructure the workforce.'

Father Duval's eyes water for a moment and I think maybe he is crying but then I see that it's the dust. He goes back to polishing the false St Frances.

'What about this new arrival at the Priory? The mud-brown type. You've heard?'

'He's been here for weeks. But never goes out. I've seen him now for the first time – on the beach.'

'Not good news. The Priory Hotel is heading for ruin. André can't keep it up. And he knows it. Monsieur Cherubini has made several good offers and met blanket rejection. And now André takes in these odd guests. As if all those little baggage-carriers (so-called) he hires in Lyons were not enough! This black man is some potentate, I believe. If it goes on like this Monsieur Cherubini will take action and I for one will not blame him! Nor will the people of this village. The Mayor's already making enquiries. What does he do, this man – when you see him?'

'He sunbathes.'

'Does the pot need more glaze? Has he spoken to you?'

'He speaks to no one.'

'What does he look like?'

'His face is round and rather puffy. His eyes bulge, his jaw is bony, the mouth cruel.'

'He's ugly?'

'I've never seen anyone like him. So . . . otherwise.'

'You know the hotel is closed to further bookings? It's intolerable! We have all sorts of people coming to the rally on Saturday and we can't put them up at the Priory. André refuses! He gives no reasons.'

Father Duval slaps the face of the sleeping lady in his agitation.

'As to this business of prayer, Bella, there is another side to it. If you want to pray – pray! Let me assure you, there are many who can't do it. To them I say, if it fails to come easily, don't force it. Prayers from guilt are a bad business. But those that come naturally will do little harm. Will we meet at your grandmama's on Friday night? I hope so. We are invited, Monsieur Cherubini and I. Will you be there? We will practise our English together. Now I must deal with these terrors.'

I watch him walking away, seemingly anxious to assert his authority, but actually keen to get away from me.

'Kemal, Abdul, Mustapha – come to me! Today we will talk about hell.'

I remember when the most recent attack of the weeping sickness hit me. I can date it because it coincided with an event of pretty well primary importance, the day I had news of the arrival of the stranger.

It happened as I sat watching television in the lounge of the Priory Hotel. Like all other secular pursuits of that holy place, watching TV was an odd business. It took place in a room that had once been the office of the Prior himself. His table stood there still; a sturdy oak affair, a great seamed slab supported by fluted columns which burst into acanthus leaves. The television was placed on the Prior's desk, the heavy honey-coloured curtains were drawn against the fierce sunshine because the room looked out on the garden with its green-and-white umbrellas, and across the lake beyond. In the rather yellow, slightly liquid light which strained through the curtains the guests occasionally sat uneasily to watch selected programmes. This didn't happen often. The lure of sun and water were too strong and perhaps the people themselves were too grand. Usually they tended to watch programmes they'd made themselves, or that featured them. They might also assemble to watch ceremonial displays by branches of

European and British royalty: christenings, matings and funerals of televisual idols; presidential inaugurations and papal visits. The sight of the Pope on the windswept tarmac of some foreign airport, stooping to kiss the ground, rising and clutching his hat against the breeze, always drew a sigh of admiration tinged with something that might have been relief. But for the rest of the time the TV lounge was a good place to escape to. Somewhere I could be alone.

I was watching a programme about Aids and the progress made among American homosexuals in alerting them to precautionary measures against the disease. The speaker was a man in a blue suit called Geoff. He wore a black toupee and shone with geniality, not to say gentle mischief. He recommended the condom, he urged its widespread adoption, he took one out of his pocket and stretched it thoughtfully between his hands, he plucked it gently with his tongue producing a plangent, not unpleasant note. Great strides had been made in getting people to use condoms in the United States. He had been working to improve acquaintance with the condom which was so simple in its operation, if properly employed.

'I used to blow 'em up when I was a kid,' said Geoff. 'Or we'd fill 'em with water and bomb passers-by. Gone are the days. This is serious. These things work. They could save your life.'

He tossed the musical condom behind him and pulled another from his ear with the stylised fingerplay of a professional magician, lifting an eyebrow and tapping ash off an imaginary cigar in the manner of Groucho Marx. He would like to share with us, he said, a simple procedure needed to operate the condom. From the empty air – I know this sounds melodramatic – but from nothing at all he snatched a large banana, still in its skin. He grinned again, rueful, apologetic, modest, but still with that hint of wickedness that intrigued me.

'I have here a friendly banana,' said Geoff. 'Let's give him a name – let's call him Byron. Hullo, Byron.'

'Hullo, Geoff,' said Byron.

Geoff, it seemed, besides being a magician was also no mean ventriloquist.

'You know what this is, Byron?' He dangled the condom.

'Sure, Geoff, that's a condom.'

'Slip it on, Byron.'

Geoff did just that, easing the rubber along the yellow curve of Byron's body.

'How you doing there, Byron?'

'Just fine, Geoff.' The banana's voice was muffled.

I had to admire Geoff's professionalism. The man was a perfectionist. I suppose if that was as far as it went, that would have been okay. But there had been that slightly mad gleam in Geoff's eye and the reason now became clear. He held the banana tightly in one hand. With the other he stroked it gently, grinning and muttering to himself.

'It's safe, it's easy, it's fun,' crooned Geoff. Then his eyes misted over and he held the banana close to his cheek. 'You just love it, don't you?'

But Byron had fallen silent. I can't say I blamed him. The spectacle we were witnessing was embarrassing. When Geoff started kissing Byron I couldn't watch any longer. It was the coy glances he kept shooting at the viewer that did it for me. I switched off the set.

My legs were shaking and I sank to my knees and buried my head in my hands and began crying – for myself, for Geoff, for the fucking banana, I couldn't be sure. But there I was on my knees in the TV room, with the cooling grey eye of the dead TV set beaming down upon me from its perch on the Prior's old table, praying my head off: 'Lord God in Heaven help me! Save me from the world that turns into particles and collapses. From the Angel who is fat and disgusting. Save my mother, too, wherever she is. And my father, even if he's dead. And help Clovis, because if he goes on taking that stuff it's the end of him . . . And help me. To eat properly, to go for long walks and not start crying, to stop worrying about whether there's enough dark matter in the universe to keep it open or make it close, because I don't really care for either of those possibilities. When I tell Uncle Claude that I won't accept that we're just bits in a bubble of nothingness, he tells me not to disparage myself for I am the sum of all the accidents of matter that have occurred since the universe began and that is a pretty impressive end-product. But I'm not having that – and neither should you. Because it's you he's after, crunching ever closer to the precipice where you are clinging by your fingernails. He talks to me, but that's because he can't talk to you. He knows that I'll pass on the message. He believes he has the law on his side, the law of science, and he's going to have the law on you. He's out for blood. Help me, Lord. Above all, help me to help you.'

I was disturbed by a faint noise behind me and for a minute (well for a split second) I almost thought – well, enough to say that in my terror I clutched at the twisted leg of the Prior's table and almost brought the television set crashing down on top of me.

'Bella, what has happened? You look as if you've seen a ghost.'

André was smiling at me from the doorway, faintly and apologetically. He had materialised from nowhere. In his eyes was a look of tenderness and pity, though he also seemed slightly embarrassed at having walked in on a private moment. He was wearing a white apron. I got slowly to my feet and rubbed my knees. He stood framed in the doorway with his arms held out, palms exposed. I think it was then that I began to notice that there was something increasingly monkish about André.

'I thought I heard a cry,' he said.

'I was watching television.'

'Ah well, that explains it. One sees such terrible things on television.'

'I turned it off.'

'Have you been crying, Bella?'

'I've stopped.'

'Good. Deluges can be exhausting. Like the falling sickness. Or someone given to fits. You fear not only the embarrassment you cause others, but the shock to your own system. And yet you can't help yourself. Oh yes, I sympathise. I went through something similar, years ago, when I was on the Bourse in Paris. Well, you can just imagine how embarrassing tears were in such circumstances. What my colleagues said! The clerks on the floor are a tough lot, financial hoodlums of a sort. And their controllers in their suits back in the offices are no better. So it does not help to liquefy in front of them. Tears are never appreciated in the arena.'

I had seen pictures of the yelling, barging young men howling their prices on the floor of the Stock Exchange.

'When the brokers are roaring like beasts on the floor of the Bourse.'

'Exactly, Bella. Well put.'

André peered at the dead television screen, grey as a corpse with tiger stripes of sunlight across its blank face. His face loosened in that alarming way I had noticed on other occasions, as if the shell protecting the flesh had been hit too hard and fractured into thousands of hair-thin cracks and might at any minute slip from his head; and perhaps that was the reason why he went and sat down in one of the rather horrid mustard chairs available for the telly viewers and placed his fragile head in his hands.

'We lived in the tenth arrondissement just where it borders on the ninth, a place of brothels, churches and newspapers. In the thirties it was no longer a fashionable area, it had been going down. Actually it had been going down since the First War. It was close to the Bourse you see, so my father decided to stay on although everybody else, of our sort that is, had left. The *boursicotiers*, the jobbers, the *agents de change*, the brokers had been going, well, to tell you the truth, they'd been clearing out since the turn of the century, going west, where it was smarter. Round our way it hadn't been smart since the Third Republic when the brokers dressed in bowler hats, spats and coats with fur trim and puffed fat cigars. My father kept a set of old caricatures of the great tycoons hanging on the wall in our house. We were in a place midway between the public baths, the old Neptuna and the Sarah Bernhardt Theatre. There we sat, my father and I, because that's where they had sat, my father and his father, because this had always been the stockbroking quarter and my father believed that a gentleman should always be able to walk to his place of employment, and it was an easy stroll to the Bourse. There we lived. There was no question of moving.'

'Where was your mother?'

'Dead.'

'I'm sorry.'

'So am I. I think we would still be there if the war hadn't come. June 1940 and France fell. People left in droves, Paris became silent, nobody seemed to speak, except my father, he was as usual optimistic. "The Marshal has in mind a plan to protect the historic destiny of France," he announced, almost as if he were the Marshal himself.'

André turned his sad eyes on me. 'I think for every child, at a certain age, fourteen, say, or fifteen, there should be a ceremony in which the child is allowed to repudiate one parent. Or both.'

'What about uncles?'

'Parents are more generally available.'

'Not in every case.'

'Shall we say one close relative?'

'Good.'

'War evoked a spirit of declaration in my father. "Business as usual," he cried. Though the Bourse was still functioning, it was a charade. Then one day he told me he'd heard that there were opportunities in Lyons. In the *zone libre*. The Bourse in Lyons was doing business! Do you hear the word, Bella – opportunity? Watch out! Such words are dangerous. Language is the mask of life! I went to stay with a cousin in the country. My father wrote to me of his great opportunity. He sent us money and food. He was busy opening a branch of our offices in Lyons, he said. I never saw him again. In 1945 he died.'

'What did he die of?'

'The war. When the war was over I went to work in the old office in Paris. I heard no more from Lyons. My father had died there. I thought no more about the branch. It died with him. At least no more was heard of it. I began to wonder if there really had been a branch at all. I put the talk of it down to my father's loose manner in the age of declarations. I became a broker like him. Only later I found the truth about our Lyons operation.'

'Is that when you became a terror?'

André gave a ghastly little grin and shook his head. 'Not then. Later. A beast. What did you say – when the brokers are roaring like beasts on the floor of the Bourse, that's well put.'

'That's not me. It's from a poet, an English poet, we read at school.'

'Ah poetry.' He looked crestfallen. 'Forgive me, but I don't touch poetry.' He spoke in the tone of a man refusing a drink. 'I'm afraid I steer clear of music, too. And I never look at paintings. It's not that I don't love them, on the contrary, but they're distractions. After my years in Paris, I simply haven't the time, and after discovering how I had lived off the profits of our offices in Lyons — well, I didn't have the stomach for these things. Take heed for you know not the day, nor the hour, sayeth the Lord. The absolute preciousness of the little time available to us to learn how to be saved is conveyed to me every year with wonderful simplicity and fierce dedication by the good fathers at the Monastery of St Bruno, up in the mountains. You know that's where I make my winter retreat. There is nothing fiercer or madder than doing just one simple thing, Bella. I look at the monks and I'm appalled. Horrified! I love what they do, but it terrifies me. Every day, every minute is measured. Like athletes they drive their bodies without ceasing. Gentle fanatics training for the perfection to come! Life by the bell — rise at two-fifteen, Vigils, Prime, Sext, dinner, then work again, supper, Compline, prayer, bed by six. There it is. All day and all night, prayer, penitence. I stay three weeks, it's as long as I can manage, when the hotel is closed in the late autumn. I want more — *months* perhaps, but the fathers don't think that's a good idea. "No, no, André," they say to me, "you've got your own place. If you come into our monastery, who will look after yours?" Except, of course, they don't really say that, or anything else, because they don't speak, Bella, as I'm sure you know. But this I take to be their advice, and I abide by it. Not my will but thine be done. Sometimes I dream that I'm keeping the Priory open for their return one day. I tell myself I'm merely the caretaker.'

He was very excited. Sweat stood out on his forehead and he dabbed at it with his apron. 'And if I didn't have enough on my mind, there is the new guest. Arrived last night and he's taken the entire upper floor.'

'All of it? Who is he?'

72

André looked vague. 'He's simply someone who wishes to avail himself of my hotel, for a short period, and desires utter privacy.'

'He must be very rich.'

'I really couldn't say.'

'But he must be! The whole of the second floor? What's that – twenty bedrooms?'

'Thirty. Twenty-four single bedrooms, where the monks had their cells, and six doubles in the adjacent wing, overlooking the lake.'

'Six suites! – he takes six suites as well?'

'He doesn't use the suites. Just one single room.'

'What's his name? Is he a sheikh or a shah or something – with a harem? Or a huge staff? Or twenty-four cousins?'

André smiled thinly. I could tell he did not like my questions. But there was something else, a kind of irritation, touched with alarm.

'He's here alone. There is no entourage.'

'Why did he come?'

André began to look embarrassed. He shrugged. 'We were given no details.'

'How long is he staying, this rich guest who has fallen out of the sky?'

'I am assured the visit will be brief.'

'You mean you don't know?'

He flushed, not bothering to conceal his anger now. 'How should I know the length of his stay. I am not psychic, Bella, and since I have not been favoured with the dates for the duration of his visit, I can't answer your question. The reservation was not one I could refuse. Don't ask me what I think about this. My views weren't considered by those arranging for this gentleman to descend upon me.' A look of real pain crossed his eggshaped face, fine cracks began spreading outwards from the corners of his eyes and rippling across the tightly stretched skin of his pink cheeks, seismic disturbances within the flesh.

'What people like us need, if we're not to fly apart, is discipline.' He took my hand. 'I sometimes feel all the familiar elements of life are flying apart at prodigious speed.' He began to pat my hand, rhythmically and rather hard. It hurt. 'Since no one else will do it, we must discipline ourselves, each in

73

his own way. Tell me, besides weeping, do you find yourself praying?'

My hand was stinging so much I pulled it away and licked it to cool it. 'Yes.'

'Aloud?'

'Yes. And I want to go down on my knees in the street!'

André shook his head. 'You see – it's impossible to live like that, in the modern world. In the monastery of St Bruno monks have their own discipline. I'm not referring only to the procedures where they confess their sins to the Prior, or are accused by their fellows of faults for which they must make reparation. I mean the little whip they hide under their pillows. It has five tails and they call it the *scourage*. And I tell you, Bella, every Friday after Lauds they whip themselves. True! Except at Christmas and Easter. Sometimes I believe that the boys who work for me would benefit by it, but I don't hold out much hope. Look, I'll show you.'

He took from the pocket of his apron a little stick with leather cords dangling from it. It looked not unlike the ceremonial flywhisks Papa brought home from Africa. Lifting it to his ear and without taking his eyes off me, André lashed himself on each shoulder in turn.

'Normally one would do this without a shirt. But I simply cannot spare the time. I must get on. Twenty-six for dinner tonight and chef has deserted me.'

He replaced the whip in his apron pocket and sighed. 'It's out of place. I know that. I keep it for sentimental reasons. A penance, punishment, discipline – call it what you like – must be appropriate. I think I have perhaps found my real *scourage*: to work myself to death.'

'Where are your boys?'

He shrugged. 'Tertius is playing *boules*, he's in the village team. Hyppolyte is unwell and Armand is in Lyons, again . . . But now I must get back to the kitchens.'

He walked me slowly along the cloisters, passed the statues of hunched, dwarfish little bishops with croziers and books who sat in stony silence on the window sills and leered as we went by.

'You mean they've left you to prepare dinner for all the guests on your own?'

74

He gave me a smile of an inexpressible sweetness. 'For my sins, yes. Tonight we're having cream of lettuce soup, followed by *filets de sole marguéry*.' He waved a hand. 'Goodbye, Bella. I'm glad you've stopped crying.'

The private beach was deserted. The empty deckchairs were orange and blue. The departed guests would now be in their rooms changing, getting ready for a cocktail and looking forward to the dinner André was preparing. The chairs opened their mouths and yawned, showing their brightly striped throats. The lake was soft and lovely as the shadows began mixing inkily with the water. It was curious the way the water seemed thicker and more solid as night began to come on and it grew to be an altogether more substantial body; darker, crueller and more private, absorbed with itself. I heard its low mutter. The many hotels and restaurants that loaded the lower slopes of the village took the force of the slanting afternoon sun which gave them a blind, somehow indecisive look; it was that curious moment of the day, that point where people had packed up and left the lake and the official evening was still an hour away from its formal beginning, when the lights would go on in the restaurants and on the terraces and the guests would talk and laugh at such establishments as the Beau Rivage and the Hotel Bellevue and at the Palace and even the famous restaurant *Les Dents Sacrés* where the rich gourmets ate and the local yokels pressed their noses to the menu boards outside and whistled at the prices of the hors-d'oeuvres. And in this non-time it was as if all had temporarily lost their identities and were waiting to reclaim them − as if for this brief period the lake alone knew what it was.

I bowed my head and called on the Lord: 'Give me the power to thwart the heathen.' I don't know why I used the word 'heathen' and the use of the term 'thwart' was even more unusual. It wasn't at all like me. Perhaps this was what they meant by 'speaking in tongues'. Or maybe it was just a matter of the comfort of words. If I say that something that brings out the reddish tints in my hair is called Copper Blush, and my foundation powder is called Warm Burgundy, my lash mascara Smokey Ebony and my lipstick Strawberry Surprise, you'd be a fool if you took away anything from this description except a very vague impression because the words are used as a kind of paint and it doesn't in the least matter whether the words used relate to, or match, or have no connection whatsoever with strawberries and blushes.

Behind me I heard shouts and wolf whistles. And there out on the lake, clambering onto the wooden pontoon that lay moored about thirty metres from the private beach, and which was used as a swimming platform by the guests, I saw Tertius, Hyppolyte and Armand, who were all supposed to be somewhere else, according to André. I'm pleased to say that my recent religious conversation did not stop me from lifting a rigid forefinger in their direction in an unmistakable gesture. They all laughed and applauded and dived off the pontoon and I saw their smooth heads breaking the water like seals playing. The stupid boys had thought it clever to lie to André, who was even then slaving over his lettuce soup and scouring mussels under cold running water and scraping off the black rope-like tufts from the shells with a small sharp knife for the *filets de sole marguéry*, which his guests were to enjoy that evening; a meal which was no doubt to be served by André as well, for the boys, whose loud catcalls and childish innuendoes, seeming in the main to refer to the way I moved, now reached me faintly across the water, showed no sign of preparing to put on their white coats and take up their dubious roles as waiters.

I walked away from the swimmers, the hotel and the private beach, along the little road that runs around the shore of the lake, dividing the Priory from the *plage privée*, skirting the waterside where the yachts are moored. The little road passed between the private wooden jetties and the big houses standing at the far ends of their gardens, their beautiful lawns, sweeping down the waterside. Most of the houses were closed up, shutters tightly secured against the wind off the water. Black and graceful streetlamps leaned over me, their pretty heads shaped like musical clefs. Everything in that corner of the lake, where the road hit the mountain and stopped dead, had been made to seem natural, a human settlement painted on the mountainside. Now I entered the picture – a daub of pink against the evening grey, visible to whatever hawk's eye swept the canvas while I kept moving, invisible the moment I stopped dead at the mountain – then I disappeared into the painting.

Many of the houses have chains around their gates, the links show rustily through ugly, yellow, transparent sleeves. These houses look like they've been shut since the nineteenth century. When the streetlamps come on they turn a warm amber. An old painted notice on a fence reads: '*Respect the purity of the Lake*'. I took a good deal of comfort from that sign. Then I turned around and walked back. All the lights on the second floor of the hotel were shining. An entire floor to himself. The guest must be made of money! Thirty rooms for one man, André had said, and no entourage!

Behind me the private beach was dark and the boys were gone from the floating island. Beyond the gates to the hotel is an open space which is used as a parking lot by day. I saw several cars still parked. It was odd to see trippers after dark, too late for bathers, too early for lovers. There were, to be precise, a Citroën, a Renault and a Deux-Chevaux. In each of the cars sat two or three men, tough-looking guys who stared at the dark water as if they were waiting for someone to arrive, a ship or something. But I knew it was too late for the ferries from *La Compagnie des Bateaux sur Le Lac* which collect passengers from the jetty near the restaurant *Les Dents Sacrés*. One came by after dark, playing music, all lit up, a floating restaurant – but it did not stop for passengers. Whatever the watchers in the parking lot were waiting for it wasn't a boat.

From that time when I first got frightened in the TV room, I have had what I think of as my 'prayer problem'. I'm God-haunted, heaven-possessed, an excess of divine grace fell on me from clear skies. The spirit took me and shook me like a fierce wind, or a fever, and my mind fluttered like a leaf or a feather. I felt increasingly called upon to oppose the likes of Uncle Claude. I heard voices calling me to become an advocate for disorder. 'Speak for the dead, Bella!' my voices told me. And I knew what they meant. For my uncle the dead were just that: dead. You might regard them as objects for study, if you were an anthropologist. But you did not weep for them. Or venerate them. Or pray for them. In my case the urge to fall on my knees overcame me in public and private places. My lips moved even when I slept. As a result I slept less, ate more chocolate, waited for something.

And this *thing*, whatever it was, was no respecter of occasions. I might be togged out in fur flying hat and distressed leather jacket and a pink soda T-shirt so skimpy it ends at the armpits; I could be swimming, dancing, sleeping, eating, when, without warning, the floods broke. The only thing worse than involuntary weeping was uncontrollable prayer. Not knowing where to turn, I wrote for advice to a magazine I liked called *N-Ova!* They printed my letter, in between one from a twelve-year-old contemplating a second abortion, and advice to someone whose boyfriend had genital warts.

*Dear 'Weepie' of La Frisette, they wrote, your condition is unusual and more suited to medieval times than to our 20th century. Perhaps it is associated with psychological problems? Or it may be an allergy. The need you also have 'to speak for the dead', as you put it, is probably linked to the praying problem. This aspect of it is not particularly advisable and is best left to the professionals. It's possible that energetic physical exercises might dampen down the urge to pray, swimming say, or riding. Avoid places like churches, shrines and religious gatherings. Tears are less of a problem and even excessive weeping will do no harm — though it plays hell with your makeup! Never mind, if you want to cry, go ahead and bawl your head off! Though we know how embarrassing that can be at a club or disco or on that heavy date, or when you're in close quarters with your lover. He/she might think (wrongly) that it reflects your opinion on their performance. Would it help to discuss this with a doctor, relative or family friend? In the circumstances, a minister of religion would not be such a hot idea . . .*

I began to learn to take steps to hide what was happening. I would bury my face in a handkerchief when the tears started, pretending I had a bad cold or hayfever, or a sneezing fit, and run from the room. If I was down by the lake, I would dive in; if I was in bed I would bury my head under the pillows; if I was having a meal I would pretend to be choking. These were unpleasant deceptions but they kept away the questions I dreaded. Only with Clovis did I once allow myself to cry unashamedly and he patted my head soothingly and seemed rather pleased by it all, though I must say he did try to remove my blouse at the same time and I had to restrain him. I jabbed him in the stomach with my elbow and winded him quite badly. He fell over and had trouble getting up again. Through tears in my eyes I saw tears in his eyes. I don't believe in hitting cripples, as a rule, but I had to defend myself. It's not easy to be firm when you're rubbery with inexplicable sorrow. However, the floods never lasted long and when they passed I always felt rather lighter, as well as a bit older and somehow wiser, if rather curiously rusty. Far from complaining about my treatment of him, Clovis always looked back on the shared occasion with delight, calling it 'the day the rains came'. He seemed to have forgotten that I'd hit him and was hoping that it would happen again.

# 5

Pass through the entrance arch of the Priory Hotel where the menus stand to attention in their glass cases on either side of the arch, fixed to the brickwork which is crumbling picturesquely like pink cheese (today we have jugged hare) and cross the tarmac parking lot where the three cars occupied by big men still have not moved, and you will see the rickety jetty where the pleasure craft are moored: paddle boats, windsurfboards and darkly varnished rowing boats hired by the old cross-patch Leclerc. On the other side of the jetty, before you come to the restaurant *Les Dents Sacrés*, lies one of the landmarks, or one of the watermarks, really, of La Frisette, the drowned boat, a dinghy lying in a few metres of water. She's been there for as long as I can remember, perfectly preserved and seen as if through a plate-glass shop window behind which someone has made a rather theatrical scene supposed to represent Davy Jones' locker. The tip of an anchor is peeping through the sand, a school of small fish investigate her ribbed belly, oars repose peacefully in the rowlocks and little crabs scuttle across their blades. So clear is the water you can read her name painted on the side, *La Belle Indifférente*. It's only when a breeze shivers the surface, or a paddle boat with a couple of kids, their knees pumping like mad, churns away from the jetty destroying the surface calm, that the illusion of shop windows and painted scenes melts as the drowned boat dissolves and crumbles, crabs run for cover, the fish swirl and vanish and you see that *La Belle Indifférente* isn't a prop at all. She really is lost beyond recall. But the funny thing is that although she lies in the shallows and could be got at very easily, no one has ever interfered with her. She is my guardian spirit, my protector, sister, friend. Her preservation is miraculous. She doesn't seem to rot, there are no holes that I can see in her timbers, her body holds together and the villagers of La Frisette regard her as a kind of monument. They pause as they walk by and stare into the water with a feeling of sadness, affection, gratitude that although she's gone, she's somehow still with us. The attitudes of the children of tourists who have never seen her before is very interesting because they come by, pause and perhaps giggle a bit at first as if they'd seen someone undressing. It's so strange: here is a boat not on the water but under it, and that's when they start to quieten down, when they realise they're staring into a transparent grave.

It is about ten in the morning, the shadows are just lifting from the water, and the lake, like a giant machine, is being cranked into action for another day, when I stop briefly to pay my respects to the drowned beauty, *La Belle Indifférente*, in her glassy coffin. Perhaps I should add that as I stand by the water's edge I'm leaning forward slightly, as is my habit, in order to get a closer view of the shadowy water spirit, resting my hands on my knees.

I'm wearing a pair of tight, long lemon shorts with brass buttons on the back pockets and an imitation snake-skin belt which, when pulled tight, gives me the wasp-waist look I am trying really hard for. I'm wearing as well (should you care to know it) a circus-tent top in red-and-white stripes, really floaty and light. Though I intend to spend a few hours on the private beach I'm not planning to swim this morning, the curse having descended with its usual irregularity the evening before.

'What a charming prospect,' says a voice behind me, in English.

More a growl than a voice, water over stones, or gravel, deep yet flowing. I straighten pretty smartly. I do not take kindly to voices at play and I take a dim view of words like 'prospect' which I thought went out with the California goldrush. But all straightening up does is to bring my ear into almost nibbling contact with his lips. And then I realise it is not on my body that this approval falls – his eyes are fixed on the drowned boat.

'It should be lifted and preserved in its entirety, like the wreck of the *Mary Rose*, pride of the Tudor navy – Henry VIII's royal flagship – which I watched being raised from the deeps on an October morning some years ago. On the television. At the time I was esconced in my coastal retreat, not very far from Nice, a pleasanter spot was never spied.'

Now let's just hold it right there. I had also seen the *Mary Rose* being raised from the ocean floor, in bad weather with TV cameras nosing through the depths like sharks, and this big yellow mechanical cradle breaking the surface like a cat with a mouse in its mouth. The remains of the ship were no more than a few old bits of wood. Talk of an excess of technology over artefact! It was like sending a bulldozer into a reliquary. The scientists went fishing with a computer-controlled cage and bags of balloons and came up with this sad little fishbone saved from the deep. The mountain of media laboured and brought forth the backbone of a mouse. And for what? In order to dredge up the spirit of the past they sent in a mechanical digger. Maybe one day they'll invent a robot archaeologist, like the sort of mechanical dog they use for sniffing out bombs, and cut out the human factor altogether – 'Hullo, my name is Colin, I'm a remote-controlled researcher investigating the pollen count in a cess-pit of an iron-age settlement – press my nose for a print-out . . .'

It's at times like this that I vow to put on my earphones and never take them off again. I distinctly object to finding strange men in my ear. I move forward sharply and return to my study of the drowned beauty but not before taking a good look at the invader.

A white suit and panama hat sporting a black-and-gold ribbon, a pair of enormous wrap-around sunglasses. His shoes are white with gold laces. This is the first time I've seen him with clothes on. He moves beside me, places his hands on his knees, and we both now bend and stare into the water. We must make an odd sight. Several passers-by give us curious glances.

'Do you believe it to be an antique?'

'No. Just an old rowing boat. She's been there for years.'

'Pity just to leave it there to rot. Of course I know what you're going to say. Why bother? After all, this is a disposable age. I dispose. You are disposed. We are disposed of! You in the West live off your technological cornucopia. We in Africa are tossed the fag-ends and they are not, if I may say so, finger-licking good. But allow me to place my finger on what I sense to be the root of your objection to rescuing this craft from the water and at the same time give me the chance to correct the old assumption among those who know nothing about Africa that it's a place of warring tribes who run around with bones through their noses.' He lifts the finger referred to, big and round, like a black cigar tube, and lays it across his nose. In fact all his fingers are distinctly tubular. 'I happen to know that once the timbers of this ship are exposed to the air they can be preserved by an application of a solution of polyethylene glycol, after which the relics are freeze-dried to preserve them for posterity. Freeze-drying is a process which is used, as possibly you know, to preserve instant coffee. Coffee is an interesting case, since it's an important cash-crop of several South American as well as of some African countries and its price is manipulated by brokers in the West to the detriment of its growers. Coffee, I might add, is also a by-product of the cocoa bean whose origins are magnificently South American, though we have made its bronze acquaintance in Africa. The bean was first used by the ancient Aztecs and other South American Indians. The tree from which it comes was a gift of the feathered snake god, Quetzalcoatl, who gave it as a gift to man. From the bean the Aztecs made chocolate, not as we know it, but a hotly spiced, rather bitter beverage which was frothed up before drinking. In this form it was presented to the conquistadors as a royal drink. Coffee came from the court of a king whom Cortés killed.'

He likes this ghastly alliteration because he repeats it twice. I do not need to be lectured on the history of chocolate. Besides, the thing to do is not to study it – but to eat it.

'Montezuma.'

'Monte – precisely – Zuma. As you say. You know about these things?'

'I more or less have to live on chocolate. I don't seem to be able to eat anything else. Well, maybe a little fish. And fruit. But mostly chocolate.'

'Ah well, then we have something to share.'

'You also?'

'I eat more than I should. I break the taboo when I eat it. I belong to the Wouff tribe. D'you know them? They are the number one people in my country of Zanj and, as a rule, they do not touch it, *cannot* touch it, believing it will kill them to eat it. I've tried to coax them out of this superstition, but they are traditionalists, the Wouff, and do not change easily. It's a damn shame. We could make a considerable success if we introduced the cocoa plant in my country. We know it well. My people were among the very first to raise the crop on the African continent. Now others do it, like Nigeria and Ghana, but we were the first. We learned the hard way that the young cocoa trees thrive best when planted in the shade of yam or banana trees. As the green armoured pods begin to swell and glow, we watch like mothers! We see the golden hue that speaks of the ripening seed within. We carefully cut the pods, scoop out the beans from their envelopes of rubbery white pulp, ferment them, dry them and pack them in bags to feed the chocolate-crazy thousands of Europe.'

'You grow cocoa beans in your country?'

'Not the beans, no. What we did was to grow the slaves. Then our slaves went off and grew the beans. *Voilà!* as the French say. The first cocoa was grown in big amounts on the West African Islands of São Tomé and Principe, off the coast of Guinea. They were owned by the Portuguese. In my country of Zanj, the tribe known as the Kanga, who are Moslems, were developers of the African cocoa trade. Do you know the Kanga? They were converted by the Arab slavers who visited our part of the world for centuries.'

'Which is your part of the world?'

'Do you know where Uganda is?'

'More or less.'

'Well, we're not more than about a thousand miles from Uganda. And not far from the Central African Republic either, as distances go in Africa. The Arab slavers were pretty free around those parts. Picking things up. Passing things on. They passed on to the Kanga, up in the central highlands of my country, a taste for the laws of the Prophet – and a big love for the business end of slavery. When the slavers left towards the end of the nineteenth century, the Kanga took over. The Kanga would kidnap members of my tribe. They say the Wouff are idiots and pagans! That's what they said, because we worship the sacred stones, and so they marched us to the coast. The

Wouff are a brave strong people, and great fighters, but the march killed many and those who grew too weak to walk were murdered. The Kanga had rifles! Yet the Kanga disliked this aspect of the work because they love to stay at home among their wives or their mosques. And the trek to the coast took weeks, even months! The Kanga count like this.' He lifted one cigar finger after another: '"One-day-away-from-wives, two-days-away-from-wives, three-days-away-from-wives . . ." and that's all. They do not count more than three. They just say "too many!" Also the Kanga hated the Portuguese who were Catholics. But the Kanga are lucky, lucky people. They brought the Ite to work for them. The Ite were very, very primitive. Fetishists. They worshipped snakes, until they became Christians. Christians are sensible. And they need money, so the Ite took on the transport of Wouff slaves to the coast. To this day, in my country, when an Ite person comes creeping into a Wouff village it makes the children run screaming for their mothers. Maybe you say this is ridiculous, you might say "you live and learn".'

'I don't say that.'

'Good. It's a stupid expression. Our Wouff children long past, in the slave years, understood that if you waited around to learn, you might not live. To this day chocolate and death are twins. Not only sin and guilt and luxury, as it is in the West. The Wouff believe chocolate is made from the blood of their fathers. They believe that this blood was taken from the bodies of their sons, together with certain fats, and sent to the Quakers.'

'The Quakers!'

'Yes, the Quakers, across the seas in England. It sounds silly, but you see it was the Quakers who bought so much of the cocoa crop from the islands of São Tomé and Principe. For their chocolate works and their cocoa factory at Bourneville. As Hamlet might have said, if he had been a Wouff, the souls of the Wouff slaves are fled to a Bourneville from which no traveller returns. Not that my people are particularly superstitious, they don't see visions of angels in baobab trees like the Ite, they don't cut their women — you know the Kanga circumcise their women? — hence the Wouff proverb: "When a Kanga makes love, his wife makes bread" . . .

*85*

And here he laughs. He is one of those men who laughs with his shoulders and chest, and his head shakes as if it's on a spring. 'I did what I could to change their minds, I said to my people: Look, I will be your example and eat! I ordered chocolate to be brought to me in front of the tribe and melted into a golden bowl.'

'Like Montezuma in the presence of Cortés?'

'Well read! Well read!' he says, rather as an Englishman will say 'Well played!' 'Exactly. But it didn't work. The very word for chocolate in the Wouff language means "death of fathers". So one fine cash-crop goes out of the window and we're left with our palm oil, our diamonds and our poverty.'

'I suppose you could say I have an addiction. I'm a chocolate junkie.'

'Then you are as much a victim as anyone else. As much as the poverty-stricken peasant toiling to produce it beneath the pitiless sun. You are the victim targeted by the merchants for its consumption, the ultimate casualty of an economic system which feeds some children of the world on chocolate and thousands of others on nothing at all. Remember the words of your former queen, Antoinette: let them eat cake! Well, let them drink chocolate! I have a good memory for the remarks of royal personages – be they Henry's boat or Antoinette's cake. Victims crying out to be saved. Like this drowned boat here. She's so little. A man could lift her in his arms, a crane would not be needed.' He steps forward. 'Shall we save her?'

'No!' I put out my hand. 'She mustn't be touched. She's perfect as she is.'

He stretches out a hand as big as a soup plate and tries to pat me on the head.

'Poor child!'

I have to move pretty bloody sharply to avoid catastrophe. I mean I spent absolutely hours getting it up this morning, getting it moussed, scrunched, dried and really wild – but fixed. This is not easy without Catherine the Great of Finchley around to lend a hand. And here I am faced with the destruction of my morning creation.

I stress *my* creation, for it is mine. Even as I am yours (whoever, wherever you are), for which you cannot expect flowing gratitude, my ever-present, invisible maker who seems to have made me only to leave me in the lurch. However often I call on you, you remain elsewhere, out of reach and out of touch. Omnipotent you may be. Omniscient, too. But hells bells! Can I rely on you?

The black man and I stare at *La Belle Indifférente*.

'I don't say she can't be raised, or even that she can't be preserved. I'm saying that if you pulled her up now she wouldn't be with us any more. She'd be something else, which means somewhere else. I want her here, where I can stop and look at her as I pass and pay my respects. So I say leave her be, let her rest in peace.'

He considers this proposition gravely and I get the feeling he's surveying me from behind the black curved screen of glass that hides his eyes. Then abruptly he holds out his hand again. 'I've been for years an inhabitant of the South of France. Almost long enough to call myself a citizen, but not quite.'

I shake his hand. It's warm, like a glove.

'Bruin,' he says. Or 'Bane' or 'Brown'.

Frankly it might also have been something quite different. Boon? or Brain? Or even Bone? Anyway I settled on Brown – and Brown he shall be. Maybe the acoustic within the small concert hall of my head has not been improved by the constant broadcasts of groups like Giuseppe and the Lambs and the heavy metal lot, like Embolism, blasting away on my earphones. Perhaps moving between English and French all the time has also done damage, maybe linguistic lane-switching hurts the hearing centres of the brain.

My Uncle Claude has these pictures from inside the brain, he carries them around in his wallet and pulls them out and makes me look at them. His tomographs, he calls them. They show a blue oval ocean with red islands top and bottom, left and right. 'These are electron scans of the brain, Bella – here, look at them!' He holds them cupped in his palm because he knows that they frighten me and he is not really supposed to do it. He does it when no one's about. He did it a lot when I was younger and I couldn't understand what he said about things like positrons. His pictures of the secret life of the brain showed that when you weren't being stimulated in *there* the islands were very small, maybe they disappeared altogether. When you hear something exciting the island on the left gets about as big as Madagascar, but if you are dumb, or not hearing properly, it shrinks to the size of the British Isles. The cards are really greasy because he carries them around in his wallet.

He gets really excited by them. They're his equivalent of the yellow baskets they sent down to pick up the wreck of the *Mary Rose* from the ocean floor. I think he's on to something. Because if you can use them on the brains of living people why not on the dead? Think of the day when they exhume a Neanderthal child from a cave floor. They retrieve the little skeleton buried in a foetal position cradling a deer antler and they find a bit of brain tissue still preserved and they run an electron scan and they say, 'Look, when this child died the cortex glowed violet and tests on living brains show violet means associations with food, so this little creature died thinking of dinner . . .' And everyone will fall about with excitement and wonder at the cleverness of it all. But the child who was sick and was given an antler to hold, the light that went out – the grief of those who loved it are gone beyond recall and will not show up in the tomographs.

Anyway, according to Uncle Claude's snaps of the cortex, looking sometimes beats listening. When your eyes are open really wide something like a coral reef is formed around the front of your brain. And I am looking really hard at the black man when we shake hands. He is so grim!

'You have a name, too?'

It's a heavy face, droopy, round, massive; the nose sits there waiting – with its wide wings like a jet plane on a runway, grounded – even the lips are heavy and dragged downwards at the corners under their own weight. Those lips are overweight. Ears are firm flaps of flesh stuck a long way back. Altogether he is as solid as a tree. A black oak darkening to violet. A very beautiful bruise. Plum dark, smooth as caramel! I lick my lips to let out the words.

'I'm called Bella – Bella Dresseur.'

I rest my pink hand in his black mitt with its long tubular fingers. He beams at me as if the name is an entrancing piece of information.

'Bella, Bella, Bella! This is delightful. A name quite outside my acquaintance. And you speak such perfect English, if I may say so. My French is non-existent. In my country, in the circles in which I was raised, it was regarded as rather low to speak the language of Molière and Hugo. Can you imagine that? It was our protest against the colonial power.'

There is a curious mixture of styles about Monsieur Brown. He is affable and rather talkative but at the same time he is also somewhat lofty and even haughty. He has a way of cocking his head and nodding wisely as if he can see into your mind and soul, can sum you up with clairvoyant accuracy, as if he knows a great deal about people and 'reads' them easily.

'I'm half English. French father, English mother.'

He clasps his hands delightedly. 'A mixture. Then you will understand. My country is a linguistic record of our conquerors. The Wouff speak some English, a gesture of defiance, since the French took over from the English as our masters and we detested them. The Kanga, naturally speak French like – shall we say like natives? – not because they felt any more kindly towards the French but because the Wouff speak English. And the Ite, well, what would you expect of the Ite? They speak French and English and a smattering of Portuguese picked up in their cocoa dealings. Of course, we all speak our own languages, sometimes numbering five or six different types. Slavery is a fine language school.'

'But you are, strictly speaking, an African.'

He laughs, a sound of water draining. 'Bless you, my dear. African? What's that? We didn't know we were anything but ourselves, until you came along and named us. Cape Hottentots, Congo pygmies, Wouff, Kanga, Ite. We had our own names for ourselves until the strangers came and declared, "Let there be Africans" . . . and there we were! We didn't even consider ourselves black – or even brown, until you told us so.'

'I'm sorry.' The moment that's out it sounds so silly I laugh. 'No, never mind. I didn't mean to say I'm sorry. How could I be?'

'You can feel sorry, if you like.' He is amused. 'I tell you what – I forgive you! How's that?'

He clasps his hands again, though this time less out of delight than in a kind of summons, as if he expects retainers to come bounding out of the air in answer to his command. When no one comes he starts walking slowly along the lakeside as if it really doesn't matter and it seems churlish not to walk some of the way with him. And so we come to the jetty.

'I had thought of hiring a rocket boat and taking a leisurely tour of the water, with views of the noble Priory,' says Monsieur Brown, 'but this may prove difficult.'

A rocket boat? At first this rather floors me. But then I get his drift. The boats the kids use are made of two white metal cylinders which look a bit like missiles. And I take the hint. What he wants is for me to arrange the booking because his French isn't good enough. I speak to old Leclerc the boatman, who pulls one of the boats hard up against the rubber tyres of the jetty.

'It's called a pedal boat. You sit in it and pedal, as if you were driving a bicycle on the water.'

'You are a poet,' says Monsieur Brown gratefully. 'Why do you laugh?'

'After years in the Midi, I'm surprised you haven't seen one of these before.'

He immediately lifts his chin and stares at the sky in his haughty way. 'We kept ourselves much to ourselves. We did not mix. Or venture out very often.'

'Why not?'

'It was not appropriate. Unpleasant characters lurked as well as honest admirers. One was liable to be accosted, not always for the best of reasons.' He sighed. 'Jealousy!' He shakes his head and the dark curve of his sunglasses proudly throws back the sun. 'Shall I step aboard?'

We both stare at his brilliant white shoes. Doeskin, I guess, with golden clasps at the ends of the laces. Without a word he bends down and removes his shoes and socks. Something happens when he takes off his shoes – but I can't put my finger on it. His socks he stuffs into his pockets. He knots the laces and hangs the shoes around his neck and old Leclerc the boatman, with his huge belly and mud-brown skin, hands him down into the boat. Monsieur Brown looks vaguely at the pedals.

'Is this the engine?'

'Put your feet on the pedals. Really it's just like a bicycle. That's the way, first your left and then your right.'

He stares admiringly at the creamy, churning wake flowing behind the boat. 'This is the most enormous fun and so healthy, I imagine.' He is pedalling furiously.

'Please, Monsieur, wait until I cast off!' barks old Leclerc. Then he turns to me and says in French, 'Really, Bella, he doesn't know that he must steer the boat. Show him the rudder. Or better still, go yourself and work the tiller. He will only threaten life and limb otherwise. This one is really more accustomed to swinging through the trees.' And with that the irritable old lizard hands me down into the boat and pushes us off from the jetty.

'How delightful,' Monsieur Brown beams. 'You're coming sailing with me? We'll take a turn upon the waters.'

'I'm going to drive,' I say.

Our turn upon the waters lasts a couple of hours and takes us in a series of shallow circles across the mouth of the little bay sheltered by the headland. We move in and out among the skiers and windsurfers and around the moored yachts awaiting their weekend owners. Looking back across the thick green water I see again how the site of the Priory had been wonderfully well chosen for dignity, concealment and defence, tucked into the shoulder of the hill with the mountains rising behind it, choked with that tough wiry alpine timber that flourishes in these parts. And beyond the nearer mountains, bigger mountains still. Monsieur Brown has a particular eye for the evidences of battles and he points excitedly to the forts, towers and castles to be glimpsed here and there upon the nearer shoreline.

'This is fighting country?'

'I suppose so. In fact all this country you see around you here, until about the middle of the last century, actually belonged to Italy and not to France at all. Then during the last war these mountains were full of Resistance people fighting the Germans.'

He waves a large hand. 'This country was owned only by Italy? Why, my country has had so many owners we lost count. We were pillaged by the Arab slavers, attacked by the Portuguese who shot their way across Africa crazy with dreams about golden cities. We were colonised by the French, sold to the Dutch, lost to the English and they, it is said, returned us to the French in the hopes that this would over-extend their forces, and their empire in Africa might collapse. It is said by others we were returned simply because the English couldn't think what to do with such a small, poor country. Certainly the French did not know what to do with us, so they maintained a loose association before and after independence, believing that they might as well do so in case somebody stepped in. I speak of the days before we had anything, only our cattle and our palm-nut trees. Both those products were dear to our hearts. Oh yes, I speak of a time when dear Uncle Richard, or poor Dickie as he was known far and wide, was leader of our first independent government. May his souls rest in peace.'

'Souls? How many did he have?'

'Three, of course. Every man has three souls. There is the blood soul transmitted by the female, which is also the voice, character and spirit of the clan. Then there is the male soul and finally the heavenly soul.'

The three fingers Monsieur Brown holds up to illustrate the Trinity lie like black bars across the sun, their shadows resting on my knee. They really are the strangest fingers, large, tubular and terribly regular. From base to tip they do not taper in the slightest. He is clearly very pleased that I have noticed because he holds up all his ten fingers to the sun and the bars imprison me entirely.

'Curious, no? Each of the fingers has the same width all the way up and down. Result: I cannot wear a ring. It falls off. This might seem a small thing but in a Head of State it has profound consequences. Our people are in the habit of seizing the hand that steers the ship of state and kissing it. Some are superstitious and would run from the naked hand. For this reason I was made to wear gloves on formal occasions and when pressing the flesh, taking as my model in this the present Queen of England. But, into my gloves were built strategic knobs and protuberances which, to the touch of the uncomprehending, felt like rings. Ah yes, it is very moving to observe the strong need of simple souls for illusion.'

'Yes,' I say, 'and very sad.'

'Sad?' He is amazed. 'My dear Miss Bella, I can assure you it is not sad – it is essential!'

'Why? In order to deceive them even further? To make fools of them and laugh at them behind your hand because you know so much more than them?'

It's a mistake to get emotional. It brings on the floods of tears. It doesn't help to weep in a paddle boat. Among other things, it interferes with the essential knee action. To his credit, Monsieur Brown pretends to notice nothing of my distress, and boy am I distressed! He unfolds a huge creamy handkerchief from his pocket with a flap and hands it to me and then, squinting into the sun, he continues as if nothing could be more natural than to be paddling barefoot across a lake with a weeping teenager by your side.

'It is simply because people have enough to bear without frightening them further with chosen facts, because they have to get by somehow in the world and how can they do that if you bully them with what I call Tuesday's truth? I call it that because it's invariably different from Thursday's truth. Such is the progress of science and politics. Once upon a time a man who insisted on Tuesday's truth on Tuesday but changed his mind on Thursday could be burned as a heretic, or tortured as a traitor, or beaten as a fool, or put in the stocks until he admitted his mistake. People believed to be true what they were told on Tuesday and you could not go about lightly upsetting them. But nowadays we are told that truth changes with each day of the week and these changes come about as a result of research. But what shall we say to those who died believing in Tuesday's truth? Or worse still – what shall we say to those we killed for not believing Tuesday's truth? Who will speak for the dead? Who will apologise to the dead? Ah – sometimes I think that those who reject research and science have hold of a deeper truth. Once Uncle Dickie was president-for-life of Zanj, and all paid tribute to him. Where is he now?'

'Where is he now?'

Monsieur Brown raises his eyes to the blue, indifferent sky. 'His souls rest with the ancestors. He symbolised for our country the old times. Good and bad. We remember his reign in Zanj as a sort of innocence. Arcadian times, Miss Bella. At the time the staple crop was the palm-oil tree, the basis of our economy, and our art, and our industry. It provided us with all we needed. Palm fronds for our roofs, brooms were made from the strands, palm wine fired the loins of our young men, the wine when fermented provided yeast which was an efficacious remedy for blindness, so much so that the oldest men tell how the father of my uncle, president-for-life, Richard, was cured by this method and threw away his crutch, cut of course from the palm-oil tree, and walked unaided in his ninetieth year! Oh yes, the palm nuts glowing red like jewels in the upper branches of the tree provided soaps, detergents and dyes for the lovely dresses of Zanjian women. It was an idyll, a garden of Eden . . .'

Under the pressure of his memories, Monsieur Brown throws himself about in the boat, rocking it violently, and for one or two moments I fear for our safety. But then he calms again and we drift peacefully. He is very much the engine of our boat, so squat, broad and powerful that it is really his legs alone that have been driving us for some time and I have just been pretending to help. But he doesn't notice.

Above us the hawks sail like black blades. Two small white clouds hang motionless over the twin peaks of St Joan making them look as if they are smoking and giving them the rather menacing contours of volcanoes.

There is something rather phoney about the picture of perfect innocence of the country of Zanj and the benign rule of President Richard, and anyway it's my experience that when men over forty go on about nuts and trees and lard their conversation with references to the joys of palm wine and the loins of lusty young men, what they really mean is people are getting slammed and women raped. And for all the sweet talk, the man Brown does not seem to be a man entirely given over to the pleasures of palm oil.

'Who overthrew Uncle Dickie?'

He looks surprised. 'Why I did, of course. Just as he had chased out the colonial invaders. I won our independence.'

'You!'

'Myself. It was my patriotic duty. I formed the Committee of National Redemption. Don't think that it cost me nothing – after all he was my relative, but I put the good of the country first. My uncle fled to London where he became known for doing social work in the East End. After which he died. Shortly before the end he confessed that he would rather have done social work in the West End. He was a witty man. I miss him.'

We drift and the water slaps the rusty cylinders beneath us with a hollow tinkle. In this corner of quiet water lies a small, brown, rather ugly little yacht with a skinny scrap of dirty grey flag drooping from her mast. We are close enough to read her name, *Minnie III*, and close enough to see her deck where two figures lie and because our boat is drifting and we are not pedalling and there is no sound at all the couple on her deck do not hear us even though they cannot be more than twenty metres away. But we can hear their harsh breathing, the man and woman coiled like golden snakes, their naked bodies glittering in the sun.

I simply don't know where to look and in my confusion, because I can think of nothing else to do, I begin paddling furiously and at the sound of the water beneath our boat the couple on the deck stop, freeze, aware suddenly of our presence and then she slides from under him and vanishes over the side into the water, out on the far side where I can't see her, while he turns his back on us and sits quite naked on the deck. Whether Monsieur Brown has seen them or not I can't tell because the blind sweep of black glass over his eyes gives nothing away, but I can see them and I know who they are: Raoul the escapee from the Foreign Legion and, unless I am very much mistaken, she is the youngest of the Dutch daughters, whom I call Ria. I can see the sweat shining on Raoul's back. On the far side of the boat I can hear her splashing in the water and although I do not like what I see and try to put the pictures out of my head I can see as well the semen drifting from her as she swims, floating in milky ribbons through the green water.

It is Monsieur Brown who finds another subject to interest him, pointing to the plaques screwed into the rock of a cliff face that drops sheer into the water. 'What is that? What are "plongeurs"?'

'Are you saying that you lived under French occupation for years without learning a word of the language?'

He looks delighted. 'Yes. But I know when I'm being insulted. You can tell the boatman that if he were in Zanj

I would puncture his jugular vein and paint the walls of my palace with his blood. Now what are "plongeurs"?'

'They mark the places where people jumped from the rocks, divers. You see, each gives the date: 1917, 1924, 1933. They drowned and their families marked the spot. Sometimes you find flowers here, underneath the plaques, or perhaps drifting in the water. It's very sad. Nowadays nobody uses this spot for diving, but once it must have been popular. I can't think why.'

'It must have been the desire on the part of young men to prove their strength. Their manhood. Some kind of initiation ceremony. Yes, I'm quite sure that's what it was.'

Monsieur Brown's capacity for being quite sure, even absolutely sure, of things which I knew he understood very little about, and often nothing at all, and his willingness to declare his certainty with a great flourish of his head and a tone of utter and complete conviction is one of those irritating qualities about him which makes me suspect that I am going to dislike him intensely.

'We should head back to the jetty. Our time is nearly up.'

'I must say I admire the pendant you wear around your neck.'

I touch the diamond. 'Yes.'

'Is it a gift?'

'From my father. He brought it from Africa.'

'He has good taste. I admire a man who knows how to choose a stone.'

'You know about diamonds?'

He nods. 'In my country we began with palm-nut oil and avoided cocoa. Later it was discovered that we also had diamonds.'

For some reason the tears come again and out comes his hankie and the rains pour down so hard the shoreline disappears. This time he pats my knee, a big black baseball glove swallows my kneecap and oddly enough I find it rather comforting. The floods pass.

'I'm sorry. I was thinking of my papa who is dead. I loved him, Monsieur Brown. Very much.'

'And so did I,' he says.

I turn cold and a buzzing begins in my ears. My finger tips are cold and I blow on them. The buzzing gets louder. I can feel the sun on my body, but it's like paint, it doesn't warm me.

'Are you saying you knew my father?'

He does not look at me but he gives this smile – big, trusting, happy.

'Come and have tea with me. I'll tell you about it.'

'When?'

'Any time you like. You just come down to the hotel and ask for me. I'll be waiting.'

# 6

'Imagine my surprise when I saw little Bella, floating on the lake, with a stranger,' says Uncle Claude, 'sailing across my field of view like a swan.'

We are waiting for the arrival of Monsieur Cherubini in the dining room, where the floor is like the eye of a fly, black-and-white diamonds standing on their points and where Uncle Claude broke my chocolate cup. Grand-mère is preparing salmon in the kitchen for our special dinner. The table dazzles with the best silver. Fruit reposes in its crystal bowl, a waxy pyramid. The papaya lies down with the blushing mango and the dainty kumquats circle, keeping their aromatic distance. I'd like to believe the grapes, in their lustrous purple bruising, are poisoned and Monsieur Cherubini will slip beneath the table at the first taste or fall forward with his forehead in the butter. A wonderful selection of cheeses is on the sideboard, some so ripe and soft they seem to throb within the glass walls of the bell beneath which they have been arranged, like a flower with irregular buttery petals, an after-dinner bouquet for the Angel. Some say keeping a cat is relaxing. But if I could I would keep a soft fat cheese – in a cage – and try to imitate its lovely, happy ooze.

'I tell myself,' my uncle drones in that silly way, in a tone I call audio-reflective, pretending to be talking to himself, 'that Bella is with someone. I look closer and find he is none other than the visitor to our village! The black man. And so I say to myself – now hold on! – that's the type everyone is talking about, the man who has bought his way onto two floors of André's hotel. There he is, out on the lake, in a pedal boat with our little Bella. Fancy that!'

I walk over and examine myself in the Spanish mirror that hangs above the sideboard; in the mirror the cheeses are reflected from above, seeming to swim in yellow light, like fish in an aquarium. The mirror is somewhat spotted and was bought in Spain, I think, years ago and is in a frame of some savage foliage, the tousled leaves roughly entwined, rudely fashioned from tin and studded with garnets. Looking at myself in the mirror is a riposte to my uncle. In the language of our family I am making a gesture of defiance. But I wish the grapes were poisoned instead.

My grandmother emerges flushed and harrassed.

'Come, Bella, leave yourself alone,' she begs, 'help me with the salmon. It is after all for you that we eat fish instead of meat tonight. Come into the kitchen.'

We have this language of our own because without it we've no means of getting in touch with each other. Our aims are so different. My grandmother, for example, cares only to protect me from corruption and win me for France and likes me to look up to her in the way that Bernadette looked up to our Lady of Lourdes, as a repository of dignity and grace. For his part, my uncle inhabits such distant reaches of outer space that the only way of making contact with him, if at all, is by sending out a series of systematic pulses, rather as scientists will beam radio signals to the stars, in the hopes of convincing distant listeners of our existence. Only when my uncle can read my pulses as being mathematically coherent will he believe that there is intelligent life somewhere inside the dark spaces of my cranium. Without such signals we would be locked within our own universes, my grandmother inhabiting a world which begins with Joan of Arc and ends with Marshal Pétain; my uncle who sees people only as molecular clouds; and me, wandering some vale of tears, addicted to chocolate, hooked on cheap lyrics and a slave to style.

'What are you talking about?' my grandmother demands.

'Nothing,' I say.

'The stranger. Down at the Priory,' says my uncle.

'I believe he is Algerian,' says my grandmother, holding up a wineglass to the light and frowning. 'These are not suitable, I am afraid. It is Monsieur Cherubini who dines with us, after all.'

'And I regret, Maman, they are our best glasses.'

My grandmother leaves the room and returns with goblets of heavy Venetian crystal with a lovely toothed, or chewed texture to them, a glass with the look of leather, bitten by old women to give it soft, supple lines. 'A wedding present from my husband, God rest his dear soul. Bought in a little shop on the Cours de Verdun in Lyons in 1920. Doubtless the little place has gone now. So much has gone. A relic of former times, a sign of grace, wrecked and pillaged.'

'That's the fate of relics, Maman – to be stolen by the faithful. Think of St Theresa of Avila, her body was dismembered almost before it was cold. And it was done by her confessor! What demented times they must have been, when the faithful scrabbled for the thumb or the knee of a saint, because they believed it was a lifeline to paradise. Or a kind of *jeton* to be inserted into a slot machine for admission to the gates of heaven!'

'My dear Claude, if I thought that this discussion of the bones of saints means you have softened in your scorn and scepticism about the mysteries of God, then I would pause to talk about it.' Grand-mère shows him a sweet smile only slightly tinged with irony. 'But I'm more concerned, just now, with my mousseline sauce. If Bella knows the visitor at the Priory, perhaps she can tell us if he is an Arab? What is his name?'

'Monsieur Brown.'

'English!' My grandmother is appalled.

'African, Maman,' says Uncle Claude, 'and he's taken a dozen rooms.'

'Two dozen,' I say. 'And I tell you his name is Brown.'

'At five hundred francs a night? His bill must be astronomical! On top of that there are the suites. There are at least six of those, and they cost a thousand each. Six thousand francs a night, just for the suites! This means six plus twelve ... !' – he shakes his head disbelievingly – 'Eighteen thousand a night!'

But grandmama is already moving back to the kitchen; she has more important things to think about. 'I can't hear unless you speak loudly. But I hate to be shouted at. No doubt he has an entourage, tribes of offspring? Perhaps he has numbers of wives? Do they wear veils? I'm sure they kill chickens in their bathrooms and practise the unsettling dietary rites required for their cuisine. Signs of the times.

And portents. All I can say is, thank God for Monsieur Cherubini!'

Her gown is black velvet with a high silver collar, two fat milky pearls swing from the lobes of her ears and her eyes are shining. They always shine when Monsieur Cherubini is expected to appear. When he moves into her vicinity, she lights up like a star; seventy-nine years old and she switches on whenever the Angel pays a visit. There is something about this pompous slug that so appeals to her that she spontaneously ignites whenever he sets foot in the house, she becomes skittish, she won't use her stick, she blushes and she even tries to disguise her limp. In short, Monsieur Cherubini restores her to life.

So why is it then that we think of the life-giver as beautiful? He might look like a snail. To see my grandmother scooting about the house, checking on the coolness of the wine and on her precious poached salmon with a gleam of adoration in her eyes is to know that she finds him utterly beautiful. We know that when the Angel of the Lord declared unto Mary that a Saviour was on the way he took a human form, but do we have to think of that form as pink and rounded and Italian with long hair and almond eyes? Maybe the angel who appeared to Mary looked like a pork butcher, or a brush salesman, or maybe he had the brilliantly shifty look of a small-time dictator. Beauty surprises not because it is beautiful, but because it is surprising, out of the ordinary – and it's out of the ordinary, because everything about it is astonishingly, fatally, appropriate. Just for once, however oddly, everything fits. Not to everyone else, perhaps, not in anyone else's eyes, but to you who look on it, the lucky observer, it is shockingly surprising to find everything so perfectly in place. So when the Angel knocked on the Virgin Mary's door and said, 'By the way, I am the Angel Gabriel . . .', maybe he then went on to say, '. . . and I am running for mayor. Can I count on your support?' And when that message went down really well, then he turned to the frightened girl in front of him and he whispered in her ear, sweet and low, 'And you're in the family way, my dear,' and Mary knew he was telling the truth because he said what she, in a sense, had known all along. But it didn't have to do with his looks, necessarily. Let somebody real and very ugly approach with an astonishing message that exhilarates and suddenly, by magic, the messenger is lovely. My grandmother and Monsieur Cherubini are locked in that embrace. She talks all the time of his open, cordial, honest look, the look, she says, of a sportsman and a soldier. Yet there is nothing of those qualities to be seen in the man, not a trace. So I begin to think that maybe we can know nothing of what others know, that there are for each of us universes beyond universes, much in the same way that Uncle Claude suggests that ours is quite possibly not the only cosmos but that we occupy one of a countless number, a foaming plenitude of universes, like bubbles in a head of beer. Or in an *Aero* chocolate bar . . .

When I am quite sure that grandmama has gone to the kitchen, I face Uncle Claude. 'I want to know how you saw me on the lake?'

Before he can answer, my grandmother returns with the Chinese lettuce and radishes for the salad, glowing within a cut-glass bowl. She hears well enough when she wants.

'I think if you've seen Bella out on the lake with a certain person and especially if she reminded you of a swan, please tell her what happened to Leda.' And off she goes, pretending that the wine needs more attention.

'Leda?' Uncle Claude calls after her, perplexed, he hasn't the faintest idea what she means.

'Leda and the swan,' I inform him. 'It's a Greek legend. She was raped by the swan, who was actually Zeus in disguise, the god in feathers. Even I know that.'

'I regret to say that my education has been scientific and not artistic,' and he gets that peculiar little facial tic, a contemptuous ripple of the eyebrows, which signals his hatred for the unholy trinity made up of gods, arts and foreigners.

'Tell me, Bella, is there some masonic ritual behind the need to roll up one's trouser legs and hang one's shoes around one's neck, is this perhaps some tribal custom in the black man's country, when a warrior goes sailing?'

Now I understand! He's been up in the attic where he's built an astronomical observatory to study the comets. He's mad about comets, he believes that the origins of life on earth began in the distant past when a comet donated a cargo of living matter to the newborn earth. Our planet, according to Uncle Claude, was fertilised in much the same way as a sperm fertilises the female ovum. It was impregnated by meteorite showers which carried the seeds of life, the molecules and the amino acids needed to animate matter, to get life stirring in the primordial soup. It's curious how Uncle Claude always uses these homely instances to describe the mysteries of everything. Once there was a tiny speck of matter of unimaginable density, out of which the cosmos exploded. After a long time cooking and condensing, the solar system was formed maybe ten billion years ago; then about four billion years ago, out of the mixture of steam, rain, storm, gas, water, sunshine and lightning, out of the lava and the mud, life was born on this planet. Out of the soup. So much for starters. At the end of the day, the sun will swell up as though someone turned up the gas in the oven, and will grill us to a cinder. It's frighteningly domestic, isn't it? You start discussing the origin of all things and what you get down to is kitchen talk, cookery terms.

'You were spying on me through your telescope.'

It occurs to me with a shiver of nausea that he probably watched as my black friend and I approached in our paddle boat the couple recovering from their lovemaking on the deck of *Minnie III*. Raoul the escapee from the Foreign Legion and Ria, the second Dutch daughter. Maybe his telescope is powerful enough to have seen the liquids of their lovemaking floating in the water until eaten by the fish, by the little silver shoals which darted and flickered in and out of the shadows just beneath the surface of the water. Fruits of the lake. Little do the tourists and diners who visit the restaurants around about imagine that the local delicacy upon which they feast has itself lately fed on the mingled spermatozoa and vaginal fluids of an escapee from the Foreign Legion and a Dutch girl with beautiful breasts. Cuisine again!

'It is an accident,' Uncle Claude insists. 'Or if you like, it is a scientific observation. Curiosity is the basis of science.'

I don't like it, not one little bit. Heaven knows what other nooks and crannies in the village are visible from his observatory. I don't, of course, expect to embarrass him by pointing out the voyeur that he is. The scientific spirit is shameless. But now there are footsteps on the path and

*103*

knocks on the door and Uncle Claude may run away and open it.

'Look, our guests. Monsieur Cherubini, Father Duval, welcome!'

In the kitchen, my grandmother shrieks softly and drops a plate. Uncle Claude throws open his arms and embraces the Angel and the priest.

Rafael Cherubini is a champagne millionaire, they say. Known to all as the 'Angel' and to his closest followers simply as *'patron'*, he is big and square with rather beautiful silvery hair, his cheeks are high and full and he has a dimple to the left of his mouth. When he smiles the blue of his eyes brightens and his teeth are regular though he never opens his mouth without giving me the impression that it is full of metal. Of course, Uncle Claude will prove to me beyond doubt that the Angel's teeth are composed of nothing but the finest enamel, and I will tell you that they are composed of a steel as yet unrecognised by science. He is perhaps in his sixties; since he founded his party a few years ago branches have sprung up in the villages of these mountains and the big rally on Saturday will draw crowds and supporters from miles around. The police chief, Pesché, and his salmon-suited assistant, the only member of the new order of postal workers, alias Clovis, are working around the clock to prepare the platform, the parking spaces and the seating plans for the hundreds expected.

The PNP is the party of reason and progress. It requires of its members only that they be French. Although Monsieur Cherubini is descended from the Dukes of Savoy, who once governed this territory as part of Italy, he wittily turns this to his advantage by stating that he would fight as hard today against ceding France to foreigners as his family once fought against giving the country of Savoy to the French in 1860. He has twice made offers to buy the Priory Hotel and twice André has refused. Monsieur Cherubini's paper *La Liberté* has recently returned to the attack asking '. . . *If the proprietor of our oldest hotel has neither the will to make extensive and imaginative changes, nor the money to restore this old house to its Carthusian prosperity, then has not the time come to yield to one with bolder plans? We trust that, when the owner of the*

*Priory Hotel contemplates a third refusal, he will not hear the cock crow . . .'*

When my grandmother sees the Angel she goes pale and loses at least fifteen years. When I see him I want to put on my earphones and listen to something really heavy, something really dead – like Grimm or Oedema, that's the black punk lot with that great transvestite drummer and a rhythm section composed of droids who learned their trade from fakirs and like to pass steel pins through their cheeks on stage. He makes me want to do something quite outrageous, like threading neon lights through my pubic hair, or putting my head in the hands once again of Catherine the Great of Finchley for one of her very special treatments, the one called 'Rampage'. That's the one where some of the hair gets spiked and the rest is gathered into an armour of steel pellets, where she makes it into a thatch of blazing colours and lets you loose looking like an insane toucan. When the Angel enters a room I don't see him as a soldier, or a sportsman, or a champagne millionaire, or even as a dangerous politician, which is what they say he is. I just see him as bad news, like the early darkness of winter, as a room full of shadows. I think his teeth too metallic, his face too full, his eyes insincere, and by all these things I show myself utterly out of touch with the general opinion of him, for here in La Frisette, and elsewhere, he's a hero. And coming up behind him now is his accomplice, Father Duval, bringing up the rear like his page-boy or accolyte, keeping a couple of steps behind him. This sense of protocol leads Father Duval to be called by some in the village 'the boat boy', a name he gets from the altar server who accompanies the priest carrying the vessel or 'boat' of incense which is ladled onto the glowing charcoal within the thurifer. Duval is carrying a large bunch of flowers wrapped in cellophane to which beads of water cling like rain on a windscreen. The priest gives them to the Angel and the Angel with a flourish gives them to my grandmother, whose eyes fill with tears. She has trouble speaking.

'Yellow roses! Like my bridal bouquet!'

The Angel says in his big round voice to me, 'Welcome back to our village, Miss Bella. Welcome to France! How they shoot up, Madame, these children.' He turns to my grandmother,

'They're comets. I'm sure my friend the mayor agrees. Racing across our aged skies.' He bends and kisses my hand, a firm warm pressure that sends shivers scurrying up my back and into my hair.

'It's an apt metaphor, *patron*,' Father Duval agrees. 'I must say that to me the young sometimes resemble rushing streams. Like those torrents that race down the mountains behind the village after a storm. You see the little rivers running every day and they're quiet and tame and predictable, their space is sluggish and peaceful. It takes a little rain higher up the mountains and you have a flood, a rampage, where once you had a backwater, the result of some violent storm of which we adults know nothing.'

'Or perhaps have forgotten,' the Angel suggests. 'After all, there are people who once believed that children remembered something of the heaven they had recently left and it was only as they grew older that the memories faded. We laugh at these things today. Perhaps we shouldn't. What's the scientific opinion of this? I mean it's at least possible that it is we adults who really do forget the paradise of youth with its emotions comprised of honey and volcanoes. And in forgetting we begin to die. Perhaps the Mayor will tell us?'

'Such expressions passed for philosophy in the nineteenth century,' says my uncle, 'but they are utterly discredited now. The extraordinary picture, for example, that the newborn child comes down to earth stepping from some fairy heaven, clothed in clouds of immortality. What a cruel pretence! Tell it to the woman dying of childbirth. Tell it to the peasant who has ten kids already and can't feed any of them! You know sometimes I get the feeling that until the late-nineteenth century mankind was caught in a long dream, the victim of the most vulgar witchcraft. Imagine: for these past seventeen thousand years, ever since sensible beings first began exploring their environment using stone tools – and I'm referring of course to the older form of primitive man, archaic homo sapiens – right up to the time just a century ago, the long sleep continued. And then suddenly Darwin shouted: "Mankind awake!"'

'Please, *patron*, sit here. Claude, do not bellow so.' My grandmother ushers the Angel to the head of the table.

'But no, no. That place is for the Mayor. Please, Monsieur le Maire, take your rightful place!'

For a moment I think my grandmother is going to weep at this display of modesty.

'But *patron*, my son yields his place to you in his own house. It is right, surely?'

But he will have none of it and Uncle Claude is obliged to take up his position at the head of the table where he sits rather uneasily and I know he'll be happier upstairs peering through his telescope or inspecting the tank of water in the corner of his den into which are mixed a variety of substances duplicating, so my uncle believes, the early soup that covered the earth at the beginning of time and out of which life crawled. Or studying the photographic plates, artfully coloured, which he sends for from some scientific lending library, showing vivid subatomic particles arcing through the darkness of a cloud chamber, the curious scratchings on phenomenally expensive cave walls tracing the brief careers and invisible appearances of protons, lamdas, neutrinos and pi-zeros. I don't think he'd be mayor if the Angel and Grand-mère weren't so insistent; in fact I think he'd hardly ever emerge into the light at all.

Despite the pain in her joints, my grandmother insists on helping me to serve and will not sit until the men have their plates well heaped. It is very good, the poached salmon perfect, the mousseline sauce winning high praise and the Chablis perfectly cold. The Angel is quick to compliment her on her Venetian glasses.

'I got them from a little shop in the Cours de Verdun. I doubt it's still there. Like so many good things gone a long time, I fear.'

'But I remember it well!' cries Father Duval. 'Two doors away from the railway station entrance. It was popular with German soldiers during the Occupation.'

'Say what you like about Germans,' the Angel announces, 'they appreciate fine glass.'

'It's precisely because there are so many things gone that the *Parti National Populaire* is determined to restore to France something of her former greatness and integrity,' says Uncle Claude suddenly.

'Bravo!' cries Father Duval, raising his glass. 'I give you Monsieur Cherubini, our *patron*, founder of the PNP and, if I may say so, hope of the nation!'

The toasts are coming thick and fast. The Angel is on his feet, beaming around the table.

'I'd like to reply to that generous, gracious salutation from Father Duval, with an official toast, or shall I call it a promise? At any rate a message. The message at the heart of our Party is quite simply: France, Motherhood, Liberty! We must never again allow history to tell us the terrible tales that came from the Hotel Terminus. Tales which we may see, in the words of the Bible, as we gaze into these beautiful Venetian goblets, through a glass darkly.'

This is all Greek to me. I haven't a clue what he means, but they talk in speeches, those men. It's like being caught in a sudden downpour and there is nothing to do but wait until it's over, and then attack.

'What was there about the Hotel Terminus that makes people so odd when they talk about it? What else did you find there?'

They stiffen at my question, and the Angel immediately stops talking and sits. He begins to slice his cheese with fanatical precision, measuring the angles by fractional adjustments of his knife. Father Duval clears his throat and shifts in his seat.

'Bella!' My grandmother is anguished. 'You've eaten next to nothing. You've barely touched your food. You've played with your salad. Surely it can be said, in all fairness, that my poached salmon passes muster? Even if I must be entirely objective and say that I think the mousseline sauce is perhaps a shade too bland.'

'The sauce is superb, Madame,' the Angel insists, breaking bread and mopping his plate with relish.

'The trouble is that my granddaughter takes too much chocolate,' says Grand-mère. 'She is fixated. It kills the appetite.'

Father Duval wades in. 'We had a little talk today, Bella and I. Perhaps she is inclined to overdo things a bit.'

'The tears,' says my grandmother.

'The prayers,' says Uncle Claude.

'I deduced that perhaps she is suffering from a mild form of religious discomfort,' says Father Duval and begins delicately to peel a peach.

'Mania,' Uncle Claude breaks in. 'In my opinion, she's God-fixated.'

The slippery yellow globe of the skinned peach spins in Duval's fingers like a tiny planet. 'Let me be honest. I'm not a Shaman, a psychiatrist or a faith-healer. I am simply a village priest and Bella came to me for help. I never promised to cure everything or anything. But I did what I could to reassure her. I think she is probably confusing psychological stress with religious aspirations. She tells me that she feels that God is speaking to her.'

'He is,' I say, 'all the time. He never stops.'

'This sort of disturbance is not uncommon in young people,' says Father Duval smoothly. 'Perhaps it has something to do with adolescence. Then the girl has been, and you all have been, cruelly bereaved. Perhaps she seeks some sort of presence to replace the father she's lost. It's also possible that the removal to England and her rude introduction to the Protestant temper of things has had the paradoxical effect of stimulating her Catholic faith to a somewhat overheated degree.'

'But why the chocolate?' Uncle Claude demands.

'It's possible that her diet is being affected by her psychological condition. She's in need of reassurance. Above all, she needs to cheer up. Remember, Bella, God loves a cheerful heart. Morbidity has no place in our faith.'

Seeing that his bright, glassy chatter doesn't impress my uncle, Father Duval spreads his hands and gives his most Pol Pottish smile. 'After all, Claude, we're talking of chocolate, a mixture of ground cocoa beans and sugar. There are far worse substances, surely?'

'You miss my point,' my uncle says crossly. 'It's just as well to note the fact that chocolate is the food of the lovelorn. Did you know it contains a chemical also found in the brain, called phenylethylamine? A natural substance similar to amphetamines. It can trigger surges of joy, troughs of depression, emotional highs and lows. According to the literature, which I've consulted, people with a history of depressive illness and a taste for amphetamines quite often go on chocolate bashes. Like Bella. The phenylethylamine stokes them up. You could call them chocolate junkies.'

Imagine my reaction. No, on second thoughts, don't bother, because you've already done it, haven't you? Both foreseen and predicted my reaction. But I don't have that advantage. You reserve that to yourself.

'Why am I being discussed like some kind of lunatic gerbil who has offended with her lack of house training?'

I can feel the tears coming on and I don't want that so I get up and make for the Spanish mirror, because in the face of these sorts of inquisitions that presume I'm not here I only know one answer and that is to insist that I am here by showing myself, straightening an eyelash, flicking a curl, consulting the image in the mirror.

'Mirror, mirror on the wall, who is the fairest of us all?'

This question from the Angel is so unexpected and so inappropriate that everybody stops talking and eventually he has to explain.

'It's the question asked by the Wicked Queen, the nasty story of Snow White and the Seven Dwarfs.'

Uncle Claude immediately takes refuge in science. 'It's an interesting sideline on fairytales that they were once dismissed as childish nonsense. But researchers have found them to be therapeutic in the treatment of people who have been badly traumatised, shocked and abused. I suppose the most famous example is in the treatment of former concentration camp victims. It seems that there is something in all of us that makes us long to see the mighty put down from their seats, the evil punished. The child in us longs to see the wicked stepmother destroyed. The savage in us wants to see the irrational, illogical, indifferent universe made to conform to comforting patterns of rewards and punishments.'

'In my opinion,' says Father Duval, 'stories of the concentration camps have been exaggerated to serve the purposes of special interest groups.'

'What I want to know,' I say loudly, still examining myself in the mirror and making minor adjustments to body, face and costume, 'is why is it that women always get the bad press in fairytales? Why always wicked queens and cruel

110

stepmothers? Why are there no men doing the damage? Like depraved uncles, for instance? Or poisonous nephews? After all, in the real world it's generally men who abuse children, and little girls in particular. Left alone with them, when no one is looking . . .'

Then I take out of my bag my tomato-blush lipliner and apply it confidently around my lips and pout at my reflection. Catherine the Great of Finchley cut my hair very short at special request before I left England and it testifies to her ability that the style has held well in the weeks I have spent in La Frisette. I go on to repair my navy-blue mascara and to deepen the rather nice plummy shade around my eyes. Because I find my cheeks have a round peachiness to them, which I hate, I slush on tons of strawberry blusher to soften the offending peaches and to give a better line. This wanton display of face paint can always be relied upon to enrage my French family. They sit there pretending to be eating their fruit and cheese, but I think my little scene makes its point. Besides, I believe that the urge to beautify oneself often disconcerts pupils of scientific certainty. To them – what else? – it's all so pointless. That's why I think there is something rather vulgar, yes *gross*, a willingness to lead with the chin, which you will find among possessors of the one true faith, whether they believe in pixies or molecules. There's always something about them that's so horribly forward. Of course Uncle Claude knows who this is aimed at and he takes diversionary action, reaching for the facts like a man going for his guns. Flesh always disconcerts him.

Now Father Duval is on his feet, taking from his inside pocket a large yellow envelope which he waves. '*Patron*, as you know, our parishioners of the Church of the Resurrection have been collecting for a year now to begin to repair the fabric of our beloved edifice. It looks a bit threadbare, I know, a bit patched. But we also know that God is eternal, which means he can wait, but you, *patron*, are dealing with more pressing problems, they cry out for our attention! For that reason I would like to present you, on behalf of our parish, with the money we have gathered.' And he formally presents the Angel with the large yellow envelope.

My grandmother sobs quietly and she comes over to me and puts her arm round my shoulder and leads me back to the table and makes me sit and she keeps lifting her hand and opening it and gesturing towards the Angel as if there is something she wants to say or to give him but which she can't express, only symbolise by the movement of the open hand.

The Angel gets to his feet now. 'Monsieur le Curé, you may absolutely and entirely rely on us. And on the PNP. We're not taking this money from you, we're merely holding it in trust. We remember that we owe it to you and to the Church. I assure you that in accepting this gift we stand ready to repay our debt because one day when your old church is threatened with more than damp and neglect, we'll be there to save it.'

And then he sits down and carefully eats an orange with a delicacy unexpected in such a square, hearty man. And Father Duval feasts on lychees which he eats with a sucking sound and a little shake of the head as the flesh goes down.

'Did you know, *patron*, that Bella has seen our very own Ethiopian, the wandering one, who's settled in La Frisette,' Grand-mère announces. The Angel takes me in with interested eyes, my canary yellow and very baggy shorts, my sloppy Joe shirt, my green sneakers.

'I don't think he's an Ethiopian, Madame.'

'Well he's from Africa, we know that,' says my Uncle Claude. 'Our chocolate chum who's moved into the Priory Hotel. You've met him, Bella, you tell the *patron* about him.'

The Angel is suddenly very attentive and his voice gentle. 'Yes, tell me, my dear.'

'My uncle is right, he is exactly the colour of chocolate. And the texture. He's dark and glistening. I wonder what he tastes like?'

'Bella!' My uncle is scandalised. 'Don't be absurd!'

'Come, come, the child likes confection. You know how she feels about chocolate. It's only natural,' my grandmother remonstrates gently. 'Black and bitter, I imagine, that's what he tastes like, my Bella. There's not much sugar in that one.'

'Have you seen him then, Grand-mère?'

She taps her forehead with her finger. 'Only in here.'

'He's so ugly. You cannot imagine how superbly ugly he is. Do you think he'd soften if he stayed in the sun too long?'

'Well, what would you say?'

'Certainly, I say that he would. Besides, one shouldn't expose chocolate to a naked flame. I want to tell him that each time I see him lying there on the private beach. I notice it when he's been in the sun for a little time, he begins sweating and shining and it makes him look as if he really is – you know . . .'

'Melting?'

'Yes. And I sometimes wonder if I shouldn't tell him that he's in danger of liquefying and running between the cracks of the jetty and disappearing.'

The others listen in silence to our conversation. Such is the silence I can hear Uncle Claude moving in his clothes. The dining room commands a fine view of the lake and the warm watery breeze stirs the lace curtains carrying on it very faintly the distant growl of motorbikes. As the sun sets, the surface of the water has a dark, glassy appearance and shadows begin spreading swiftly, mingling like ink with the water. Opposite us on the further shore of the lake stand the two conical mountains, one slightly behind the other, which we know in these parts as the breasts of St Joan. I never could see why. They look more like volcanoes. The clarity of the day is always to be judged by the view across the lake and when the breasts of St Joan stand up above the water in perfectly sharp detail, you know the day has been good, and you know that you are looking at least thirty kilometres across the water.

My grandmother goes on considering the black man melting between the cracks on the jetty. Eventually she nods and sighs, 'It serves him right.'

The Angel's broad face takes on a look of simple dignity that is really quite beautiful. It's the sort of look which leads to descriptions of him which are flamboyant to say the least. *La Liberté*, his own paper, speaks of him in intoxicated terms which actually are not all that inaccurate because they catch something of the curious attractiveness of the man. *La Liberté* speaks of the look of a 'sportsman and a soldier', it raves about his bluff and attractive directness, his natural manner and it says that he is perhaps *somewhere between a saviour and a hunter, easy and generous yet formidable in the smoke of battle. Someone who destroys without compunction the foolish and the idiotic. A lithe hunter who despatches his prey with precision,*

113

*yet who turns to a woman or a child with touching sincerity and manly gentility . . .'*

'Madame, I know I speak for many when I assure you that I am a simple patriot. I make no secret of the fact that I prefer my own family to my neighbour's. I prefer my neighbours to the English tourists. However I prefer the English tourists to those members of an alien culture who are unable, or unwilling, to respect the duties of citizens even while claiming the rights of native-born Frenchmen. One does not have to be racialist or a xenophobe to believe that the French are entitled to claim France as their own.'

'I met old Laval in the village earlier today and he told me that the man at the Priory has taken thirty rooms!' says Father Duval.

'He told Bella his name is Brown,' my uncle chips in. 'I find that unlikely – although appropriate.'

'I didn't say that he told me his name was Brown. I said that I called him Brown. I think that's his name. At any rate it's my name for him.'

'My niece has a habit of subverting reality in this way. She believes words carry the capacity to change things. She lives in a world of imagination where stones speak and rivers dance, but no one knows how to add up or subtract. Bella has an aversion to facts, figures, details, accuracy. She has an allergy to the truth. She believes she has only to name a thing and it becomes whatever she likes. She assumes the powers of the defunct Creator. She believes in magics, spells, witcheries whereby people shape and govern the world and by which other people are enchanted. You can see it in everything she does, the rather vulgar and perverse attachment to emotion, the prayers, the tears, the devotion to the animal spirits of popular music, the hatred of what must be verified or what can be analysed. It is as if looks alone are enough for her. Sensation. She behaves as if one can give to things whatever shape one finds pleasing. How things look to you. Worse still, how you look to the world is everything. She wants to sweep away the power of reason and have everybody run mad!'

My uncle takes an apple and squeezes it till the bruises show and then he stabs it with his knife.

'She's got the sort of looks that may very well do that,' says the Angel calmly and he looks very hard at my breasts. 'You're a very pretty girl, my dear Bella,' he says with a directness that no one dares to contradict since he is the *patron* and directness is his strong point.

'Well said, *patron*! I warned her about Leda. Or at least I asked Claude to do so,' says my grandmother. 'You see, *patron*, she was out in the boat on the lake with this Brown man. I felt she should be reminded of what happened between Leda and Zeus.'

'I'm the only one who knows what happened, it seems,' I say. 'Uncle Claude doesn't.'

'Zeus got Leda pregnant, I seem to remember. She laid an egg,' says the Angel.

'And from that egg were hatched Helen, Castor and Poly-deuces,' Father Duval counts them off on his fingers. 'And afterwards Leda was given a place among the stars. She became the goddess Nemesis. I really can't help feeling that the delightful embroideries of the Greek gods are so much more inventive than our Christian monotheism.'

'I gave him the name Brown. The name is mine.'

'There you are,' says my uncle excitedly. 'There is exactly the process of naming to which she always gives way. It's no good discussing the world with Bella. For Bella's world is one continuous selfish invention.'

'But my name does very well. You see, the important thing about my name is that the man in question answers to it. What do you say about that!'

The Angel looks at me with those bright blue eyes and I get the feeling that he thinks that I am some kind of smart but weird child, a sly kid, full of tricks and surprises, one with odd tastes in clothes and appalling leanings in music. I've got my earphones round my neck, they are my necklace and I want to lift them up now and put them on. But I promised Grand-mère. It's hard though with the sonic interference reaching the pitch it does with me in a world where everybody is beaming signals the whole time, wanting me to do this and that, and I wish I had my phones on right now and was gassing it with someone like Garotte, the new Hispanic trio from Cologne, synthesizers and plainchant, really just the usual 'blood on the ceiling, blood on the floor' boys, who actually sincerely want to be very, very rich. But OK listening for about ten minutes. Then just as you get to the point of melting them back into the industrial waste from whence they came, you hear something in their voices which tells you that they've just shown the bishop what the choirboy has got under his frock, and suddenly you don't feel so bad about being exploited by three kids who learnt their American English by numbers and you don't feel sorry for the bishop, just glad there are people too bent ever to straighten out, who are beyond Uncle Claude and the Angel, who is now eating a peach. Would you look at him eating this peach which is so terrified by the experience it doesn't dare drip off his chin but slips between his lips like it has been expensively trained. Look!

But then you are looking. You're looking at the Angel who's looking at me and you know what's coming next.

'I'm not talking about the name of our visitor,' says the Angel softly. 'I'm talking about somebody else, a friend of Bella's Monsieur Brown, back in his country of Zanj. I've heard that the country is rich in diamonds, in nothing else, but its jewels are highly prized. I understand that this little state is amongst the poorest in Africa. France gives considerable amounts in aid. It's a custom in that country to make presents of diamonds to those who are regarded as friends. It's whispered that certain Zanjian leaders tried to further relations with certain French officials . . .'

'It's plain now,' Uncle Claude cuts in. 'Bribery! Are you listening to this, Bella? Well now – I forbid you to have any more to do with this man until we get to the bottom of this.'

'Let's agree to call them gifts,' says the Angel. 'For the moment, at least.'

'Very well, let's call them gifts,' says Father Duval. 'So this man, this official, during his tenure in this benighted country, or land, Zand or Gang, or whatever you call it, bribed some French official with diamonds?'

'One official in particular. A government employee who travelled extensively in the country and knew its ruling figures and, it seems, enjoyed excellent relations with the dictator of Zanj himself.'

I reach up and touch my diamond pendant. It has a curious cold and warm feeling all at once. The way I felt in the paddle boat. Then I see the Angel is watching. It's all horribly obvious now, hideously clear. The visit my mother and I had paid to Paris, the uneasiness of the official with the face like a shoehorn who could tell us nothing and would give us no explanation. The loss of our house, the reclamation of my mother's jewels.

'I think we can guess the name,' says Uncle Claude. 'Perhaps now is not the time – '

But he is too late. My grandmother begins to moan. 'My poor, poor boy. Dead among savages and thieves!'

Then she gets up and comes round to the Angel, goes down on her knees and lays her head on his lap. '*Patron*, what must I do?'

No one answers.

It's much later that I leave my grandmother, when I'm sure she is sleeping. I can hear the men up in my uncle's den. I find them clustered around the telescope. They've been drinking brandy.

'Come and look here,' my uncle commands. 'See, Bella, we've found a meteor shower.'

Through the telescope I can see the skittering, glancing fuzz of lights which seem to be falling directly out of the black heavens and into the lake looking for all the world like a fireworks display, they could be shooting rockets through the roof of the Priory Hotel.

'The medievals held comets to be the smoke of sin,' Father Duval giggles.

'The ancients had a bewildering variety of explanations for meteorites,' my Uncle Claude explains. 'The Greeks thought that they looked like flowing hair, and they reminded the Arabs of flaming swords. They were blamed for everything from wars to weather. When they appeared people panicked. When the great comet of 1466, which was really Halley's Comet, returned, all Europe was terrified. But I think I like most of all the English philosopher Hume's belief in them as a kind of cosmic sperm, a stellar fertilisation programme. In fact, in a way, he might have been correct. As you know there are many theories about the origins of life on earth. I am a meteorite man.'

'It makes such a pretty show above the Priory Hotel,' I tell them.

'I think we'll call on the owner tonight,' the Angel remarks. 'As a leading member of the community I think André owes it to us to tell us anything he knows about his new guest.'

'We should take something with us,' Father Duval suggests. 'It would look natural if we expressed our interest by showing hospitality.'

'A very good idea,' says Uncle Claude, the meteorite man. 'As Mayor of La Frisette I will present him with free tickets for a ferry ride on the Lake.'

'And I will give him a bottle of *pineau*,' says the Angel. 'And a little piece of glass from Lyons. Bought in the same shop which your Mama remembers with such affection.'

'And I will offer my blessing,' Father Duval smiles. 'From the sounds of things he might need it.'

A little later I hear them setting off in search of André's guest. They don't walk the five minutes down the little hill to the lakeside, they travel instead in the Angel's big Mercedes.

# 7

André is standing behind the reception desk with Tertius, who is dressed in lemon − a colour that does not suit him. André's pink shirt is creased, his eyes bloodshot. The deputation of the night before has terrified him. Before long I know that this is what they wanted. When he had told his visitors that his guest was seeing no one they attempted to pass on to him their gifts: the bottle of *pineau* from the Angel, my uncle's complimentary ferry tickets, and Father Duval's blessing. But it's the little piece of glass that seems to have upset André most.

'With its long thin neck, intended for a single flower, no doubt. But would have done as well for an arrow to pierce my heart. It comes from a little shop in the Cours de Verdun. Simply a little vase, of Venetian crystal. Bought with a purpose. Monsieur Cherubini was careful to point out where it came from.'

'I know. They told me. The shop near the railway station entrance.'

'Two doors away. When my guest refused to see them − they forced these gifts on me. What could I do? Order the man to meet them?'

'But why should it upset you so?'

'The little shop was near my father's offices, of which I have told you, Bella. Though I have not told you all, by any means. It was a warning. They're moving in.'

'Like a dead cat through the window,' says Tertius unhelpfully.

I want to say, 'You haven't told me anything,' but I'm put off by the boy Tertius, who stands grinning. It's a horrid smile, curved downwards, flat and thin, a potato peeling of a smile. So all I ask is: 'Near your father's offices? When he was a stockbroker, in Lyons?'

The smile on the face of Tertius changes into the sort of snagged toothed smile they carve in pumpkins at Halloween. 'Stockbroker! That's rich!'

It's clear to me that Tertius is pretending to be the reception clerk today. André, with a sad distracted look, fondles Tertius' shoulder and then his neck, as if tenderness will silence him.

'I have never said that we traded in shares in the city but only that we had offices in Lyons.'

He's stroking Tertius' cheek now. I don't know if he hopes that this will shut him up or calm him down or make him fall asleep. He seems quite unaware of the fact that the sight of the hotel manager fondling the desk clerk is new to me.

'I've come to see Monsieur Brown.'

'You may not see him without permission,' Tertius announces pompously.

'Whose permission?'

He thinks this over. 'His permission.'

'Tertius has told me that he intends to become a hotel manager,' says André with paternal delight. 'I'm planning more of this on-site training for him. It's an ambition on his part that makes me very happy.'

'They wandered up to the door last night. The lords of La Frisette – your uncle, the mayor, the *patron* and the boat-boy – and demanded to meet the black chap,' says Tertius, 'like they owned the place. So poor André trots upstairs and tells him, and d'you know what? – he told André to throw them out! There's a head-on clash coming, Bella – don't you think?'

'He won't see anyone without an appointment. Best run along home, Bella.' André shrugs. 'I'm sorry.'

'I'm invited to tea. I'm expected.'

'Is that why you're dressed in those funny clothes? You look like a squaw.' Tertius ogles me while André goes upstairs to check. I can tell by his slow tread that he does not believe me. Tertius lounges.

He's such a little prick, is Tertius.

'That's because I am a squaw.'

I am wearing a black-and-white print blouse, a black string tie, with a medallion showing the head of Chief Sitting Bull, in onyx on a silver ground. The medallion is pinned at my throat, threaded through the print blouse on a long and beautiful pin. I also wear a black bandana. The Indian look. Give me an occasion and I dress for it and I have an idea that this will be an occasion, so I have done my hair carefully and it is wild! It took me hours last night, first with curlers and then, afterwards, the somewhat unruly coils wrapped tight around a finger and clipped to the scalp while I slept, and then in the morning because it was, well, more *mad* than wild, I compromised with a wide-toothed afro-comb to soften it slightly. Very slightly.

André comes scampering downstairs, the cracks of concern widening on his eggy face.

'Well, it seems you are expected, Bella. You can go up.'

'Be careful,' Tertius warns. 'We call him the cannibal in the attic.'

'The attitude of the boy towards our guest is one of camaraderie,' says André apologetically.

'Go suck yourself,' I tell Tertius and sweep upstairs.

'Room twenty-two,' André calls after me.

The long gallery where the monks once lived as close neighbours in their little cells is built in two tiers, lines of little rooms like kennels or chicken coops, but it's a lovely, dark and wooden space. Number twenty-two looks like all the other rooms, twenty-four in all, each with a dark oak door, a wooden hook where perhaps the monk hung a cloak or cowl which he doffed before entering his cell. The whole place creaks like a ship.

He answers my knock immediately, as if he has been waiting. 'How delightful to see you, my dear Bella. Shall we stretch our legs, as the English say, before taking tea?'

A monk's cell is spartan, even if you add a few touches of comfort, and André has added hardly any. The little room contains no more than a bed, covered in a stern white counterpane, a little green chaise longue, a fireplace, table and washbasin. The curtains are new, pink and floral, but that's the only gentleness.

At first I think he's suggesting we take a stroll along the lakeside or potter about the garden but instead he intends us to walk around the gallery. We walk in silence, passing ancient oils of popes and cardinals which stare down from dark wooden

121

walls with sad yellow faces. They have the painted concrete immobility of garden gnomes. We promenade creakily, our footsteps echoing in the chamber. Monsieur Brown wears a blue-grey woollen suit the colour of cigarette smoke and his black shoes are pointed and highly polished. He is a vision of shining elegance, his shirt cuffs protrude an inch or two and have the crispness of communion wafers. In the gloom his heavy, round face with its black glasses and full lips is aloof and relaxed. I can't help noticing how his neck rises from his perfect collar, like a column of pure – well, what can I say? – chocolate! No, cocoa-butter! In the shadows he is solid, silent and shorter than I remember him, pure Bourneville, utter Nestlé, simply Suchard from nose to toe, the lines of his jowls and chin etched as if newly cast from a mould, as if I am seeing the face just before it is wrapped in silver paper to be sent off to delight children, a walking, talking chocolate troll . . . a most lickable fellow . . .

'I don't want to go downstairs. Forgive me, it's not my policy to mix with the other guests. The natives here are curious but they will have to contain their curiosity. I'd have been happier if the hotel had been cleared entirely before my arrival. Sadly the owner wouldn't agree. I suppose we have to get used to a world where tradesmen put profit before affairs of state, and the security of the state. Besides, what we have to say is between us, alone.'

'Why are you here, Monsieur Brown?'

He laughs, a dark and milky sound. 'Monsieur Brown! Is that what they call me?'

'You don't like it? I thought that's what you said – Brown, or was it Boon, or Bane – or even Brain?'

'It doesn't matter. If that's your name for me, then that's the name I answer to – Brown!'

'Why are you here?'

'Ah, that comes later.'

'Tell me about my father.'

He put his hand on my arm. 'My poor child – you hope he might be alive still, don't you?'

'Yes, I hope that.'

'You mustn't. You must face the fact that your father is dead. I am here to bring you messages from beyond the grave. I am – how does the saying go? – being brutal only to be kind.'

'I think you mean cruel to be kind.'

'No. Brutal. Your father was killed by the banditry. Dissident elements who put their military ambitions above the good of my country, overthrew its elected and traditional representatives, let loose such a reign of terror that mothers' milk dried in their breasts and babies died before they could call down vengeance on their murderers!'

'Who are the bandits?'

'To answer that I must tell you something more of the history of my country, up until the time of the insurrection which brought ruin on us all. The country of Zanj is poor but, as they say in the old song, it is honest. I've explained a little about our three main tribal groupings: firstly, the Wouff, which is my tribe, they're animists, they worship the sacred stones of their fathers. The Christian Ite are a sad disappointment to me, a milky, soppy, preachy congregation of hypocrites, but my countrymen right or wrong, as the old saying goes, and a group I have struggled mightily to save from their own weakness and stupidity. And finally there are the Kanga, Moslems who go in for a good deal of bowing and scraping to Mecca, then put a knife in your back when the praying is over. But enough. I am not here to condemn, I am here to explain. The Wouff are the smallest of the tribes, but being clean and brave, they have generally provided the soldiers of Zanj, and its rulers, from the time of the ancestors. Inhabiting the central highlands, the Wouff are a proud, fierce people, the Spartans of Africa they are called. Perhaps you have heard the expression? No? Well, I can tell you, that if you go anywhere in our part of Africa and ask after the Wouff, you will be told they're Spartans, real Spartans. And this is the tribe to which I have the privilege of belonging. This little band with its great responsibilities, which they have never complained about, which they have borne however great the weight, like a stack of firewood. It is the Wouff who have intervened to save the Ite from attacks by the Kanga during religious riots. The Ite are southerners, supplicant yet greedy, merchants, shopkeepers and traders. They control the markets in which the Kanga must sell their produce and because the Kanga are subsistence farmers and herdsmen in the inhospitable north of our country, the Ite exploit them. And so the Kanga turn on the Ite for strangling prices and throwing farmers a pittance, they fall on the Ite with spears and rifles, and when this happens it is the Wouff who must step between them – brave, uncomplaining, alert! You can picture it, I feel sure.'

I'd like to say that I can picture it, that I can see in my mind's eye the strange country of Zanj with its warring tribes, its brave Wouff, soft Ite and sullen Kanga, its sacred stones and its strangled prices. But I don't, I see nothing of it. I don't even see my father, dead in some unmarked grave, somewhere in Africa. I simply see the black bulky figure of Monsieur Brown frowning at me in the gloom and holding up five fingers in front of his face, all of them exactly the same width, dark, tubular fingers, inches from my face, fingers from which the rings always slip, fingers which the gloves cover and which his subjects press to their lips.

'You will be amazed to hear, no doubt, that you see before you the ruler for life of Zanj. Let me explain my elevation to that position. My enemies will tell you that I claim to be king or emperor. Lies! Five times I refused the offer, five times I turned aside the proffered crown, five times I put by the laurel wreath until at last my people forced me to face my responsibilities and accept their command, not to become king or emperor, but something far more modest, more in keeping with the tribal traditions of Zanj – I became, by popular acclamation, the Redeemer! I can tell you it was a golden afternoon, it was a love feast, it was a happy time of the sort you people in Europe are said to have enjoyed before the Great War. It was at this time that your father became my friend. More than a friend, he was aide, confidant, counsellor, the only man who was permitted to approach the Leopard Throne with his eyes open, all others having to enter on their knees with their eyes closed, guided solely by the sound of my breathing, which you will notice is not excessively loud.'

And it's true. It isn't excessively loud. It's more of a soft, sighing sound like the wind across sand, soothing and rather lonely. Now that he's stopped walking and stands so stock still, and behind him the windows are filled with the brightest blue, he looks as if he were part of a giant picture someone has hung there at the end of the hall. And so I stand listening to his breathing and he stands holding up his five fingers and somehow I know that we're going to be friends, me and this fat, black ugly man who stands so still he might have set solid.

'I like your black headband. You're a young widow, perhaps?'

'It's supposed to be the Indian squaw look.'

'You enjoy dressing?'

'Not especially. But you know what bodies are. Your own and others.'

'Never there when you want them?'

'Yes. Grandmama says Marshal Pétain made France the gift of his person – he was personally present in the gift, like God in the communion wafer.'

He snaps his fingers. 'That's not so unusual. I've made my people the gift of my person many times. In return, many people have made me the gift of their . . . persons.'

'Well, I don't feel sure enough to start giving away my – person . . . My body sometimes feels like it's working loose, floating off. So I keep checking in the mirror. I'm always hoping to find somebody worth dressing.'

'Who?'

'Me.'

He looks at me closely. Now Monsieur Brown has his looks, the panoramic, the aerial, the microscopic, the spy satellite capable of zooming in and focussing on the smallest detail. It's my pendant, the blue diamond my father gave to me. And he gives it the look of a lawyer and a lover, it's a tender, almost dewy-eyed stare. Instinctively, I reach up and put my fingers around it. It's all I have from Papa, the rest they took away, the shoehorn men in the government, our home, Mama's jewels, everything, including my Bapuna mask.

'I am a fancier,' says Monsieur Brown, 'not unnaturally, being a member of the Wouff tribe. I read stories in stones, the sacred stones of my people, something which we never buy or sell, but may give only to our friends.'

I keep my hand round the stone. A girl with only one jewel is not easily placed. Leave it in some secret place and you risk robbery, keep it on you and risk its confiscation. Diamonds are not always a girl's best friend.

'You are very modest,' he says again, 'your father told me so himself. At the end, when we were exchanging promises.'

Under the sweet, soft flow of Monsieur Brown's voice, luscious and muddy, there is a sudden serration, as if beneath the smoothness lies a bed of gravel.

'Tell me how he died!'

He begins walking again. He's really rather short, only an inch or two taller than I am. His polished shoes shine like little black ponds as we promenade beneath the thickly varnished eyes of the dead cardinals, eyes in which the fire has dimmed into single points, like eyes pressed to keyholes or the eyes of fish on slabs, cold and starkly amused. The old oak floor groans like a ship's deck.

'As the tanks closed in on my palace with rockets landing in my wives' apartments, mortars bursting among the tapestries, your father and I embraced. I was determined to go down with the presidential palace, in the manner of a ship's captain with his vessel. As was no doubt the case with the late-lamented *Mary Rose*, or the *Titanic* – but your father, preserve his memory, wouldn't have it. "You're too humble, Majesty," he said, "you've given me countless gifts. Now let me give you the gift of my advice – your country will not sink if you survive. Save yourself!" And that's what I did, escaping by the help of loyal friends, sailing by night in a dug-out canoe smelling of barbel, down the River Zan, which flows through our capital city of Waq. Your father fled into the interior, straight into the hands of the rebels. A ragtail bob and bag of traitors, renegades from the Ite and the Kanga. So much for turning the other cheek! So much for Mohammed! Led by a hot little parcel of noncoms, privates and sergeants. Wouff it seems they were, if that isn't to insult the name of my people! May the stones of my fathers fall on them and grind their bones to paste! May their wives bring forth pebbles! May the walls of their houses revolt and fall on them as they sleep! In the hands of such creatures your dear father could expect no mercy. That was the last ever seen of him. I smelt of fish, for days.'

I begin crying.

'That was the last ever seen of either of us.'

I think he means to console me but I can hear the tone and the tone makes me realise that any consolation is inner directed. Well, that does it, the stopcocks are blown on all the pipes. I become a walking sprinkler system.

'But my papa is dead!'

'And I was once Redeemer of Zanj!'

I cry all the more, an absolute flood. He stops walking and takes my hand in his. Warm, soft hands like mittens they are, with their beautiful regularity, his cigar fingers settle on my wrists and an amazing thing happens, my crying stops. It dries and vanishes, I can feel the tears drying on my cheeks. He has cured my sobbing sickness and, though I know this sounds silly, I go weak at the knees, I have to command them to stiffen, to keep me up, not to buckle, not to let me fall, collapse at his feet, knocked over, out, by a feeling of ridiculous gratitude. It's really only my mind that keeps me upright, my mind that keeps telling me, yes, you were once the Redeemer of Zanj, and for all I know may be again. But Papa will not be anything again.

Tea is a reward, taken among talk of coups, in his bedroom, his monkish cell. Served by André, but brought upstairs by Tertius who, though he has carried the tray, doesn't come in though I can hear him outside the door. I am *meant* to hear him outside the door, giggling just loudly enough while André arranges the tray with its bone china and its little plates of patisseries, little rainbows of delicacies, pastries with the lightness of moths' wings, little cakes decorated and filled with mocha buttercream, and rose-shaped *petits fours*. 'My *dujas*,' André calls them proudly. Each is crowned with a button of candied violet. They look like little sea plants, sugar seaweeds or sweet algae, edible corals and in the clear soft light that fills his bedroom, lying so beautifully neatly on the plates they could also be microscope specimens, to be studied not eaten. But they will be eaten, as I suppose all things that eventually come to be studied are at first eaten. Scholarship begins in the gut. Soon. But first I have to excuse myself while André is fussing with milk and sugar in cups, and go outside where I find the slug Tertius wheezing with laughter beneath the portrait of a yellow-faced pope and I say politely: 'Stop,' and I add firmly, 'Immediately.'

127

'And if I won't?' Tertius tosses his rather lank hair in a gesture which he no doubt believes to be flirtatious.

'Then I will drive this shiny pin from my black bandana deeply within your parts. I will split a testicle like an olive, possibly two.'

Tertius says nothing. I am rewarded with the instinctive, protective gesture, crossed hands like butterfly wings across the top of the thighs, the footballer's gesture when faced by the penalty. Why, I wonder, does affection inspire insolence? Watching André leading away the sullen Tertius I cannot understand why someone reputed to have been such a terror in Lyons inspires so little fear in his young friends.

The Redeemer's room really is very plain without even a view of the lake and I see he has his pictures up and his books, lives of generals, politicians, dictators: Hannibal, Cromwell, Napoleon, Lenin, Mazzini, Gandhi, Mussolini and Hitler.

'I devote much energy to the study of revolutionaries and their methods,' he says and eats a *duja* with its button of candied violet.

More like dictators, it looks to me. All the pictures are of women, photographs framed in gold. The poses are pretty weird.

'Sit down, please. Take that little sofa in front of the fireplace. I will sit on the bed.'

His bed is raised on bricks, two red bricks beneath each leg.

'I observe the custom of my country. We believe that by sleeping high we escape the horrid little spirit who haunts bedrooms and steals the souls of men while they sleep. A trick our mothers teach us.'

'My uncle lines the floor of his room with aluminium foil. That's my Uncle Claude. He's an astronomer. And an atheist. He believes that the earth's magnetic currents affect him, and so does radiation. It's something called geopathic stress. In fact the best way to guard against it is moving about a lot, that way you don't get cooked in the same place night after night. Like you move the food in a microwave oven. Strictly speaking he should shove the furniture in his room about every week or so, but that gets to be a bit of a drag, so he puts down the aluminium foil instead and bounces the rays back into space. That's the theory.'

'You live with your uncle?'

'If you can call it living. And with my grandmother. I'm really their prisoner. I used to live with my mother, in England. But then she went off to America, and got lost. So I came here. Everything's gone wrong since Papa died.'

'Has your uncle always had these ideas? About moving the furniture?'

'He's full of ideas.'

'Europe is riddled with superstition. Full of blood and darkness. Sometimes a person dares not venture outside.'

'My Uncle Claude's a kind of scientist. He believes we're all descended from viruses.'

'Germs?'

'Yes. He says human beings are probably just here to keep the germs immortal. They live on in us. We're just by the way. When the earth was young and hot, about a billion years ago, these germs got into the early cells that swam around in the primal soup, drilled into them like crazy with their little tails that go round and round, and took up residence – those they didn't kill, they consorted with. I'd really like to drill into Uncle Claude sometime. But my aim wouldn't be to consort, let me tell you.'

'I don't think you like your father's brother.'

'I don't like being accosted by someone with his views. About how he's going to finish off God. And how man is really just the germ's Eiffel Tower. Uncle Claude has two views of us: cosmic and planetary. Cosmically speaking, we don't rate at all – a minor planet of an indifferent sun in a tenth-rate galaxy. In planetary terms we're really just a means for getting the microbes about. And we serve as manure.'

He's shocked. 'Dung?'

'Yes. Mammals are just here to fertilise the planet. To keep the plants growing.'

'In Zanj we have punishments for these mockers and madmen.'

'You do? What punishments?'

'If I were in Zanj I would feed him to the crocodiles.'

'You would!'

I don't believe him for a moment but I have to say I'm warming to the idea of Zanj. 'Tell me about these creatures who steal souls.'

'Tiny little men – but their genitals are large.'

I love the idea of this horrid, horny little black troll. Now that's what I call something to worry about! In fact I think everyone should start building their beds on bricks, it really makes sense if all these funny little guys are running around all night.

He waves a broad black hand around the room to include his gold-framed portraits of women. 'My wives. Dear girls. To be seen in the National Gallery in Zanj. I started it. We are poor and can't afford originals. So I brought science to the rescue. My dear consorts, whom you see here displayed before you, are photographed after the styles of certain famous paintings. Some modern. Some after the Renaissance masters. I often thought it wasn't so much a collection of wives as an orchestra. Here is my wife Viola, posing in the manner of the Degas painting of a woman drying herself after her bath. Isn't she nice? And here is Tympany, portrayed as a Roman Venus. What they call a *Venus Pudica,* hence the hand rather carefully draped. Now this is my third wife, Harp, in her recreation as Venus with Cupid, after a painting by Correggio. The man you see standing beside her is Mercury.'

'It looks like you!'

'It is me. I am Mercury.'

And indeed he is. Wearing a strange cap, and not much else.

He sits on the white counterpane, on the high bed, with the tray beside him and I look at his pictures. His orchestra of wives. We might be in an art gallery. Two people, tired of looking, resting between pictures.

'I hope you will give me the pleasure of painting you, one day.'

'What painting will I become?'

'I have just the one! It's called *Les Beaux Jours,* by the modern master Balthus. You will be perfect in the part.'

He looks at his pictures fondly. 'I adore art. So did my wives.'

I understand. There had been other casualties when the mortars began exploding among the tapestries.

'Sitting among my wives I feel like a child. In the mountains.'

I see this. They do rather loom. Viola turns her broad back on the camera, Harp shows her enormous breasts with pride and he sits beside her on the rock wearing a funny kind of feathery baseball cap.

'Harp wears the wings of the goddess Venus. And my cap signifies my godhead.'

'Who is the child standing between them?'

'Cupid, played by one of my sons.'

'What's his name?'

'I forget. I have many children.'

'How many?'

'Over sixty-five, I think.'

'Where are they now?'

'With their mothers, I expect. When the rebels moved in on the presidential palace, my surviving wives went back to their villages. To melt among their people. To wait.'

'Wait for what?'

'For my return. And here is my fourth wife, Dulcimer. She is a copy of St Ursula, a very fine carving by the Master of Elsloo from the sixteenth century.'

St Ursula, alias his fourth wife Dulcimer, wears an elaborate head-dress. Her breasts are small and high and she carries a book, looks down modestly and wears a diamond pendant around her neck. Her pendant is the image of my own. Her eyes are downcast modestly.

'Ours is not a rich country. To decorate the presidential palace I was determined to hang the very best art. We have one of the lowest standards of living in Africa, a position which our first leader, my Uncle Richard, did very little to alleviate. He was more concerned with playing off the French and the British against one another to see which side would give him more aid, which he spent as quickly as they gave it to him. He negotiated independence for our country from the French in the sixties. He gave us a parliament based on the British system and a constitution based on the French model. He ignored the fact that the Wouff, the Ite and the Kanga desire nothing more than to skin each other alive. Though not himself a member of the Ite tribe, he appointed most of his ministers from that group. A fatal mistake. It took into account none of the traditions of our country. When I was

*131*

approached by a small band of patriotic colonels from the national army I told them, after due thought, that I could drive a Lagonda through the constitution, and I did. When I came to power, all appointments of any importance were made from the Wouff tribe. This is the way it had always been done and I am a great respecter of tradition.'

'Isn't that cheating?'

'Not at all. Take my wives. First wife Viola was a Wouff. My second, Tympany, was an Ite, so I converted to Christianity. Harp, my third, belonged to the Kanga tribe – though you'd never think so to look at her – so I became a Moslem.'

'And Dulcimer?'

'A Wouff. Back to stage one. You see how even-handed I was? One of the first things you learn as a redeemer is that you must be everything to everyone. It's not easy.'

The tea turns out to be chocolate. I can feel the gratitude rising in me, warm and strong.

'I remembered what you said. That you liked it. I am a great respecter of addictions.'

So we drink chocolate and talk. Talk of one coup leads to another, I find. You drive a Lagonda through somebody's constitution and somebody else drives a tank through yours. That's how it seems to go. And here he is washed up in France. But why the funny little room? Not even a view of the lake. What there is though is a fine view of the front gates of the hotel and beyond them the carpark where the watchers sit in the Citroën, the Renault and the little Deux-Chevaux.

'I see you are keeping a little eye on my friends, who are keeping an eye on me,' he says.

'Do they want to hurt you?'

He smiles. 'On the contrary. They are here to look after me. It's very touching, this concern. But I have tried to tell them it's no good, I'm beyond help. You see the Wouff believe their leader or ruler to be the son of God. They further believe that when he abuses his authority he should be killed, because he shows that he is no longer the son of the great God.' Suddenly he looks like a child, a fat, black, ugly child, his shoulders sink and he blows out his cheeks and his big lips turn downwards. He is for an instant the perfect baby.

# 8

I spend the morning as usual on the private beach by the lakeside but no longer at ease despite the fact that the wooden platform creaks beneath the same weight of oiled, gleaming, familiar flesh as it did yesterday and the day before. My cast of characters on the *plage privée* are settled, named, content. They've not been consulted, I know. But then this is not a democracy. You can tell they like it by their relaxed, easy, affable behaviour; Edith and Alphonse sleep with the sun gleaming in their purple rinses; Wolf is reading the life of Bismarck – his little daughters look happier; the breasts of the Dutch sisters, Ria and Beatrice, are no longer quite so distant. Raoul looks a bit shifty – he knows I have my eye on him . . . We are at that point in the season where time seems to have stopped and no one is ever going to leave. Early in August the days get this way, the hawks fly higher, the sky is pale and powdery above the breasts of St Joan and it seems as if everything will continue, but I know that the perfect weather cannot last. Summers past are proof of that. The less time left, the faster it runs. These perfect moments mean the end of things. The sun pierces the wooden slats and lets down its dusty, silver nets into the green water but catches nothing. The fish flash past quick as thinking and there is no calling them back.

The fish are hungry and I am famished. Hunger is the mother of knowledge. Thinking is hunting.

My poor, dear Clovis now comes equipped with the new boot that the Angel presented to him.

'Crystal, Bella!'

'No, Clovis – plastic.'

Through the transparent boot Clovis' withered little foot in its grey sock shows like a mummy. According to the Angel, beauty through disability is achieved by showing, framing, *exhibiting* the deficiency.

*

Because I'm eating tonight I starve myself, lock the big silver trunk beneath my bed, that bed now raised most impressively on two bricks beneath each leg to guard against the little black troll who haunts bedrooms ... as Monsieur Brown teaches ... It's been diet day. I have to be strong. It's worst, the craving, just before a period, I notice, and bad during it (very tender breasts), a burning in the back of the throat tells me to stop, but I can get over that. I take them out of their wrappers first and build branches with them, whole trees, and then eat the trees, twig by twig and the wrappers fall around me like leaves, each one about three hundred calories, and a batch of weird stuff, as Uncle Claude never tires of telling me, caffeine and theobromine for pep, phenylethylmine for love, faint feelings of nausea, but I can live with that, though I can't *bear* to look at the scattered wrappers afterwards, twelve, fifteen, because I know I can't have eaten all those, not one girl on her own, not me! Perhaps two or three, and one for the road, and a nightcap, just a nibble, perhaps ...

Yes, Clovis, who has no money and for whom the chances of there being a tomorrow are slight, takes me to dinner at the most expensive restaurant in La Frisette, *Les Dents Sacrés*, because he wants to talk to me about the future! He arrives in his new uniform, on his new bike, wearing his new boot and we eat *fruits de mer*, the little cousins of these same silvery flitters which pass for thoughts in the watery mind of the lake.

I am on view in the new bottle-green, off-the-shoulder velvet dress, a red rose in my hair and, of course, my earphones, briefly occupied by the emissions of four lovely boys in six-inch stiletto heels communally called Ape! They operate at a level that would give a deaf man tinnitus — raunchy guitars and circular riffs being their stock in trade, and singing, sometimes in unison, 'What do I do to please ya?/You and Mother Theresa!' Actually I only wear the earphones to annoy the *maître* and take them off the moment we sit down and Clovis begins telling me about his future, and love.

Love for Clovis is summed up in a single word, 'her'. It is with her that he has been riding around the village, the Dutch peach, on his pillion, his grassy wedge of hair is newly retouched in spanking apple-green, wearing his salmon-pink overall, issued by the Angel's party to its association of communications workers, of which Clovis represents the first, and only, member, the sole recruit of the Postal Workers for the Fatherland, as well as being the favourite son of the Angel's 'beauty through disability brigade', and, again, its entire membership.

The restaurant lies close by the water. Swans float by, their necks curving into question marks as they put on speed. The waiters mutter to themselves as they step over Clovis' new boot which sticks out proudly beneath the table. They stare at his freshly painted hair.

'Did you know, Bella, that your shoulders are very like the chocolate mousse you're eating? I see things so much more clearly since I met "her".'

'I don't think you must take everything you believe about "her" to be true. Well, not absolutely everything.'

'Of course it's all true. If it wasn't I'd die. Because if you lose your salvation what is the point of saving your life? You should look to yourself, Bella. What is going to happen if your mother doesn't come back for you? Will you stay here? For good?'

'Never!'

'Then where will you go?'

'I don't know. Somewhere. Maybe I'll ask the new guest at the Priory if I can go home with him?'

'Don't be ridiculous. He's not going anywhere, that one. Haven't you seen the watchers at the gate, in the cars? They never sleep. They're his guards, Bella. He's a guest maybe, like a prisoner is the guest of the state.'

'Who told you?'

'Pesché, of course. We're on the best of terms, the chief and I. Did you know that I'm in charge of the forward planning for the Saturday rally? They can use me. The PNP give me work, trust me. I owe all this to the Angel.'

'And that ridiculous pink overall? And the plastic boot?'

'Not pink – salmon. And the boot is crystal.'

'Why should the Angel give you a crystal boot?'

'Because he's a generous soul. And he loves beauty.'

'It's not even practical, a glass boot. What would happen if you smashed it?'

'I've been issued with this boot by the PNP. If I break it or lose it I have only to tell Monsieur Cherubini and he will issue another one.'

'Listen, the PNP is the creation of three men: the Angel, who hates immigrants, strangers, foreigners; Father Duval; and my Uncle Claude, who is frightened of people who aren't quite right.'

'What do you mean?'

'The physically handicapped.'

'You mean cripples – don't you, Bella? But my very employment shows that's false. The Party wants what is its own. Sure. Own family, nation, country. Anyone who accepts this may join. We'll become the party of the future because we want what is modern.'

'And what's modern?'

'A computer for everyone. A video phone. Information storage and retrieval, the facts of life collated, stored, accessible so that society can be made orderly. A census each year. Statistics of everyday life, income, illness, age, debts, beliefs, crimes, all registered. Monitoring of the destitute and the dangerous. Online concern for the underdog, electronic surveillance of offenders. Are you coming to the Rally? I'll be there – with her!'

Of 'her' Clovis speaks in reverent terms. She has saved him, he says and his voice is full of devotion. He adores her in the way that savages once worshipped the moon, when the moon was still cold, naked and unattainable, before men began shooting things into her and dumping garbage on the rocky beaches of her empty seas. At one point in his litany he touches my knee beneath the tablecloth.

'Beat it!'

'I've been cured by her, Bella. No more drugs. No more heartbreak. See?'

Three hypos gripped in his fist beneath the tablecloth, a quiver full of miniature rockets. This is Clovis! He has not snorted, shot or swallowed a noxious substance in three days. He does not ask me for money. In fact he says he will pay for our dinner! And this a boy who has been ingesting whatever dust came his way with a perfectly American abandon for as long as anyone can remember. A miracle!

'For heaven's sake, put those damn things away!'

From the vantage point of my white chocolate mousse I watch him ploughing his way through *Galatine de Canard* stuffed with pork, veal, truffles and pistachios. My mousse is excellent, flavoured with a hint of cinnamon, just a delicate touch, like a fragrance of woodsmoke at dawn.

'Poor Bella, you look sad. Would you like to tell me about it? Would you like to consult your analyst? Have you heard from your mama?'

'She writes to me. Or rather she sends me notes.'

'That's nice. What does she say?'

'She doesn't say anything. I don't mean she writes notes. She sends me banknotes. Sometimes she writes on the banknote: "I hope you got my last note?" She's in America with her camera, searching for beauty. When she finds it she will bring back pictures.'

'I understand,' Clovis nods, 'it's like people going with cameras to photograph the Yeti in the Himalayas, to prove he exists.'

'That boot is not crystal.'

'It is.'

'Very well, we'll conduct an experiment. You know how the roof of this place reaches down almost to the ground on the other side of the building?'

'Sure. You can climb up there. We used to do it as kids.'

'Right. So we climb up there tonight and drop the boot.'

'What if it smashes?'

'Then you've won. And, like you said, the Angel will issue you with a new one.'

'Right,' says Clovis. 'And he will, too. You are really crazy. I wish I could help.'

Sympathy amid the duck and the mousse and the waiters who stare at me and glare at Clovis is difficult to take. What you love becomes beautiful, Papa said, and that is assuredly so. Clovis loves the Dutch girl – but does she love him? Certainly she walks with him and rides on his bike and talks with him, but equally surely she does not sail with him. For not only can Clovis not swim but I have already seen her sailor and swimmer on the deck of the *Minnie III* on the day that the Redeemer and I went for our voyage on the lake and the

137

Foreign Legion plucked the Dutch peach and the little fish fed on the remainders, on the seed that fell by the waterside. Shall I rephrase, Papa? What you love becomes beautiful, if it isn't beautiful already. Or maybe it's when you love that you become beautiful? Mama would know perhaps, but then she is not here either.

'Happy boy,' I tell Clovis later that night as we stand on the roof of *Les Dents Sacrés* and prepare to drop his boot. 'I am glad for you, and of course for Ria.'

'Who?' Clovis asks, and drops the boot. It doesn't even chip. I am sorry I made him do it now. He has set his heart on it being crystal. It prompts me to think that maybe I have something of my Uncle Claude in me and that makes me very unhappy. There is nothing in the least useful about the snappy identification of molecular structures. It leads only to trouble and heartbreak. Even so, Clovis irritates me by pretending not to know the name of the Dutch peach is Ria.

'Her name is Sophie,' Clovis insists.

'Plastic,' I say cruelly, 'your boot is made of plastic.'

Thursday morning shows early signs of being remarkable. Take, for example, the Redeemer's toes. They are what I see first when he comes out in his robe to take the sun, making his ritual appearance on our private beach. Though we've taken chocolate together, we don't talk about it, at least not in public. But word has been spreading that there is something strange about Monsieur Brown. You can tell by the way the other guests ignore him. He remains lofty, silent and apparently blind to the *cordon sanitaire* which now exists between the other flavours of humanity and his sainted, soft, brown, sweet self. Several metres of wooden beach are now the stranger's territory and we all respect what politicians call its sovereignty. The distinction is as sharp as it would be if we had drawn our boundaries in spit or garlic, menstrual blood or sacred salt. The border could not be more clearly set if it were built of bricks and topped with barbed wire. This has come to pass since the guests of the Priory discovered that plain Monsieur Brown was once a president and a dictator. He has now become the dark continent, to be avoided at all costs, the subject of a hundred horror stories.

Only I am in possession of the facts. At least some of the facts. And you, of course, I suppose, you who made us, all creatures great and small. What I know is that he once had gaps between his front teeth, and that the gap was bridged years ago by a Boston dentist when he studied in that city, back in the years when the French ruled his country of Zanj and Uncle Dickie was still planning to lead the country to independence, and thus claim the Leopard Throne, whose legs were piles of the skulls of slave enemies. I know that he is the ninth child and not the first – and the significance of this:

'Because, Bella, in our culture, the first child is somewhat dim. My uncle was a first child. Do you say dim? Yes, the third then is pretty go-ahead, the ninth brings luck and the tenth misfortune. I was number nine. The day of the week is also important and the newborn child is named accordingly for the weekday of his birth. In the Wouff language I am named Wednesday.'

Wednesday Brown!

But as I say, take his toes. His toes are unexpected, especially in view of the other marvels of which he is compounded, that is to say the startlingly pouting, toady features, the luscious, Bourneville sheen to his skin, his three souls, the blood soul, the clan soul and the platonic soul – otherwise known as the male soul. However, it is his toes that I now see, curved and powerful like the toes of an anteater lying so beautifully stacked within a hair's breadth of my right arm as I stretch out on the warm wooden beach planks and hear the red and grey canvas of his chair creak, for the Redeemer is moving into a more comfortable position above me and I watch and see a drop of sweat gather in the curiously soft fine hairs of his leg it swells and hangs trembling until gravity calls and it disappears leaving only its gleaming trail. I come as close as I can without touching, crossing a line the others have drawn, while I know that above me the cruel, rubbery face behind its dark glasses turns this way and that, staring out across the lake. My basking lizard, my lighthouse-keeper! His toes, unlike his fingers, are properly formed and though he can't wear rings on his fingers they wouldn't fall off his toes. This is something I intend to take up with him when we next speak. I hope there's time

139

for that because something occurred to me when we talked together. He doesn't intend to stick around for very long. He's just waiting for something.

'What do you mean I can't come in? That is ridiculous!'

My uncle's voice is high and hateful. You can hear it, can't you? It really is most terribly shrill and he is clearly hopping mad and I can't for the life of me think why they are holding him up at the gate, and I shan't look either.

My uncle's face is a horribly neat little assemblage, with its light blue eyes, rosebud lips, soft sooty eyebrows and firm pink clean flesh. Uncle Claude is not one of those about whom you can say that he does not have very much upstairs, he has too much upstairs for his own good and it all goes on in this sort of attic behind his forehead where I think he is building a kind of partition made of this lousy material which, in cerebral terms, you might call the flimsiest plywood around, the sort of thing they make walls from in cheap hotels, the sorts of walls which shiver when the heroine slams the door on soap-opera sets. And up in this room, in the attic in his head which he is partitioning, lies the divine figment chained to the bed, I suppose, like some poor hostage in Lebanon, fearing every minute will be his last. In the other little room he keeps his idea of Monsieur Brown, whom I think he sees as a kind of alien lodger from Mars and who grows daily more sinister and dangerous. I notice that, from time to time, Uncle Claude, though I am sure he is unaware of it, lifts his shapely hand and bangs himself on his forehead and when he does this I get the idea that he is bent on knocking down the partition between the rooms in the attic, allowing figment and alien to flow together and become one.

'But I insist on going through! Kindly get out of my way. Don't you know who I am? I am the mayor! Aha, I can see you did not know that. Where are you from? I can tell you're not from around here or you would know who I am.'

The loud and astonished voice of my Uncle Claude. If you lifted your head just a little and turned over ever so slightly to your right, you would be able to see him out of the corner of your eye. But you do not look up, you do not even – what is the word – ah yes, *deign* (thank you), you do not even deign to look up, do you?

140

'Very well, if you won't permit me to pass in an ordinary, civilised manner, you will oblige me by taking a message to the manager.'

A few minutes later André is standing above me wearing bright peach colours that do not suit him and I would swear from his red eyes that he has been weeping. Hyppolyte has replaced Tertius as desk clerk and stands beside him dressed in a pair of very brief silvery shorts, a horribly cheap gold chain and crucifix. He doesn't wear a shirt and his muscles move under his thatch of chest hair like snakes in a sack. He scratches the black hair of his chest with the crucifix and yawns.

'We were asleep and the goons at the gate started yelling. Surely you heard them? They've been making enough of a row.'

'It is the mayor,' André whispers, feeling this is the sort of news he must deliver privately. It seems you have an appointment. He is asking for you, at the gate.'

'I bet she heard him,' Hyppolyte grumbles. 'Go on, admit it, Bella. How could you not have heard him – he's been yelling his head off! You just turned a deaf ear, didn't you?'

All around me they're listening though they don't move; everybody on the beach is deathly quiet, carefully not staring at André and Hyppolyte, not noticing that they've just woken up, though Hyppolyte goes on giving his ridiculously exaggerated yawn and stretching, not noticing that André has forgotten to button his trousers. Everybody keeps looking elsewhere. The Dutch family oil themselves, I can hear the edge of Beatrice's hand strike each vertebra as it glides down Ria's spine. The German family huddle and Gudrun peers across the water as if waiting for some Viking to sail into view. Raoul, the deserter, is rapt in a study of his balding knees. The lizards, Edith and Alphonse, turn in the sun the fleshy dials of their body clocks. They're all pretending to be characters in other people's paintings. Wise move. You don't expect sense from oil on canvas. Hidden in their frames, they pretend not to hear my uncle arguing with the men who will not let him through. And I guess they need this period of silence and reflection because, among other things, they want to get over the shock of learning that (a) the guys at the gate who've been clogging up the drive for the past few days are not simply impoverished tourists who have to sleep in their cars and (b) that Monsieur Brown is under guard and (c) so are they . . . Someone somewhere has decided that people may leave the hotel; however nobody but the guests are allowed in.

When Uncle Claude walks me home I can tell he is good and mad because he talks about numbers. He talks about something called fractals, which he says will provide future models of reality because they allow us to get round one of the problems of a purely mechanistic interpretation of phenomena: the view that reduces everything to plain quantum mechanics and then can't explain the complexity of certain systems, like networks, and the odd way the universe seems to organise itself, despite the command of Newton's Second Law of Thermodynamics that says it should be running down everywhere.

'Don't get me wrong,' says Uncle Claude firmly. 'I still believe in entropy. Ultimately. And absolutely. But first you have to deal with this problem of order. A tap drips, OK? So you get some disorder. But speed it up a little and it flows. Then there's water which boils, but doesn't fly apart. Or heat a gas, and it lights up. Push it way past its stable equilibrium, where each atom is acting for itself, and what happens? Does it go crazy? Certainly not. Pump up the atoms and zillions of them suddenly fall into step giving out their waves of light like a marching regiment thousands of miles long, and you've got a laser! The thing is, Bella, that things left alone don't fall apart. First they are organised. But they organise themselves.'

'Why have you come to fetch me? Why have you pulled me away from the beach?'

'It's the fourth of August. And also Monsieur Cherubini has made certain discoveries about the black man.'

'What discoveries?'

'Those men at the gate who wouldn't let me pass. They're not just watchers. Those guys are warders and this place is a gaol. Those gorillas are the keepers in what is fast becoming a sinister zoo. This whole business smells of something and I tell you what: it smells of Paris. They're cops. Supercops. You can be sure that the local gendarmes know nothing about them. They are letting people leave, I noticed that. The guests can come and go. But nobody else can go in.'

'But I went in.'

'Yes.' He gives me an odd look.

We walk up the hill to our house on the square and most of the houses we pass are shuttered against the heat. The sun stands small and brightly powdered in an ashy blue sky and seems to burn into the top of my head. I barely hear Uncle Claude who is talking angrily. One word I do catch is 'fractals' and then he says 'Feigenbaum's Constants' several times. They sound like criminal charges.

My grandmother is beside herself with anger. 'Ah, Bella, Claude found you. Come, we go walking. It is my saint's day – remember, August the fourth?' She's in pain, I can see it, it seizes her heart. 'I wish to talk to Monsieur André. His behaviour towards us, towards Monsieur Cherubini, is an insult!'

Nothing we can say will calm her. She clutches at her heart in her beautiful blouse of violet watered silk and her nostrils quiver; this agony is due as much to the feeling that an act of discourtesy has been committed, an act of *lèse majesté* towards the Angel, the Priest and the Mayor.

'Please, Maman, it really doesn't matter.' Uncle Claude makes her sit in the chair. 'Besides, we drank the *pineau* on the way home! So we enjoyed it even if he did not.'

'And Father Duval laid his blessing upon us. I suspect we probably need it more than the owner of the Priory Hotel,' says the Angel in a show of magnanimity.

But my grandmother will have none of it. She snorts and orders me upstairs. 'Bella, kindly change your clothes into something suitable for our saint's day promenade. Let me tell you, Monsieur Cherubini, that André has more than enough to answer for, some of us remember, oh yes!, those of us who were once prominent in Lyons at the time of his father, we recall very well the former associations of that family, when they had offices in Lyons, not far from the Hotel Terminus.'

Upstairs in my room I change and then raid my supplies in the silver trunk under the bed, where it is dark and cool. I change into a lily-green crêpe button-through dress and black stockings. I take as well, for a little show, a mint-green straw hat with a scarlet band and a group of three rather sugary

*143*

roses like jewels on the crusty scarlet velvet hatband. Clearly this must please somebody, because when I get downstairs the Angel compliments me rather confusingly.

'You sparkle like lakewater.'

'Perhaps she ought to be told what we know about her Monsieur Brown?' my uncle enquires anxiously. 'They've stopped people entering the hotel. They wouldn't even let me in. The guards at the gate are stepping up security. Tell her, *patron*, what you've found out.'

But the Angel is not to be rushed. 'Walk first, talk later,' he says.

And so we progress down to the lakeside for our annual promenade, Grandmama and I. It's something she only does once a year now since arthritis made walking increasingly difficult, and besides she hates the pleasure resort for what it has become. But she always makes this exception, on the fourth of August each year when we go down to the waterside, unsuitably and formally dressed. Today she wears a silk blouse with a high collar and several pieces of her rich collection of costume jewellery, much of it cast in the form of insects: butterflies with ruby eyes and a giant scarab, whose body is a cool, fat emerald, upon her shoulder. Her eyes scan the glittering surface of the lake as if there might appear around the corner some pirate rig, or as if she were some anxious wife awaiting the return of her sailor husband. But there is nothing to be seen except the noisy play of pleasure craft, the water-skiers ploughing the surface of the lake, a few speedboats and the windsurfers. My grandmother sometimes shakes herself when we go down to the lakeside as if she has just woken up from a dream and found herself walking among guests or Sunday trippers or pockets of Japanese tourists, and when this happens she raises her eyebrows at their excellent French with a kind of frowning perplexity, as if she has just heard children discussing their expense accounts. She averts her eyes from the girls sunning their breasts and touches her hands to her ears when the speedboats rocket past.

'Today, Bella dear, we commemorate the feast of our beloved St John Vianney, once said to be the most stupid priest in Lyons. But do you think that he allowed this insult

144

to overcome him? Of course not! He went on to become the world-famous Curé of Ars. Thousands made the pilgrimage to hear him preach or to kneel in his confessional. To repent their sins. To receive his forgiveness. Such was his saintliness it was said he could see right into their souls. So great the boldness and humility of the man that he overcame the whole world. When he was young he was called up for the army. Can you believe it? But he was sickened by the excesses of the French Revolution and so turned his back on war and went off to fight for Christ. These are the qualities of the old Lyons, my dear Bella. The Lyons into which upstarts such as André's father came and made their name and their money. But in the Curé of Ars you have a real child of France. In Monsieur Cherubini there is another.'

My grandmother gazes at the pleasure-seekers thronging the waterside and says bitterly: 'As for these, they ought to be locked up.'

We began these walks in the years before Papa died, when I was still a child and when Grand-mère's only worries were that I would dirty my white dress or eat too many apricots. That is to say, before she decided that I had become a woman and was thus a danger to myself and others. I have always thought it strange that my grandmother should worry so much about me and so little about my uncle. I wondered how, with her strong simple faith, she managed to cope with Uncle Claude's wish to polish off God. Gradually I realised that however much they might have disagreed about some things, mother and son came together in their political feelings: both wished to do something very violent to someone else. And quite possibly my Uncle Claude was careful to keep his dream of deicide to himself. He was, as they taught me to say at the North London Academy for Girls, a canny bugger. Grand-mère also quite happily ignored his attempts to molest me with his loose talk of sub-atomic particles. It really got him going, did the talk of particles, he was the only man I knew who would come out in goose-flesh when he tried to explain to me how a phototube in a bubble chamber detects the arrival of a particle called a pi-zero. To talk of the neutrino gave him a patch of extremely bumpy and not very pretty goose-flesh stretching from his collar to his earlobe in which the little hairs stood up like anaemic grass. And merely to mention quarks made his lips tremble and excited a curious circular motion in the area of the knees and thighs, which as a young child used to amuse me, until I grew up and then it frightened me.

My grandmother's method for deciding that I had passed from my girlhood was pretty clinical. She had a checklist. I had menstruated? I had breasts? I had lost my father? Very well, it remained only for me to think of Joan of Arc and all that she had already accomplished by the time she got to my age, and I would willingly grasp my destiny. Joan had already heard her 'voices' commanding her to save France from the accursed English. Before her lay glory, martyrdom, sainthood. Quite how I was to achieve this great goal was not made clear, though the expectation was there.

The men in the cars at the front gate of the Priory Hotel look hard at me but make no attempt to stop us. André is behind the desk when we enter.

'Madame, how pleasant! Can it be that a whole year has passed since you took tea with us? And look at Miss Bella! My heavens, she is a young lady. I fear they are like clocks, Madame, these children, they measure the diminishing years of their elders.'

'She lived in England for a time,' my grandmother replies drily, as if this is a far worse fate than the mortal ruin which we fleshy chronometers are said to measure. André and my grandmother examine me, their eyes sweeping my face like searchlights, or telescopes probing the black, cold and empty sky (empty of everything, if my Uncle Claude is to be believed, and warmed, if at all, only by the human imagination).

Our meeting with André is to be a contest, a trial, an excoriation, an inquisition; Grandmama is to thread his soft pink body with her spiky enquiries, he is to her now what the English were for Joan of Arc and she intends to do to him what they did to her. For his part, André is soft, smiling, charming sociability and his face gleams like a wrapped Easter egg. He orders a rather sullen Tertius to bring us coffee and insists that we sit beneath the chestnut trees in the garden. The wooden beach is clear now of its human freight, swept bare of golden, oiled bodies, and a few swans drift past with their poised, fastidious air of investigation. It is too hot to be out of doors and the guests are up in their rooms taking siestas. On the second floor, which Monsieur Brown occupies, all the green shutters are closed. Only the watchers at the gate in the Renault, the Citroën and the Deux-Chevaux are awake. In the face of my grandmother's coldness, André's smile deepens and warms: there is really something wonderful and terrible in his need to spread amiability and kindness, to make others feel better, stronger; to encourage, cheer and support wherever possible as if kindness were a kind of paint which you need only apply liberally to make the human picture smile and glow. As if by sheer will, by application alone, you can bring into the world the good, the right and the happy.

So we sit under the chestnut tree which throws grey shadows across the white iron table and coffee is served by Tertius who, it seems, is as tired and as grumpy as Hyppolyte was earlier. He now wears a pair of sky-blue shorts and his dark hair has been peroxided in patches which gives it a kind of basket-weave effect.

'He's a good boy at heart, but he tires easily,' says André, as Tertius places the tray on the table. 'These little confections you see are something that he has prepared for us. He is very clever that way.'

I can see by the expression of surprise on the boy's rather yellow face, which he does not bother to hide, that this compliment is unexpected and quite untrue.

André looks after him fondly, as Tertius slouches away. 'I trust you had no trouble getting in?'

'Who are the men at the gate, André?'

He shrugs unhappily. 'They don't tell me, Bella. In fact we are not supposed to know about them. The man with the red ears, he is the one in the Renault, he said to me: "Just ignore us. We're invisible." I don't know, I don't ask and I try not to see, but I can hardly be unaware of the fact that they won't let anybody pass the gates, except you, Bella. You seem to have the key, for some reason. Why they should let you pass and nobody else, I can't imagine. Mind you, you look lovely. Perhaps you appeal to their aesthetic sense? Pure peppermint you are today!'

But my grandmama has no time for pleasantries. She bangs her stick on the ground: 'Why should anyone try and stop me? I saw no one, I would have stopped for no one. I have been walking this village for half a century – who would dare to stop me? This is still a free country, I believe, praise God. And it will remain so while there are men such as Monsieur Cherubini determined to protect the lovely heart of France! What I do know is this: last night a deputation called on you made up of Monsieur Cherubini, as well as the Mayor and Father Duval. They came to pay their respects to this new guest of yours, this Nubian, or Ethiopian, or Arab, or whatever he is. But you refused to allow them to see him. I don't understand. It was discourteous, it was unimaginative, it was unnecessary! Now it turns out that this man is connected to some African kingdom where my dear son lost his life, Bella's papa, trying to bring civilisation to the savages who inhabit that place. And yet we, his relatives, are not permitted to see this African chief. It seems you have in your house one of the last people on earth to see my son and yet you forbid us to meet him.'

She scans the closed shutters. 'He's out of sight again. No doubt locked away in the thirty rooms he occupies, with his wives and his goats and his chickens and his hateful food.'

André, always anxious to please, seizes on the word food and pushes the plate of pastries towards me. 'These are called Rigo Jancsi Squares. Try one.' He turns to Grandmama. 'But I didn't prevent them, Madame. My guest refused to see them. He said he wouldn't receive delegations of officials. He's here on a private visit. I can't force him to see your son and his friends. Though I must say I am surprised that they wanted to see him. From what I learn of Monsieur Cherubini's new party, my guest is exactly the sort of man he doesn't want to see any more of in this part of France. And in this instance, and only in this instance, Cherubini and I see eye to eye, because I can assure you that the sooner I get rid of him the happier I will be. Anyway, your information isn't correct. Someone from your family has met my guest. And at his request. Isn't that so, Bella? You met him for tea.'

'For chocolate.'

Now up to the front gates comes Clovis mounted on his new green bike. It is no faster than the others and more flatulent, but it is also somehow flashier, trimmed with chrome and blinking with mirrors, and he arrives in his perspex boot with Ria sitting on the pillion, her long bare legs stuck out on either side of the bike like a compass, in an apricot skirt and a dill-green bandana, shrieking and giggling, hanging on to him, and somehow she looks fatter with her clothes on. Clovis doesn't try and pass the guard at the gate but lets her off and watches admiringly as she flounces up the path and into the hotel.

'Bella, is this true!' Grand-mère is scandalised. 'You've seen this man – again. After we discussed the dangers? After your uncle spoke to you of Leda!'

Terrified now that he has given something away, André pushes over the plate of chocolate cakes towards me. 'I can see you like them. Have another. See how she tucks in, Madame? I must tell Tertius, he'll be so pleased. Do you know the story of these cakes? They're named after a Hungarian violinist called Rigo Jancsi who played so beautifully and seductively that a princess eloped with him! They take simply ages to make and need the very best bitter chocolate, double cream, rum and vanilla. Yes, take another! Please, Madame, won't you try one?'

Grandmama, to my surprise, does so. She lifts the solid creamy cake to her thin blue lips and bites. There is so much violence in the action that I half expect to see blood spurt from her mouth. She turns to André.

'You remember stories, of another hotel, some years ago? The Hotel Terminus in Lyons. Yes, I see you remember! It looked across the square, the Cours de Verdun. It was in this hotel that your late father, Monsieur, opened the Lyons branch of his offices. It's a chapter in the career of your family that few of us old enough to remember will ever forget.'

Suddenly he is hurt, angry and frightened all at once. But mostly he is angry. I watch as the fragile eggshell of his forehead fractures, he makes fists of his hands and rubs his fists across his pink shirt in an agitated manner. I can hear his nails clipping his shirt buttons.

'Why do you bring this up?'

'You wouldn't let my son enter your hotel. You insulted the village priest. You offended Monsieur Cherubini, the best friend our village has ever had. And now I discover that you have allowed my daughter to visit the Nubian. Why should I consider your feelings?'

'You speak as if I were a dictator. I'm not a god to give permission or to refuse access. I am an hotelier, who has been told to accommodate this man. So why should I be blamed? If you want to spread stories then let me say, Madame Dresseur, you had better be careful. You of all people shouldn't talk of collaboration with the enemies of France. Or I may tell my story.'

Grandmama gets up. Her hand is on her heart and her lips are blue. She takes my arm and she shakes her silver-headed walking-stick in André's face.

'Shout out your story! I glory in it!'

'I can't think why. It's as shameful as mine. Please, Madame, let the dead sleep, let's not lay their corpses by the lakeside.'

'Don't you dare mention your father in the same breath as my husband. What your father did was to lick the boots of the German monsters.'

'And what did your husband do, Madame?'

My grandmother's smile of triumph is terrible.

'He gave his life for France, for his beloved chief and for his faith!' And then, suddenly, she clutches her chest and seems to faint.

I run to stop her falling and I shout at André: 'You've killed her!' My cry brings Tertius running.

It's not true but I can't help myself. I want it to be true. The watchers at the gate regard us steadily. Strangely, it is Tertius who keeps his head. 'She's not dead, she's breathing. Get the doctor.'

'Shall I call Dr Valléry?' André's eyes are wide with anguish.

Grandmama opens her eyes. 'No. Call my son. Or Monsieur Cherubini. I wish to go home. I don't want to pass away in the garden of the Carthusians. Her face is chalky white and she grimaces with the pain in her chest.

A few minutes later Monsieur Cherubini arrives in his Mercedes with Father Duval. The watchers at the gate make no attempt to stop them. But nor do they make any attempt to help us. They must be under orders never to leave their posts, no matter what happens.

'We were just about to leave for the rehearsal. For Saturday's rally,' says the priest. 'You caught us just in time.'

We carry my grandmother to the car. Her reaction at seeing Monsieur Cherubini is profound. By the time we reach the house her colour is better and the pain seems to be easing. Her breathing is regular.

'You are feeling a little easier, Madame?' asks the Angel.

'Certainly. Though your rescue was only just in time, *patron*. I had my little talk with the owner of the hotel but possibly I did not allow for the evil atmosphere of the place. It affected me. However, I was determined that they had claimed enough victims, that family, with their offices in Lyons. They were not going to get me as well. Never!'

'Bravo, Madame!' says the Angel.

Grand-mère's smile is pure delight, open and adoring. The miracles of faith are more awesome in our day-to-day business than anything the saints could comprehend.

# 9

We gather in the dining room. As the sun sinks, the lake grows dark and heavy, closing down for the night, taking on a deserted, shuttered look like the old houses above the little lakeside road. Grandmama is helped to a chair by Father Duval. I want to call Dr Valléry but she won't have it.

'My confessor is here, my family is here. And my *patron*! Enough. Onwards into battle, let's ride the English down, at last we have a general in the field!' She turns a softly affectionate glance on Monsieur Cherubini.

'The *patron* has such information as makes the ears curl,' says Father Duval, 'little scraps of knowledge, even if one needs to put on gloves before handling, the sort of thing that may help us to understand his game.'

'I don't want to understand it,' Grandmama says. 'The thing to do with Monsieur Brown is not to understand him, it's to get rid of him.'

'Spoken like a philosopher!' Monsieur Cherubini approves.

Father Duval is dressed tonight like a master of ceremonies, or a campaign manager, which is one thing as sure as hell he wants to be. He's wearing a snappy dark wool suit and cream shirt with terracotta tie and ivory cuff-links. Tonight he's ringmaster, television floor manager and warm-up man rolled into one pink rotundity.

It is Monsieur Cherubini's gift and perhaps his genius that he applauds in others all the parts they wish to play. He stands now and acknowledges the applause he hears, though we do not, and acknowledges it with a modest wave and a smile. Part of him is already on the platform receiving the adulation of his followers.

'I call on Monsieur Cherubini to speak to us!' announces Father Duval.

'How pleasant to think that an angel should be deemed worthy of his own annunciation.'

This little jollity so entrances Father Duval that he can't help applauding. 'Bravo, Monsieur! Bravo, chief!'

'But where is the Mayor? We cannot begin without him,' the Angel says.

'Upstairs catching comets,' says Father Duval. It seems that the weather will be perfect for viewing tonight. 'Bella, please call your uncle. The *patron* is about to speak. The North African secrets of the funny guest at the Priory Hotel are to be revealed to us, one and all, tonight.'

Up in his attic laboratory at the top of the house, Uncle Claude takes an age to open his door to me. It has at least three locks on it and he makes a tremendous fuss before letting me in and even more of a fuss when I tell him he's wanted and he looks remarkably distracted, a little shy, almost angry, and oddly embarrassed.

'Bella, I can't be disturbed. Tonight, two or three hours after sunset, will give me by best chance in years! I'm on the track of a comet, I think. I really do. I'm pretty sure it's not a globular cluster or just a faint elliptical galaxy. In a region around 36° of the western horizon. It doesn't have a tail, as far as I can see. But then on the other hand you don't always have to see a tail straight off because really what you're looking at is a kind of chalk mark on the blackboard of the heavens. If you're looking at a comet at all. But I've checked my sky atlas and there's nothing marked there. So who knows?'

'Listen, you had better come down. Grand-mère was taken ill at the hotel.'

'What? You see, I told you she should not have gone there. I knew it! What happened?'

'She had words with André. She got really mad. I don't understand exactly what they were talking about, except that they both have stories about each other they'd rather not tell. Or hear. I don't know which. But they clashed, and then she collapsed and we called Monsieur Cherubini and he came and fetched her in the car. She's downstairs now and I think she must see the doctor but she won't let me call him. And now the Angel's going to tell her more stories about Monsieur

Brown. It's bound to upset her because she thinks of Papa. Come down and put a stop to it.'

'But Bella I must set up.'

'Uncle Claude, she might die!'

'Very well, I'll come down – but no one can stop this. It's a reaction which has to run its course. We must face the consequences. But I blame André. He will suffer for it.'

'Something bad is going to happen.'

'The truth is never bad.'

Here are his fat telescope, his books, his calculations and his experiments. In particular the thoroughly nasty job of work which stands in the corner and has stood in the corner for as long as I can remember. Some people have pot plants, Uncle Claude has his soup, his secret solutions in glass jars, his garden of molecular surprises, conspiracies of simple sugars, nucleotides and phosphates out of which he hopes to grow a living cell, the solutions changed every week according to a new formula, every week a little closer to the secret of life. It is, if you like, Uncle Claude's very own, very early version of the primal cosmic gruel out of which the microbes came that became us. Bionic fishtank aglow with hope. All Uncle Claude's life spreads before him in this den. Here he spies out comets, believing that it was in the tails of the comets, or in the arrival of meteorites, that the organic compounds and the lively molecules first migrated to our planet maybe three and a half billion years ago and the magic ingredients fraternized and became life, viruses, microbes. Inanimate salts combining, as he hopes they are combining even now in his fishtanks, tubes and retorts in the corner, and eventually these lucky organisms will grow up to be able to understand the secrets of the universe, relativity, the speed of light, gravity and the Grand Unification Theory which one day ('I'm utterly confident of this, Bella. Mark my words. You watch and see') will satisfactorily describe, in mathematical form, the forces which bind the universe: gravity and electro-magnetism, as well as the strong and the weak nuclear forces. ('Then you just watch and see what will happen to that old figment!') And my uncle dances across the room, boasting about the figment's fate, waving his fists like some skinny George Charpentier of the cosmos. My boring, bloody, abysmal, murderous Uncle Claude.

I can tell you that on my trip downstairs I stopped off and tucked into the supplies in the steel trunk beneath my bed and consumed in pretty short order two bars of *Côte d'Or Chocolate Extra Superior* and a handful of *Lindt Bittersweet* and thus geared up I prepared to expose myself to the Angel's sermon.

Downstairs we all assemble, my grandmother is the colour of icing sugar, hard and shining, her hand permanently to her heart. I think for a moment vaguely of plugging in my cans and spinning something like Thomas and the Apostles, you must know their really funky big one called 'Jesus On The Cheap!', with their heavy lead guitarist, Raymond Whatsit, who made it big in 'I Never Went to Paris' and who treats his instrument like a sailor who's just been forbidden shore leave. But then *of course* you know what I mean. And you'll know what I mean when I say that to complain that T. and the A.s are over the top just because T. tries to couple with his bass guitar is to believe that balls are only for bouncing . . . I don't believe that. And yet do I put on the cans, despite being Bella the one-woman walkman, because I can tell that my ears have been lent on my behalf to the Angel for his speech.

'The man that we know as Brown, Brown according to Bella, not christened, I cannot say that in the presence of the clergy, not sanctified by the Church, no, no, especially not in the light of what is to follow, but named, for convenience, Brown, is as I told you before the dictator of an African country with which France once had dealings. That country has dwindled now to the status of a distant debtor. But until recently it was still a place to which government officials were posted for obscure reasons, some associated with the country for purposes of French prestige, others were there to see to the more mundane need of this client state to pay its way. Now the man that we know as Brown was, until a few years ago, known to his subjects, whom he ruled with whip and sword, as the Redeemer. I apologise to Father Duval for this blasphemy, but it seems the title is not unknown in Africa.'

My grandmama appears to have fallen asleep at this stage and only her flickering eyelids tell me that she is listening, though at what cost, I hate to imagine. Her concentration is quite horribly rewarded when the Angel, holding up his hands

*155*

to silence, and then joining them together beneath his upper lip in a prayerful gesture, says softly:

'The charges against him are very impressive: murder, corruption, anthropophagy.'

'I don't understand the last,' says Father Duval.

'Cannibalism,' says my uncle.

Grandmama opens her blue eyes, sits bolt upright in her chair and then shrieks and falls back again in a dead faint. There is no question of Monsieur Cherubini going on or of Grandmama being allowed to stay downstairs, but first we must revive her and make her put her head between her knees, her lips are now very white, she has a twitch in her cheek she cannot stop. Uncle Claude and I carry her to her bedroom and I put her to bed and sit with her while Uncle Claude calls the doctor. When her eyes open, she reaches out and strokes my cheek, then with the other hand she strokes her three pictures, her holy trinity, Marshal Pétain, her young husband in his military cap and Joan of Arc astride her horse, sword drawn, a look of ecstasy in her eyes. Taking my cheek between thumb and finger, she gently pulls me down to her and whispers fiercely in my ear, I feel her lips brush my earlobe:

'If I die it will be another death that our little hotel-keeper will have on his conscience.'

'Grandmama, what is this talk about the Hotel Terminus? What happened there, in the war?'

Her blue eyes now are full of rage. 'It's best not to ask, my little Bella. Best not to know. There are horrible secrets of the Hotel Terminus. Third floor, suite fifty-eight. The father of our little hotelier knew it well. He was a knower of such things, a money man. You know he moved down from Paris after the Fall and he took root in our part of the world, like a weed. It was to Lyons that he came, because that was, until November 1942, part of Free France, the *zone libre*. The country of opportunity for some, of death for many. André's father came south when the Bourse closed in Paris and he found business to do in this part of the world. First as a *passeur*, one who arranged the flight of refugees across the Swiss border, frightened people, often loaded with gold and jewels; he took shares in their safe passage. Sometimes they didn't make it. And nor did their gold. Escaping was as dangerous as being caught. It was an expanding industry. Then, when the Germans marched into Lyons, the *zone libre* was finished, but the *passeurs* were busier than ever. And you must realise that the factories ran, and the offices and the industries. It was all business as usual and it needed managing. André's papa had shown himself to be a fine manager. It was not long before the new guests at the Hotel Terminus employed him.'

'Germans?'

'Gestapo. And when the war was over, what did he say to explain his role? He denied ever having collaborated with the Germans. Collaboration? Never! All he had done was to liaise. The reward of his profitable liaison was to die in bed with his socks on, leaving a fortune to his little son, while those who had given their lives for their country died like dogs in the early morning rain and people spat on their faces – '

And here she lets me go and sighs deeply and her eyes fix for a moment on the photograph of her young husband before filling with tears.

At last I begin to understand her anger and grief. Her husband in the Resistance, captured, and shot.

And André? I know now the riddle behind the Beast of the Bourse and his offices in Lyons. It was not in fact André but his father who was the monster, and the offices were not his, but belonged to the Gestapo, they were not for dealing in stocks and shares, but belonged to a business that ran on blood.

The doctor arrives, little Dr Valléry, our local socialist, a man of hair the colour of beer, and thick glasses. Entering our house is a trial for him: he's going into the lion's den; he pales visibly at the sight of Marshal Pétain in the silver frame and I know just by looking at him that his medical skills are undermined by his political shivers. He can't wait to leave. As it is, he is one of those who has tried to rally support against the Angel and his new party. But in the village of La Frisette, everybody worth mentioning is Angel-bound to a degree that nothing will shift and the voices of the opposition are faint, they may mock and jeer, but do not carry. Valléry's position is weakened still further by the fact that he has recently abandoned his wife and taken up with Louise, the brunette with the prodigious cleavage who works in the *tabac*. She's one of those women so utterly sexual that she resembles more a running stream than a person of flesh and bone, and she presented to the doctor something like the sight of a bubbling brook on a stifling day and he no sooner set eyes on her than he flung himself into her and was carried away. Since the good doctor drowned himself in liquid Louise, his wife has taken to attending the Church of the Resurrection like a reproachful, straight-backed ghost. Poor woman! As if angry virtue would somehow recompense her or punish the philanderer, when, in fact, his utter surrender to the lubricious Louise (legend holds she partnered Clovis at one time and is known as a watery wonder in whom even that demented boy once dipped a toe, or some other appendage) is enough to rust the doctor's political reputation, from which all other assessments in La Frisette proceed. To fall is one thing, to leap another and to drown something else entirely, and such was Dr Valléry's immersion, so utterly comprehensive his seduction, that it played hell with his standing as a socialist. Even now as he comes into the room and takes my grandmother's pulse, I can feel, tell, almost smell that he's come from the warmth of Louise and his tousled irritation signals that he yearns to be back there as soon as possible. I'll bet he floats in her the way Uncle Claude says the sea creatures do, who may be our real ancestors, the blind red tubeworms who cruise the sandy bottom of the Gulf of Mexico where the searing magma of the earth's hot heart bleeds and congeals, veiled in steam and gas, thousands of metres under the sea. Give the giant red tubeworm a pair of thick glasses and a cheesy wink and you've got Dr Valléry to the life. No wonder I go downstairs, no wonder I can't go on looking at him, his politics undermined, his doctoring deeply suspect, and all that remains a quivering desire so palpable it's positively embarrassing.

We wait for the medical opinion without any hope that it will be anything more than conventional. But that's wrong. Because when the little doctor scampers downstairs he has clearly thought about his diagnosis. He's considered his position and is determined that both should be respected.

'Angina, arthritis, old age. You'll appreciate I can't do much more than alleviate any of these conditions. She's old, sick, stubborn. She won't listen to me. So I tell you that if she's too excited or overly stressed it may be fatal. No, I correct myself, it will be fatal.'

Terse and even impressive as this is, it doesn't help him much. One cannot threaten an angel with death and a physicist devoted to entropy is used to such things and Father Duval long ago dissociated himself from death as a form of political scandal. So Monsieur Cherubini's silent nod is also a gesture of dismissal and the little doctor scurries away back to his big wide bed where Louise waits for him willing, warm and wet.

'Well, we've decided, Bella,' the Angel announces, 'you will have to go to the man whom you call Brown and find out what he's doing here.'

'Why me?'

'Because you're the only one he's willing to see. He's invited you to take tea with him. We didn't even get past the door,' says Uncle Claude. 'The family honour depends on it.'

'He's up to something, Bella. We know that,' says Father Duval.

'Go,' says my uncle shortly.

'But I thought you had objections. You don't like me seeing him. And Monsieur Cherubini says he's a cannibal.'

'He was and maybe still is,' says the Angel. 'The world is full of strange tastes. Only time will tell. I admit my information is disturbing.'

'Tell her about the lions,' says Father Duval.

'He fed his opponents to the lions,' the Angel says. 'And then one day he tried to feed their keeper to them. But the animals recognised their friend and refused the morsel offered.'

'And so he fed the keeper to his crocodiles instead – what d'you say to that?' asks Uncle Claude, with a look very like satisfaction.

'It sounds too good to be true. Stories to frighten children.'

'Bella, this man killed without compunction. He's a monster. An animal. He sliced his opponents into pieces and kept some of them in the refrigerator to adorn the presidential menus. Human corpses stuffed with rice and ready to be served. Prepared meals, you might say. He killed children, and first he poked their eyes out. There was nothing he wouldn't do!'

When Father Duval tells me this he walks about throwing his hands to left and right as if getting rid of the little bits of the Redeemer's menu that have somehow stuck to his fingers.

'He was a good friend of my papa's.'

'Bella, Bella' – the Angel is all kindness and at his most reptilian when he softens into kindness – 'it is precisely this connection with your father that worries me. If he involved your father in any of his attempts at bribing officials, if this news came out, here, now, it wouldn't look good. It would kill your grandmother.'

'You mean it wouldn't look good for you. And for Uncle Claude, the Mayor. For your rally on Saturday. And for your new party. You talk of my family – what family? My father's dead and my mother is missing somewhere in America. And then I make a friend of Monsieur Brown, who is kind to me, and who knew Papa, they were very dear friends, together almost to the last. But my uncle warns me about him, he tells me to keep away from him. Now you tell me he eats people and in the same breath you say I must go and find him and see what he knows. I don't understand.'

'I don't want to be blamed for my brother's errors of judgement,' says Uncle Claude. 'This is guilt by association and I am not guilty. But someone has made the connection. Who do you think those men at the gate of the hotel are? They come from Paris! Government people. There's something dark and troubling about this. I don't like it, I don't like the way that he has some kind of official protection, a bodyguard maybe. They're tough guys sitting in the parking lot. They're after something. We've had trouble in the family, we don't want any more.'

'They've taken everything already, our apartment in Paris, my mother's jewels, even my Bapuna mask which Papa brought for me. Gone. What more can they possibly want from us?'

'What more do you have to give?' the Angel asks. 'Because if one thing is clear about this it is that someone has got something that someone wants.'

Before we can work out the interesting convolutions of this last comment the door opens and Clovis enters in fine high spirits, clapping his hands and beaming. He's been helping the police plan the parking arrangements for Saturday's rally and insists on telling us everything immediately.

'The plan is proceeding wonderfully, *patron*. Clovis is in control! We've been having a full dress rehearsal tonight with the fire brigade standing by and a band, a great big band blowing brass instruments, made up of all the local hunters. We've worked out how many cars may be parked by the lakeside so as to keep all traffic from the centre of town. The dais on which you will speak is draped in red and blue and there are patterns on it arranged in chevrons and many flowers of different kinds are ordered. Poinsettias and lilies predominate, according to your orders. We're now ready to check your position on the platform for security and for camera angles. Clovis is here to escort you, chief!'

And with that he does a strange thing, he balls his hands into fists, crosses his arms at the wrists and bangs himself on the chest. Once, twice, bou-boum! For a hollow-chested boy he gives off quite an echo. It's some sort of salute, I realise, and I don't like it. Not one bit.

'Not now, not now,' Uncle Claude snaps, waving him away, 'come back later.'

'No, no,' says Father Duval coming forward, 'he's been told to escort Monsieur Cherubini to the podium and it would be very bad for his rehabilitation if he were to be encouraged to disregard orders. Can't he perhaps just wait awhile? Can't he go upstairs?'

I can see Uncle Claude is about to refuse when the Angel says, 'Yes, it will be better if we briefed Miss Bella in private and the parking must wait until that's done. She must go and she must be told what to do.'

'Yes, she must be briefed,' says Father Duval, 'it's a special mission.'

At the mention of the words 'brief' and 'mission' I can see my Uncle Claude stiffen slowly to attention. Perhaps it's because scientists always must stand passive before the workings of the universe unable to do anything more than observe helplessly, however happily, the immutable operations of unshakable laws, that they must sometimes ache to push somebody around.

'Very well, young man,' Uncle Claude says to Clovis, 'you may continue on up the stairs, go to the very top of the house and there you'll find my den. Go quietly, mind, for Madame is ill and may not be disturbed. And nor may any of the equipment in my study. It's all very important. Top secret. Dangerous! It can kill silly people who touch it!' And here Uncle Claude throws up his arms and locks them, fingers rigid and hisses like a cat, his blue eyes wild and staring, then his body shudders as if he's having a fit. It is his way of warning Clovis what will happen if he messes around with his equipment. It's really strange that he should go into this man-in-the-electric-chair routine to suggest danger. I mean, why doesn't he just draw a skull and cross-bones on the door of his room? And anyway what is a man who understands the significance of Feigenbaum's Constants and the mysteries of Quantum Chromodynamics doing putting on this show as if Clovis were some brain-damaged monkey instead of a very intelligent, if somewhat flighty boy with a bad limp. Indeed my Uncle Claude's horror of sex and disease are such as to make me wonder whether modern scientists are not perhaps plunged so deeply into the miasma of superstition and dogma as to make the most hide-bound medieval theologian seem positively skittish by comparison.

But all this is happily lost on Clovis who, with a skip and a grin, dances, no *flies* up the stairs, his salmon-pink overall clashing so weirdly with his staring white face beneath the glowing pampas of hair, and his flashing perspex boot, which hits the wooden walls of the staircase as he ascends with a hard, satisfying sound, and, leaving behind him a trailing and cheerful 'Yessir!' he disappears aloft.

'Now, Bella, let's talk,' says the Angel. 'Let's go through the factors that make it essential that you do as I ask. Something very strange is happening. The man you call Brown, the dictator of Zanj, as we know, was until recently retired in the South of France, where he has lived since his overthrow. Without family as far as I know, without friends. In all that time he's not been heard of. He dropped out of sight, went underground, disappeared. I suspect the politics from which he emerged makes it essential that he keeps his head down. If you spend a good deal of time murdering your opponents and stripping bare the treasury of your country, then I suppose there are always going to be those who wish to complain.

'Well, all of a sudden, out of his hidey-hole he pops, he takes off one day and comes here, to La Frisette. Why, and more to the point, why now? What does he want? We know that Paris know that he's here because it is undoubtedly they who have effectively commandeered the Priory Hotel where dear André plays the unwilling host to the Redeemer. Paris have also supplied a guard. Which means that they must worry about his safety. Paris also know, and would prefer to keep quiet, the links between this Redeemer Brown and your Papa. We know something happened out in Zanj and we know it's something that our government wants to conceal. Remember that they were sufficiently worried to move in on you and your mother after your father's death; as you pointed out, they forced the sale of your apartment, they took your mother's jewels. And here I have to point out that we must remember that diamonds are one of the few treasures of the curious country of Zanj. The clear implication of all this is that this man had some hold on your father, perhaps some unpaid debt. And now maybe he's run out of money. So he comes here, looking for the family. He wants something, Bella. You must find out what it is.'

'And then?'

'Then we can fight him,' says Father Duval. 'The *patron* has plans.'

I have returned to the Priory to find out why *he* is here. Not for the Angel, but for my own sake. I've taken the precaution of dressing carefully for the part I'm to play: the innocent enquirer. I'm wearing a dress of blush-pink velvet with a low neck, flat white shoes, and my hair is elaborate but chic. It's a style damn difficult to fix on your own; first it has to be spritzed then scrunched, moussed and dried naturally, and finished with a little wax rubbed through it for control. Two tortoiseshell combs complete the effect. It took all of an hour with Uncle Claude and the Angel muttering impatiently downstairs while they waited to drive me to the Priory. It was only when we got to the Priory that I remembered Clovis, upstairs in Uncle Claude's den.

'I locked him inside,' says Uncle Claude.

'He won't come to any harm,' the Angel promises as I leave the car. 'Father Duval is standing guard.'

André shows little surprise when I tell him what I know about Monsieur Brown.

'They may plan to fight the Redeemer,' André says solemnly, 'but first they want to finish with me. Have you seen this?'

He holds up a copy of *La Liberté*, the house organ of the *Parti National Populaire*, and with a trembling finger he points to an unsigned editorial:

\*

A STRANGE PERFUME FROM THE GARDEN OF THE CARTHUSIANS?

... *A troubling, foreign and unhealthy cosmopolitanism has begun to invade the precincts of our dear village. Not only do strangers from abroad find it increasingly easy to take up employment in the local industries, such as the nougat factory, thus depriving native-born Frenchmen of their rights of employment, but there now comes from the garden of the Carthusians a most provocative scent, a perfume androgynous, unhealthy and, moreover, one which would not be recognised by the good fathers who once inhabited the holy house by the lakeside. The present Prior of this establishment has a somewhat unusual taste in novices, or acolytes, a band of mendicants drawn from the lesser suburbs of Lyons, who together practise a brand of heresy which once drew down on its protagonists the cleansing fires of the stake* ...

'It's sad, Bella. The old cures for sin and suffering are not available any more. This ancient monastery, once the house of Carthusians, had its little punishments, its flagellations, its mortifications, its routes to salvation. All off limits to us now. You know the story of St Benedict, who founded the Cistercian Order? It was said that he was very troubled by lust and when his lust became apparent in company – '

'Do you mean he had an erection?'

'Yes. He cured himself of it by jumping into a bed of nettles. It never troubled him again. The simplicity of the very holy ones is quite frightening, isn't it? Everything final seems too easy. After all,' – his smile is awful – 'it's not the fault of the dear boys who come to work for me in the summer – all the way from Lyons. They're good boys . . .'

I can't resist it, I say: 'I'm glad some good comes out of Lyons.'

'So you know my family story? Your grandmother has told you about our branch in Lyons?'

I nod. 'You should have told me yourself. I wouldn't have blamed you.'

'Why not?'

'Because it wasn't your fault.'

André's eyes roll and he begins to tear the newspaper.

'When a child discovers his inheritance is a death sentence, he must go on living under it! And he must live *on* it! Won't you even allow me to feel pain? To refuse to help those who suffer is never kind, but to refuse to allow someone to suffer! – Bella, is that why you've come, to bait the bear?'

'I'd like to see Monsieur Brown. If he'll see me.'

'Of course. He's always willing to see you. I think that's why the men at the gate let you in without a challenge. It's a funny thing, Bella, but I would say that you are continually expected.'

André throws the bits of newspaper into the air and the little scraps rain down on us.


And certainly he does seem to be expecting me because my soft knock on the door of his cell is answered instantly. He is dressed in red shirt and green trousers and carries a copy of the autobiography of Kwame Nkrumah of Ghana, it's a book in a loud red cover. On the table beside his bed is a tin of drinking chocolate with a picture of *La Belle Chocolatière* carrying her tray of drinking chocolate, a lovely homely picture of a plump pretty girl in cap and apron who comes bearing her hot, dark, sweet, blissful sleeping draft in just the way my grandmother would carry it to me each night in bed in the days before my father died and my mother fled, before my doll Gloria was kidnapped, before my uncle broke my mug with the intelligent bear being led by the fat man, a picture in which all the beastliness seemed concentrated in the man.

'Still with those funny earphones on, still listening to your music. What is it this time?'

I give him the earphones.

'Who are they – witches?'

Actually it's that three-woman group Vulpine who made it big with 'Trauma', last year sometime – they all wear blonde wigs and black leather, bicycle-chain belts. The usual S & M lookalikes. They're a gothic triad, a middle- to heavyweight metallic lot who fell out of the air somewhere above Ealing last winter, like space debris, and made a bit of a splash when they came down.

'This is the barbarism of the West,' Monsieur Brown says. 'Doesn't this noise make it difficult for you to hear what people are saying?'

'That's the idea. Have you started making yourself hot chocolate in the evenings? I see that *La Belle Chocolatière* keeps you company.'

He smiles. 'No, the tin is empty. But the dear proprietor, for whom my every whim is his command, as he often tells me, seeing that I admired the portrait of the girl with the tray, gave it to me. But I can see you know her. Who is she, please?'

'She lived quite a time ago. She's known as *La Belle Chocolatière* and she was a real person, Anna Baltauf, a girl who worked in a chocolate house in Vienna. Each day the Prince came down to the chocolate house because he loved the liquid of the gods, the fashionable new drink, and he fell in love with the waitress Anna who served him and he carried her off and married her. For a wedding present he had her painted in the same uniform she had worn when she was just a humble chocolate server.'

'She is . . .' he searched for the word, 'just right. Beautiful.'

I look at *La Belle Chocolatière* and I see that what makes for beauty is the yoking together of unlikely things that suddenly become appropriate. To make them seem as if they could never have been otherwise. To create necessity from the elements of chance meetings. The union of the most unlikely is brilliantly vindicated. Sense and necessity are born.

'It's a chocolate fairy-tale!' He claps his hands like a child. 'A marriage born of the sacred bean. If I were in Zanj tomorrow I would have someone painted like the girl on the chocolate tin.'

'Which wife would you use?'

He doesn't answer, just gives me his big, slow smile and sits me down on the little green chaise-longue. 'Now you must tell me why you've come to see me. Is there something I can do for you?'

I look at him then, this solid, dark, slab of a man with his wide, turned-down mouth, the waxy ridges of jaw bone, the corduroy quality of his skin close up, the flapping ears and the heavy jowls. Behind him is a photograph of him in all his glory. No doubt another portrait taken by delayed-action camera. And he is so ridiculous in this picture, in his white uniform blazing with medals like hub-caps, and braid, epaulettes and insignia, a broad snowy belt studded with jewels around his plump middle, the peaked cap crazed with gold; here are the familiar heavy round harsh black glasses, and behold also he carries a thick wand, or a baton, or a club, or maybe a truncheon, of midnight blue flecked with silver stars held up before him in his hand, neat in a white glove. This is the man who killed and ate his enemies. Kept them in the fridge. I should be frightened. I want to be frightened. But I'm not. All I want to know is – did he cook them first? Before he served them up with rice? I take off the diamond pendant Papa gave me and hand it to him.

'Why are you giving me this?'

'Because I think it belongs to you.'

'It doesn't. It's yours.'

'Yes, Papa gave it to me. But you gave it to him, didn't you? All the jewels he gave to me and my mother came from you. The stones of the Wouff.'

'Gifts. It's a custom among my people, the people of the stone.'

'Gifts for favours. Bribes.'

'There's no such word in our language. Besides, these stones for us are not what you regard them as: treasures, valuables. They're the sacred signs of our gods and they represent marks of friendship and affection that we felt, your father and me. Freely passed, freely accepted. Given like promises. Why do you want to return it to me now?'

'After my father died the men from the government in Paris came to see us and they took all the diamonds and

167

jewels away from my mother. All except this one. So I want you to take it because I feel it's yours. It doesn't belong to me. Please, we have enough trouble here. My grandmama is very ill.'

'You believe that this is why I came? You give me the diamond because you hope I'll take it and leave?' Very gently, he takes the pendant and replaces it around my neck.

'Ah, no, my dear. I will go – but not yet. Keep it. One day you might be glad. It's a special stone. Only certain people may wear it.'

'I don't think you understand. My uncle and the Angel and Father Duval – they're powerful men. My uncle's the mayor and Monsieur Cherubini runs him like clockwork. They have a new party, the PNP, which many people in the village belong to, and the police chief too. And they're keen to begin to stir things up.'

'My compliments. You have important tribal relations.'

'There's a big rally on Saturday.'

'And you wish to invite me? Very well, I will come.'

'There will be trouble. You must get out.'

'You worry for me! You are a good girl.'

'Please.'

'My dear young miss, it is you who don't understand. This is not something I can decide myself. Those men out there in the parking lot – why do you think they watch me day and night?'

'For your protection. Because you have enemies.'

'Yes. But also so that I should not slip away and never be seen again. So that I shouldn't run home to my own country where my people cry for me. I hear their voices on the wind – ' He cocks an ear to the silent, velvet night beyond the windows. 'Come home, Redeemer! – they cry – Save us from the tyrant . . . I hear their cry but I cannot reply. Believe me, if the door stood open I would fly tomorrow. Tonight. This second! But the watchers are ready. I do not move without their knowledge. You see how I am in this place. They chose it, took it over for me because of its position. A fine place to imprison a man, an easy place to guard, no access except by the little lake road, the water before, the mountains behind . . .'

'There might be a way.'

'Can you see such a way? They have patrols on the autoroutes outside the village, people standing by to catch me at the airports. Yet if I could get out then they would have trouble stopping me, this I know, because people don't recognise people they are not expecting to see. I would glide by them like a ghost. If, and I say *if*, I could get away ... If I had help, a friend, a guide ...'

'By water,' I hear myself say, 'that's the only route. Late at night, tomorrow night, Friday. That would be the time.'

'But how do I get clear of the village? The lake, yes, possibly, to escape from the Priory. But how to get from the village thereafter?'

'You don't, not immediately. You wait, hide, until Saturday morning when the rally begins and when everyone is fully occupied. The entire village is expected to turn out. No one's allowed to park in the square, so there will be motor cars all over the village, unattended, available. You understand?'

'Such consternation when they find me gone! The scandal!'

'Monsieur Brown, if we do this properly there will be no consternation. No one will know you've left the hotel. You will spend Friday night quietly in some hiding place and then when the rally gets underway, you disappear.'

'Where will you hide a person of my prominence?'

'Leave that to me. Come down to the private beach tomorrow night, at two in the morning exactly. Don't bring much – just what you're standing up in.'

'And a song on my lips, hope in my heart and my people's voices ringing in my ears!'

He takes up a position in front of his picture, the one with the wand and all the medals, and he beams like crazy. I think in his own mind he's already back in Zanj, back in his uniform. Back getting ready to chew up some opponents? Well, I don't ask that question. You appreciate my diffidence, it's not easy suddenly to turn round and ask someone if he eats people. You need to nudge the conversation along. And anyway, what do I say if he says 'yes'? Between the two of us, I think I'd be even more worried if he said 'no'.

'May I paint you?'

'What?' For a moment I don't understand because he has a camera in his hands, one of those cameras which gives you prints immediately and he's examining me through the viewfinder as I sit on his little green settee.

'Something to remember you by. Something to take away with me. The daughter of my friend whom I have travelled so far to see. My rescuer!'

'We haven't done it yet.'

'I have faith. Please, just one picture. Let me arrange you. Excuse me but you seem to have newspaper in your hair. May I remove it? What lovely pins! There!'

So he arranges me. I have a little pillow behind my head and I sit on the edge of the settee with my left knee raised. Very gently he takes the right shoulder of my dress and pulls it down, baring my arm and showing the pendant around my neck. Then he goes over to the fire and lights it. He gives me a mirror to hold and I look at myself, glad to see I am still there, still in one piece. Once the fire is blazing he sets the camera on automatic and crouches in front of the flames with his back to me. He takes several pictures before he's satisfied. He constantly feeds the fire. The room becomes terribly hot, I can feel the flames playing along my legs, I have beads of sweat on my lip and forehead. His red shirt is the colour of the flames crackling in the grate.

Afterwards he shows me the original. A picture torn from a magazine.

'*Les Beaux Jours*'. I like the title,' says Monsieur Brown. 'And I recognise you in the picture.'

'But her hair is redder than mine and I think she's quite a bit shorter. She's wearing a pearl necklace, not a pendant. It isn't me.'

'It is now,' he says.

I am walking through the darkened cloisters of the Priory towards the front door, after leaving him, and the whole place is deathly quiet, the guests asleep, André absent. Then, in the dark of the Prior's garden, through the glass walls, I see him lying by the well, beneath the virgin who examines the foot of the Christ child. Clovis. Out for the count, stoked to the eyeballs. Has he been taking Chinese heroin or durophet or LSD or the whole damn caboodle? I can't say, but he is out cold. He's become again the old shooting, popping, sniffing

Clovis, stoned out of his unstable little mind. Where is the new Clovis of the salmon-pink overall and the perspex boot, full of life and high hopes? My first thought is to wonder how on earth he got past the watchers at the gate who would let no one in. But then I guess Clovis was so high he was flying and simply soared over their heads, Mercury, the messenger of the gods, only he wasn't wearing a funny hat like a golf cap, which Monsieur Brown wore when he played Mercury in the painting. Clovis just wears his hair as green as Ireland and is lying now on the ground as if he's dead, or has given up all hopes of life and happiness.

I go ·upstairs to André's room and knock on the door. It takes him some time to answer and when he does he is wearing a lavender silk dressing-gown and his eyes are red. It looks to me as though he has been weeping. He opens the door just a little but when I tell him about Clovis he comes out immediately, though not before I see behind him the big wide bed, and I mean really wide, and there tucked up like the three bears without Goldilocks are Armand, Tertius and Hyppolyte, sleeping like three little mummified babies stuck in the womb, sleeping soundly and smiling broadly, tucked up in the mammoth bed under a white blanket pulled up to their chins. All this I take in and he sees that I do and he doesn't care. He helps me to carry Clovis inside to the empty television room on the ground floor and we call the doctor.

Twice tonight Dr Valléry has stepped from the tepid depths that are his mistress and he is not best pleased. I think that he's beginning to imagine that I'm a bird of ill-omen.

'Heroin,' says Valléry after a while.

'Come, we will carry him to one of the rooms and put him to bed,' says André. 'I will nurse him.'

'Will he die?' I ask.

'If he's lucky,' says Valléry.

At home I find no sign of my uncle or the Angel. Father Duval sits downstairs reading an old copy of the *Life of Charles Maurras*. When I speak to him his eyes fill with tears.

'A terrible thing, Bella. A sacrilege has been committed! He was wailing like an animal so I went upstairs. I feared he would wake your grandmother. I opened the door of your uncle's study and he ran out into the night. A mad creature. Go and see for yourself.'

My grandmother is fast asleep. The door to my uncle's den is open. His telescope is not pointing at the sky, the moon is out, the light good and the magnification beautiful. What I see through the telescope is the deck of a yacht, on the lake. I know immediately that it's the *Minnie III* because I recognise the couple who move together like oil and shadows on her deck, I swear the image of them is so clear you can see her mouth open and I tell myself I hear her groan of pleasure. Now I know what Clovis saw and why he went back to the needle. My uncle's passion for astronomy has given Clovis a glimpse of uncharted universes.

'Your uncle is searching the village. It is terrible! What did the cannibal want – did you find out?'

'I think I know.'

'Well?'

'He wants me.'

'But Bella, what could such a person want you for?'

Before I can begin to answer, Uncle Claude bursts in, his face mottled with rage, and stands grinding his teeth. 'Please find him!' he cries to Duval. 'Where is he? I must kill him! Nothing else will do.' He sees me and rushes over and drops to his knees. 'Bella, you're his friend. Tell me where he is! I will give you chocolate, money, clothes, anything – find him so I can strangle him soon.'

'Who do you want?'

'The post boy, the cretin, the motorised idiot with the hoof!'

Everyone is mad.

'Clovis?'

'The assassin! The virus! The defective!'

'What did he do?'

'My flasks!' Uncle Claude's voice rises to a howl. 'My formulas. Years and years and years of work. My solutions, my primordial soup! Gone, all gone, forever!'

'He damaged it? Knocked it over?'

He shakes his head. 'He drank it!'

# 10

The dark lake opens its mouth. Lap, lick, a gulp and we're gone! The invisible one beside me, black on black, coalhatch man, king of the caramel islands, snuffles in delight as he slips aboard and we head out.

'Keep as low as possible. I'll do the paddling.'

The watchers sit in their cars and do not sleep, I can tell by the little glow from their dashboards. Ever alert, but looking the wrong way. I didn't expect any more of a break than this and that's why I've laid my plan so carefully, manoeuvring the paddle boat silently alongside the *plage privée*. Number 66, stolen earlier in the day from old Leclerc the boatman and moored around the headland which juts out into the lake. Into the waterproof tanks of number 66 I have introduced several small holes with the help of Uncle Claude's drill, though I have never been one for do-it-yourself. These punctures are sealed with patches of rubber from my bicycle-tyre repair kit. At eleven o'clock I left the house and walked to the little beach where the paddle boat waited under the headland from which the divers plunged into the lake, some never to surface again.

At three minutes before two, on the *plage privée* of the Priory Hotel, he is waiting for me, a bag over his shoulder, his shoes slung around his neck, his trousers rolled, one of Uncle Claude's precious black holes of such gravitational power that not even light can escape from it, and with one hand on the jetty he kneels down, pulls me alongside and then he's aboard.

We must be at least a hundred metres out now, passing the lovely lawns of the restaurant *Les Dents Sacrés*, rounding the jetty where the ferries pick up their passengers for trips upon the lake. The guest, or prisoner, of the Priory Hotel has been sprung, there is no way we can be followed and little chance that our pursuers can organise a boat at this time of night to give chase.

'Wonderful idea — escape by water! I am remembering my flight from the presidential palace, down the river Zan, away from the city of Waq, also by night and by water, in a dug-out. Praise be the memory of your papa! You are his own true daughter.'

'You smelt of fish for days.'

'Yes! And the Wouff do not eat fish.'

'Why's that?'

'Because we believe fish to be the children born of the marriage of rocks and rivers. And the Wouff do not eat the fruit of the gods. Unlike some people I could mention.' He grunts sarcastically. 'Like the Ite, who make it a practice to eat their gods. It's part of their religion. But we are very careful about what we eat.'

'Or whom you eat, I suppose?'

I can feel him stiffen beside me, what was warm velvet turns to coal. Then the moment passes and he is all delight again. I'm wearing black velvet trousers and black silk blouse, and my pendant is tucked inside my blouse lest moonlight strike it. But there is no moon tonight.

Once past the restaurant I steer for the shore and beach the craft. I push him out, drag the boat back into about five feet of water and remove the rubber patches from her floats. She sinks without a whimper, bedding down in the water as her floats fill, with a sideways shuffling motion like a fat woman settling herself on a crowded bus seat.

'Why drown the boat?' He is distressed.

'Because to leave her here on the shore is to allow them to work out where we landed and maybe even guess where we're headed.'

'Sure, sure.' He gives this great big sigh, the kind of sigh, I am beginning to think, in which there is more air than feeling. 'So the little ship must be sacrificed in the cause of freedom. Sad but true.'

174

Almost more unnerving than his attachment to inanimate objects is his willingness to 'sacrifice' for the sake of freedom. Freedom seems to mean letting him do something he wants, and to invite sympathy for the suffering this causes him. What makes a monster are little human touches. This results in the clashing emotions you feel when you hear about the hangman's tennis elbow, or the janitor who complains about his back while having to gather up the victims' teeth or the charlady with asthma who has to swab away the blood ... How many died for freedom? Died, were cooked and dished up, maybe with rice? Am I the wrong person to be taking Monsieur Brown out and about in the world? Maybe it should really have been my Uncle Claude, who takes a fairly unsentimental view of things, up to a point. He's also really big on unexpected titbits, unorthodox cuisine, maybe he and Monsieur Brown would have got along a lot better than they think? Maybe they could have talked menus?

He snaps his fingers. 'Do you think this is how she ended – the other little boat, *La Belle Indifférente*? I'm thinking perhaps that she gave her life to let someone escape. Important personages. Even lovers, perhaps?'

'Who knows? Now you must stick very close behind me because I'm going to take you home through the lanes and backstreets.'

'Home through the lanes and backstreets,' the darkness beside me sighs. 'I'll stick closer to you than your shadow; lead on, kindly light!'

And he follows in my wake, lumbering along, snuffling happily in the night, barefoot, all the way home, through the dark lanes overhung with clematis and bougainvillaea. I realise now why his shoes make such a difference. Something that's niggled at me ever since we went sailing together. Without them he's shorter than I am. Monsieur Brown wears platform heels.

So tell me then, did he who made the lamb make thee? Did he who made little Bella, just fifteen, though somewhat developed for her age, with a weakness for chocolate, questions, rather inferior heavy-metal rock and a soft spot for oppressed tyrants and beleaguered monsters who come her way, also make Monsieur Brown? And cannibals, murderers and corrupters of persons innumerable? I mean, just who is in charge around here? No, on second thoughts, perhaps you'd better not answer that.

'We are in your house?'

'Yes. We must be very, very quiet. Perhaps talk into my ear.'

'We are in your very room?' His whisper lifts a tendril of hair on my forehead.

'Yes.'

'Where can I put my bag?'

I open my cupboard. He catches my eye.

'It's a change of clothes. Are there others in the house?'

'My Uncle Claude. He's asleep above us. My grandmother's in the bedroom below. She's not well. Perhaps even dying. At one stage they thought she would die before the rally, but I know she won't do that. Tomorrow morning at twelve the leader of the *Parti National Populaire* steps onto the platform. Hundreds of people are expected. Everyone will have their eyes on Monsieur Cherubini, the leader, down there.' I open my curtains. 'Look. But stand back from the window.'

'Slogans!' He claps his hands. 'Beautiful!'

'Please – no noise!' I switch on the little reading light above my bed.'

Below us the town square waits for the triumphant entry of the Angel and all his hosts, lit by the lamps left on overnight. Everything is ready: the platform with its flags and bunting; the lectern and the microphone. Rows of empty chairs face us, happy to receive the faithful, the banner is proud of its golden legend: LIBERTY, FAMILY, FATHERLAND. And on every available streetlamp, spike, rooftop and railing the initials of the party, PNP, also in gold, with the Ps slashed with silver crosses, a design said to be inspired by the sacred symbols on Father Duval's Parisian vestments.

'I love a good slogan,' he says. 'I had lots but one of my favourites, I remember, was MOTHERHOOD, MIRTH, MAJESTY. It worked for a time, at least until Tympany tired of it, and we found another. Uncle Dickie's drive for independence made for some dull slogans. He favoured: VIVA MARXIST LENINISM! But of course this meant nothing to the masses, only an aristocrat would think it could. But I can't be cruel. To my Uncle Dickie, God rest his souls, we owe our successful struggle for independence. Oh yes, it was just after the war when the imperial powers still felt that they were in the driving seat for an unforeseeable period. Such was the cloudy optimism of the colonialists they thought they could go on exporting our diamonds and cocoa slaves forever, and so, when my uncle rose up against them, with his New Freedom Party, they were, well, I suppose they were out for coffee. At any rate, they didn't know what was happening.'

'Was it – very violent?'

'Bless you, my dear, of course it was! We weren't making our First Communions, you know. It started off quietly enough with Uncle Dickie going around the slums of Waq rousing the rabble. Again, it takes an aristocrat to really stir things up. Next thing we knew, windows were being broken, cars overturned, government offices set on fire. The fire engines came to put out the fires and we slashed through the hoses with cutlasses.'

'Like pirates!'

'Exactly. The colonial powers really knew things were on the hop when they saw us with our cutlasses slashing the fire-hoses. Until then fire engines were for attacking fires. When they saw the people preferring fires to fire engines, our masters went pale. The leaders of our rebellion carried the fight to the government. We broadened our appeal among the people and changed the name of Uncle Dickie's Freedom Party to the Party of National Salvation. A modest suggestion of mine, I remember. Uncle was wonderful. Everyone was for salvation. He went about the city making speeches, he was smart, Western-educated, a superior public performer, full of rhetoric and beautiful gestures. And a linguist. When he went to speak to the people it was in their own language, in the vernacular. He never used English or French. Under his direction we all began to do it, to speak in our own tongues. Or to yell in the vernacular. Well, the Wouff yelled, the Kanga muttered and the Ite mumbled. Do you get the picture? This terrified the government. I remember a little clerk named Fabrice running out of Government House screaming: "Speak French, you swine, speak French!" Oh happy days, I can tell you. And

177

we had our different youth groups. I was in the Wouff group, of course, and we were called the Action Troopers. The Kanga formed the Action Groupers and we fought the government forces. Sometimes we fought each other.'

'What about the Ite?'

'The Ite made a lot of money by selling flags and badges with the party insignia. Six months later we had a new constitution, and our independence.'

'Was that the constitution you drove a Lagonda through?'

'Yes, later. When it went rotten. The government ministers were soaking up public cash, housing ministers were taking ten per cent on contracts and cheating their own civil servants. I abolished all that. And them. But back in the early hours of our independence my uncle wished us simply to be free. Free black Anglo-Frenchmen he thought us. Western and superior. He wanted us to be free citizens of the Republic of Zanj. Later we saw that it needed a stronger broom than my uncle and I was that broom in the hands of destiny. And so it was that the old order gave way to the new. Not that I spat on the old verities, or deliberately offended cherished beliefs. Nothing could be further from the truth! I did my best to respect the customs of others. With each wife I married I embraced a new religion. And then there was our flag which incorporated the sacred rocks of the Wouff, the Crescent for the Kanga and the Cross for the Ite. And we always sang "Lead Kindly Light" at my political rallies.

'Motherhood, Mirth, Majesty! Ah yes . . .' He comes away from the window muttering sadly, wrapped in memories of former days. 'We didn't have banners as glorious as those of your uncle and his Angel, made from such rich stuffs, but then we are a developing country.'

I draw the curtains and sit him down on my bed. My room is very plain, I have a long pink counterpane on my bed and pictures of Papa, suave and smiling on the wall. Mama is here too, as Miss Torquay 1967. But there is little else except the silver trunk which used to stand underneath my bed and which is now beneath the window. Cupboards to hold my clothes and rack upon rack of cassettes like dark giraffe stripes across the silver chevrons of my wallpaper. I get the feeling he's becoming rather emotional. I hope he's not going to cry. There really is nothing worse than a weeping Redeemer, a tearful monster. I raid the silver trunk and the sight of the chocolate cheers him up.

'We'll have something to eat.'

'You've put bricks under the legs of your bed.'

'Yes. To protect me against the spirits you told me about.'

'Very sensible. Those little devils get everywhere. As you know, I had it done the moment I entered the Priory. I had those useless bumboys belonging to the owner go out and forage bricks for me. You should have heard them complain! You'd think I'd asked them to build the Cathedral of Reims! Is your uncle still sleeping on silver paper?'

'Yes.'

'The world is full of ignorance. And helpless superstition. A man sleeps on silver paper and moves the furniture around. This place is full of savages. Now tell me: is this my hiding place? Very well, where do you want me to sleep?'

I point to the space under my bed.

He laughs.

'With my bed up on bricks there's plenty of room. I've moved my trunk. I usually hide the trunk under my bed – it's for my chocolates. And my money. You'll be safe here, out of sight. But please be very quiet. My uncle has the rather worrying habit of putting his head round the door.'

'You above, me below?'

'You'll be quite invisible. Somebody could walk right up to my bed and never see you.' I lift the pink bedspread that reaches to the floor and show him the second bed that I have made underneath mine.

'A double storey!'

'And in the morning you'll have a fine view from this window. Only don't come too close or you might be spotted. As soon as the people are in the square and the rally's underway, you creep downstairs – and disappear!' I reach over and turn off the light above my bed.

'Pouf! Like magic!' He snaps his fingers in the darkness. Strange the way he hovers between excitement, sadness and amusement. I begin to wonder how far this plan is mine, and not his.

'Yes, I suppose it will seem like magic.'

'Shall I walk, run or fly?'

'Whichever is easiest. I'll give you the keys to Monsieur Cherubini's black Mercedes. You'll find it in the parking area behind the square. You can't miss it, it's the biggest, baddest car around. You don't know him, but he owns this town. He'll be arriving with my uncle in the mayor's car.'

'Bella, you are a genius! Would your papa were living at this hour . . . to see his daughter save me . . . in style!'

'It's my pleasure, I promise you. I can't wait to see the Angel's face when he discovers his car's missing – and you've gone home!'

'Home – ' He takes a shaky breath, gulps and begins to sing, 'Just a Closer Walk with Thee . . .', but he hasn't the heart to go on and lets the hymn trail off like water freezing in a tap.

'Was that another favourite at your rallies?'

He nods, so fiercely the bed sways on its bricks. 'Beloved of the market-stall holders. It was ear-splitting, you know, in their mouths. What time will you go to the rally?'

'My uncle wants me there at ten.'

'What about your sick grandmother? Will they leave her here?'

'No. She won't miss it. Deathly ill though she is, they're going to move her on a litter.'

He is puzzled. 'Explain please – what is this litter?'

'It's like a stretcher. Grandmama is to be carried onto the platform. The doctor has warned her it may kill her. Grandmama disregards the warning of the doctor because it's tainted by socialism. She trusts instead that the aura of the Angel will heal her.'

'To reach down and touch her, to raise her from her sickbed?'

'Something like that. Why do you ask?'

'Because I do the same thing myself. People were forever pushing forward demanding the sacred touch, expecting to be healed. I did what I could. In my day leprosy was slow to yield to the touch. Goitre was more congenial, and river blindness. Do you say – congenial?'

'Easier to cure?'

'Thank you. I am trying all the time to improve my English. I am most humble.'

'Grateful.'

'No, not grateful, I've never been grateful in my life. Grateful feelings are something people give you after you're dead or when they want you to kill someone else . . . In Africa, gratitude is not a virtue, it's a weapon. No, I feel humble to be curing people. All the people pushing and yelling and dying for my sacred touch – "Redeemer! Redeemer!" they would shout. And of course they would be pushed back by one's bodyguard who got real mad when this happened. Or they did worse than pushing. I had a lot of trouble with bodyguards. You don't find them like you used to. Palestinians were the best. If you're ever stuck for bodyguards, always you go for Palestinians. But you can't get them any more. East Germans do OK. Fine equipment, but slow to move without instructions. Not good if you know that you've got a few days coming up with what we call a high-loon factor.'

'What's that?'

'Every ruler has them. Days when the crazy people, who always wanted to kill you anyway, suddenly multiply. Because of the weather maybe. Or the breeding season for loons. Anyway the assassins line up to do it on what we call high-loon factor days. When that happens give me Cubans.'

He calls them 'koobins' in his rough, growly whisper, biting off the name in the middle with a smile like it tastes nice, like it's a sweetmeat that he's fond of. It's amazing what you learn if you listen to a former redeemer. Did you know that, in Africa, it's when the parties of Russians and South Africans slip into town that you know the leader's dying? Birds of ill-omen arriving with a flap of leathery wings, and promises of trade credits. And coffins, I suppose. Shopping for political influence when the shades come down and night falls on the big man in the presidential palace. Then there are the games with names. Take his own Public Audit Committee, who seem rather fierce, especially for a bunch of accountants. Why should people run in terror from the Public Audit Committee?

He's still rather emotional and inclined to raise his voice and I have to keep putting my finger to his lips. When I do he kisses it. Or pretends to nibble it. That's really weird! Bits of me disappear inside him. From my silver trunk I now fetch two plastic cups and the flask of hot chocolate I've prepared and, for safety's sake, I move really close to him and we sit there in the darkness.

'But why do you have to import bodyguards? If the Wouff are such a warlike tribe, why can't they do it?'

'Well you see the Wouff believe their leader is a god-king. So therefore it is impossible to kill him. He does not need protection. Simple. And if perchance you do kill him, by some strange magic, then he will re-arise. So they don't see the point of becoming bodyguards.'

'And what about the Kanga?'

'They're the sort of people who'll shoot you before the loons can reach you.'

'And of course the Ite wouldn't do.'

'If you arm the Ite, they just sell their weapons.'

But it's not all politics, I'm pleased to say, as side by side on my bed we sit sipping hot chocolate from my thermos and extolling the virtues of the bean.

'A Swedish botanist called it the "food of the gods"!' he tells me.

'What was his name?'

'Linnaeus. Do you know which vitamins and minerals the good food contains?'

'Protein, calcium, phosphorous, iron, vitamin A, riboflavin.'

And he takes up the litany: ' . . . theobromine, sodium, starch, potassium, thiamine and caffeine.'

'To the botanist Linnaeus!'

And we bump our plastic cups together. I suppose it's the joy of knowledge that one hears about, the love of a subject that keeps you warm as it goes down. It's especially helpful to have a friend who shares a secret, to sit in a room late at night, in the darkness, with your enemies all around, knowing that nobody else realises what's going on is very exciting. Anyway, we all have to eat. Starve a saint, feed a tyrant. Believe me, it works. How often do you see a fat saint, or a thin tyrant? I kiss his cheek. I don't know why, except that it tastes good.

'A dinner of chocolate in the darkness.'

'Isn't there something wonderful about the way the word itself melts in the mouth and slips down the throat? What was its name among the Aztec Indians?'

'Xocolatl.'

'Very musical, Bella. And knowledgeable. I'm never too proud to learn. Tell me more.'

'And the Mexican Indians called it Cacuatl.'

We sit on in the darkness repeating to ourselves the Aztec and Mexican words for chocolate – Xocolatl and Cacuatl.

'A pretty reasonable slave could be bought among the Aztecs for a hundred cocoa beans.'

I hear him snort. 'Well, the Ite never got such good prices when they sold us off to the Quakers.'

I apologise for the tacky thermos and plastic cups.

'Nonsense. I would not enjoy it more if we were supping from golden beakers with tortoiseshell spoons.'

I know what he's talking about. That's how Montezuma took his chocolate when Cortés and his invading armies destroyed his country. Montezuma thought they came from heaven. That's the trouble with heavenly apparitions. You never know if they're after your chocolate or your blood.

'I often wonder what would have happened if Montezuma hadn't listened to Cortés, but simply killed him. That might have made a difference.'

In the darkness beside me I can feel him shake his head so vigorously the bed sways on its bricks. 'It wouldn't have changed things. Cortés was not a man, he was just a name for the future. If not him then someone else would have done it. Behind him, coming next, walks the big disaster. Look at the fellows in New Zealand who killed Captain Cooke. Well done, you might say. But behind Cooke came the riff-raff of the Empire with their sheep and their rugby balls. One dead Cooke does not stop time. By the way, did I tell you what the Quakers, who made their chocolate from the sweat of our slaves, who were marched to the coast by the Ite, called the benefits of this delicious substance?'

'No.'

'They called it flesh-forming. Ha! What does that make you think of – flesh-forming?'

I don't know what it makes me think of, or if I do, I don't, if you grasp my meaning. It seems about time to haul out of my silver trunk further supplies of chocolate, a selection of *Callebaut Dessert*, *Côte d'Or 'Extra Dry'* and the very last of my *Suchard Velma*. And it goes down a real treat, I can tell you, if you need telling. And when we're licking the last crumbs from our fingers he speaks to me in his low, gravelly, growly voice, and takes my hand and holds it just like he did when we walked around the gallery and he cured my crying sickness, only this time he holds it and holds it like he's never going to let it go, and he says:

'You're a good girl, Bella, just as your father promised you would be good.'

And the thing is, I don't care. He can sit and hold my hand in the dark for as long as he likes. And the feeling I get is a bit like swimming in black milk – and remember, this is a man who has quite probably eaten hands like mine and *still* I don't care! But then as if to show he means me no harm he lets me lick the last of the crumbs of chocolate from his beautiful fingers. A most lickable fellow! And perhaps for the first time in months I don't feel hungry and I don't mind even if he strokes my arm, or touches my cheek very gently with those amazing fingers. Just what Papa promised I would be good for I can't imagine. And sitting here in the dark I don't have to close my eyes to pretend he's here or that he's not here. I can open my eyes as wide as saucers and still believe he's not here, if that's what I want. But if I do want it, then he is. And he'll speak to me if I want him to. I have only to speak to him:

'I don't think you should do that.'

'What am I doing, my dear Bella?'

'Feeling like that.'

'Like this?'

'Yes.'

'But what is this tightness into which you're packed, my dear? I don't seem to be able to find my way.'

'That's because the buttons are around the back.'

'Ah yes! There – that's better.'

'Oh, much.'

The tiny luminous claw print on my wrist shows the time is after three. And he is almost asleep now beneath me in his curtained alcove, an especially comfortable place and completely private. It's odd how things work out. From him I have got back all the things I missed so much – my Bapuna

184

mask that hung on my wall in my bedroom in the old days, before the plastic shoehorn stepped in and took it all away; my doll Gloria whom Uncle Claude lost, or stole, or killed – and the bear who visited me when Grand-mère brought my hot chocolate every evening, the sad, wise, human bear. All come back to me now. Gifts travel in threes, like wise men. Then just before I sleep I remember something.

'What happened to Fabrice? The clerk who ran out screaming at you to speak French, during your rebellion.'

The answer comes slowly and drowsily. 'We hung him from a baobab tree.'

I suppose he must feel me tense above him because he adds quickly: 'But someone put a recording of Racine on an old wind-up gramophone and sent him to paradise with the language he loved singing in his ears.'

I feel rather strange. Warm but strange. The sound of his breathing under my bed is very soothing. I love it, I love –

# 11

A perfect, dreamless night; no aminos chased me, no figment howled in the abyss, blood blushing beneath the divine finger-nails as Uncle's cleated boots clopped closer; no Feigenbaum's Constants hunted with teeth of digital numerals and liquid crystal eyes. Nothing but peace. I have been awake since dawn when the first light crept into my room and shook me awake like a friend, or a sentry, or a jailer, because the day was waiting to begin.

Under me. I think I can hear him under me, though his breath is faint. It lifts the corner of the bedcovers that hang to the floor. I could look, but I don't because I know he's sleeping safely, soundly. See the covers shiver. Look!

But of course you see. Yours is almost certainly the voice that says softly in my brain, 'Bella, let sleeping monsters lie . . .'

Around seven, before the house begins to stir, I slip from my bed and dress very quietly, like a ghost, and I don't think I disturb him because the counterpane continues to shiver in time to the long slow breathing of my friend, my sleeping beast, my bear in his cave. Really, if you didn't know, you could be forgiven for thinking there is nobody here.

'Well, well – up, dressed and waiting? Good, good. But why out here in the passage? Come, breakfast! We descend at ten. Father Duval and I will carry Maman on the litter. It's madness, but she insists. Loyal to the end. The square is filling already!'

Yes, you've guessed, it's Uncle Claude, dressed in a dark blue suit, wearing his mayoral sash, pale and freshly shaved, his eyes clouded with pain and anger, smelling muskily of some appalling potion he slaps on after his shave. Since the loss of his soup and his failure to kill Clovis, he has gone into a kind of irritable trance.

*Plus*, there seems to have been trouble with the forces – the four forces of the GUT – or Grand Unification Theory which, if we truly believe in them, will one day lead us to TOE – the Theory of Everything.

The trouble is there are *not* four.

'Maybe five – or even six!' cries Uncle Claude, 'according to the very latest theory! Damn! Damn!'

I take this as a good sign. It seems people have been doing measurements, dropping weights over the sides of cliffs or something and the measurements – don't ask me which measurements – will not add up. There are discrepancies! Thank God for those discrepancies! If I were you I'd get lost among them.

'Tried to draw a bead on him, sir! But the doggone critter disappeared into those darn discrepancies.'

I am wearing a halter-top in cream silk with buttons up the front, a beige skirt in cotton and rayon mixture, and very high red sandals. I've put my hair up and this can be tricky and took all my small skills (I do miss Catherine the Great!). Anyway, for what it's worth, I've put it up, working on it slightly damp, twisting it into a pretty chignon, low on the neck, to create what Catherine would call 'a small silhouette', ruffling the sides with my fingers to soften the look and then planted the whole creation full of a garden of pretty pins, brass daisies and silver scarabs, gold bees with glass eyes. No make-up this time, I don't want complaints, just enough powder to keep the shine away.

I eat my last pieces of chocolate for breakfast. Well, I eat *almost* all of my last pieces of chocolate for breakfast. I leave a little bit for him, debating which he should get. Does he get the *Marks & Spencers Swiss Plain* or the *Lindt Excellence*? He will be hungry when he wakes and who can say when he will eat again after he leaves the house? In the end I give him the *Lindt*, it seems only right and I swallow the Swiss fake myself. A rather pretty girl with pale red hair and grey eyes waves goodbye from the mirror.

\*

The village square is crowded by mid-morning. Despite the absence of Clovis, leader of the motorised battalion of communication workers in the Angelic divisions for a new France, Pesché has nonetheless organised things perfectly. A ruddy-faced man with tiny regular teeth that gleam unexpectedly when he lifts his heavy lips in a slow, wavelike motion to shout orders to his men, a modest soul, who tells Father Duval:

'God willing, Father, we'll pack them together in the square like strands of rope, they will twine in a human chain to welcome Monsieur Cherubini,' and he laces his fingers together to illustrate how closely and beautifully people will be packed.

'Not the deity. Science is responsible for this organisation, I think,' Father Duval replies. 'Forward planning, Chief. It's won more battles than masses in the front lines, believe me.'

'But surely Father would agree that some divine vision is useful, even in a policeman?' The Chief of Police is an agnostic but he is also very stubborn.

'The poor see visions when they don't have enough to eat. The drinker sees visions in the bottom of his glass. The voter sees visions when he swallows the cheap remedies supplied by the other parties which promise him that his living standards will improve, that his old age is secure, his birthright as a free Frenchman is safe and the uncontrolled admission of foreigners to our country won't infect and weaken the national identity of which you and I are so proud. So much for visions! That is why the *Parti National Populaire* believes in clarity, reason, persuasion, logic and truth. French qualities.'

'French exports maybe,' says the Chief of Police drily. He is known for his rueful wit.

'I promise you that under the direction of Monsieur Cherubini such virtues will once again become home industries providing for local consumption. You may be assured of that, Chief.'

Father Duval is dressed today in a dove-grey tracksuit and running shoes and a salmon-pink cap, a party cap with the letters PNP embroidered upon the peak, one of the many souvenirs on offer today from a stall near the pizzeria presided over by the De La Salle sisters with the help of a number of the Gramus children. There are also badges, scarves, pens, books, pictures, balloons, flags, bunting, many of them carrying pictures of the leader. Top of the market is a watch with the Angel's craggy face sporting a pair of hands, like weird whiskers.

Seating in the square is being arranged on the exclusion/participation principle: everyone may participate but only after certain people are excluded. First in, and allowed to take up the majority of seats around the platform, are the party supporters who have been arriving by bus and car since dawn. Here now come the party chairmen, accompanied by their wives, burly men in their best suits, faces scrubbed and their hair showing clearly the teeth marks of their combs. Their wives puff along importantly beside them in linen costumes and cotton frocks. Many of the crowd are young men in jeans and leather jackets; there are plumbers, waiters, white working-class boys with their girlfriends, or their mothers, sisters, aunts and children. Some have their heads shaved or dyed red and blue, others wear the party initials emblazoned on their skulls like cattle brands. The single heartshaped drop-earring, out of which the face of Monsieur Cherubini beams happily, is especially popular. There are lots of children. Many buy picture-postcards from the market stalls, and the children love their free balloons with frosted messages that look like they've been written in toothpaste: *'Give them hell, patron!'* and *'We love the Angel!'*

Now here come groups of the disabled drawn from the hospital and homes in the area, the blind, the halt, the lame, the mentally defective and the terminally ill from hospital and hospice, accompanied by drips and nurses. They are always invited to his rallies, living proof, says Monsieur Cherubini, that all French people are God's children and we owe a debt to our old and our ill, that despite their disabilities they are our brother citizens, and that there is strength and beauty to be attained through disability.'Our people are at home here,' says Monsieur Cherubini, 'but *only* our people are at home here.' When most of the seats are taken, the 'public' are admitted. In fact, they are the opposition, a small crowd of perhaps sixty or seventy socialists and communists, enemies of the Angel, here to barrack and scoff but seated so far back that their cries will barely carry to the platform. Behind

*189*

them the Chief of Police lines up his men. It is known as the sandwich tactic.

'Tell me, what happened to the mad boy? The one you saved?' Pesché asks Father Duval. 'The one with the glass boot and the funny hair? He did a good day's work for me, despite having so much powder in his veins. I think sometimes he was so high that he thought he'd come down from outer space. Some sort of celestial being who'd returned to earth.'

'He took something which did not agree with him,' says Father Duval.

'Heroin?'

'Soup,' says the priest.

'It couldn't have been bouillabaisse.'

Everything has been most carefully timed. At ten o'clock my grandmother is to be carried through the crowd on a litter by Uncle Claude and Father Duval. She is semi-conscious, her breath coming in harsh, choked little patterns, her eyes flickering weakly, yet she is enough herself still to issue instructions.

'This is yours, child. Yours to keep and remember. A small token of my love. Keep it always by you as I've done.'

It is the picture of my grandfather which always stands by her bed. Other gifts are handed out and Uncle Claude receives the photograph of Marshal Pétain. Doubtless the statue of Joan of Arc is destined for the Angel. My grandmother is divesting herself of her treasures. It's plain that she expects to die but she isn't sad or frightened, rather she is seized with a fierce joy so wonderful and immense that it makes her half hunch up on the litter as it is carried through the crowd, her hands are wings that beat against her chest like a child overcome by excitement, a child who can hardly wait for some huge event to come. And it isn't either that my grandmother is eager to meet her maker, or that her heart is set on heavenly things, far from it, for Grandmama is frantic with joy and anticipation simply and solely because she is going to lie by the side of her beloved. At last! And if it takes dying to do something so wonderful, then die she will, with an emotion very like pleasure.

And no one, not even her son, is going to interpose good sense or reason between her and her desire. Though he tries in a feeble fashion:

'You shouldn't stir. We love you, Maman. The *patron* knows you wish to come and he will take the wish for the deed. But please don't go out. Please remember what the doctor said! You must not move!'

In reply she merely stretches out her hand towards the podium, towards the platform that awaits the arrival of the Angel, towards the microphone and the row of chairs and in that gesture includes her dream of paradise.

Because he can't make any headway with her – yes, you guessed it – he picks on me. He begins raging on about the current state of the controversy as to whether the universe is going to expand indefinitely as it has done since the big bang when it blew up from something as infinitesimally small as a proton, to a grapefruit, to a galaxy, to everything we know now, all in a billionth trillionth of a second. Or will the balloon burst and it all collapse again one day into the big crunch?

'It's a question of matter. It's question of critical density. If there's enough matter then there'll be enough gravitation to pull it all together again. We think today that there is enough, but we can't find it.'

'Where is it? This missing matter?'

'Hidden. Maybe it's there in the form of neutrinos. We've been counting neutrinos since the explosion within the Large Magellanic Cloud of Supernova 1987A. We think the missing mass may be found in the neutrinos. If, that is, neutrinos have any mass. We know they're almost massless. But are they completely massless? They're so tiny, Bella, that even as you stand here trillions of them stream through your body, through the earth and out the other side like machine gun bullets through smoke.'

'But why can't we find this missing matter?'

'We will,' he says grimly. 'But just at the moment we can't find it because it's invisible, it's cold dark matter hidden somewhere out there – ' he jerks a finger heavenward. 'Don't you worry about it, though, we'll track it down one day. And when we do we'll know the answer to one of the few remaining mysteries about the universe.'

191

This is said with a glare which suggests that I might have seen the missing matter recently, and if I have I should be sure to pass on his warning.

'It can run, but it can't hide.'

Luckily, this is when Father Duval drags him away because Grandmama is to be lifted onto the litter and carried to the platform, now ready to receive the Angel, who is reported to be drawing near. No expense has been spared to make the litter as rich and impressive as possible. It has gold coverings and a satin cushion with tassles upon which her head is propped and where, with her white face and her eyes flickering, she looks no more than she is, an elegant, dying lady, but most regal, and goodness how the people cheer as she is borne to the platform. Even Granny Gramus, who is in fact a good deal older than my grandmother and might have been expected to feel just a twinge of jealousy at the attention being paid to someone so many years her junior, can scarce forbear to cackle and raise a thumb in the air as the litter goes by and the sunlight striking the white hairs on her pointy chin makes her look more witchlike than ever, notwithstanding her good cheer. And Old Laveur, the drycleaner, is overcome and cries openly. Even Brest the butcher, who does not, as they say, compete with the fountains of Versailles in his flow of water, looks distinctly moist-eyed. Uncle leads the way and Father Duval follows, carrying her easily on their shoulders because she weighs so little. The crowd falls back and some, thinking perhaps that they are watching the passage of a saint, fall on one knee, others cross themselves. I bring up the rear, walking some way behind so that the full focus of attention falls on my grandmother. I carry the photograph of my grandfather.

Halfway up the aisle André steps from the crowd and puts his hand on my arm. 'Bella, I'm very worried about Clovis. Have you seen him? He left his room and somehow got hold of his motorbike. The old one. The one they gave him at the Post Office. Then he tried to persuade the Dutch girl to come with him but she laughed. When he insisted and tried to carry her away, the young accountant hit him.'

'The young accountant?'

'You know him. Over there. Dark hair, standing very close to the Dutch girl. Name's Dupont.'

I look. There must be some mistake because the boy André points out to me is the escapee from the Foreign Legion, randy Raoul of the easy erection and the greasy bathing trunks.

'What did you call him?'

'Dupont,' says André. 'He's an accountant from Grenoble. Bella, we must do something. Clovis has gone away and I fear for him. The boy is shattered.'

I also worry about Clovis, of course, but this is not the time or the place to begin to discover again that many universes run parallel to the one in which I am most at home, because I invented it, and because I do not wish to live in worlds where accountants from Grenoble masquerade as escapees from the Foreign Legion. I spot other guests from the Priory Hotel in the crowd, all of them, no doubt, as unreliable as the accountant. There is the German family, Gudrun and Wolf, and the two lizards from Monte Carlo, Alphonse and Edith, and the very last thing I want right now, thank you very much, is for André to wave his wand and to turn all my princes into frogs.

'I can't stay.'

'You mean you won't. You hate me! Your friend! Well, you'll see today what lies in store for your friend. Don't worry, I'm not staying for this meeting, I don't need to hear it with my own ears. They plan to pillory me, Bella. From the platform today they'll set this mob on me. Watch! The Angel will weave his spell and move with all the cunning of a beautiful snake to sting and poison the minds of these people. He wants it, you know. My hotel. I think I could take their hatred, and I think I could even take their fear, I could pray for the strength to stand up to their attacks on my beautiful things, my boys and my Priory. But what I can't stand is to be hated by you for something I didn't do. I'm not blaming you. It's the penalty. I prayed for mortification and for suffering. Remember we talked about it? And look now what's happened: my prayer's answered!' He gives a ghastly smile. 'And you'll see what you want. You'll see the Beast of the Bourse destroyed. There's only a little more time to wait. It's funny, Bella, I haven't it in me to pray that this cup be taken from me. Yet I'm frightened.'

'You're hurting my arm, please let me go.'

'I see you're carrying a photograph of your grandfather.'
He takes his hand from my arm, defeated. And then he says,
angrily, bitterly: 'Well, things are difficult, things are complex.
There are many views of everything. And never less than two.
Here – this is another view.'

And from his pocket he takes out an old, faded black-
and-white photograph and pushes it violently into my hand,
crushing it. I have to smooth it out on the glass front of my
grandfather's picture before I can make out what it is. It's a
picture of a young man, in fact there are several young men,
but this young man is right in the foreground. He's tied to a
stake, in a village square. The heads of all these young men
are shaven and in the distance I can see a row of soldiers who
stand with rifles. The riflemen are wearing tin hats and they
seem to be waiting for something.

'This was taken minutes before he was shot. You see
the firing squad is making ready. It happened in a village
not far from here, after a trial before a court drawn from
the Resistance. Several hundred were shot. Executions began
at dawn and went on until after eleven. Many were young
men. All were guilty of murdering their own countrymen and
collaborating with the Germans.'

Though he is here without his cap, the prisoner at the
stake is the same soldier who watched over my grandmother's
sleep from the heart of her holy trinity on the bedside table.
My grandfather is very young. The light strikes his face from
the right, illuminating the clean, handsome profile. He looks
up, over the heads of the firing party, up to the wall on his
right; it is the corner of a house and on the wall of the house
is the advertisement for the chocolate my grandmother always
spoke of when she recalled his last moments on earth. *Chocolat
Cémoi . . . Un Régal Chocolat Cémoi.*

'Well, you have it now. I'm sorry, Bella, but I wasn't
going to my grave letting you think the most terrible of
all thoughts: the thought of one who believes she knows
the truth about another – who believes that the truth she
knows is pure. I couldn't bear it that my friend, perhaps my
only friend, should remember me with horror. I'm a soul in
torment, Bella. You wouldn't deny me water?'

'I thought he died for his country? For the Resistance?'

'Your grandfather was among the fascist Militia. Do you understand what that means? He worked for the Germans, he was a volunteer, a follower of Pétain and of the Vichy clique. They were terribly fierce, the Militia, and they were often used by the Germans for tracking down dissidents in the mountains. It is said that this lot died bravely shouting before they were shot, "Long live Christ the King!" and "Long live the Marshal! Long live France!"'

'I thought he died fighting the enemy.'

'For a good many in these parts the Resistance was the enemy.'

His face is chalk-white. He puts his fist in his mouth and when he takes it out I see blood on his knuckles – he has bitten down to the bone. I can think of nothing to say. It is sometimes kinder to shoot people. Because I must do something I lean forward and kiss him on his broad pink forehead. That's all. There isn't time for more.

Behind me I hear unmistakable hints of the Angel's approach. The crowds are noisy with the socialists, who see him first, shrieking, 'Down with the new fascists! Down with the Angel of Hate!' I must hurry if I'm to make it to the platform before he catches up with me. Now his supporters see him and set up a counter-clamour, '*Patron! Patron! Patron!*' They stamp their feet until the square trembles.

I reach the platform unnoticed by anyone but Uncle Claude who frowns gloomily at me and motions at me to pull my dress down over my knees when I sit. That's always the trouble with these skimpy mixtures, they will ride up, but with my hands full, adjustments for the sake of modesty are awkward to make.

And now here he is, the Angel, in a blue suit and – oh my! – but he's been on a diet, he's so much leaner, craggier and his eyes show like bluebells on a river bank, rich and strong and – and what the hell is this? – I don't believe it! He has with him none other than Domitian, the lead singer, or should I say the big yeller, with a group called Record Damages, which is, I have to say, a piss-poor little sewing circle masquerading as a rock group and imagining it has some weight, whereas in fact it wouldn't even register on the post office scale. But it's Domitian all right, in mufti, in deep disguise. Gone are the butcher's hooks through the earlobes that used to swing with a low jingle, vanished are the jodhpurs with the swastika spurs, gone too is the shrunken-head necklace with all the little noses buried in his chest hair. He is in a suit even bluer than the Angel's and a pink tie with dolphins leaping from a salmon sea. And this, can you believe, is the mighty presence from Paris whom Uncle boasted about. *Of course!* Now I know what he's up to on the platform. Domitian has one platinum disc, the kind of thing that stinks of the studio and was done so nakedly for the cash that you can almost smell the producer's cigar wafting across the lyrics. Oh, I know, it's got a pretty enough little circular riff arrangement, that's if you like being reminded of the lesser-known rhythms of, say, 'Maid Of The Mountains'. But it's the lyrics that made Domitian rich and made the *Parti National Populaire* embrace him as their troubadour, a style which *Les Temps*, with the wry understatement affected by those who are intelligent enough to know that they're powerless, without being brave enough to do anything about it, described as '. . . not a form of versification likely to appeal to the cous-cous voter . . .'

No indeed.

*'They say that Africa's the mother of man/So I say this to the Africa lover/We're gonna pack your bags real soon/And boot you home to mother . . .'*

Isn't it a reflection on our times that a group of the heavily unwashed, who once set out to be the end of civilisation as we know it, spaced-out rockheads, who believe that talent amounts to showing the audience your dental fillings, are now turning up on platforms like this, disguised as friends of the dolphins and displaying a degree of grace you would normally associate with an electric cattle prod?

But it's the time of platform kisses: Father Duval kisses the Angel, the Angel kisses Grandmama, who closes her eyes and smiles seraphically from her satin pillows and the crowd erupts again into whistles and applause and cries of *'Vive Monsieur Cherubini!'* and since they do not know who the aged lady is, perhaps some suppose that they are going to witness a miracle cure, for nothing is beyond the power of the Angel. Uncle Claude does not know who Domitian is and so does not try to kiss him. Domitian kisses me because I am under forty-five and female and therefore must be a fan *and* he calls me dear child, and the nasty little virus is himself not more than twenty! But fame ages people, I notice . . . Domitian does not kiss Grandmama because even he can see she is very ill and illness is the closest you come in Domitian's world to bad taste.

Uncle Claude steps to the mike and announces that Father Duval will open the meeting with prayers. More cheers from the Party faithful and far away, at the back of the square, cries of anger from the hecklers but they are faint and distant like mewing gulls helpless against a booming surf. Father Duval bounds to the mike. He has spent some time warming up the crowd and they love him. The little Father of the micro-phone:

'Friends, patriots, Frenchmen and women, I won't detain you long because you wouldn't forgive me, nor I myself were I to do so. I'm not here on my own behalf, but on behalf of another whose very laces I am not fit to tie,' and he waves his hand at the Angel who responds genially by lifting the leg of one trouser a little to reveal that he is wearing black moccasins without laces. The crowd love it. They always appreciate this side of him, the down-to-earth country humour.

'But I'm here to pledge myself to our Party, the *Parti National Populaire*. With it we will march into the future, free, proud, purposeful. Free because it is French, proud because it is free, purposeful because at its head there marches one who leads, like the Maid of Orleans once led the fighting men of France against the enemy, our dear, no our *beloved, patron*! And another thing, remember that the PNP is growing, it is strong and it grows stronger across the country. We grow like the rejuvenation of cells in a person recuperating from some illness who is in the hands of a great expert. The miracle of our cure comes from our faith, faith in national identity, or in other words, in ourselves. A last word: we are free because we revere that most precious institution, the family. Ours, yours and the greater family of France. For us the family is holy. It might be said that our mother is France and our father is our beloved *patron*. As a result our demands are natural and
197

modest. All we ask is to be allowed to remain French. Therein lies our freedom. I will remind you of what the Africans said during their struggle for independence – they said: "Africa for the Africans". We say the same. France for the French! But to achieve this, firm leadership is essential. Let me quote that considerable patriot of the 1920s, Pierre Taittinger: "France wants a fist!"

'And this brings me to my prayer – if I have a prayer – it is this: let us press forward with the terrible modesty of our proposals, let us allow nothing to stand in our way. I, for my sins, am the parish priest of the little village of La Frisette to which we welcome you today. Some of you know that. That is to say that I am "a father". Well, that may be so. But let me tell you that in the presence of our *patron*, I feel like not a father but a child. This is what I meant by my earlier, perhaps clumsy allusion. If it was clumsy, forgive me! And I want to tell you further that my congregation has been collecting money together for our little church. For the roof, you see. For cleaning the gravestones. For stopping the draughts that howl down the aisles. Yet we have decided by popular decision to present our savings to the PNP. And why? you ask. Because we see the Party is the guarantor of our future. We give to it and we know our gift will be redoubled in the giving. Remember this when you leave here today. Facilities have been made available to receive your gifts. Forgive me for having trespassed on your time. Here is the man you have really come to meet, our *patron*, Monsieur Cherubini! May God bless him!'

I see that not only has the money from the church gone to the PNP but Father Duval has lined up various collectors with church plates.

But it's still not time for the Angel to approach the mike because now my grandmother interrupts. That is to say, she lifts her hand as a child might in a classroom. She wants attention and I get up but she won't let me come near her, shaking her head and struggling to lift herself off the pillows. She is far too weak and falls back. By this time the crowds are pointing and whispering. The Angel calls to Father Duval to carry the microphone across to Grandmama. Something rather odd is happening. I can see her struggling with the ring on her finger. Father Duval bends closer to her with the mike. Now, suddenly, we can all hear her voice, echoing around the square. It's very, very ragged:

'Dear Monsieur Cherubini, *patron*, dear Angel. Let me present you with something worth more than life to me: my wedding ring. It has not left my hand since the day I married my dearest husband. He died, as you know, for France, the name of Christ on his lips. Take it! Not because it is worth much, but because it is all I have.'

Monsieur Cherubini is overcome, he raises wet eyes to heaven and then he crosses to her and raises her hand to his lips, then he lifts the ring to the sun. The crowd erupt again. Men and women begin removing their wedding rings and depositing them on the collection plates now passing swiftly along the rows. Grandmama sinks back onto her pillow, exhausted, and there is on her face such a look of happy triumph that I can feel nothing for her but admiration. To have so forced through her view of the world, to have blasted through the brute facts of the matter which suggested that everything she stood for, loved and believed in, was false, foul, fraudulent, and then to come out on the other side of the horrible comedy of her life, smiling and happy, is a great and terrible achievement.

'Dear Madame Dresseur, I thank you from the bottom of my heart, not only for the generosity of your gift, but for its sacred appropriateness. This gold ring is a symbol for all we desire and hold dear. This shining band signifies the marriage of true minds, the reverence for the family which is the fruit of marriage, your family and mine, the little family of the PNP and beyond that the family of France! The funds raised here today, of which this ring is a precious example, go to fight for the preservation of that sacred family and the freedom it cherishes. The Chaplain of the Holy Church of the Immaculate Conception, my good friend Father Duval, has mentioned the great patriot Pierre Taittinger. Well, the example is well chosen because I can recall something else that Taittinger said, and which is apposite to our struggle for freedom. "France," he declared, "requires a leader who can make himself obeyed, who can exert his will, a leader with French character, with, yes, a degree of stubbornness and even roughness, and above all the will to say no!"'

Then he lifts into the air the fist that France demands. The people in the square make similar fists and wave them enthusiastically. But this isn't all. Far from it. For out of his chunky fist, growing like a strange flower, there appears a single finger glinting with gold.

'And to remind myself yet again of my sacred mission, here renewed today, I will wear this ring throughout the meeting, a bond between myself and a good strong woman who has given herself for her country.'

By turning my head slightly to the right I can see behind me the shutters of my bedroom. In the shadows, my Redeemer stands looking down on the square.

'Let me, ladies and gentlemen, dispose of this idea that Monsieur Cherubini, of popular report, of vilification in the newspapers, is a xenophobe, a racist, an anti-semite. Ask yourself: how a man with a name like mine could be against foreigners?'

Again the obedient laughter.

'Why do our opponents always concentrate on the negative? Why don't they believe us when we say that the PNP is open to all people of all colours and creeds, with one proviso: that they are first and foremost French. We are not against others, we are for our own!'

Now this is where my plan begins to go badly wrong. Remember, I most clearly told Monsieur Brown that the moment he saw the people in the square intoxicated by the Angel's oratory he was to slip quietly from my room, find the Angel's car and disappear. He has the keys, he has my instructions. But this is not what happens, for the window behind us now discloses shadowily, obscurely, but visibly, a man who has taken up his position very carefully so that the square of my window surrounds him like a frame, and he does not move.

'It is said by some that we are the party of fascists. Nothing could be further from the truth. Modesty and reason are our twin virtues. Fairness and negotiation characterise our dealings. We wish to attune ourselves to the future, we wish to be ready for what is to come as surely as night follows day. As to our business in the village of La Frisette, our aims once again are modest, even domestic. We wish merely to set up a home here. A headquarters. We have been negotiating for some time for a suitable property by the lakeside. This property is one which suits us perfectly. It dates back to the seventeenth century and we would preserve it in all its beauty. This, too, is the aim of the present owner. Unfortunately, he is unable either to restore the building completely or to maintain it in a style to which this daughter of the Church is accustomed. I am speaking of course of our own very beautiful Priory by the lake, the former house of the Carthusians, the hotel of Monsieur André.'

The sunlight plays on the window frame. I estimate he has only to take one step forward and everyone will see him.

'I am sorry to have to tell you that an infection, a bacillus, a deadly germ has entered the house of the Carthusians. It is an illness which our Party is resolved to prevent. Just as the human body has an immune system for repelling disease, so it could be argued that the State must have its own built-in immune system lest contagion take it over. Sadly, this beautiful daughter of the Church is threatened today. A virusical presence inhabits her. A bacillus – '

'A lot of bumboys, you mean!'

That interjection comes from the butcher Brest at the back of the tenth row and draws an appreciative round of applause and some laughter.

The Angel holds up his hands for silence. Grandmama's ring gleams on his finger. His mood is sombre. The sunshine makes his hair silvery. My grandmother's eyes are closed. I fear she may have died. But I can't move. She would never forgive me if I interrupted the Angel with news of her death.

'Consider the nature of the problem,' the Angel shows his fine large teeth. 'It's one of hygiene. Of taking preventative measures against a disease for which, as yet, no cure has been found. Imagine an infection which does not attack any particular part of the organism. Instead it destroys the very defences which are necessary to preserve life within the body. A hidden invasion vehicle. It attacks the immune system and thereby renders it helpless. We all know of just such a disease. I do not have to tell you where it comes from – '

'Africa! Africa!' people shout from the crowd.

'It's time to ask whether any good ever came out of Africa. It's too much to expect the Government to protect its own. Instead it permits the pollution of our towns and cities by foreign entities. Among the more recent of its guests is a certain gentleman, one of that tribe of dictators in which Africa is so fruitful, to whom our Government extended hospitality some years ago and who went to earth in a comfortable hole in the South of France. Few of you will have heard of him. He is known as the Beast of Zanj. Others called him the "Cannibal King". Among his victims he was called by a title as blasphemous as it is sad: "the Redeemer"! Never mind the names. They're all disgusting! I say that this disease shall have no free passage in our country. No political asylum for monsters. A virus has no civil rights. You will no doubt have heard of strange goings-on at the Priory Hotel – '

' – You mean it's a bordello for boys!' This comes from Old Laveur, not to be outdone by the outburst from the butcher Brest.

The Angel looks cross, he doesn't like being interrupted. 'To the already prevalent malaise which afflicts the Priory Hotel, that is its owner and its guests – add another! We have become aware lately of the very peculiar conditions under which certain people have been living there. Of the heavy guard on the gate. Of the refusal by the authorities to allow anyone to enter. What is going on? I'll tell you, a monster is in quarantine. Has the owner infected the guest – or the guest the owner? Do we want in our village a creature who, it is said, poked out the eyes of schoolchildren? Murdered his opponents and then drank their blood and ate their flesh? Or do we send a message to the powers in Paris? Do we tell them that this is our place and we reserve the right to defend it, protect it and sanitise it!'

The crowd shriek with happiness.

It is too late to stop him. My face is burning, my hands icy, 'Go back! go back!' I can hear myself – perhaps the others can too. The sun strikes the top of the window and there Monsieur Brown stands, illuminated. The speakers on the platform cannot see him because they have their backs to the house but the crowd are beginning to notice him. Pesché has spotted him and is moving swiftly down the aisle towards us and I distinctly hear Granny Gramus, at the back, by the table with the flags and the watches and the Party paraphernalia, give a low and not unmusical scream. Who can blame her? There he stands, in the window, perfectly framed and, can you believe it? – in full uniform. That's what he will have been carrying in his bag: white tunic, great gold belt, a cap and medals, stars and stripes and epaulettes. Now I recognise it – it's the uniform in the photograph. He holds the squat baton, midnight blue and adorned with silver stars, the sunshine reflects on his thick glasses and he appears – and this is the enormity of it – he appears as if he were at home, looking down on his subjects – the Redeemer rules again!

I am trying to understand why he is doing this. He risks his life, it's as if he is challenging the crowd to kill him. He is offering himself as a sacrifice. The only way I can explain it is in terms of science. Please forgive me! But I suddenly imagine the pursuit of a particle known as the neutral pion in a cloud or bubble chamber. The object of the experiment is to get particles, which are normally invisible to the observer, to disclose themselves. The trouble with the neutral pion, sometimes known as the pi-zero, is that it is so impossibly shortlived that you can never tell what it is since it never stays around for long enough. In less time than we can measure, it decays into two photons, energetic gamma rays which, like it, are invisible. Uncle Claude and the Angel take the places of the invisible particles. They are never here long enough for me to get a positive identification of them. Nor are they visible to the naked eye for what they are. Maybe this is Monsieur Brown's way of forcing them into the open, of getting them to leave tracks. In the real experiment a physicist would make use of a sheet of lead placed in the path of the invisible photons. When the photons strike the lead they turn, individually, into an electron and a positron and their paths are clearly visible in the bubble chamber as two tracks curving away from each other in a beautiful V-shape. By tracing back their flight paths we can infer the routes of the missing, invisible particles. None of this research is my own, of course. I owe all this to Uncle Claude, who is still worried about the way my skirt keeps riding up my legs:

'Bella, for heaven's sake, make yourself decent!'

Ignore him. I do.

The crowd are on their feet now, many of them are gesticulating, some of them are laughing and the Angel is losing them, he can feel himself losing them and as the Chief of Police begins running towards the platform he turns, and Father Duval turns, and my uncle turns, and they all see what I see.

Something will have to be done. The yells and whistles from the crowd are deafening. 'The monster!' they cry, and 'Look, *patron*, the King of the Cannibal Islands is there!' But it is not done to turn and stare. Well, not too quickly, too obviously. Now Police Chief Pesché reaches us, and dashes past without a word, leading a patrol of his men. On they rush, through the door into our house.

In the window of my bedroom he lingers for one last moment and then he vanishes.

Something is to be done. The Angel can't continue with his speech, he's lost the attention of the crowd. Ah, but we have resources, we have reserves. Father Duval steps to the microphone:

'My friends – listen to me! Straight from Paris, that extra-ordinary artist – Domitian!'

Domitian sings: *'They say that Africa's the mother of man/So I say this to the Africa lover/We're gonna pack your bags real soon/And boot you home to mother.'*

And for that he gets a platinum disc!

I'm reconciled to the worst, to the door of the house opening to show Chief Pesché and his prisoner, perhaps in chains, like the bear on my chocolate cup. When this happens, I have already decided, I will not know Monsieur Brown. If he did not do as I told him, if, after all my efforts to rescue him from the hotel, he chooses to get himself arrested then he needn't come running to me!

It seems forever before the door opens. Pesché comes out followed by his men. He looks hot, sheepish, puzzled.

'Well?' My uncle's voice is high and hard.

'Report, man!' says the Angel. 'Where is he? You got him?' Pesché shakes his head. 'There's nobody in the house.'

'In a few minutes he flies away? What do you think he is – some sort of genie?' Again my uncle's voice is shrill and threatens to break.

'We were up the stairs in maybe ninety seconds. We've searched the house from top to bottom. It's empty, I tell you.'

'Well then, where is he?' the Angel demands.

'This is the mystery. You remember that there are certain people also watching the Priory Hotel? I thought they ought to know what was going on. So I sent a man down to tell them their bird was loose.' The Chief shakes his head again. 'This is very strange. I don't understand this. And yet I saw him, you saw him – we all saw him!'

'For God's sake man, tell us!' My uncle now grabs him by the coat and shakes him.

'Well, the watchers at the gate of the Priory Hotel, they tell me that he's still there! Inside! He's never left. They think I'm crazy, they think we're all crazy. They asked me if we'd been seeing visions. Father Duval, you're a religious man – tell me if we've been seeing visions. You, me, the Mayor, everyone here? Like Bernadette at Lourdes when the Virgin appeared in the rock!'

'I hardly think this is the moment for religious speculation,' protests Father Duval.

And, behold, I think he may be right. I think, further, that I am coming close to understanding what is going on here. The Redeemer has, by his appearance in the window, taken it on himself to make Uncle Claude and Monsieur Cherubini disclose themselves; he has played the part of the sheet of lead, they are the invisible particles, and we are the observers of the experiment.

You see the possibilities, don't you? You who do not play dice with the universe but rather enjoy Russian roulette. You can do just about anything with science, once you get the hang of it. I'm quietly excited by the possibility.

'If the black man isn't here, or there – where is he?' Pesché demands. A flooding wave of relief makes me giddy and I speak:

'Maybe the mistake we've been making with Monsieur Brown is to imagine that he must always be in one place at the same time. Here or there. Perhaps he is continually in movement, and if he is a quantum force then we must apply Heisenberg's Uncertainty Principle when we analyse the reality of this creature. When we know where he is we cannot also know how fast he is travelling, and when we know how fast he's travelling we cannot say for certain where he is. What do you think of that, Uncle Claude?'

'I've never heard such nonsense in all my life,' says the Angel. 'We *saw* him. In the window. Standing there! It was a deliberate, calculated insult. He was there and we will find him.'

'No, no, *patron*,' says Uncle Claude slowly, 'perhaps Bella has a point. Some of my lessons in physics seem to be taking hold. Maybe we should rethink this. Later. But now you must give yourself to your supporters who have come a long way today to be with us. When the village is peaceful again, some time this evening, we will get to the bottom of this. I have in mind a little experiment. If Monsieur Brown is where the watchers at the gate tell us – the hotel – then this would be an ideal chance to test whether he can be in two places at once. If he is experimenting with us, we will return the compliment. Let's test the hypothesis to destruction.'

'Do as you like,' I tell my uncle. 'You can't touch him now.'

I speak as I do, certain that the Redeemer has got away. I see him roaring down the autoroute in the Angel's Mercedes, singing some favourite Wouff song – or humming snatches of 'Lead Kindly Light'. Imagine my horror, then, at the discovery that the Angel's limousine has not been touched.

# 12

It seems a long time before the local brigade arrives, because I suppose, at half-past ten in the evening people are hard to find and the firemen have to be summoned from nearby villages. They are a scratch crew pulled from their homes, and out of bars and cafés, dressed in a variety of outfits ranging from smart blue serge to denim jeans, and a few of them are wearing helmets. First comes the advance guard in a little truck which has to fight its way past the cars parked outside the gates of the Priory and it's at least another ten minutes before they can get their water tender through. The firemen have literally to bounce several cars out of the way and they are helped by the watchers in the Citroën, the Renault and the Deux-Chevaux, though as soon as they have done this, I notice, they go back to their cars and lean on the door jambs, put their elbows on the roofs as if they have come to an election rally, or a bullfight, or the scene of some ghastly accident, and like everybody else they stare. Everyone stares. By the time the big hoses are connected to the main water supply from the lake, the fire is raging in the kitchens and lower floors of the Priory. Smoke pours from the windows and hangs in the sky. The guests scream and run into the garden. Tertius has been burnt, his hair is alight and he has to be sprayed with water by the firemen. Hyppolyte and Armand stand shaking with fear, never has reality brushed so close. They were in the kitchen when the fire started and a sheet of flame leapt at them as they stood peeling potatoes. This seems particularly to have enraged them, the fact that the fire broke out while they were working, really working! It's as if they think the fire has waited until they were genuinely busy before attacking them. They feel that they have been doing their duty and have been endangered. I get the impression that this is a mistake they will not be making again. Last night they were pretending to be waiters, tonight they are pretending to be chefs — and tomorrow night? For them there will be no more nights. Armand puts it for them all:

'We might have died. The bastard's got no concern for his staff!' He holds in his hand a peeled potato and with a sudden movement turns and hurls it behind him, curving upwards and into the water.

People are sitting out at the cast-iron tables under the trees, watching the progress of the fire. People will watch a fire. And there seems little else to do after the first panic is over; perhaps the guests are now beginning faintly to relish the relief that comes when danger is past and, feeling that they can now be quite safe, they sit back and look at things objectively. I can hardly blame them. There is always an element of carnival in a fire, particularly when you have the knowledge safe and sure that however fiercely it burns, beside you lie several million litres of water. Little boys begin to form a crowd around the fire-fighters who have now put on breathing apparatus and are preparing to enter the hotel. Suddenly Gudrun leaps to her feet and begins screaming. Her anguish is terrible. She runs to the front doors but the firemen turn her away and so she begins walking up and down the path in front of the hotel weeping and gnawing her knuckles and calling for her children, though as far as I can see all of them are here. Her husband is at a loss and he goes and speaks to the *pompiers* who tell him that nothing can be done until they enter the hotel and begin to search the rooms. Gudrun weeps bitterly and covers her eyes. Then, suddenly, around the corner there appears Raoul, or, as I suppose we must now call him, Dupont, the accountant from Grenoble. His face is sooty and he is carrying on his hip the little blond boy. Gudrun screams 'Francois! Francois!' and runs and snatches the child away and hugs him frantically. Raoul/Dupont beams as the Dutch girl runs to him and embraces him.

I really can't look. That's why I turn around and it's because I turn around, away from the fire, that I see Clovis. He's up on the headland that forms the right-hand arm of the little bay. He is on his motor-cycle. The last of the evening light glints on something — of course, the glass boot. As I watch, the bike shoots forward and Clovis soars into space. For a long moment he stays on the bike, riding it through the air, Hermes flying through the heavens, but then the machine, being heavier, begins to fall away beneath him and both of them twist and turn through the air as they drop towards the water. One force in the Grand Unification Theory we can absolutely rely on: gravity. It's over very suddenly, there's no noise, they're too far away for that, not even a splash, boy and machine simply aren't there any longer. I turn back to the fire and the guests at the tables. Am I the only one who saw Clovis fly? Certainly no one else gives any sign of it, they have eyes only for the fire. I want to do something. Of course I want to do something but Clovis is too far out, no one can reach him in time, even by motor-boat, and, besides, the surface of the water where he disappeared is as clear and as clean as a newly swept floor.

Now the front door of the hotel opens and two firemen carrying a stretcher come down the steps. One blue espadrille protrudes from beneath the white sheet and I know at once it's André. Tertius, Hyppolyte and Armand jump to their feet as the stretcher is carried down the slate path between the tables towards the ambulance. They stare, and point, but there's no sign in their faces of grief or concern. Shock, yes, disappointment certainly, and more than a touch of anger; they're watching the one person to whom they wish bitterly to complain being carried past insensible, quite possibly dead.

The crowd outside the main gates of the Priory where the ambulance waits is even bigger now. There are many people from the village but they still don't come into the garden because it is, after all, private property and even though the property in question looks as if it is about to be razed to the ground the people of our village always observe the proprieties.

'Is he bad?' someone asks.

The fireman turns to the questioner the great goggle-eyes of his monster face in its breathing apparatus, and very slowly lifts the mask. He shrugs hopelessly. 'He is hot to the touch.'

Hot to the touch!

The words sink into my head where, despite their meaning, they fail to warm. Quite the opposite. I believe everyone who hears them shivers. To the villagers gathered around the front gates of the hotel the menus upon the gateposts speak from behind their polished glass frames of Veal Soup with Pasta and Cheese, of *Paupiettes de Sole Déglère*, the dishes for the day, the specialities of the house; they speak, in fact, of another cooler, happier period when fire and smoke and ambulances were unknown. The ambulance accepts the still figure on the stretcher and speeds away up the winding hill, its siren wailing. I begin to recognise people: old Laveur, the drycleaner along with the two De La Salle sisters who run the pizzeria and the florist at the top of the village; young Brest, the butcher, who must have been working because he's still in his apron with blood in the creases across his belly; the entire family Gramus are here, father and mother and several children as well as the granny with the warts and the pointy chin. Because the Gramus family in years gone by had provided all the undertaking services in the village, their presence in any number, even today, is regarded as a bad omen.

The works of man are insensible to his grief. Several of the villagers studying the menus give low whistles over prices of the dishes. They do this sort of thing across the way at *Les Dents Sacrés*. The air of festival is growing.

'He smelt like burnt biscuit,' says the younger of the De La Salle sisters, a lady of about seventy who wears strings of dark metal jewellery around her thin throat and wrists (it makes a harsh crunching sound when she moves, like the clash of boots on gravel). The other sister smells always of cold flower water from her florist's shop.

Hot to the touch!

The Angel, Uncle Claude and Father Duval arrive in the big Mercedes which should not be here. The watchers at the gate, who had been standing guard over the Redeemer, become quite excited at the sight of the Mayor although they still do not leave their cars but stand beside them in an attitude of patient expectation, feet on the bumpers, hands hooked into waist-bands. For the first time I see their guns visible beneath their jackets and for the first time it is as if they do not care who sees them. The unexpected has broken in on routine and its reward is this revelation of metal in trouser waist-bands and in holsters under the arms.

The Angel, seeing the assembled crowd, and still smarting from the major interruption of the rally, climbs onto the bonnet of his car and begins addressing the onlookers:

'My friends, we meet in unhappy circumstances. One of the monuments of La Frisette is engulfed in flames. Our ancient Priory stands gasping for breath! For hundreds of years it has endured in holy tranquillity, a hospice for weary travellers, a refuge for the sick, a light to passing ships on the lake. Who knows if we are not today here present at its death? You have seen, I believe, its owner and its dearest friend, carried away on a stretcher, overcome no doubt by smoke and flames as he fought to contain the blaze. Our valiant fire service are risking life and limb to bring this catastrophe under control and we are proud of them. But this is not the time for words. However, let me say that I give you my pledge – and I know that Monsieur Dresseur, the Mayor, who is also here to comfort his young niece, will support me – the Priory will not die! No matter what the damage, no matter what the cost, it will rise again from the ashes. No part of our beloved village of La Frisette is disposable, or dispensable. Its fabric is as precious as our bones! Be it our little church on the hill, or the old Mairie, we fight to preserve them.'

The crowd hear him in silence and applaud politely. Old mother Gramus speaks for many when she asks: 'Did he start the fire on purpose, *patron*? For the insurance? This place must be costing him a packet and we all know it.'

And young Brest, yellow-haired in his white plastic apron, calls out, 'What about the black fellow – the one with the disease? Is he also burnt?'

'You are referring, of course, to the hotel's foreign guest,' the Angel observes.

'To the dictator,' says old Laveur. 'The one they call the King of the Caramel Islands. Where is he?'

The Angel shrugs. 'Who knows? You see the firemen entering the hotel. Perhaps they will find him.'

'If he's still there he'll be all melted by this time,' suggests the elder of the De La Salle sisters, throwing up a hand to her mouth, pale and transparent and delicate as a blue-veined leaf.

She is renowned for her salty humour and the crowd love the joke. There's no doubt that there is now a real carnival atmosphere and it's not just the exhilarating effect of the fire that brings it on. There's another reason for this festive mood. I see it now, all the village people are taking part in an old ritual, something they surely remember in their bones because it was in just this place that the villagers would have once gathered in the middle of the seventeenth century, and again early in the eighteenth during the Revolution when the last remaining monks were expelled by the Revolutionary Council.

On June 30th, 1793, all the village came down to the lakeside, summoned by drum and trumpet to a kind of people's free rock concert. It must have been, in a way, just as if a group like, say, Neanderthal were playing a waterside gig, you know the lot, pretty good on bangs and brass and a soul-scouring synthesiser (I'm thinking especially of their all-time smash 'If I Had Double Barrels Would You Press Me To Your Heart?'). Because that's how it must have seemed, two hundred years ago on this spot with the crowds and the music and the flames, everyone pushing and shoving under the chestnut trees to get at the wine the monks had left behind them when they fled. All the officials were here, the municipal officers with boots up to their thighs and coats picked out in dazzling designs, red, white and blue belts, hats tufty with feathers. And of course there were the flames, the big bonfire they made to receive the treasures of the Priory, the vanities which were pitched into the fire, the maps, the paintings, books, scrolls, statues. I could hear them cheering, the ancestors of Laveur and the De La Salle sisters and, yes, of my own family, the Dresseurs, as they snatched up the wooden madonnas, the painted Christs, the canvasses and the priceless brocades, eight centuries of treasure, sacred and profane or simply silly, saints' molars, the crutches of visiting cripples who had put up in the Priory for a few nights and had been miraculously cured of their afflictions, chalices, silks, croziers, all pitched into the flames.

Quite a night it must have been. They also set fire to the Priory itself but the blaze was doused by municipal officials using a chain of wine skins passed by hand from the lakeside. This was mainly due, the old story goes, to the fact that they feared that the mounting hysteria of the crowd might make them start raising fires all over

212

the place and a horrid conflagration would consume their beloved village.

From that time on it was expected that the ruin would stand, blackened and empty, as a warning to succeeding generations about the idiocy of the Church and the terrific cleansing and destructive power of the Revolution; all was to endure until Kingdom come. In fact this state of affairs lasted only until André arrived on the scene, kissed the old ruin awake and breathed life into it. It must annoy the various gods, the God of the Bible, or of history, that Man is such an incorrigible optimist, well-meaning interferer, short-term artist incapable of taking a long view, must always be up and doing, fixing and refurbishing, never heeding the warnings, never letting well alone, always having to be stopped and warned and, when he won't be warned, destroyed ... Only for him to get up out of the ashes and try again.

Hot to the touch!

'Come into the garden with me, Bella. We get a good view from there. The firemen are inside the house now, searching room by room.'

My Uncle Claude takes my arm and leads me over to one of the tables under the chestnut trees where, like all the other guests, we sit as if waiting for service.

'You did this, didn't you? You set fire to the hotel.'

'For the moment,' says my uncle with hateful, heavy calm, 'your chocolate friend is in the position of the cat in the paradox to which the physicist Schrödinger gave his name over half a century ago. This paradox goes as follows. The cat (for which in this case read Redeemer) is put into a sealed box (for which read Priory Hotel). No one can see inside the box or open it, or in any way affect what will happen when the pellet of poison drops (for which read fire).'

'Poison?'

'Yes, a pellet of cyanide is suspended above a beaker of hydrochloric acid inside the box.'

'With the cat?'

'Exactly. Also inside the box is a radioactive element which, within the hour, may or may not send out a signal. If it does the pellet drops and the cat dies. If it doesn't, the cat lives.'

'Two worlds?'

He nods. 'Parallel worlds. If our observer discovered a dead cat then he and the late pussy constitute one possible world. This is what we call the observer effect. Quantum mechanics means that things keep flowing until we look at them, and when we look at them they stop. The host of possible universes simply flows on and the flow is everything until it's arrested by the observation of the enquiring human.'

'So in another world the cat may live happily ever after?'

'Yes.'

'In other words we only find out about something when we interrupt?'

'Quite so. But when we interrupt, the experiment is over. We've painted ourselves into the picture.'

I can see the firemen moving about through the smoke. They have broken a window on the second floor and a stream of smouldering, charred debris rains down. Chairs, books, pictures spattered with mud, sodden with water. The leather-bound books have a greasy brown look to them, like smoked mackerel, their pages licked into charred solid blocks and yet I recognise them easily despite this disfigurement. Here are the lives of the great dictators, Caesar, Hitler, Alexander the Great and Mussolini. And here also are the pictures of his musical wives: Viola, Tympany, Harp and Dulcimer, smiling bravely through cracked, seared, mud-flecked glass.

'Have you found anything?' I call to the fireman at the window.

'Nothing yet.'

'They're all naked,' old Laveur whistles as he inspects the Redeemer's wives. 'Come here Etienne,' he calls the butcher Brest, who splashes through the puddles and whistles his astonishment. 'I think the monster enjoyed white meat,' Laveur says.

'Pork above chicken if you ask me,' is Brest's opinion.

Old Granny Gramus, with the pointy chin and the copper sulphate eyes, speaks for all when she observes, 'I believe it's an affliction of savages to be haunted by human flesh.'

The De La Salle sisters say nothing but I think they ought to pull their skirts over their heads and give way to wailing and keening.

'These are pictures of his wives,' I explain carefully. 'What you are actually looking at are photographs based on paintings by famous artists. French artists, some of them!'

Uncle Claude stands beside me and begins turning over the pictures and books with his toe as if they are little corpses, small dead bodies of squirrels or gophers or rats. 'Yes, it does rather look as if these pictures are influenced by a number of European artistic styles. Isn't this Degas? This lady with her cheek turned to us while she dries herself with a towel?'

'Yes, that's his first wife, Viola, posing in the manner of the Degas painting of a woman drying herself after her bath. You must have seen it on postcards. He has even gone to the trouble of getting an old tin bath. Next to her is Tympany, she's portrayed as a Roman Venus.'

We all look down on Tympany.

'She looks more of a stocky German type, to me,' says the butcher Brest. 'There are several hectares of flesh.'

'At least she uses her hand to cover herself,' says Granny Gramus.

'She's modelled on what was called the *Venus Pudica*.'

'*Pudica*? I'll say.' Laveur laughs and the others join him. 'Obviously some kind of African joke! Who would have thought that the chocolate one kept all this in his little room. I must say his taste is not bad, if somewhat florid. I prefer my cheese a little firmer than this.'

'The word *Pudica* means "modest" – in Latin,' I tell Laveur.

'Oh yes? Doesn't look very modest to me,' says Laveur.

'It's very interesting. What we have here is a copy of a copy of a copy,' says Uncle Claude. 'We see a photograph of a modern woman posing for a painting in the attitude of an idealised Greek goddess.' He turns another picture with his delicate little toe. 'And who's this? She's more modest.'

'Dulcimer, wife number two. She's a copy of St Ursula, a carving made by somebody called the Master of Elsloo in the early sixteenth century.'

'A saint? In a blouse like that?' Now it's the turn of the elder of the De La Salle sisters, a woman so frail and thin, dressed in white lace which shakes when she speaks like the feathery, flimsy wings of flying ants.

'I like the detail on this one,' says the butcher Brest as
Uncle Claude unearths another picture. 'I think her wings
are actually very good. They look like real feathers. Are they
real feathers? I'd guess at goose though of course they may
be duck. Who is she, Bella?'

'That's Harp, his third wife. She's seen here as Venus, after
a painting by Correggio called *Mercury Instructing Cupid Before
Venus.*'

'Hey, that's him, the one in the funny hat, the jockey hat,
that's the black fellow!' says old Laveur in astonishment. 'And
who's the little kid also with the wings?'

'That's one of his sons. Playing Cupid,' I tell him.

'I think it's the flesh that really catches your eye,' says the
younger of the De La Salle sisters to the butcher Brest. 'Let's
be frank about this. We're all grown people. These so-called
classical poses that painters talk these girls into are nothing
more than disguises through which the audience of males look
on. Voyeurs! That's what they're meant for! By dressing up a
whore as the goddess Venus you can gape all you like under
the cloak of culture.'

The butcher Brest has gone a muddy brown colour and
is breathing hard. 'I'd like you to know, Mademoiselle De
La Salle and Monsieur le Maire, that what interests me about
this picture is the question of accuracy – is it goose feathers
or duck? I take pleasure from the accurate identification of
such things, feathers, fur, flesh. It's my trade. I handle them
daily. The very last thing to arouse me is the sight of flesh.
A moment's thought will show you why. Butchers are like
mortuary attendants. I suppose like painters too. They look
on things in death all the time and death is cold and naked.
I have a professional interest! May I take another look at the
Venus? I think now they are probably duck feathers.'

But my uncle isn't listening, he is pulling at his lips as if
he has swallowed something acid and it won't go down, or
it has gone down and threatens to come straight up again.

'Bella, what does this mean?'

And there in the mud I lie, at the end of Uncle Claude's
pointed toe. It's the photograph the Redeemer took of me
on the hot afternoon, when, despite the heat, he'd insisted
on making a fire in the grate. I recline on the little green

*216*

chaise-longue. To my left the window with the curtain drawn back lets in the fierce lake light. At the corner of the window stands a small brown table carrying a white basin. My right arm drops over the edge of the chair, fingers extending almost to the green carpet. I can feel it now under my fingers as I look at myself, I can feel it like a skin or a fur, it is almost as if I can touch the short woollen hair of the green carpet straining upwards the way real hair does when it's charged with static electricity. My uncle and the others are staring at my open dress, at the bodice cut low, falling off the right shoulder. They're staring as well at my raised left knee climbing from my skirt. How flat my shoes look, and white. The fire warms my legs. I remember feeling the heat along the insides of my thighs. The little mirror I hold in my hand shows me the clouds drifting past the open window behind me, drifting past my face which is quiet and composed. Over to my right, kneeling on one leg before the fire which he is working up into a terrific blaze, is the Redeemer. He has his back to me and he ripples inside his dark red shirt as he feeds the flames with his left hand. His right hand holds the edge of the mantelpiece for support.

'Always use your left hand to feed yourself,' I remember him telling me. 'That at least is the custom in my country.'

And he uses his left hand to feed the fire.

Hot to the touch!

My uncle's voice is a wounded bellow:

'Four wives he has – Viola, Tympany, Harp, Dulcimer – and now Bella! Wife number five!'

Disgust is a wonderful diversion. At first Uncle Claude doesn't notice the chattering, smoke-stained firefighters heading for their engine, stowing their hoses, gathering equipment. Only a few are left in the house punching holes in the windows. But clearly the worst is over. They're not looking for anyone. The people at the gate are moving off. Now the Angel and Father Duval are conferring anxiously with the firemen. The people in the Renault, the Citroën and the Deux-Chevaux have noticed. Look at the way they're yelling down their radios which, for once, they don't bother to hide. It's really exciting. I put on my earphones and stick a tape in the cassette, one of those dreamier numbers from an outfit called Jurassic, they've got these lovely, sliding, sucking rhythms that make you think of, oh, Father Christmas in petticoats, or the Pope in drag. And I'm so happy! It's at times like this when I can profess my love for you! It's miracle time. Do you hear? I can say now that there is you and only you and never a stand-in. You alone – you do all your own stunts!

Uncle Claude's noticed at last. He begins yelling at the firemen, 'What do you mean he's not here? Are you telling me he melted maybe – and slipped through the cracks and disappeared? He *has* to be here. He can't be anywhere else!'

In the midst of all this the De La Salle sisters and the butcher Brest continue to argue.

'The trouble with the women in these paintings,' complains the older De La Salle sister, 'is that they know they're being looked at.'

'You mean they want to be looked at?' Brest rejoins.

'I mean they're painted by men for men. They show so much of themselves. If this weren't art, it would be disgusting.'

'You are among nature's natural killers, Madame,' says Brest.

'By men for men,' the De La Salle sister repeats.

This brings out the worst in Brest, or perhaps the best. He looks down at the portrait of the Redeemer and Harp as Mercury and Venus, and he licks his lips. 'Do you know what this picture makes me feel, Madame? It makes me hungry, look at that flesh, the texture, it's like milk – you want to taste it!'

I think I'd like to record just what I told my uncle on this score. You'll see the particular advances I've been making in my study of particle physics, now that I've got the hang of it, now that I realise that the point about it is to make predictions which later experimental evidence will confirm. I offer the following on the subject of Schrödinger's cat, as explained to Uncle Claude:

'Perhaps we've just added something to the history of particle physics. Maybe there are not just two parallel worlds with the cat and the observer alive in one world and dead in the other. Perhaps today we've stepped through a hole into a third world, a new dimension. Because when you think about it there aren't just two possibilities facing the cat, are there? It's not just a question of whether the radioactive element fires, the cyanide pellet drops into the acid and you get one dead cat – or if it doesn't, you don't. That's to say it's not a question of either/or, either the cat's alive or it's dead. There is another alternative which I'm surprised nobody's thought of until now: when the scientists inspect the box maybe there's no cat at all.'

'Bella,' says my uncle speaking through his teeth. 'There is *always* a cat. The only question is – alive or dead?'

'Or escaped?'

Axe blades smash through wood and glass with a dry coughing sound and the splinters of glass land on the pavement below. Wherever a hole appears in a window, smoke pours out while we wait and watch. Many of the tables still have drinks on them, cocktails smelling slightly of peppermint, doubtless Emile's *coupe maison*, now returning to its original constituents which show up as different bands of colour in the large beakers Emile favours for his evening libations.

We suffer and our works look on; these drinks, the menus at the front gate, the very appearance of the tables beneath the trees all insist on business as usual. We make our engines and set them going. But when disaster strikes and removes the makers our works continue as if nothing has happened, go on inviting us to pleasure, or advertising happiness, mocking our expectations, our sheer bloody nerve. You started this, they say. Don't you still want to play? And this will happen on a much bigger scale one day, when our sun runs out of fuel and expands and roasts us all. Our engines will go on running, powered by varieties of energy as yet unthought of; they will play our tunes and show our pictures and talk to each other along their super-cooled ceramic synapses, telling the time, checking our credit ratings, measuring the weather which, by then, will have proved terminal. Even our cheapest music will survive us because it will doubtless have been taught to compose itself and will go on doing so; there will be singing robots, and brighter versions of groups like Oedema and Giuseppe and the Lambs will go on belting out their stuff to the stars as the noisy planet, lights blinking, floats through space like some deserted ship, a *Marie Celeste* of the solar system, music blasting out, television on and the trains still running for years, decades, after we have departed.

# Zanj

*Close the gates*
*With lacari thorns,*
*For the Prince,*
*The heir to the Stool is lost!*

Okot p'Bitek

Atkins International Airport stands in a vast saucer-shaped plain surrounded by a circle of low hills behind which the sun is just dipping and applying delicate colour, like a touch of oyster-pink lipstick, to the saucer's rocky rim. Mine is the only footfall to echo around the big arrival hall. Behind the desk an official in black jacket wearing a peaked cap offers a small careful smile. It is cool in the hall and quiet and empty.

'Good morning, dear young person.'

He takes my passport between thumb and forefinger and by his touch makes it slim, wafery and strangely edible. He has a cricket's mandible for a mouth and papery fingers and he holds up the book as if uncertain whether to read it or eat it. He seems to wish to savour it first, to linger for some time over the job in hand. He sniffs the passport, riffles through the pages as someone in a bookstore might before deciding whether to buy.

'Dresseur – Dresseur ... A French name. You speak English? I have to speak English to you. It's now our official language.'

'I don't mind. Speak either.'

'Thank you. You are most civil. Welcome to Zanj. Would you like to buy a copy of our official history?'

'No, thank you.'

'Then I must read it to you.' He picks up a printed card and clears his throat. 'Our country was the victim of twin colonialisms, French and English. As if it were not enough we were divided among three tribes, the Kanga, the Ite and the Wouff, and we were beset by the mongrels of Europe and obliged to master the tongues of our invaders. Happily, tribal distinctions have been abolished under the beneficent administration of Comrade Atkins. In

223

the interests of modernity it has been decided that English should be our national tongue. So be it.' He peers hard at my photograph and hands the passport back. 'Your picture doesn't do you justice. Please step forward into the customs.'

Customs turns out to be a large wooden table with a drawer facing outwards; the handle is made of well-rubbed brass. Waiting for me behind the table is the same man except that now he has taken off his black jacket and is in a white shirt and I suppose he looks something like a customs officer.

'Anything to declare?'

'No.'

'I think we'll just have a look in your case.'

He hoists the case onto the wooden table. I like the way he blows on his hands and rubs them together before springing the locks as if he doesn't want to touch them with cold hands. He's less sensitive with my things, holding up my clothes and reading the labels. Sometimes he whistles, sometimes he clicks his tongue, though whether because he approves of the fabric or dislikes the maker I cannot say. He looks inside the fingers of my pink leather gloves.

'Is this your first visit to Zanj, Miss Dresseur?'

'Yes.'

'Are you on vacation – or have you come on business?' He's busy now with my make-up. The black hands dip into the bag like feeding birds. He touches a finger to one of my hairpins and whistles at its sharp point. He unscrews the cap of my 'Contouring Creme-jel' – a non-greasy jel which moisturises, shines and controls my fly-away hair; he *tastes* my 'Kiss And Tell' lipstick, a strawberry stripe on his tongue. He runs a finger along my tortoiseshell comb and makes a little tune in which I think I hear echoes of 'Lead Kindly Light'.

'I've come to see a friend.'

'How long are you staying?'

'For as long as necessary.'

He holds up a box of eye-shadow. 'What is this, please?'

'I put it on my eyes. I mix the blue with the deep purple and I use 'Fort Knox Gold' on my brows to get a subtle, stylish effect.'

'Is your friend meeting you?'

224

'I don't know.'

'I should point out that you will find the forecourt innocent of vehicular traffic.'

Whatever that means it sounds vaguely disappointing. I say, 'OK.'

'As a woman very much in the fashionable swim,' – his eyes rest briefly on my turtle-neck top – 'you'll be fascinated to know that our leader, Comrade Atkins, has commanded that an end be put to the prettifyings and face-paintings among our women. He says, "Woman of Zanj, return to the modesty of your mothers and grandmothers!"'

He is particularly fascinated by my diamond pendant and keeps staring at it with quick, hard eyes.

'Your jewel is going to get a lot of attention. It is very unusual. You put it inside your dress. OK?'

I do as he says.

'Some of our people are crazy – for jewels. Stone crazy.'

I watch him repacking my case, taking special care to square off a patterned red shawl. He has a passion for neatness, this man. The way he kneads the toes of a pair of my best black tights gets me seriously mad.

'Listen, have you found something you don't like?'

He closes my case and snaps the locks. 'You're absolutely fine.'

'Can I go?'

'Just one small thing.'

'Yes?'

'You're overweight.'

'Overweight? But that's something they check before you fly. I've already landed. I'm here. How can I be overweight?'

'Don't worry. You're only a few kilos over the limit. Shall we say a charge of one hundred Zanjian dollars?'

'I don't have any of your currency. They wouldn't give me any, they said the banks here were closed.'

'US dollars will be acceptable. Twenty. OK? Open the drawer in front of you and place them inside.'

I count out twenty dollars from my purse. The drawer slides open with a delicate, subdued hiss.

'Now close the drawer. And open it again.'

I do as I'm told. The drawer is empty.

225

He grins delightedly. 'Magic. And you're my witness, I didn't touch it.'

'Can I go now?'

'What's the name of the friend you're going to meet?'

Now it's my turn to look at him hard. All sorts of options are open, I think – well? – shall I tell you the name of the friend whom I'm here to find? Your dear departed ruler, the lively, lickable fellow, the king thing, the edible dictator?

'Brown.'

His face is hard, beaky, without expression.

'Some people in Zanj called him the Redeemer.'

A tray of cups smashes. He opens his mouth. He's laughing – I see that now.

He laughs long and hard and in the darkness of his mouth his teeth twinkle like landing lights. 'Miss Dresseur, someone's been fooling you. Maybe you've been reading lies in the Western press. There is no one answering to that name here. The only leader we possess, our Head of State and beloved helmsman, is Comrade Atkins.'

Oh yeah, I think, and Mohammed is his prophet. 'How long has Comrade Atkins been in charge?'

'For as long as anyone can remember.' He pushes my case across to me and indicates that I am free to go. 'I wish you a very happy stay in the People's Republic of Zanj.'

At times like this I wish I had my music back and had not plunged it into the lake along with poor Clovis. On the day I left La Frisette I hired a boat from old Leclerc and paddled out to the spot where I estimated Clovis had disappeared. The hawks watched me as I took off my walkman. I would have liked to put up a plaque on the rocks above the deep water where he drowned. Instead I gave him my walkman and all my tapes. Heavy metal sinks fast. What I think I'd like to be listening to now is something good from the soft lips of Divina and his latest chartbuster, called 'Suck It And See', which, as the entire universe knows, is the big one from his first film of the same name. OK, so they say he keeps this collection of frozen dwarves in a special cryptogenic chamber, that he's got these mummified corpses of these famous dwarves in there and talks to them like his friends, calls them his ancestors and kneels and prays to them. At least, that's the story you get in the music sheets that specialise in peddling in this dirt. The sorts of papers that print the stories about his latest leading lady in *Suck It And See* before she got fired in favour of Wanda Tremoy for refusing to go nude in the big bed scene and they say that Divina ran shrieking from the set, because the boy may be the most tender lover in the world but he's also a blushing violet. Just because I drowned my walkman along with poor drowned Clovis doesn't mean the music won't go on. The spool between my ears keeps turning.

I walk out into the main concourse which is big and utterly empty; there are no chairs, no flightboards, no people. At the far end of the hall a notice above a little stall tells me that coffee is supplied by the Consumer Unit of the Department of Trade. A second notice tells me that there is no coffee. On the wall is a picture of Comrade Atkins, who wears a tunic which buttons up to the neck and has a high collar; the face is young, boyish, and looks very like that of a fat peacock, the lower lip juts, almost touching his nose which is thin and beaked. Altogether Atkins has a pavonine look about him. The inscription beneath the portrait reads: *'Comrade Atkins, Number One Peasant.'*

Well, what do you think, as you look down on us from your great height, from study or cell or stage or wherever you sit in judgement? No doubt you feel there are things to be retrieved in even the most hopeless and horrible cases because you don't see things in terms of black and white, as we are constantly being told, but understand that man is meant to be saved. You could, I suppose, if it came to the push, show redeeming qualities even in the Number One Peasant of the People's Republic of Zanj. I mean maybe he's good at maths or works tirelessly for the eradication of the tsetse fly, or perhaps he plays the flute with majestic virtuosity, his fingers flying over the stops with the athletic assurance of a spider running? Though looking at that hard, beaky face, I have my doubts. But if you have this in mind you do not speak of these virtues, and the portrait on the wall of the Zanj International Airport gives no credence to such hopes.

Which is putting it mildly.

Outside the airport no expense has been spared in laying out the parking facilities. There are magnificent concrete erections marked Long Term Parking, and Buses, Freight and Taxis, but there's not a single bloody vehicle to be seen. It's also very hot and I begin to have my doubts about wearing the swing-coat in dogtooth check, although I'm glad of my black straw picture hat. And Divina's fluting voice vibrates in my ears: *'Who says there ain't no Christmas fairy?/Don't knock my faith/Suck it and see.'*

I put him on hold. This needs serious consideration, here I am in the middle of the bush without a car, contacts or accommodation and the only living soul I know is some guy who doubles up as passport control and customs and excise, if that is not to overstate his claim to sentience. The sun stands upon the distant ring of hills and shows their rocky peaks and for miles there's nothing to be glimpsed but rock and sand, not a tree, not a blade of grass, not a petal interrupts the sameness of the scene. I feel like the first woman on the moon except that the people on the moon had a radio and a control tower back home in Houston and a lot of folks rooting for them. Moreover, they were properly dressed. I can feel the sweat beginning to trickle down the inside of my thighs, I always sweat there when I'm overcome by heat – and when I'm scared out of my bloody life.

I might have known that Passports and Customs would have another string to his bow. He draws up in a slew of pebbles in a green Datsun Sunny with a large pink plastic butterfly spreading its wings on the bonnet and, more alarmingly, a compass mounted on his dashboard.

'How was I supposed to get into town?'

He does not answer until he has loaded my luggage and we are bumping down the dirt road.

'I warned you about the innocence of vehicular traffic. Most persons arriving at the airport arrange to be met. But as soon as I heard the name of your friend, I knew there'd be no one to meet you. It doesn't matter. I offer a first-class taxi service between the airport and the capital.'

'But surely just because you haven't heard of him doesn't throw his existence into doubt?'

'Oh, what do I know?' he asks wearily. 'I just drive a taxi.' And that's all he has to say on the matter.

The road is long, rutted, dusty and empty. A few thorn trees are dotted about here and there and the soil is red and seamed by erosion. We could be on Mars but eventually we get to the outskirts of the city. I know this because there are little shacks of wood and tin dotted around the place, and I mean *around* the place: everything here seems to spread out, as if the only thing they have plenty of is space. Also lying by the roadside are skeletons and the decaying carcasses of buck, a couple of bush pigs, and what looks like the remains of a donkey. Is this the result of a drought, a blight, a pest?

'They got shot,' comes the laconic reply, 'by bandits.'

'Why do they kill animals?'

'These brigands are elements of the Zanjian defence force who can't accept the lead given in restructuring the army by our leader, Comrade Atkins. They've deteriorated into scavengers and dissidents who machine-gun their food wherever they find it. They come from the Wouff tribe, mostly. They're animists. They worship stones.'

'Which tribe are you from?'

'We don't have tribes any more. Under the new order of Comrade Atkins they've been abolished.'

After the business of passport control, then the trick drawer in the customs department, and now the taxi service, I reckon he's an Ite, and I hear the Redeemer's voice: 'A people not worthy to go on two legs, a milky, soppy, preachy congregation of hypocrites.' But then he'd been pretty ratty about the Kanga as well. 'All that bowing and scraping to Mecca, and a knife in the back when the praying's over.' Only about his own tribe, the Wouff, had he been poetical. 'A lovely strong community, not since ancient Sparta has there been such a fierce and beautiful people, with a special reverence for poetry and the sacred rocks of their forefathers.'

'Where are we going?'

'Kingdom Towers, it's the Hilton of Central Africa, best place in town.'

When I say 'town' I don't wish to be misunderstood, this place is a cross between a slum, an industrial estate, a *bidonville* and a mud hut citadel. The place is pure Timbuctoo with Bon Marché making a takeover bid. The houses have mud walls painted with peacock tails and stippled with dotted lines in what I suppose has some aesthetic or religious significance but it gives the effect of painterly perforations, a zippered look as if they are made for tearing into sections. Here and there are attempts to build in what I suppose is regarded as the modern manner, in what I can only call English post-war style, flat roofs and walls in the sort of concrete the rain stains, and in this neck of the woods once the rains have fallen, the storm waters rushing past the foot of the buildings leave a highwater mark perhaps a metre up, a smudge of powdery rouge. Modernity has never amounted to much here, it has been born into the world wearing a flat roof, its edges sharp, its sides square, it has shot up above the mud houses for about the equivalent of two minutes, African time, and then it has turned into a vision of emptiness and despair, deserted bunkers with their windows smashed, their walls covered with posters and paintings and political cartoons. Karl Marx and Lenin and a fat rather jolly man I don't recognise who looks a bit like Alfred Hitchcock.

'Who is the tubby bloke?'

'President Podgorny of the Soviet Union,' comes the wholly unexpected reply. 'He made a stop in Zanj when he was on an extended African tour some years ago. He visited one of our diamond mines and there he was presented with an uncut stone of considerable worth which he spat upon and rubbed on his trousers. I think he was just polishing it but there was a terrific debate about the meaning of this. One party said that the President had shown us all how much he hated material things by spitting on the stone. The other party said he had spat on the stone and then rubbed it on his trousers to look at his reflection in it. And this proved he was as greedy for the good things of life as anyone else. The argument led to blows and blood.'

'You mean people killed each other over this?'

'It was known as the War of the Stone. It turned mother against son, brother against sister. Of course the Wouff made it even worse. But then what can you expect of these primitives? They decided, on the basis of his performance, that President Podgorny was in fact their long-lost river god come back to them. But that's the Wouff all over. Show them a politician from Moscow and they've got themselves a new god because his head looks like a river boulder, or whatever, and the next

230

thing you know they're building shrines all over the place and painting his picture on the walls of houses. The Wouff have gods the way a cow has ticks. Let them catch a glimpse of someone who looks the least like a pebble, or a bit of rock, and bang! They've got themselves another deity. I tell you, their heaven must weigh a ton!'

'A heavy heaven. I'm surprised it stays up.'

'It doesn't. The Wouff say that every so often the gods have a clear-out. They throw down to earth the lesser gods. You and I would call it hail, but not the Wouff: they say the gods are clearing out their cellars and the little gods are being hurled down to earth where they turn to water and this water then begins to erode the rock and turn it into new shapes and thus new gods.'

I look up at the sky which is like hot blue steel. 'It can't hail here very often.'

'Once in ten years, maybe. And then you should see the Wouff! They run round with their mouths open and try to catch some of the little gods and swallow them because they believe that some of the divine power will pass into them. The storms here can be very violent. The damage done to the worshippers is pretty bad. Old women and children often die. The Wouff think this is hot stuff. I'm sorry to say that such sad, outlandish beliefs were encouraged in high places in the days before the coming of Comrade Atkins and his Committee of Salvation.'

'Committee of Salvation?'

'Right. It's what we in Zanj call the Government. Why are you smiling?'

'Oh I just think it's a good name. Maybe your Committee of Salvation can tell me where to find my Redeemer.'

He gets out of the car and fetches my bags, grunting significantly at their weight. 'Listen, young person, go to other places if you wish spiritual enlightenment. Go to India if you want a guru, go to Kathmandu and get stoned. Go to America and fall in love with a television preacher. But don't come to Africa looking for redeemers.'

'Why not? Do you think I won't find him?'

'Of course you'll find him. You'll find any number of him. Africa has enough redeemers to fill the national football

231

stadium. In Africa you could probably demand one man one redeemer – and you'd get it!'

'Where are we now exactly?'

'This is the centre of town. Most of those newer buildings you see across the road from you are government departments. The one there is the Ministry for Water and next to it is the Ministry for Herds and Grazing and then just down the road is the Ministry for Peasantry.'

'And where would I find the Number One Peasant?'

'He's safe and sound in the Presidential Palace, top of the town, Patrice Lumumba Drive, you can't miss it. You'll see the guards outside. Walk around town as much as you like, only don't go into the country unless your trip's really well organised. It's quite safe if you know what you're doing, but as you saw, you get these Wouff bandits ruining the country-side, shooting up things. That'll be ten dollars American or five hundred Zanj, plus ten.'

'What's the ten for?'

'I told you, you're overweight.' He reverently takes the dollars I hand him and perhaps out of some obscure feeling of gratitude says in a loud whisper, 'Don't go out after dusk. Our curfew is very strict. And keep that diamond out of sight if you don't want people to get the wrong impression.'

Kingdom Towers has a curving drive that leads past the front entrance where two dead palms in pots stand on either side of the door like deceased sentries. A doorman should have patrolled the area between the palms and he probably has once done so because on the tip of one of the withered palms hangs his grey top hat and this gives the tree a gruesomely cheerful look, like a skeleton wearing a wristwatch. And the town had architectural pretensions even before the glass stump called Kingdom Towers was built, because across the road are the remains of a nineteenth-century colonial villa, a gracious and pretty place once. The house seems to have been attacked on three fronts. It has been set alight. That's clear from those big black streaks of soot darkening the crumbling walls which had once been painted a kind of ice-cream pink. It has been fired upon, and the bullets have made craters in the soft powdery pink plaster. And it has been neglected; much of the upper storey has collapsed, leaving only the window frames, which are incongruously protected by heavy wire mesh against which the blue sky presses. A spread of rather tired washing hangs along the balcony rail which runs the full length of the decrepit first floor and tells me that the place is still occupied. A tiny section of roof overhanging this catwalk is propped up by a rotting plank which bulges at several points with termites' nests. In front of the house runs a hot red river of dust and out of the dust grow tall emaciated shrubs with broad green leaves.

Whatever you do, don't believe what you hear about the Kingdom Towers. The place is a dump, a pit, a flea-bag. Above all, do not believe what the barman tells you. It is not the 'Hilton of Central Africa'. The barman's name is Kwatch and he is, I think, my friend. A little man, a gnome, a mannequin, and he doesn't seem to have feet because behind the bar he bobs rather as if he were weighted like one of those dolls you can't knock down, sad whiskers and buck teeth, a most delicate pink nose that you associate with rabbits, and he dresses in olive-green safari suits. His bar is surprisingly modern, smoked glass and a chromium counter, Congolese beer and Egyptian peanuts, beer mats from Albania. The swimming pool has been left to stand and has turned a poisonously milky green, the sort of colour which suggests that if sprayed on fields it would kill locusts or if introduced into the diets of rats would kill those scavengers in their hundreds. It was one of my first suggestions to Kwatch the barman, shortly after my arrival.

'I haven't seen any rats.' He gives a sour little smile.

Kwatch is without doubt the twitchiest barman I've ever met. I can't resist seeing his face lose colour. He does it so quickly! I ask about my father, being careful to spell the name.

'Never heard of him. I'd remember it otherwise.' He watches the door.

'But you must have! He lived here for years. In Waq. He was a friend of the President – the one before the Peasant.'

Kwatch bobs along the bar in some agitation, and leans across. 'Best not to talk of presidents here. You get people who object – like the police. And worse.'

'Do you mean the Public Audit Bureau?'

He goes quite pale. I find that very interesting.

A group of little black boys use the swimming pool notwith-standing the venomous olive sheen upon its surface. Almost every day I see them leaving their games beside the rusted railway engines which stand alone in a field not far from us. They slip into the hotel grounds and dive into the poisoned green milk that was once chlorinated water and spit on the notice which says that costumes must be worn in the pool at all times and reserves it strictly for the use of the guests.

Those railway engines in the middle of nowhere really intrigue me, rusting up and waiting for the creepers to crawl all over them. Flowers poke out of their smoke stacks. The little boys clamber all over them from dawn to dusk, hooting and chugging and pretending to pull the bell and steam away into the blue distance, though of course these trains are going nowhere, they've come to the end of the line, it literally peters out in the dust beneath their big steel wheels. Perhaps the remaining track has been stolen, levered up and sold. This is Kwatch's suggestion. Maybe there was a real station here once, he says, or a siding, and the whole damn thing has been lifted. This is Africa, says Kwatch, which is his way of explaining everything. As if that were a way of explaining anything.

The guests don't miss the pool. They are too few in number. There is the Albanian delegation on the fourth floor, all short hair and smiles, young too, they look like American college boys, with crew cuts, black blazers and red ties. In fact they bear a striking resemblance to the Four Preps; they are bouncy, cheery, and one longs to know if they can harmonise. Instead they go about the place handing out propaganda. Kwatch says that they have been sent over here to subvert the existing order, whatever that is. I think they have merely been abandoned, someone forgot them here, or perhaps there isn't the money to fly them home so they wander about the marketplace pushing bits of paper into the hands of shoppers. It doesn't do much good because the next thing you know, these Albanian tracts have been folded into funnels and used to carry salt (which is the way it's sold here) or they're bleeding soggily in the arms of a woman who's just bought a load of monkey meat, or lizard or bushmeat or the variety of brilliantly feathered birds which are eaten in Zanj with great appetite. But I understand why the Albanians visit the marketplace with their propaganda which no one reads: it helps to pass the time.

I pass some of the time by dressing because I believe one is made, almost commanded, to look one's best whatever the circumstances. I keep myself in trim. So what if I wander about the place exciting curious stares from all and sundry dressed in my Prince of Wales cropped jacket, a fake fur hat and riding breeches? Or if I choose to wear pink leather gloves despite the heat (if we took account of the heat we'd never wear anything). Or if, in the evening, I wear a ruby dress, red suede court shoes and a cummerbund when I wander down to the bar for a drink, who is to say me nay? Certainly not Kwatch. He knows I'm the brightest thing to have hit his bar in light years. But if, by contrast, I set off exploring dressed in a pair of black denim jeans and a silk camisole with shoe-string straps, well then what could be more sensible in this stewing weather?

I'm not here to wait, among my virtues you won't find patience, I'm here to look, to seek, and I do a fair amount of seeking. Without much luck so far. I haven't a car, and no transport is available outside the city of Waq except for a fleet of dusty yellow buses that arrive each morning in the marketplace with peasants stuffed into every corner, carrying their produce, yams, monkeys, snakes and anteaters tied up with string. The anteaters are a local delicacy. I hate the way their snouts are bound, the string wrapped round and round, giving them the look of mummies or muzzled dogs, and their eyes are wild and sad. The buses depart each evening belching black smoke, scattering chickens and urchins as they race across the huge baked floor of the marketplace. The people are a cheerful lot and jabber away in a local vernacular. I believe there are twenty-three languages in all, according to Kwatch. Alas, I do not understand a single one of them. Though a few of the people do speak English. The people in charge are the soldiers who drive around Waq towards sunset when the cur-few is about to come into force, a bunch of arrogant bastards, they loll about in their jeeps. A soldier will ride through town with one leg thrown over the side, a green helmet cocked over one eye, thumbs hooked in his belt, machine gun on the seat beside him. The soldiers signal the beginning of the curfew by firing their guns in the air and everyone scatters to their shanties, tenements, holes, or they run down to the river where some of them live in houses perched on stilts. The River Zan flows through the town of Waq, a dull swirl of brown water, whipped to a dirty cream when there are rains up-country. There are supposed to be thousands of miles of navigable waterway in Zanj but the uncertain levels of the water make this an unreliable asset.

Waq is full of signs, you find them at bus stops and hanging from hedges: 'Zanj is the Tomb of Imperialism' and another popular one is 'Self-sufficiency above all'. Kiosks by the roadsides sell eggs, fruit and vegetables and even these carry slogans urging people to eat Zanjian food only: 'Get your frozen Zanjian rabbit here – 21% more protein'. For a while I feared that they ate worse things still. I studied the meat on the butchers' tables and was convinced it was provided by the rats that I saw outside my hotel. The meat is not red, but black with congealed blood, and the flies are awful. But this is not rat meat, it's bushmeat. It comes from a rodent called the grasscutter, Kwatch tells me, which is not a member of the rat family but is related to the porcupine and the chinchilla. It's much prized and is twice the price of beef or pork, but I'm glad that I'm managing to survive on toast and tea, Egyptian peanuts and beer. Strange thing is, I seldom think of my chocolate days; I think instead of the Redeemer and this gives me strength. Another thing that gives me strength is Kwatch's determination to persuade me that I won't find him.

'For one thing,' says Kwatch, 'if you've got this God, then remember you've got to split him three ways. To the Ite, he is the Lord, right? Because they're Christians. To the Kanga he's an Imam, or something that the Moslems go for. And to the Wouff he's a bloody rock! So what you've got is not a redeemer, you've got an entire holy trinity!'

'I know he's here.'

'I admire your faith,' says Kwatch, 'but can you prove it?'

Kwatch claims to be Lebanese though he speaks English with a German accent. The large lobes of his ears are covered in soft down. 'I mean, do you really think that there exists a cannibal king in Zanj, one that everybody knows about but won't tell you? Do you really think, delightful young lady, with eyes the colour of smoke, and hair – my god, little lady, what hair! The colour of firelight – do you think that you will find your lost cannibal king here? Whoever filled your head with these stories deserves to be flogged. We couldn't afford such a luxury. The country of Zanj is little, land-locked and backward. We grow some coffee, but we don't have enough insecticides, our roads are impassable, we have some diamonds, they say, somewhere in the mountains, but we have no railway system, all our goods must flow down the river through three countries on their way to the sea, when the rivers flow at all. Our population growth is frightening. We have already three million. Maybe to a smart French miss that doesn't seem a lot. But let me tell you that when the World Bank visited us ten years ago, we had only half that number. The World Bank doesn't come here any more. That's why we're so pleased to see you. Maybe you're the start of the tourist trade!'

I sit in his bar and sip my beer. For a week now I have been the only customer. According to Kwatch, trade fluctuates and the hotel fills up unexpectedly, depending on developments. What sort of developments? 'Political developments,' says Kwatch heavily. 'That's the only development we have.' My days are divided into roughly three periods, of which sitting in the bar after curfew is the third. In the mornings I dress slowly and eat in the dining room where bread and coffee is provided for the Albanian delegation and myself. Sometimes there is no sugar for the coffee, sometimes no milk. The manager, a portly little Roumanian, comes into the dining room and apologises for the late arrival of whatever is not there and craves our indulgence. We know then that whatever has not been forthcoming won't be, and go forward into our day; the Albanian delegation to the marketplace with their pamphlets, I to walk about town, pretending to be looking, pretending to be sightseeing, when I know that like the missing sugar or bread at breakfast, the sights I wish to see will not be forthcoming. But then looking is a good disguise, I find. If you do it well enough no one dreams that what you are really doing is waiting. Mr Adelescu, the hotel manager, was not always a hotel manager, as he tells me mournfully, but he was 'sacrificed'.

'I came out here to rebuild the capital of Waq, sent by my president, President Ceausescu. I was gift of the president. I came out here soon after most of the Western diplomatic missions closed, when Comrade Atkins broke off relations with France. I came to spread the Roumanian gospel of socialist architecture based upon the Roumanian plan. Knock down the slums and hovels of Waq. Replace with people's city, spacious streets and serviceable quarters. But the bulldozers we were promised by Hungary never arrived. And I was sacrificed!' He spreads his hands and shrugs apologetically. 'This morning we have no milk. The ferry has broken down twenty kilometres up-river.'

Kwatch gives me reasons why Monsieur Brown can't be here; he speaks in the language of scepticism, of science, of observation: 'If there's no sign of him, he can't be here.' His urgent attempts to convince me of his non-existence, his kind-ly, laboratory approach, give me quite another idea, because if you listen carefully to the language of persuasion you can hear that through the deep subterranean caves of his grammar runs the river of fear. In fact, the denials he offers me continually provide clues and pointers to the presence somewhere of the Redeemer.

And so this talk of his absence excites me. And I'm getting ready for something, I can feel it, it comes to me that if he is to appear then I must be ready for him and that's why after one of these disinformation sessions with Kwatch I go upstairs to my bedroom and stretch out on my bed. I may be wearing my leopard print bodysuit and leopard print leggings, the thick black belt with the dragon clasp and a pair of purple leather gloves. Or I may be wearing my black lycra mini-skirt and black opaque tights. It doesn't matter. From my bed I am afforded a view of myself in the freckled mirror of my brown wooden cupboard with the wonky left leg (I have propped that leg with a copy of *The Life of Mussolini*, one of those salvaged from among the poor burnt books after the fire at the Priory Hotel) and I watch myself lying on the bed. It's my spiritual exercise. And even without my walkman I hear the music in my head as I remove whatever I am wearing and stretch out on the bed and lie there naked, hearing the sounds of something appropriate, say an electronic 'Four Seasons', or early Presley, the only acceptable sort, say 'Milk Cow Blues Boogie', or Gregorian plainchant done reggae-style. Sometimes I think my musical education has not been very complete; maybe more attention should have been paid to the lyrics we love and learn, especially since for so many of us they are the only form of religion available.

It's vital that I lie in the middle of my bed and then spread my legs in a V, checking on my central position in the mirror so that its freckled eye bisects me: I did not arrive at this position without experiment. In fact, if I were as scientific as my Uncle Claude, I would say that I have achieved what I call this ideal position by a series of experiments, ceaselessly manoeuvring myself on the bed so as to achieve precisely the right position, just as a radio antenna is adjusted until the signal is received, or as the emulsion is laid on the photographic plate to record the flight of elementary particles, or as the gas in the bubble chamber is made ready to allow us to see the passage of invisible neutral pions and the dance of charmed particles. Of course we do not 'see' them at all, but only their passage through the universe we have prepared for them. We record their tracks and then fall over and adore the obvious. The will to power has disguised itself as the search for knowledge, and the love of the obvious is what has eaten at Uncle Claude, his weakness for props spun into a dramatic theory and narrated in the self-satisfied tones of a man sick from his own certainty. I prefer to remember that there are particles which reveal themselves only when they have changed into others. Before then they are invisible, their presence is only detected when they decay into visible tracks, which are the tracks of new particles entirely. In other words, it is only after their death that they come to life, it is only after they have disappeared that we can see them. I have learnt something after all from Uncle Claude. The bastard!

And what am I positioning myself for? Well, I'm not entirely sure except, in some way, for *him*! Though I do not join my uncle's church of cause and effect, his cult of erectile tissue, his temple of psychological delusions. I sail by internal tides, the salty, bloody ocean within me. When the time and the position are right, he will come!

There have been signs. There have been times when I have been pretty depressed having to endure the impenetrable bonhomie of the Albanian political hucksters, the lies of the manager about breakfast, the heat, the loneliness, and the smooth evasions of the barman Kwatch. But there *have* been signs. The first came one afternoon as I wandered around the perimeter of the hotel, and found that the River Zan, which floods the mud flats at the far end of town in what is laughingly called the harbour, where the stilt houses cluster, in fact runs past the back of the Kingdom Towers, runs silently and almost guiltily, like so much in this country, as if it did not want to be observed, or as if it carried on its thick muscular current a cargo of dead babies or human limbs, a hateful, hidden contraband. Behind the hotel it flows through a narrow pass that it has cut for itself over the centuries and which can only be reached by scrambling down a steep bank thick with thorn bushes and grass as tough as rusted wire. Into the side of this bank there has been scooped out, perhaps some years ago, to judge by the secondary growth of grass and shrubs, a shallow pit, and into the pit there have been thrown hundreds and hundreds of used sanitary towels. Once they must have been covered over but the occasional rains and scouring winds have revealed the tangled mass of blood-stained bandages. The pit gapes, it's grievous, the blood on the bandages has turned brown where it is not black and some towels have been almost washed clean of it and show only the faintest pink tinge.

I can't tell you what this discovery did to me. (Well, even though you can be told nothing, I am going to do so anyway. You whom nothing can surprise since presumably such discoveries are arranged by you, like everyone else, long in advance. At least allow your creatures to bore you dreadfully by telling you what you have known all along, and they have not.) The pit of towels spoke to me of time and women. They told me that there had been a time when things were ordered differently in the country of Zanj, certainly among those lucky enough to live in the city of Waq, a time when the elementary comforts of the outside world were available to the women I see here today in the marketplace with their thin faces and their skinny children, their bushmeat and their monkey meat

240

reddening the advertising brochures of the Albanian Revolution. I knew then that the oppressive insistence of everyone and all I saw in the country of Zanj, that this place was sunk in poverty and torpor from which nothing could arouse it, that things had always been this way and always would be, that its people were wretches who might bleed where they stood – all this was a lie and it vanished at the sight of the secret of the river bank.

Let me tell you right now that I wasn't dressed to be exploring the river bank, not in a white silk organza blouse, more suitable for evening wear, and navy gaberdine jodhpurs and, as you can imagine, my pants were soon covered in a mass of spiny black thorns that gave the material a bearded look, but I went on down to the water's edge anyway, after I had discovered the pit, and there I found a little boy fishing. He wore a shirt only and the curve of his buttocks was like marble. He caught a fish while I watched and held it up, small, dark and very ugly with an aged whiskery face. I felt he was going to throw it back into the river which curdled past his feet, its little rugged waves capped with dirty, creamy foam. But he suddenly bent down and smashed its head on a rock. I called out but he didn't turn. Perhaps he didn't see me. I think sometimes that people have no idea I'm here. As I watched he pulled from the fish's whiskery mouth a wicked three-barbed hook and cast his line back into the river. I went away again, scrabbling my way up the bank, using my hands to pull me up quickly, breaking a nail, which made me curse. As I passed the pit of towels I reached out and touched one; it was stiff, like a dead person, but warm.

I knew then, without thinking, what I had to do and that's when I went upstairs to my room and locked the door. I lay down on the bed and took off my clothes, kicking and throwing them into the corner as I dragged them off. As soon as I had got my clothes off and lay there sweating slightly, listening to the sound of my breathing, I reached for my bedside mirror and looked at myself. The breeze that you will often get in Waq in the early afternoon was cool across my body and I stroked the inside of my knee. The mirror showed me in pieces and I put them together by moving it across my body, adding a breast to a shoulder, joining a body from navel to collarbone and a face somewhat pale and white around the lips, adding an eyebrow seen from above, bristling over the eye socket. Some bits are more difficult to connect — my pubic mound, an atoll surrounded by a fleshy sea, and a chin more pointed than I had suspected. This was all experimental stuff, but of three things I was sure: I should wait, I should be ready, and he was close to me.

Naturally they follow me, crazy little white girl strolling around town. The job's down to the sad little tyke in the dark woollen suit who watches my window from the ruined villa over the road. They suffer for security's sake here. He's my first glimpse of the Public Audit Bureau in action. The classes in Zanj are two: the poor and the armed. The armed take it in turns to wear each others' clothes. It's my first introduction to the knowledge that tyranny likes to dress. Today there are soldiers riding around before curfew; yesterday these soldiers were accountants in suits and glasses, carrying briefcases, and from whom even the children run in fear.

'Who called them by that name?'

Kwatch shrugs. 'Somebody liked the sound. Sound is everything here. They do the books — understand? Settle accounts.'

'Who was the somebody?'

Kwatch raises his eyes to heaven and sighs heavily. 'Give it up, Bella. He's not here.'

But there are great gaps in his pretence which I can expose when I wish. He can be trapped pretty easily.

'Who are those guards they have patrolling the Presidential Palace? They're not Zanjians.'

'No, they're Moroccans.'

'What happened to the Palestinians? You used to have Palestinians, didn't you? They're the best.'

'Who told you about the Palestinians?'

'Somebody.'

He swallows hard.

See what I mean?

The glacial melt of time, seeming slow only at first, suddenly sweeps us away. My first weeks in Waq are when time waits, while I pray for signs and wonders. Prayers have an odd way of turning into theories. I have a theory and it runs as follows.

242

Having explored over several weeks the city of Waq, I have come to the conclusion that all is not what it seems. I am sure, on the basis of my observations, that there is simply not enough here to explain the mystery of Zanj, there is not enough visible matter to explain the totality which Waq claims to be. Note, *claims to be*, because there is something very odd about the city of Waq. Number one mystery is the whereabouts of the Number One Peasant, Comrade Atkins. Visit the Presidential Palace at the top of town and you will see there a squat, concrete bunker that looks to the innocent eye of your reporter like a gaol, stuck away at the end of Patrice Lumumba Drive, with all the foreign legations crouching around it like village houses around a grand château, the embassies of the Yemen, Albania, the People's Republic of the Congo, and there is obviously a swift trade in these places because the Yemeni Embassy was once occupied by the Belgians and before that by the Dutch and the coats of arms of these countries remain there still, and if you look closely at the pock-marked brick gateposts of its entrance, an Austrian eagle is to be discerned, wounded in one eye by a stray bullet which still protrudes from the stone.

The President is said to be in residence, bored soldiers patrol the entrance, notices appear written by hand, and stuck to the security fence: *'Number One Peasant, Comrade Atkins, today welcomes the Ambassador of Libya . . .', 'Three Bandits were executed at dawn! Long live the People's Republic of Zanj!'*

Now this sort of thing is all very well, but it's simply not enough, is it? So I say again, there is not enough visible matter to hold the so-called universe of Zanj together. The observable material amounts, in my estimation, to no more than about twenty per cent of the total. So where is the missing matter and why can't we see it? Well, I believe that it exists beyond the confines of Waq itself and that we can't see it because it is dark matter. This then is my theory. It may sound a little unlikely, but my position is that we can show that my theoretical extrapolations point to a hidden universe, much larger than ours, an invisible neighbour. How can I know this? Well, you will understand that the universe has a propensity for arranging itself in patterns and sequences which have the mysterious power to conform to whatever the observer expects to find. To the anthropic principle that things are the way they

243

are because we are, I add the fairy-tale principle: that things will look just as you wish them to look, so long as we provide ourselves with a special way of seeing. God does not play dice with the universe, someone insisted. My Uncle Claude replied that, on the contrary, the universe plays poker with God, and it's about to call his bluff. I don't think either of these things is true, God may not play dice, but I believe he does play hide-and-seek. I don't expect you to take all this on trust, you will want some scientific proof, a clue, a sign that this hidden universe which I am investigating exists at all.

My sign comes to me one evening about a month after arriving in Zanj. I am sitting having a drink in Kwatch's bar. It is his habit to give me change in local currency, converting my American dollars into Zanjian money. Among the notes he hands me is one rather older than the rest, leaf-brown, wrinkled and rather frail, and this leads me to single it out before putting the change in my purse, smoothing it on the bar counter. Staring back at me, without his glasses admittedly, without his cap and without his field marshal's baton, now with his head crowned, or haloed in a wreath, perhaps of laurel leaves, which gives him a rather Roman look, is Monsieur Brown. Now I know that my Redeemer liveth! And this is no trick, watch my hands carefully, check that I have nothing up my sleeves. The fact is that my friend has sent me a note from the other side. A window opens on the world next door and I am on my way, I am going through that window. Glass and all.

The question is where to start? Actually that's not very difficult to decide because, as we know, the universe looks much the same in every direction. I use the astronomical 'we' so that it should be understood that mine is a real scientific investigation and to alert the careful observer that my voyage is based upon the firmest scientific principles, for it is clear to anyone but the blind that there is something outside the city of Waq which draws things to it, something or someone, and this gravitational force must have an explanation even if we can't yet say with any clarity what it is. Or who it is. I pack immediately.

I've not told Kwatch of my plans but I think he knows. He's taken to following me around the place with a hang-dog expression, the look of someone who hasn't quite come to terms with himself. I can't decide whether he gave me the banknote by accident, or was it a Freudian slip? Or did he want me to know? There's something strange and apologetic about his manner and, although he doesn't actually apologise, this sorrowing attitude of his worries me and so I make my departure arrangements quietly. Out of the mouths of barmen!

In a little bag I pack a few changes of clothing, among them a little black cotton tulip-skirted dress with pink spots, a green silk jacket and trousers, a pink crepe button-through dress and rather pretty, dark-blue lycra stockings. I hide my bag of clothes at the back of the hotel on the river bank. On one of these sorties I see soldiers repairing and painting, sweeping and washing the main road that runs from the Presidential Palace to the hotel.

I'm not exactly bowled over when I see from my window these guys marching up the main steps. They're soldiers from the Presidential Palace, except they are soldiers no longer now. They've taken off their metal helmets and their boots and they wear dark-grey safari suits and carry briefcases. The Public Audit Bureau is on the march. Times change fast in Africa, it's a matter of hats. I hear the little Roumanian manager shrieking at the auditors.

'But the presidential suite is unfit to receive His Excellency. Please convey my joy at the suggestion, my grief at the unreadiness of the rooms. If only you'd given me some warning!'

I slip out the back, claim my little travel bag and head for the marketplace. With an hour to run before curfew, I get on the yellow bus called *Sweet Little Me*, its roof piled at least two metres high with bags, pots, boxes, bicycles and blankets, which gives the bus a distinct list to the left. Climbing aboard with me are about thirty other people all carrying their goods and chattels, hens in baskets, snakes in basins, supplies of bushmeat, manioc and cooked maize. I am dressed for the road in crisp, classic tailoring, a long lean jacket, tapering trousers and fitted blouse; my scarf is covered with turquoise butterflies on a creamy ground and I wear a black straw hat. The beggars who haunt the marketplace give us a rousing send-off. They possess an incredible variety of disabilities, goitres, stumps, ganglions. There are blind old men led by boys, there are limbless babies carried by girls, there are here the champions of the thousand ills to which the flesh is heir, the marketplace is a terrible trading fair of infirmities and deformities. Yet the beggars are surprisingly cheerful, determined and imaginative. One plays tunes from 'Orpheus in the Underworld' on a nose flute; another with no eyes but round, milky sockets carries a tape-recorder and has gone high-tech, slipping a tape into his ghetto-blaster and broadcasting at tremendous volume his appeal for alms for the love of Allah. Before boarding the bus I scatter small change like the sower with his seed.

'You're generous,' says the driver, who introduces himself as Sessou. 'You give for the love of Allah.'

'No, just because I feel sorry for them.'

We take off in a storm of dust into which the beggars dissolve. I can hear the luggage on the roof, tied down with rope and wire, creaking protestingly; our list to the left is even worse.

I ask the driver what I should pay.

'First stop is Bamba. Where are you going?'

'Wherever you're going. I want to explore the country. How much, please?'

'It doesn't matter. When you know where you're going, you'll know what to pay. You will recognise the place when you get there?'

'Certainly.'

Perhaps I haven't dressed very wisely because the bus is twice as full as it should be and smells to high heaven. It's not only the crush of people and goods, the stale sweat and dust, but one of the anteaters has diarrhoea and the packets of bushmeat give off a strong gamey aroma of blood and skin that make me feel pretty queasy. Mr Sessou speaks English, French and a number of the vernaculars. The people on the bus are a tribal mix: there are Wouff, tall, dark and silent, semi-naked but for little leather skirts, wearing round their necks a small stone with a hole bored through the centre strung on a leather thong. There are Ite, mostly in Western clothes, the women with their heads swathed in bright turbans. And there are the

Moslem Kanga in flowing white. I sit beside a lady as wide as she is tall, her feet on a can of paraffin which reeks with that boringly chemical brazenness, so much at odds with the smell of fruit, of cured hide and the excretions of the captive animals around me. My companion carries on her lap a caged monkey, a tiny, beautiful creature which grips the bars of its cage with exquisite hands and stares at me with passionate, bewildered eyes. Because of the pronounced list of *Sweet Little Me* I tend to lean rather heavily on my companion as we race along the dusty roads, as if I were a small white moon captured by her superior gravity, but she's soft and warm as a bread oven and pays me the compliment of appearing not to notice by keeping her eyes closed. Thirty kilometres or so outside Waq, just as the sun is setting, a golden performance in an utterly empty huge blue sky, we stop.

'Customs post.' Sessou's announcement is met with groans and hisses of disapproval from the passengers.

I walk up to the front. 'A customs post? So soon? But we've only been travelling about twenty minutes. Surely we haven't reached the border yet?'

'In Zanj,' Sessou explains, 'we've got customs posts inside the country. They're all over the place. All over! It's the way the soldiers and the official cadres gather income. The story says that one day a soldier saw a customs post at the border. He saw them collecting money. And he said to himself, because he was a clever soldier, let me start one! And he did! Now they all go off somewhere and start their own – it's the soldiers' industry.'

A soldier with a rifle climbs aboard and mutters something at Sessou, who commands us to produce our *pièces d'identité* – travel permits, passports, our papers, our permissions.

No one stirs. They all regard the soldier warily and he studiously does not return the sullen looks of the bus passengers. The anteater's diarrhoea continues noisily. The soldier mutters again and stomps off the bus, his steel boots noisy on the stairs. Sessou leaves his seat with a rueful shake of his head. 'He say all luggage must be unloaded. Taken off the roof. Examined for contraband. All. Everything. On the other hand we must pay him one thousand dollars Zanj in travellers' levy.'

It's clear that 'on the other hand' means that this is the hand to be greased.

'Offer him twenty American dollars.'

I'm surprised by the strength of my voice and its impatience.

Sessou is swift off the mark. He confers with the soldier, money changes hands, the soldier salutes and we rattle away into the sunset. My fellow passengers are so stunned for a moment that we've come through it quickly and painlessly that they gaze at me quite boggle-eyed and then they break into applause. I seize my moment. You see, we live and learn. The alternative is that we die and nature learns. I speak in evolutionary terms, of course. But I really haven't time for evolution. I'm not a cathedral of bacteria, a cloud of particles, some sort of special plastic material on which nature plays and builds simply to keep itself going. I am me, Bella, now — or never.

I take out the banknote, the sign from the other world, and show it to my companion and her reaction is a religious spectacle, a *missa solemnis* of enthusiasm. She throws her hands up to her mouth, then to her ears; she closes her eyes and then opens them again and, seeing that the picture doesn't change, throws her hands into the air once more and jiggles them in excitement and ecstasy. I get the feeling that if she could she'd go down on her knees but the paraffin can and the monkey prevent that. Her excitement spreads to the other customers who leave their seats and crowd around us, chattering and pointing and touching their hands together in gestures of reverence. The driver Sessou shouts from the top of the bus that the movement of people is adding to the list and making driving dangerous.

'All passengers return to seats. Movement will unroad us!' When he is ignored he pulls over to the side of the road and comes back to investigate the cause of all the excitement. The passengers are reaching out to touch the frail banknote from whose centre, beneath a circle of laurel leaves, a Caesarian image, my Redeemer glowers deeply at the world. How wonderful to see him so regally displayed. People kiss their fingers and reach out to touch his face and I remember then the stories that he told me about the belief in the healing powers of his person.

'They know him!' is all I can say to Sessou. 'Look, they all know him!'

'Naturally they know him. He is the Redeemer, he ruled us. Supreme ruler and great man of Zanj.' Sessou is pleased and proud to make the identification.

'But in the capital they tell me they haven't ever heard of him. He doesn't exist.'

Sessou shrugs. 'In the capital they say things because it is ordered. All memories of the Redeemer have been scratched from the mind of the nation. It is ordered from Comrade Atkins. Do you know him? The Number One Peasant? Thus it always goes in Zanj. Our Peasant belongs to the Kanga tribe, but the Redeemer, he was a Wouff, and the Kanga hate the Wouff . . .'

'Yes, I know. They regard the Wouff as slaves.'

'You know this country! It is true. The Wouff do make quite good slaves. That was once upon a time, but they needed much, much training.'

I gather from this observation that Sessou is a member of the Ite tribe.

'I have heard it said that the Redeemer was very cruel.'

His face brightens. 'He was the cruellest man in the world! This we all knew. God bless him! He was the King of blood and he made us very, very frightened. Oh yes! Now they say in the capital that we may not speak of him any longer. No more. All his pictures are gone. They take his pictures and they throw them in the River Zan: his books, his pictures, his money and his magic, they drown them all in the River Zan saying he is dead forever and no more. We must not say his name or the soldiers come and shoot us. But the people know, they remember, here in the country they know the Redeemer and who he is. They never forget him, never, never!'

'But if he was so cruel why do they think so much of him?'

'Because,' Sessou explains with superb logic, 'he showed himself to the people. OK, he maybe say to this one, "You die!" and he died. Or to that one, "Crocodile meat!" and he is meat. But he came before his people and they saw him. He was very, very brave!'

249

'He came before the people more often than Comrade Atkins?'

Sessou looks at me as if I am mad. 'Atkins never comes. Not once in his life. He is frightened, not like the Redeemer who was a great, big man. You can see the Redeemer's house, there in Bamba, where we are going. This winter palace of the Redeemer – you wait!'

'He had his house in Bamba?'

'His palace. For the winter. The summer, he goes to the capital.'

*Sweet Little Me* sways along under a night sky so vast, so mountainous, huge and rearing and brilliantly powdered, crowded and overflowing with stars, so many the sheer multitude makes me feel a little sick. But then I've been feeling off colour for some days. Look up and the galaxies are scattered across the heavens like cosmic foam, a billion trillion suns, stars, planets, moons, quasars, bits of cosmic string, black holes, white dwarves, red giants, supernova and interstellar dust, and through all this cosmic ocean the schools of particles stream like plankton: gravitons, muons, gluons, quarks, neutrinos, photons, baryons, as well as light matter, dark matter and anti-matter. All of which my Uncle Claude probes with the grace of a backstreet abortionist and the certainties of a priest of the Inquisition (here's the funny part), he scours it with the superstitious faith of some Neolithic dreamer looking in terror for the bogeyman who he believes hides in the heavens, but who all the time . . .

I think Uncle Claude, who I am sure even now is sweeping the section of the cosmos accessible to his cold eye above La Frisette, feels his telescope to be some kind of a straw through which he draws as much celestial matter as he can swallow at a gulp and then slowly digests it for signs of life, after which it passes through his system like so much waste matter. A scientist is an instrument for converting knowledge into sewage. Oh, Uncle Claude, why don't you come to Bamba! But he can't/won't! Only I come to Bamba on a yellow bus called *Sweet Little Me* which trundles through the night with a bad list, the good Mr Sessou at the wheel. My large companion is so warm and comfortable that I fall asleep against her shoulder and when I wake I find the monkey playing with my hair, its bright black eyes wide and wild.

The town of Bamba has seen better days. Nothing works. Water must be carried from the river of the same name which runs past the town. The only shop is a table under a tree selling dates, Egyptian cigarettes and Chinese razor blades. The houses are deserted. But this was a centre of substance once, there was a Sofitel hotel on the edge of town and a casino for visiting dignitaries, but both are now smashed and deserted, their windows are gone and their doors carried off. The roads are muddy but here and there a little grey macadam shows through to remind us that they were once paved.

So what do you wear for a visit to a Redeemer's winter palace? The expectation is there, whether you like it or not. I go top of the range, eventually, after much thought. A black linen halterneck top and a chocolate linen jacket plus chocolate bermuda shorts. Yes, I *know*, it is woefully inappropriate. But it's also cool and convenient. I wash my hair in tepid water and simply comb it back. The comb grates on particles of sand – this is river water!

The winter palace of the Redeemer is a series of Spanish-style villas set within a compound behind walls which were once pink, the shade of old blood stains, and mounted with spikes. You push on the big gates and they rasp noisily on their rusted hinges. A black boy scuttles out of the compound as I enter and crouches in half appeal, half bow of welcome. 'Missy, Missy, Missy! Come see, I'll show you the gaols of the Redeemer. Place of torture!'

I give him five dollars. He nearly faints and I realise it's far too much but he reminds me of Clovis and I can't help it. He must be about twenty, with a beautifully smooth face and cloudy eyes, his skin polished. He stares at me, at my clothes and when he sees my diamond pendant he becomes frantic:

'I will show you things of great cruelty, for the Redeemer was a great monster.'

Here is the same excitement I heard in Sessou's voice. To many people the fabled cruelty of their former leader is a source of pride. Because of the nearness of the river the growth in the garden is luxuriant behind the steel gates and the high walls. Lizards peer from the spreading fronds of the encroaching bush, a red bird with a bright green eye looks down its long curved nose at me and nods as if information received is being confirmed. My guide scampers before me, turning around repeatedly and calling me on by throwing out his hand, keeping it low and rubbing the fingers together as if he is spreading breadcrumbs to lure a bird. The palace is now no more than a series of empty, looted rooms around a central courtyard where a stagnant pool covered in green scum moves like a carpet beneath the hovering dragonflies.

'Come this way,' the young man beckons.

The first room shows broken taps protruding from walls and a channel, or sluice, cut into the floor and running out into the River Bamba.

'Come in, come in.' My guide pulls me into the gloom of the first chamber and then through a little passage into a second room where there are the remains of a giant fridge. In the fridge are rails and butchers' hooks which he sends spinning along the rails with a musical clash of steel.

'Here people were killed, on a table here,' – the young man shows me precisely – 'the blood and other parts were washed down the drains in the floor into the River Bamba outside. Sometimes the meat was rolled. Sometimes they hung the whole person on a hook and then the cook came here to make his choice. All this I saw, me,' says the young man and touches his eyes, 'myself.'

On the floor of the giant fridge are fragments of bones. And scattered among the bones, little white flakes of something. Rice! Next door is the dining room.

'Here stood the table.' With the flat of his hand he gives me not only the position but the height of the Redeemer's table, then a swift tracery in the air describes the glittering chandelier which hung above it and the twenty places it could accommodate. Again there is that curious sparkle of pride. 'The Monster ate here with his guests. Afterwards they watched the lions.'

The lions' cage is out in the open and the throne is there where the Redeemer sat to decide the fate of his enemies. The young man sits on the marble throne, beside which are dead fountains that once sprayed scented water and played tunes, the 'Marseillaise' and 'Waltzing Matilda', I know this because my guide whistles them while sitting on the throne. Those not fed to the lions went to the crocodile pool, now simply a sludgy trench, and those who escaped the crocodiles were thrown into the snake-pit, all now empty, nondescript, decaying, dirty, non-existent you might say, were it not for the brilliant performance of my guide, the living theatre of the Redeemer. It's all cheaper, poorer, hotter than I thought it would be. Nothing is ever like the movies except the movies and sometimes I think I made a mistake in drowning my walkman.

'Where is he now?'

'He?' The question appears to amaze him, he scratches his head, he pulls at his lips. 'He was a bad man, very cruel. An animal!'

I'm beginning to think the record's stuck. 'Where can I find him?'

I don't really expect an answer but I get one and it staggers me. 'Maybe his mother tells you.'

At first there is no way of telling whether the little old lady in front of me in the dust, in the tiny mud house, with the pink, marbled gums, smooth of any hint of teeth, and the rheumy eyes, is who I take her to be. My guide claims that she is the mother of the Redeemer and who am I to contradict him? What can we do when we are faced with configurations we do not recognise but which others insist are perfectly matched to our expectations, sorry, our theories – what can we do but watch and study and wait for the clue, the evidence which might suggest that what we are seeing is what we think we are seeing. I don't see any family resemblance. In fact if she looks like anybody she looks like the lead guitarist with Giuseppe and the Lambs – but perhaps I'm rather tired. What I see in front of me, in so far as I *can* see in this gloomy little hut, is a lady of about ninety, I guess, her old black face wrinkled and lit by the astonishing pink of her gums when she smiles. She points to my pendant and says something to the boy. He nods vigorously. The diamond seems to fascinate everyone who sees it. I remember the warning of the customs' man to keep it hidden. Except that these people aren't in any way threatening. They seem pleased to see the stone.

'Say that I know her son.'

The old woman smiles and nods as if this isn't news, that everyone in the world, if they know what's good for them, knows her son.

'Say I knew him in the country where I live, in France.'

He tells her and I can see that this information is a bit puzzling, because she interrupts the translator with a series of brief little barks and when he argues with her she shrugs her shoulders and seems to be prepared to give me the benefit of the doubt, to say, OK, so this crazy child thinks she knew him in her country, but then he is world-renowned, they know him everywhere, so if you want to know him in France, good luck to you.

'Ask her if she knows where he is now. Is he here?'

She gives a short emphatic grunt. My chest is so tight I find it difficult to breathe and my heart is loud in the darkness and noisy, it's beating so that it actually moves me as I try to stand steady on the earth floor peering down at the little lady who lifts her hands and points them in an arrow shape, fingers extended to show us where he is. Her fingers! Each and every one of them the same; tubular, uniform fingers that made it so difficult to wear rings, so difficult when your subjects wish always to kiss your rings . . .

'She says her son is near. Her daughter will take you. We go.'

Strange, again, how when one piece of evidence emerges, others follow, first her fingers and then her daughter. Daughter-in-law, more likely, for as soon as the woman approaches us outside the old lady's hut, I recognise her. Certainly she may have put on a little weight since the days when she made a wonderful Venus to his Mercury, after Correggio, the one with the wings that gave Brest the butcher so much pleasure, the recreated painting in which my Redeemer plays Mercury in the baseball cap and is seen with one of his sixty-five children as Cupid. Harp, his third wife! The very same.

'She leads, we go after,' my guide answers.

We go after, as he says we should. This outfit was certainly not the right thing to wear: the grass is high and sharp and tears at my bare legs and although my outfit is pretty light, the heat is intense; this might be winter but the temperature is surely well into the thirties as we walk behind Harp who leads us to the centre of the little town of Bamba where there

254

is a kind of rocky table of land surrounded by trees and heavily overgrown with vines and creepers. It was walled once, though there are great breaches in the walls as if this place has been under heavy bombardment. Harp, who has not spoken and only turns now and then to make sure we are following her, will go no further. The guide nods me towards the entrance, which carries the very faint sign painted high on the wall in ornate script, *Jardin de Thé* – Tea Garden.

'You go in. He is there.' My guide pushes me. 'The daughter says.'

'Won't you come with me?'

He gives an embarrassed laugh, shakes his head and says nothing. I can see he's frightened.

At first I see what I think is a glass altar set in a kind of arena or amphitheatre. There are tattered flags, their ends eaten by the winds, hanging from four flagpoles set at each corner of the altar. There is a steel turnstile, long rusted and no longer turning. In the tall grass I find fragments of statues. There is a Victor Hugo asleep on his face in the sun; and Napoleon without hands; an orb and a sceptre that can only have come from some statue of Queen Victoria of whom there is now no sign. And the altar is not really an altar, I see this as I get closer, nor is it made of glass but probably of perspex, like Clovis' boot. It's a tomb, a hero's tomb. There are also shreds and tatters of some kind of canvas in the grass, a livid green with yellow stipples, and it occurs to me that this was probably some kind of tent or canopy to keep off the sun which beats down mercilessly. Strewn in the long grass are pieces of rusting equipment, cogs and wheels. Into the frieze at the base of the tomb messages had once been cut but these have been removed by the simple expedient of rubbing cement into the carving. This tomb has been defaced and then desecrated. I step closer to the glass coffin which is covered with dust and leaves and bending over I sweep away one corner and look inside. I feel as I did when I looked through the lake water at *La Belle Indifférente* in her watery grave, so perfectly preserved and so remote, lost to us and yet so near.

The tomb is empty. Whoever was here once is gone. On one of the pieces of equipment in the grass, I can make out the words *Refriga Hungarica* ... I understand now that this was some kind of cooling plant, and here he would have lain in state, preserved under the canopy, cooled by the conditioning plant, surrounded by statues of the great ones.

He was to sleep forever, preserved against rot and damp, worms and wives, pharaohed in his greatness, ever secure in his box. Which came first – tomb or tea garden? Tea garden, of course, though at some point it was, as they say, redeveloped, the place made ready, the cooling system brought in, turnstiles erected, glass polished; then something happened. Before the remains of the old imperial tea garden could be torn away there came disaster, the clock stopped, the bush came back, the sun wouldn't go away. New times, new regimes – another ruler who objected to the old pretender had had his praises obliterated, maybe the Number One Peasant, or Number Three or Four, maybe all numbered peasants are indistinguishable, except by their numbers ... I breathe on the glass and rub it with my hand in case there is something I missed. Nothing. Not a bit of bone, a tooth, not a relic, not a grain of rice. The purple hangings that were to keep the sun off are torn, all the statues are stones in the grass. But the intention is there, the prayer is there, he was to have lain here in the way my little boat lay on the floor of the lake, *La Belle Indifférente*, and no doubt children passing this way were also to pause and gape in wonder, perhaps to giggle softly as they leaned over the grave, hands on their knees. Nothing. Nothing except the sound of the sun which has been squeezed into a hot choked ticking in the long grass. But I feel him! As I felt him when he stood beside me by the lakeside and peered into the grave of the drowned boat. Suddenly, in case I hear a voice in my ear and find him beside me staring into the glass box built to hold himself, I straighten. The boy watches. He blinks at me, quick and hurt, I think he must be crying until I feel the tears on my own cheeks.

'Ask her if she knew my father. A white man – a friend of the Redeemer?'

In answer Harp turns and moves away, giving us a glance over her shoulder meaning that we are to follow, and we go out of the garden and down a track and through thick reeds where the ducks fly upward in panic, and there by the riverside, moored in the brown waters of the River Bamba, is a houseboat. It's just like the houseboats I saw in his photographs in his room in the Rue Vandal. It hasn't been occupied for a long time – months, years perhaps. Creepers have begun to grow over it and it creaks protestingly as we climb aboard and clouds of mud float up to the surface of the water as she moves sluggishly beneath our weight. The rugs, the twirly table-legs, the settled, solid and rather pushy, overclothed permanence of a floating home. It's sweltering hot, the windows have not been opened – well, since he went away. Everything is as he left it.

On his desk the photographs stare at me. Here is my mother, young and very beautiful, posing for once for somebody else's camera, hand on her hip with the sea behind her and the wind lifting her hair. Here I am in my First Communion dress and here again on a bicycle, about eight years old, smiling toothily from a gilt frame. And here I am, a baby, sitting on Uncle Claude's lap while he reads to me from Euclid. I am crying but he does not appear to have noticed.

And here is a letter, his pen lies on the paper, uncapped, just as he left it . . .

> *'My dear Bella,*
> *Do not believe–'*

Though I try several times the pen will make no mark; it simply scratches the paper of his unfinished letter.

*Do not believe*?

The boy and Harp regard me silently. He laces and unlaces his hands. Harp hangs her head and speaks to him in a low whisper.

'What does she say?'

'She asks where you got the stone you wear around your neck.'

'From my father.'

'She says only wives wear such a stone. It is a gift from him. She asks if you are a new wife. She asks if he made your picture.'

Harp watches me and holds up five fingers. I nod. 'Yes,' I say, 'wife number five.'

The boy translates. Harp's face breaks into an enormous smile, relief, happiness and something else. It's only when she goes down on one knee that I recognise what it is, adoration . . .

*

I missed the bus. But there is a little steamer that plies the River Bamba, fifty years old at least; it was called the *Comrade Atkins* but that's been scratched out and it is renamed the *Uncle Dickie*. Signs of the developments which are everywhere in the air. Up the River Bamba, beating against the current, the steep-sided banks where the monkeys scream overhead and the tight green bush ticks like a bomb. Everybody seems to be travelling to Waq and by the time we reach the confluence of the Bamba and the River Zan, the little steamer sits low in the water and there is no space to be had. Someone has a crocodile aboard and feeds it twice a day with bushmeat, propping open its jaws with a piece of stick and tossing titbits into its jaws like a mother bird feeding her baby. The water ran out soon after we left and only beer remains. Plantain, if well roasted, is tolerable, the cooks working on deck sweating over their smoking braziers. The first-class cabins are crowded with important functionaries travelling to the capital to see for themselves the developments of which everybody has heard, although no one can say what they are. The second- and third-class cabins are stifling black holes, best never entered. Once we reach the Zan we begin stopping like a train at so many small sidings, packed villages on the banks where the looming ebony and mahogany trees have been cut back and dug-outs push from the shore to offer fish, manioc, out-of-date penicillin and even older pop cassettes . . .

*Do not believe* – the last words my father wrote. Well, that's not so difficult, I do not believe. But Lord, help my belief!

In Waq I find they are doing something to the facts of history. The facts are in a state of continual revision; like symptoms of serious diseases, if you catch them early enough, repercussions can be prevented.

I am met by a party of Wouff all in a great state of excitement, jumping up and down so that their little skirts flap

258

and the hollowed-out stones that they wear around their necks bounce on their chests; they sing and dance, and it seems that I am expected, known, and this is why they go down on one knee and bow their heads and insist on escorting me to the Kingdom Towers Hotel, even coming with me into the foyer, though the doorman who wears the hat which once hung on the tree beside the door tries in vain to prevent them. They spill into the newly painted lobby, chattering and smiling and pointing, happy as children. The Kingdom Towers Hotel is now another place, smart and sparkling. Big cars draw up to the entrance and men in suits climb out. The swimming pool has been cleaned, the urchins banished and women lie about in bikinis, sipping drinks from coconut shells. The Roumanian manager is a changed man, running up and down the foyer shouting 'Front!' and 'Good day!' and beaming horribly, and smacking his hands together with a sound of paper bags bursting. On the walls are framed telegrams praising the President of Roumania for his shining achievements: King Olaf of Sweden congratulates him on the new spirit of architecture; and Queen Elizabeth of England celebrates with him the anniversary of his accession to power. The manager wears a swallow-tail coat and pretends not to recognise me.

'Do you have a booking?'

'What do you mean, a booking? I have a room. I'm staying here.'

'Dear Miss, we are very busy. We have the President upstairs, Comrade Atkins. Up on the tenth floor, plus his entourage, plus medical staff. We have visitors from everywhere. We're having to double up. Rumours about the health of the President have attracted enormous attention.'

'But where am I to stay?'

He shrugs. 'I'm sorry. But if you have no booking . . . Are these your Wouff?'

He looks coldly at my chattering entourage.

'Yes.'

'I'm afraid we allow no one in tribal dress into the hotel.'

It's no better in the bar, where Kwatch also refuses to recognise me and it's only when I go over with my hand outstretched that I force him to see me. He takes my hand vaguely and shakes it.

'It's me. Bella.'

Kwatch stares. 'Bella?'

'Bella Dresseur, you know.'

Now he does know me, he smiles, he shakes my hand vigorously. But this recognition I do not like, this recognition is for somebody else. 'Miss Dresseur,' – he smiles widely – 'I knew your father! When did you arrive? Have you come all the way from France?'

'I have no room. The manager says I have no room.'

'It's true, the hotel is very crowded. But surely you've booked? We're packed out. There isn't a millimetre of space to be had. If we'd known you were coming . . . I was very attached to your father, he was a good friend to this country. But we have great developments going on here, you see. Many foreigners in town.' He points to a group of noisy beer-drinkers in the corner: 'South Africans. Keen observers of our political developments. And over there,' – he drops his voice – 'with the vodka, Russians. You see – it would have been wiser to book . . .'

My accompanying band of Wouff seem delighted that I have been refused entrance and I guess that's why they pick me up and carry me along Patrice Lumumba Drive towards the Presidential Palace.

Oh the city of Waq is turned on its head!

Well here I am, and here are the six bathrooms with golden taps in the shapes of swans and griffins, dozens of lavatories and crystal bidets, here are the apartments of the wives, four of them, great purple beds. Whose wives? Does it matter? Here are five thousand pairs of shoes, in these cupboards you will find three thousand pairs of pink panties. The Wouff carry me to the biggest bedroom of all: a field of a bed, clothed in gold, smelling slightly of onion.

This then is my position, I think. I am a guest of the Wouff or, seen in another light, you might call me a captive, a prisoner – but there are compensations. I have the run of the palace, except in the morning when the people are allowed in to gape at the spoils of the rulers, the thousands of bottles of anti-wrinkle cream, the boxes of toys bought for the children and never, as far as I can see, unpacked, the two hundred

260

games of table football, for instance, and the thirty-six pogo-sticks, the entire rooms full of electric trains. Curious crowds wander in each morning and stroll down the corridors gazing at the beds, the chandeliers, the dozens of coffee-dispensing machines, and the Wouff make sure they do not touch anything though they are allowed to flush the toilets, which they do with great enthusiasm and cries of disbelief.

The Wouff, my guards or companions, patrol the corridors and they line the red carpet that leads to the throne. Yes, there is a throne, it's the famous Leopard Throne. Well, it's not what you might think of as a throne as much as a wooden chair, more a stool actually, made of two parallel discs of wood, one forming the base and the other the seat, and between these discs are a circle of leopards on whose backs ride little foetal creatures, baby spirits, infant ghosts. The back of the chair is carved in the shape of a trinity; a man sits with his knees spread widely apart and rests his hands on the heads of a man and a woman. It's surprisingly comfortable and I've rather taken to it. This is where I am obliged to sit whenever visitors call. For instance, Kwatch, the barman, who drives over with hot food from the Kingdom Towers where it seems that the health of the Number One Peasant is still in the balance. I can see Kwatch would like to stay and talk but the Wouff prevent this, urging him on to the throne where he deposits my tray; it's a kind of meals on wheels service, or rather a meals on knees service because poor Kwatch is forced to approach the Leopard Throne backwards, and on his knees, guided only by the sound of my breathing. Naturally I breathe as loudly as possible and try to guide him, I'm a kind of pneumatic lighthouse. Even so, he's inclined to wander off course occasionally with unhappy results, falling over a pogo-stick or backing into a chair, and I'm afraid the Wouff seem to enjoy this.

As the weeks pass I feel more at home. I can, for example, now recognise the presence of my Wouff escort without opening my eyes; I can tell just by the swish of their little leather skirts when they are near, and the thump of the hollowed stones that they wear around their necks bouncing on their breastbones. And from the window I can see other tribes gathered outside the palace. The Kanga in their white robes, praying to Mecca, dark, silent and patient. The Ite, in jeans and coloured shirts, have set up a little entrance beyond the palace where the queues of people form. I strongly suspect they are charging an entrance fee to the trippers who wander the lower floors of the palace each morning.

All of them waiting.

The news of my condition, of my position, has been spreading. I've had a letter, which I will not read you, from Monsieur Cherubini. It seems that my uncle has been corresponding with another comet fiend in this part of the world for some time, and in the course of the letters they exchanged, his friend happened to mention the white girl who had been enthroned in the palace of the former Redeemer of Zanj. It was but the work of moments, the Angel writes, to guess her identity. It's a surprisingly friendly letter. It seems they're planning a trip to what the Angel calls my part of the world. Father Duval's coming too. It's to be a threesome. The reasons given are that the southern skies are very fine for astronomical purposes and that Uncle Claude, who has been much depressed since the loss of his soup, might here realise his life-long wish to discover a comet. But I am not fooled by this for a moment. They intend calling on me. They want to see if the rumours are true. Why else should Monsieur Cherubini ask if they should bring anything with them? If there's anything that I need?

All I need is time. Down the road the Number One Peasant continues to pass away. This is the time of trial. If he dies then the old world will have vanished. If he survives and returns to the Presidential Palace then my future is unsure, to say the least. It will mean that the universe has been put into reverse, it will be the equivalent of the big crunch. But if he dies – then! Because at my end of Patrice Lumumba Drive things are expanding every day, growing by leaps and bounds. In next to no time at all the pinpoint of life within me has grown to something like the size (and this is only a rough estimate) of a grapefruit . . . These are the early days of creation in the city of Waq, and, in that mysterious time behind the Planck Wall where telescopes may not spy, my universe is hot and young, and anything may happen.

# A Selected List of Titles Available in Minerva

While every effort is made to keep prices low, it is sometimes necessary to increase prices at short notice. Mandarin Paperbacks reserves the right to show new retail prices on covers which may differ from those previously advertised in the text or elsewhere.

The prices shown below were correct at the time of going to press.

Fiction

| | | | | |
|---|---|---|---|---|
| ☐ 7493 9026 3 | **I Pass Like Night** | Jonathan Ames | £3.99 | BX |
| ☐ 7493 9006 9 | **The Tidewater Tales** | John Barth | £4.99 | BX |
| ☐ 7493 9004 2 | **A Casual Brutality** | Neil Bissoondath | £4.50 | BX |
| ☐ 7493 9018 2 | **Interior** | Justin Cartwright | £3.99 | BC |
| ☐ 7493 9002 6 | **No Telephone to Heaven** | Michelle Cliff | £3.99 | BX |
| ☐ 7493 9028 X | **Not Not While the Giro** | James Kelman | £3.99 | BX |
| ☐ 7493 9011 5 | **Parable of the Blind** | Gert Hofmann | £3.99 | BC |
| ☐ 7493 9010 7 | **The Inventor** | Jakov Lind | £3.99 | BC |
| ☐ 7493 9003 4 | **Fall of the Imam** | Nawal El Saadawi | £3.99 | BC |

Non-Fiction

| | | | | |
|---|---|---|---|---|
| ☐ 7493 9012 3 | **Days in the Life** | Jonathon Green | £4.99 | BC |
| ☐ 7493 9019 0 | **In Search of J D Salinger** | Ian Hamilton | £4.50 | BX |
| ☐ 7493 9023 9 | **Stealing from a Deep Place** | Brian Hall | £3.99 | BX |
| ☐ 7493 9005 0 | **The Orton Diaries** | John Lahr | £4.99 | BC |
| ☐ 7493 9014 X | **Nora** | Brenda Maddox | £5.99 | BC |

All these books are available at your bookshop or newsagent, or can be ordered direct from the publisher. Just tick the titles you want and fill in the form below. Available in:
BX: British Commonwealth excluding Canada
BC: British Commonwealth including Canada

**Mandarin Paperbacks**, Cash Sales Department, PO Box 11, Falmouth, Cornwall TR10 9EN.

Please send cheque or postal order, no currency, for purchase price quoted and allow the following for postage and packing:

| | |
|---|---|
| UK | 55p for the first book, 22p for the second book and 14p for each additional book ordered to a maximum charge of £1.75. |
| BFPO and Eire | 55p for the first book, 22p for the second book and 14p for each of the next seven books, thereafter 8p per book. |
| Overseas Customers | £1.00 for the first book plus 25p per copy for each additional book. |

NAME (Block Letters) ..........................................................................................................................

ADDRESS ..........................................................................................................................

..........................................................................................................................